L

CAST OF CH

Miss Bertha Tidy. Owner of the Minerva, a teashop, hatshop, and beauty shop. A cold, calculating woman, she does not inspire affection in others.

Jane Kingsley. A "big, golden creature" with an extraordinarily sweet nature, who works in the Minerva teashop and lives with her brother and sister-in-law.

Samela Wild. A small, dark, pretty young woman, who works in the hatshop. The cleverest and most vocal of the employees, she's also a happily married woman.

Crystal Bates. Tall, titian-haired, and a gifted milliner, she's otherwise unimaginative and even shallow. She too works for Miss Tidy and is married.

Marion Oates. The youngest of Miss Tidy's employees, a tall, plain, phlegmatic, and surprisingly observant teenager, who lives with her elderly aunts.

Leonie Blanchard. Miss Tidy's long-time housekeeper, an old Breton woman.

Kate Beaton. A plain-spoken writer of crime stories, who treasures her solitude.

Mrs. Emmie Weaver. An antiquarian bookseller, who lives for her books and whose shop is next to the Minerva.

Owen Greatorex. A distinguished novelist and a bit of a snob.

Iris Kane, Colonel and Mrs. Livingston-Bole, Edith Drake, and **Beatrice Graves.** Five local people who died by their own hands before the story opens.

The Rev. Daniel Buskin. The saintly old rector of Long Greeting.

Arthur Tidy. Miss Tidy's brother, a solicitor with a heart as cold as his sister's.

Dr. Hare. The village doctor.

Superintendent Lecky. A local policeman, who resembles a benign bloodhound.

Detective-Inspector Raikes. A dark, wiry, handsome man, sent down from Scotland Yard to investigate the deaths at Long Greeting.

Plus assorted relatives, spouses, servants, police officers, and townspeople.

Books by Dorothy Bowers

Postscript to Poison (1938)
Shadows Before (1939)
Deed Without a Name (1940)
Fear and Miss Betony (1941)
The Bells of Old Bailey (1947)

The Bells of Old Bailey

Dorothy Bowers

Rue Morgue Press
Lyons / Boulder

For information on our titles see
www.ruemorguepress.com
or call
800-699-6214
or write
The Rue Morgue Press
P.O. Box 4119
Boulder, CO 80306

ISBN: 0-915230-95-X

Printed by
Johnson Printing

PRINTED IN THE UNITED STATES OF AMERICA

About the author

Dorothy Bowers (1902-1948) was well on her way to establishing herself as one of Britain's leading mystery writers when she succumbed to tuberculosis at the age of 46. Her first Inspector Dan Pardoe novel, *Postscript to Poison*, was published in England in 1938 to enthusiastic reviews ("She ranks with the best."—*The London Times*). Three more Pardoe books followed, one a year until 1941, when Bowers left her longtime home in Monmouth for London, to do war work for the European News Service of the BBC. Her fifth and final novel was published in 1947, and she was elected to the prestigious Detection Club in 1948, shortly before her untimely death.

She was born on June 11, 1902, in Leonminster, Herefordshire, the second daughter of Albert Edwards Bowers, a confectioner who moved his family to Monmouth in 1903. He operated his own bakery on Agincourt Square in that city until he retired in 1936. Dorothy's early education was at the Monmouth School for Girls. She went up to Oxford on October 13, 1923, when she was twenty-one, a somewhat advanced age for a first-year student, though one should also remember that Oxford only started awarding degrees to women in 1920. She took a third honors in Modern History in 1926 from The Society of Oxford Home Students (now St. Anne's College) and returned to Monmouth to pursue a reluctant career as a history mistress, although her first love was writing. Her happiest memories during that time were of her days at Oxford.

In addition to her writing and substitute teaching duties, Dorothy compiled crossword puzzles for *John O'London Weekly* from 1936 to 1943 and for *Country Life* from 1940 to 1946. Like her sister and many of her Oxford friends, she never married. She died at Tupsley, Hereford, on Sunday, Aug. 29, 1948, at the age of 46, with her sister May at her bedside, and was buried near her mother.

For more information on Bowers see the introduction by Tom & Enid Schantz to The Rue Morgue Press edition of *Postscript to Poison*.

CHAPTER 1

Gay go up, and gay go down,
To ring the bells of London town.

It was not until the fifth death in Long Greeting that Miss Tidy made up her mind to go to the police. And then from no sense of civic duty but because she knew her own security imperiled.

For a woman of uncommon resolution she had been slow to reach a decision; having come to it, however, there would be no turning back.

She would say nothing of her intention to the staff of the Minerva. Business was in a delicate enough condition. All this unhealthy babble spinning about murder versus suicide hypotheses was entirely alien to the chaste atmosphere she had for years cultivated for the creation and proper disposal of hats. So she had refused to subscribe to the prevailing hysteria by the very smallest show of interest in the more dubious manifestations of local activity. At first she had tried by the silent disapproval that rarely missed its target to discourage even discussion of the emphatically publicized inquests. When this failed she went on ignoring the furtive gossip, the whispered fears, the cumulative suggestiveness harbored by panicky women that rippled slyly out of the hatshop into the no less exclusive café behind, and thence gushed full course in the beauty parlor, her last and most profitable addition to the establishment.

There, it was only to be expected, tattle ran boldly and unstemmed. The passivity demanded for a reconditioned skin or the right sort of eyebrow was a notorious tongue loosener, so that even clients who in ordinary social intercourse practiced a measure of reserve found themselves in those cribbed, attractive cubicles receiving and imparting the most astonishing confidences. Miss Tidy made no real effort to check them there; she knew defeat when she met it. Besides, such slips of the tongue as occurred had at times been not unuseful to her.

But it was on these accounts, as well as for a more cogent private reason, that she herself preserved uncompromising reticence. Now that she was going to break it, it should be in the official sense only.

7

Business over for the day, she was giving a good deal of reflection to these things as she watched the staff departures before locking up.

There were only four of them now. She managed the beauty parlor alone these days. Marion and Jane from the teashop were always the first to go: Marion on foot because she had only to cross the cathedral close to Thistle Street where she lived with her old aunts, and Jane to get the bus for Stone-acre hamlet, the next stop after Long Greeting. Miss Tidy never used the bus. Season in, season out, she clung obstinately to the belief that health was best maintained by the something-under-three-miles cycle ride between Ravenchurch and her cottage in Long Greeting. The bus too would have entailed constant travel in Jane's company, mutually embarrassing at both ends of a day spent in common harness.

From the half-open café window that looked on Flute Lane she could see the two she mentally dubbed "Hats" pulling their bicycles out of the alley behind the antiquarian bookshop opposite. Samela was the first to disen-tangle, her small, dark, exquisite features as guarded as if she had not doffed the saleswoman for today. Conscious of scrutiny, perhaps, she raised her eyes and looked straight into Miss Tidy's, smiling at once with the imper-sonal courtesy that might have expected to find her there. More than that; she made, Miss Tidy was sure, a delicate signal of sorts to Crystal Bates, who, emerging from the alley, was just moving her lips for an utterance doomed at birth. For she closed them again with such deliberation and di-rected so swift a stare at the teashop that Miss Tidy, with a wintry smile of acknowledgment, decided that the girl came as near to looking silly as such loveliness could ever look.

She watched them move one behind the other down the narrow lane from which medieval builders had almost expelled the light, a brilliant shaft of sunshine firing Crystal's titian hair. They were both married women, and both, in her opinion, complete irresponsibles.

All the same she would have liked to hear whatever it was that Samela Wild had stopped Crystal saying.

The Minerva was uncannily quiet with everyone gone. Miss Tidy ap-proved it so. Closing windows and unnecessarily visiting rooms already in order, she was able in solitude to review her resources and congratulate herself again for having created this business out of nothing and made it the sparkling factor it was in Ravenchurch society. Hats ... tea ... complexions. She alone had gauged for women what a formidable triple alliance they made.

Her mind, always alert, was more than usually so this evening. It was partly the summer, of course, a memorable one this year; the morning-to-night June radiance, while physically tiring, stimulated all her mental facul-ties. She had remarked before this peculiarly gratifying compensation for torrid weather; bodily exhaustion was offset by a greater clarity of mind and will.

It was good, she thought with a touch of complacency, to know that neither time, responsibility, nor the well-mannered hostility of Ravenchurch had yet impaired her quality or the precision of her judgments. Three days from now she would be sixty years old, yet she knew unquestionably that her brain today was a more acute organ than ever it had been thirty years earlier. The knowledge filled her with gloating, for she could not recall a time when there had been as now such constant demand upon all the acumen she possessed.

Only two objects decorated the cream-washed, timbered walls. One of them, in a crooked oak frame, was a large canvas sampler worked in colored wools, not uncommonly old but distinguished by a purely secular sentiment. Miss Tidy had forgotten why she had put it there—simply to fill a space, she supposed—but she went on keeping it because people coveted it and it was nice to have the power to withhold their desire. The other was a Sheraton mirror, simple, graceful, a bit spotty, and wholly unpredictable at the angle at which it hung. When it wasn't catching useful vignettes of social life in Flute Lane, it would intercept between a couple of café patrons an eloquent glance or two seldom lost on Miss Tidy, or else it would betray Marion's fatigue and hint at how much more boredom Jane was likely to put up with.

Now it shot back at Miss Tidy the glittering whiteness of her carefully dressed hair. She viewed herself with the detachment other people found repellent. A time there had been when her pocket-Venus proportions were a source of annoyance to her; like other small women of extravagant ambition, she had in youth cherished yearnings after a Brünnhilde stature, but now, examining scrupulously her meager inches from snowy crown and full blue eyes to the arches of her tiny feet, she felt they might well be an asset. Little people suggested a defenselessness rarely in fact theirs; and this was all to the good in view of her approach to the skeptical police.

Yes, all her perceptions were sharpened to a fine point. They made her aware of a number of things at once: of the shadow of Mrs. Emmie Weaver swooping among her books at shutting-up time on the other side of Flute Lane, of the possible significance of Crystal's unspoken remark, of the empty room in front where hats were dispensed and the equally empty kitchen behind, of the absence of any reassuring footfall in the cubicles upstairs, of two letters at the moment bulging disagreeably the inner pocket of her handbag, of a large and faceless Fear groping for her among the deserted tea tables.

The air had lost its golden warmth. She shivered and, going to the door that gave onto the lane, shot its bolts sharply. At this concession the Fear loomed up in titanic form. ...

"You fool," Miss Tidy addressed herself with ferocity.

She went over to the sampler and touched with an unsteady finger the first lines of "The Bells of London," *Worked by Adelaide Bascombe Aged Eight in the Year of Our Lord 1842:*

"Gay go up—and gay go down ..."

If recklessness were gaiety—well, the Minerva had been founded on it.

"And if you *do* go down, as your delightful correspondents would like you to do," Miss Tidy whispered grimly, "let it be in the same spirit, my dear ... But—you're *not*—going to!"

2

The cottage Miss Tidy had owned and occupied for twelve years and had dubbed the Keepsake, hung with honeysuckle and deprived of personality by admirable reconditioning, stood at the bottom of Haydock Hill. There, from a sufficiently disdainful eminence, it looked down on Long Greeting. "Looked down" was the right phrase. For, with the blinds partially drawn against the heat, it did from below impress one as watching beneath lowered lids activities to which it was studiously indifferent.

Miss Tidy reached home with her shaken confidence thoroughly restored. Coming up the path between the hollyhocks, she felt rekindling in her a recognizable sensation, all the more pleasurable because it flushed her cheeks and set shining her prominent blue eyes. It hinted at a dangerous quality. It was Bertha Tidy's affirmation of faith in Bertha Tidy, in her infallibility for keeping her end up in an inimical world.

Her possessive delight in the Keepsake never failed to dispel the misgivings Ravenchurch aroused. The familiarity of things here in the country worked their old deception, suggesting stability and a refuge that was impregnable. Bees fumbling in the antirrhinums, a robin's deft journeys to and from the lily-of-the-valley bed with food for its young under the porch, from the kitchen the pleasant chink of Léonie's supper preparations ... these things were everlasting. Léonie, supper, home. If anything were needed to assure her that she and hers were invulnerable it was the thought of the old Breton servant standing by, uncritical and incurious, for over twenty years.

She squared her shoulders and walked in briskly.

"Letters?" she called, too loudly because the old woman was deaf now to all but familiar voices. There was as well an artificial lightheartedness in the greeting since yesterday's post had brought the two letters which had caused a slip of self-control marked by Léonie.

The old woman came out of the kitchen with the slow, uneasy gait that gave to her tall, masculine figure an air of fatigue incompatible with the work she achieved.

"No letters." Her voice was harsh and flat, her English without inflection. "But *she* called, Miss Bert'a."

"She? Who in the world do you mean?" Miss Tidy was impatient. Léonie, assuming her listener's omniscience, often used the relative pronoun for a name.

"Miss Beaton. She want to see you. She will come again."

"Most unusual," said Miss Tidy incredulously. Kate Beaton's infrequent calls received no encouragement, and she hoped in a fervor of inhospitality that she would forget about this one. It would be particularly inappropriate to admit her now, just when one had decided on a really frank disclosure. The letters in her bag seemed to swell a little ... Well, it wasn't impossible.

She went up to her bedroom to cool and pat and powder. Suspicion apart, she decided it wasn't merely the Beaton woman's lack of manners, shapeless tweeds, and sharp-set eyes in a red face that had never sought a masseuse to repair its ravages that made her so distasteful. What was it then? Unpardonable her ability to make a comfortable income writing crime stories which, as Miss Tidy was careful to point out, bore no relation to life as it was lived in Long Greeting, or anywhere else for that matter. Worse still, her pretentious stuff was openly approved by Owen Greatorex, in no mutual back-patting spirit either, for everybody knew how captious Kate Beaton had been about his own work, and he a great novelist of international reputation. The lion, of course, Miss Tidy reminded herself, could afford to disregard the jackal's attentions, but Mr. Greatorex had seemed sometimes to go out of his way to invite the creature's barbs. Why was she coming here? Was she on the way now?

She looked out between the chintz curtains to the known but lately, it must be admitted, somewhat sinister landscape. Across a stretch of placid beech park the rectory, disguised as a bunch of yews, sidled up to the flint-bright Saxon church with the odd wooden belfry that had been an after-thought. Beyond, the sloping ground that revealed only the chimneys of Long Greeting Place made the groves of trees on its far side look nearer than they were, and nearer too the steeples and cathedral spire of Ravenchurch that rose from their bosky summits against the melting cuckoo-flower sky. Warm, tender, no longer reassuring. For in the narrow graveyard, gleaming here and there white through the somber guardianship of the yews, were four new graves, recollection of which, and of that fifth in Ravenchurch itself, chilled Miss Tidy so unpleasantly that she shivered again with the tremor that had invaded the teashop half an hour ago.

She looked right where the dusty road ran by the Loggerheads tavern and the handful of larger houses on its route. No peace of mind was discoverable, though. Behind the inn lay pastures and mowing fields and the unseen river slipping between clumps of willow and alder; better it had been altogether unseen for shining like a plate under the burning sky was the one deadly reach of it with which everyone now was sickeningly familiar.

Dabbing lotion on skin to which resilience would never be restored, Miss Tidy hurriedly averted her eyes again. She resented these reminders jabbing at a squeamishness she resented still more.

A flash of red, and the bus from Ravenchurch rocketed to a standstill outside the Loggerheads. She glanced at her watch on the dressing table—

five-fifty. Every day at this hour the business quartet from the city alighted here. With curiously freshened interest in something she could see if she cared any weekday evening in Long Greeting, Miss Tidy watched the Ravenchurch passengers dispersing to their several teas. The letters in her handbag ... It might well be that ...

Little Beryl Hicklin from Clay's the provision merchants? She'd been bosom friend to Iris, the last to die. There she was, angling as usual for a word or two with the conductor before looking wildly up and down and all ways as if in expectation of being run over by the infrequent traffic. Miss Tidy couldn't say.

Cissie Ashwell? Because she'd been eighteen months on the telephone exchange Long Greeting credited her with encyclopedic, if unofficial, knowledge. Miss Tidy thought it not unlikely.

Young Mrs. Williams from the Pike House? She was bookkeeper to Nathaniel the furnishers, and, her XOS proportions precluding her, in her own opinion, from consulting the Minerva beauty culturist, was something of a dark horse. Miss Tidy accorded her the benefit of the doubt.

Finally, when all the ladies had tripped, floated, and lumbered to earth, Mr. Bannerman, Sr., of Bannerman, Bannerman, and Waite, Solicitors, the Bull Ring, Ravenchurch. What of Mr. Bannerman? He was as usual, with his neat little bag, at his trim little pace, making anxiously for his tea table. In consideration of his sex, age, and professional reputation, Miss Tidy, while recognizing that none of these things could be wholly discounted, was inclined to exonerate him.

Behind Mr. Bannerman today a swarthy young man, whom Miss Tidy had noticed about the Loggerheads once or twice before, stepped down from the bus. Summer visitors at the inn were no rarity and, it being a fallacy to suppose that villagers have any lively or sustained interest in other than themselves, she ceased to pay attention to him as soon as it was apparent that she did not know his name.

She managed to make a dignified withdrawal from her position at the window just in time to avoid being seen by Kate Beaton. Yes, the woman was making a beeline for the Keepsake. Up the steps cut in the bank she came, her sturdy legs seeming to thrust the hill out of her way. She pushed open the gate, perspiring, as Miss Tidy could see, in the most uncomely fashion.

With a precaution she could not have explained to herself Miss Tidy pushed the handbag containing her letters into the dressing-table drawer. Then she compressed her tiny figure into a still smaller compass and, standing motionless behind a curtain, watched through a chink her visitor's approach to the house. When the porch hid her she still stood there.

Léonie shuffled to the door in answer to the knock. When she had opened it she stood, as was her habit, a little on one side with her gaunt, knotty hands clasped loosely in front of her.

"Please, miss, to enter," she said dully. "Miss Bert'a is in. I go to tell her."

Kate Beaton, hatless and in a baggy frock no better cut than the tweeds Miss Tidy deplored, gave her a shrewd look.

"You're fagged, old thing," she said curtly. "Take my word for it and ease off a bit till the glass goes down."

She walked with clumsy self-possession into Miss Tidy's expensively furnished sitting room, while Léonie, not a glimmer of interest lighting her broad, pallid features, mounted the stairs in silence.

When Miss Tidy, who made a practice of keeping people waiting, came down nearly five minutes later she found Kate Beaton, her back to the room, gazing at the chimneys of Long Greeting Place.

"Nice little nest you've got here," she said, turning abruptly. "Though you're only at the bottom of the hill you seem as high as Haman from this window."

"What an odious simile," Miss Tidy said icily. "Though, of course, in your own line of work ..." She let the murmur, with a lift of her eyebrows, fade to silence.

Kate Beaton laughed. Like a carthorse, her hostess thought. "Oh, we all know what happened to *him!* But not what's going to happen to us, eh? And that's a heap more interesting nowadays when fact's getting to look a bit too much like fiction, if you ask me!"

"I'm not asking you," Miss Tidy said austerely, with an unusually prompt display of talon. "Though I should, perhaps, enquire, to what do I owe your visit? I gather you haven't come merely to tell me life is rather lurid in these parts lately."

"Death, you mean," her visitor corrected. "No, I haven't. All the same, I fancy I'm going to underline one or two of the known facts." She added shortly, "Mind if I sit down?"

Miss Tidy stood pointedly, watching Kate Beaton thump down on the chesterfield without permission.

"Miss Beaton," she said with the careful and tinkly enunciation equivalent to the elevation of the fighting cock's hackles, "I'm not in the least inter-ested in anything you can add to the general gossip. People here and in Ravenchurch are lost to shame."

Kate Beaton gave her a level look with a smile that did not touch her eyes.

"You should know," she said with careless ambiguity. She thrust her chin out in a small formidable gesture. "*Did* you know Iris Kane had left a letter?"

Miss Tidy went white. She felt at once the ebb of blood from her face and, inwardly raging, knew that in spite of prepared defenses it was as much a visible breach in them as blushing.

"They found it after the funeral," Kate Beaton added.

"I didn't know," Miss Tidy said, adjusting a mat on the table and pinching between her fingers a cluster of dropped rose petals. "I didn't know. And it doesn't concern me—nor you."

"No? Then perhaps something else does. I didn't come to tell you about the little Kane girl's letter, but about my own. I've had an anonymous one."

Miss Tidy looked up with oddly sparkling eyes. She had recovered a measure of composure. The letters upstairs grew in size till they threatened to burst the handbag.

"Really, Miss Beaton! Are you trying to be offensive? You know, you make a statement sound like an accusation. An anonymous letter is an un-pleasant thing to receive, no doubt, and on that account not usually broad-cast. It's a matter for yourself, or—or for an intimate friend to deal with."

"Do you think so? Yet I've called on you."

"What for? What can *I* do about it?"

"*Would* you do something about it? Nice of you." She shoved a hand into the rather lopsided pocket of her frock, pulling out a thin, folded envelope which, without rising, she held out to Miss Tidy. "Well, you could begin by reading it."

"No, thank you," Miss Tidy said on a sharply rising note. She remained rigid. "I've no wish to learn anything, false or—or *true*, about you."

"About *me?*"

"Of course. You don't interest me."

"Look here, you've got the wrong end of the stick. The letter I got today isn't about me."

"Indeed?"

"Indeed. It's all about—you."

CHAPTER 2

Oranges and lemons,
Say the bells of St. Clement's.

"Sugar and spice, that's me," said Samela, fishing for her compact mirror with the dread that her left eyebrow was a hair overplucked. "And I don't like all these dark insinuations so early in the morning!"

The Minerva was only just open. Coffee wouldn't be served for another hour and a half, but for all that Jane Kingsley had arrived because, from her rural fastness, she had to accommodate herself to a tiresome now-or-never bus service. Marion Oates, on the other hand, who was due at ten, could cut across the cathedral grass a bare five minutes, if she liked, before they began to brew the midmorning drinks. Actually, she made a practice of turning up before time for the sake of company. Crystal and Samela were always there at the unlocking, however, even though at times an hour or so passed without a customer for hats.

In the whole day this was the pleasantest time at the shop. By late afternoon everybody's eye was on home, tea, and transport, and the gregarious spirit with its collective interests had given way to a sort of fatigued *sauve qui peut* exodus that did not encourage conversation. Now the staff was comparatively fresh, leisured, and prepared to join issue on Crystal's suggestion that Miss Tidy knew more than she told.

"We all do, darling," Jane said in her slow, warm voice, gently twirling on its stand a little flutter-and-froth creation and wondering, not for the first time, if hats really were a more congenial environment than tea, coffee, and salad lunches. She was a big golden creature with superb limbs and thick, tawny hair never dressed in other than an unruly shingle. "We're all really a bit close about what we actually do know."

This, coming from the most candid of her acquaintances, made Samela stare.

"Oh no, Jane. You're quite wrong. Women always tell *more* than they know."

Crystal, a gifted milliner with an imagination reserved entirely for her work, whose mind registered slowly and comprehended with difficulty, turned this over before deciding that she hadn't grasped its import. "I don't know what you mean by that, Sammy," she said. "But if I knew anything that would throw light on—on—well, anything," she added in an unsuccessful effort at lucidity, "I should say so at once, not go about with my lips clamped and *pretending* my ears were bolted and barred to other people's talk!"

"Ah, I'm with you there," Samela said, stroking with a kind of hopeless severity the offending brow. "She *does* play possum to the absurdest degree. But listening to what everybody else says and pretending you never hear a word isn't at all the same thing as being in the know yourself. Personally, I think little Bertha's as much in the dark as the rest of us."

"Same here," said Jane lazily. "It would take someone cleverer than Bertha, cute as she is, to have the lowdown on *five* suicides in nine weeks."

"Suicides my foot!" Crystal cried irreverently, dropping in her agitation a saucy little fur felt that bowled neatly to Jane's feet and subsided there in adoration. "If you like to go on bolstering up that face-saving yarn, I don't!"

"Hush," Jane soothed in lullaby tone. "The old dear's probably pricking her ears somewhere quite close."

"No, she's not," Samela said. "You're O:K. for scandalizing. I can hear her upstairs getting ready for the beauties. But why *face-saving*, pet? Whose face?"

"Why, the police mugs, of course," Crystal retorted. Her very hair seemed tingling with excitement. "They've never wanted to do a thing in Ravenchurch. They've been used to being respectable so long."

"I see," said Samela. "One of your brighter moments, Chris. You mean— *murder* is a thing you can't be flabby over, you have to work at it?"

"Yes. You can shut shop on a suicide. Which is what they're doing.

Murder makes you sweat."

"It's a point of view," said Jane, and added too caressingly for a skeptic, "but I don't believe it. The police aren't just making it up—they *did* pop themselves off, poor things."

"Besides," Samela protested, maintaining the two-against-one argument, "what an unhandy way of committing murder! Three drownings, one hanging, and one with his head blown off and the shotgun still in his hands ..."

"Darling, must you?" Jane murmured, her dreamy gaze on the expanse of street visible through the sparely stocked window.

"Well, I ask you!" Samela insisted, her Botticelli fragility undisturbed by the catalogue of horrors. "When there's all the easy things lying about that women are quite good at, poisons and sleeping powders in overdrafts—the smooth, simple, deadly, unviolent things. Chris's murderer must *like* awkwardnesses!"

"Only as a sort of coverup, you know," Crystal explained uncertainly. Her hypotheses, never particularly rational, were already becoming too nebulous for development under Samela's assault. "The—the killer might *want* you all to think they had taken their own lives."

"Darling," said Samela, "you've been reading the Beaton too conscientiously. And not the cookery one either."

"But what I don't understand," said Jane tolerantly, "is why you pick on Tidy, Chris, as having guilty knowledge—or worse. Let's admit for argument's sake that all those people—Mrs. Livingston-Bole, her husband the old colonel, Miss Drake, Beatrice Graves, and now poor little Iris What-is-it—were done away with by somebody. Ridiculous, of course, but you will have it. Well, it just *couldn't* be Bertha—unless she had used, and she obviously didn't, the nice concoctions Sammy says women always go for. *Shoving* in the river? Up and shooting with a quite hefty gun and then fixing it all to look far otherwise? Getting a rope—and—but oh, how *horrible!* Why, Tidy's no bigger than a mouse!"

"True." Samela nodded. She looked at the bewildered Crystal and conceded generously, "Though George does say little people sometimes have *the* most surprising strength. He knows, of course, because there was a fairy of a nurse in his ward who tossed him about like a juggler does a ball."

"Well, nurses are different, you know," Crystal admitted with equal generosity, though, recalling George Wild's muscular six foot two, momentarily appalled at the vision she got. But she was grateful for having George tossed, as it were, into the scales with her. Samela, as a rule, quoted the husband she adored only in support of her own arguments. A publisher's reader and an outstandingly shrewd reviewer in the *Timekeeper* before the war, he had lost a leg in Burma and very nearly his life and sanity in Japanese prisons. Now, with Samela sticking doggedly to hats—"till George finds his feet again—no, his foot, the poor darling"—he was groping tentatively after old work and old ways and flogging an interest in them he no longer felt.

"You know," Crystal complained, "you do jump to conclusions, both of you. I never said Bertha went round bumping people off. All I said, and I stick to it, is that there's something Going On here at the Minerva, and I wouldn't be surprised if she knows all about it."

"What do you have to go on for that?" Jane enquired.

"Plenty. Look what she said yesterday about the post."

"What?"

"She said it to Samela. Sammy, you tell her."

"Oh that," Samela said. "It was nothing. Not evidence of murder, my sweet. Only a very *tiny* little straw to show the way the wind blows for making the Minerva a one-man show altogether. She told me she didn't want any of us to pick up and bring in the morning and afternoon deliveries of letters. She would do it herself in future. That was all."

"Odd," said Jane. "But there, Bertha *is* odd in those silly little ways that smack of megalomania. Lots of old spinsters are. It doesn't mean a thing."

"*Is* she so old?" Crystal put in.

"Seventy if a day," said Jane serenely. But Samela shook a doubtful head.

"Anyway," Crystal exclaimed triumphantly, "that brings me to the next point. I was forgetting till Sam reminded me by saying that about a one-man show. She *is* trying to run this place solo."

"She'd sack us if that was her game, surely," Jane replied.

"Well, that's what she has done with beauty culture. Helen Mason left at Christmas, and young Rhoda—and *she* knew her job—was sent packing in March, and here we are in June and she's still running it herself—*and* it's the only department that really does overtime."

"And," Samela agreed, "is conspicuously understaffed. My poppet, you're right about *that* being odd. Come to think of it ..." She hesitated.

"What?" said Jane and Crystal together.

"I was going to say, hats could be shut down with advantage, for they're no great catch these days when women like best to display their coiffures. Then *we* could be upstairs instead of wasting our sweetness in this lousy desert."

"Why *aren't* we up among the paints and powders?" Crystal demanded rhetorically.

"We're all beauties," said Samela reflectively.

"Mm. Especially you, Sammy."

"Oh, I'm a bit of a skinny Liz, though that goes down quite well at present. Jane's really the best of us," she added critically.

"Jane's sort's always in fashion," Crystal agreed, with an unenvious appraisal of her friend's charms.

"Like gorse and love," said Sammy. "It's that artful unsophisticated air she has. I'm better hardboiled, and a touch of the moron's quite becoming for you, Chris. But nothing goes down so well as simplicity with arms and legs like Jane's, and that lovely brown-egg tan." She frowned a little. "You'll have to be careful, though, angel. You're running to fat a bit."

"When you two have quite finished," Jane said calmly. "Here's Titus. I'll have to get back to the kitchen in a minute where arms and legs are all that matter, not airs and complexions."

The door opened with a discreet little ting. Marion Oates came in, a tall, plain, round-shouldered girl with thin brown hair knotted tightly on her neck and eyes that were quiet and intelligent. She was little more than a child, her gawkiness and pallor and an oddly independent air in company making her seem older than her sixteen years.

" 'Lo, folks," she said indifferently. Then, "You do look funny. Like conspirators."

Jane laughed. "We were waiting for you, *cherie*, to make it the Titus Oates Plot." She hissed sepulchrally, "What's Going On round here? Our Mrs. Bates is all het up to know."

Marion shrugged. "Robberies, I'd say."

Samela tottered weakly. "Catch me, somebody. I can't bear another thing. Murder, suicide, and now theft at the Minerva! Holy smoke, lass, explain yourself."

Marion was unmoved at having at once become the center of interest.

"I'm only guessing," she said coolly. "I don't know that anything's been pinched yet, or will be, but I'd say it's what she expects because she's taken to sleeping here much more often."

"*What?*" said Jane.

"How do you know?" Crystal asked.

"Not in summer," Samela objected.

They all knew Miss Tidy had slept at the Minerva at infrequent intervals when weather and darkness united to make the cycle ride home unattractive. A divan, which stood against a wall of the teashop, with blankets and a night suit in the cupboard upstairs, came in handy such nights, she had confessed. Other motives had, of course, been ascribed and, in particular the more lecherous ones suggested by Samela, reluctantly dismissed as not proven. But sleep at the Minerva in June?

"She's been doing it since—oh, the beginning of May," declared Marion. "I know because Auntie Win and I like night walks, and two or three times a week there's been a light shining in the café. You know you never have a blind down here, so it's easy to see straight through."

"I'm *jiggered*," said Samela, adding hopefully, "it *must* be a man."

"Don't be beastly," Jane reproved. "Septuagenarians don't have those indulgences."

"I don't believe she's seventy," Samela retorted. "And anyway there was Ninon de Something-or-other who sort of made her century at that kind of thing."

"Keep it clean, Sammy," Crystal pleaded. "There's children present."

"Don't mind me," Marion said with the air of being the only adult of the party. She added surprisingly, "Age can't wither the lady, perhaps, but custom staled her for me long ago."

"You don't love her, chick, do you?" said Sammy lightly.

Marion's mouth twisted in a small bitter grimace. There was an ugly flash in her eyes. "I hate her!" she said, her voice trembling to tears.

"My dear." Jane put out a hand. Her fingers closed round the girl's thin wrist. She drew them away lingeringly, glancing at the watch on her own. "Jiminy, time's getting on! Titus, old thing, *en avant*, kitchen, coffee ..."

"*Küche, Kinder*," Samela murmured after their disappearing backs. "And the Kaiser-*in*'s upstairs."

There was a stony little silence.

"I didn't know, did you?" Crystal said uncertainly.

"I guessed. I've even wondered now and again if our Jane isn't just a bit of a yoke on the lassie too."

"*Jane?* Surely not! Why, they're buddies all right." Crystal sighed. "Heigh-o ... I don't like it when nice kids like Titus suddenly look—like—like—"

"A Corsican vendetta," suggested Samela.

"Mm. That sort of thing."

Crystal began languidly to put in order that already bleakly trim room, shifting hats to equidistant points till their number looked fewer than ever, like cacti flowering sparsely in a lone land.

She hummed mockingly, " 'Sugar and spice, sugar and spice' ... Not *us*, Sammy!"

Samela grinned. "Oh yes. With modifications. Sweetness and acidity, like lots of nice things. Anyway, I take back what I said about Jane. She's all sweetness and light, bless her." She broke off quickly at sight of two figures crossing the street. "Skip to it, my child. Here's two of 'em. Only one's ours, though, and she's got her eye on my picture straw. Dear lady, it's fifteen years too late for you, but what's that? Mrs. Wardle-Phlox is coming to be bew-ti-ful. ..."

"I know," said Crystal. "The silly old hen. She's down for a mud pack."

"*Is* she now?" Samela eyed distastefully the liverish features already darkening the glass-paneled door. "Well, there's plenty been slinging around here for her."

Ting-ting, apologized the door.

"Good morning, madam," said Mrs. Bates, her lovely face wearing the precisely correct expression of anticipation properly subordinated to welcome. "The one over here? Yes—charming, isn't it? Something altogether exceptional ... Well, yes, I'm pretty sure too it's going to look delightful ..."

"Good morning," said Mrs. Wild with a dazzling beam, her soft dark eyes wide and ingenuous. "Please go straight up. Miss Tidy is waiting for you."

Mrs. Wardle-Phlox gave her a frosty little smile. The child was certainly *most* attractive, and always so genuinely pleased to see her. Absurd to think of her as a married woman ... oh well, these days ... It would be nice if old

Miss Tidy would let the gentle little creature run the beauty parlor. Now if *she* were to apply the treatments … Miss Tidy herself was hard-handed and brusque of late, overworked no doubt, though it was hard to say why she didn't change all that. A bit slapdash too, and oh, so—so—what could she call it—tongue-tied? Not exactly. Miss Tidy was never embarrassed. Morose? Perhaps. She never was chatty, anyway, as she used to be.

But, "Miss Tidy is waiting for you …" That warm little voice. Mrs. Wardle-Phlox went up the stairs with as much dignity as her rheumaticky hip would stand for, convinced that, in spite of the usual evidence to the contrary, Miss Tidy was this morning preparing exclusively for this very appointment.

CHAPTER 3

Bull's eyes and targets,
Say the bells of St. Marg'ret's.

In Superintendent Lecky's office at the police station Miss Tidy was confronting three men to whom she aired her views, or as many of them as she felt might be expedient for them to know.

To tell the truth, she was a little surprised at the degree of interest they were according her. She had come prepared for beating down indifference, skepticism, even perhaps hostility, by an impact of mingled charm and authority; for authority there would be when she produced the material evidence of the letters. But instead of the exhausting swim against the tide she'd anticipated, she was welcomed with almost painstaking alacrity. She recognized at last what it really meant to have your listeners hanging on your words. Against the tide? Why, she was swept forward on a stream of encouraging attention that might, she thought, have gone to the head of a more susceptible woman. She was too wary, however, to let her narration get out of hand. Naming no names was always a safe rule, like watching your step. Innuendo, yes; specific charge, no.

This was the first time she'd been able to observe the superintendent at close quarters. A spare, blond man, he made her own scrutiny across the table easy by seldom lifting his gaze from the torn blotting paper and pencil under his hand. He doodled lazily, with a good deal of fussy detail, making encouraging little rumbles when she faltered or repeated herself.

At a desk farther back a young sergeant industriously took notes. Once in the early stages the superintendent had addressed him, calling him Hassall. After that everybody ignored him, and the young man wrote, jotted, rubbed his nose, and tapped his pencil with only an occasional glance at Miss Tidy or in her direction, and then an abstracted one. Yet she was actually more flattered by the detached interest of the sergeant than by the more vocal attention of the other two. The invisible bond linking her words to Hassall's note pad gave her an arrogant sense of being in command of the situation, and of that permanency she had felt might be slipping from her grasp. To have your words respectfully recorded by another was something of an achievement, even a minor form of immortality.

It was the third man, however, who engaged one's curiosity. He sat, or rather lounged, in an oak Carver chair he had thrust off from the table on the superintendent's left. Dark and swarthy and good-looking in a swashbuckling fashion, he had on a well-cut and conspicuously unofficial suit. On coming in Miss Tidy had instantly recognized him for the young man at the Loggerheads. He was not, she now saw, so young as she had supposed: thirty-eight, perhaps, but something athletic and uncalculated in his movements took from his age. Her first feeling had been one of annoyance: here was somebody not a policeman who was going to strike an undesirable note of informality. Then, though nobody bothered with an introduction, the atmosphere changed. He gave her at once a smile of great charm, when she was seated it was he and not Lecky who proffered a cigarette, and from time to time his was the indolent, kindly voice that cut in with precisely the question she herself would have chosen to be asked, the sort of thing that gave her the opportunity to emphasize in her reply the importance of her own personality. The essential thing was that he took her seriously. On these grounds Miss Tidy decided that he was, after all, of official standing, and by no means of inferior rank.

She sat sideways in a shabby but comfortable leather armchair on the other side of the table. She could not catch the stranger's eye without turning her head a little, while the apparently preoccupied superintendent was under her observation all the time. His inattention, she knew, was for the decorative scribbles he was making, not for herself. The two letters, which both men had read, were now out of her handbag and lying in the middle of the table.

Miss Tidy knew she was looking pretty. That smart little navy straw poised artfully on her pile of white hair, her shining blue eyes deeper in color for the forward tilt of the brim, the cool, tight-waisted frock and navy-and-white court shoes: they all made her *petite*, feminine, therefore exacting protection.

Lecky, lifting his eyes, his chin still sunk, looked all at once like a benign bloodhound.

"Thank you. You're being very helpful. Now let me run over the main points, you checking, to see if I've got it clear."

He lifted his head and, sticking an elbow on the table, held up a hand and tapped it with the forefinger of the other. Sergeant Hassall stopped writing and screwed round in his chair for the first time. The strange man didn't move.

"First," Lecky began almost coaxingly, "in the light of after events you are convinced that five people in and about Ravenchurch have recently met their deaths by means other than the inquests determined?"

The dark man smiled, perhaps at the labored euphemism.

Miss Tidy frowned. "I wouldn't say *first*, Superintendent. My first concern is that my own life is threatened."

The stranger made comfortable noises indicative of sympathy. Lecky bowed his head.

"Of course. I mean first chronologically only. We shall get a more orderly view of it that way."

"Oh yes. I certainly hold that these poor creatures didn't die by their own hands."

"You go further than that? You suggest they were murdered?"

Miss Tidy shivered delicately. "It's horrible having to say so. But yes, I do—now."

The dark man interposed gently, "Not at first, you mean? In the beginning you too believed they were suicides?"

It was to be remarked that Miss Tidy showed no impatience at having to repeat herself to these charming but, surely, rather obtuse officers. She liked it. It was all going much more favorably than she had dared hope.

"But I didn't," she said, turning a little so that her eyes met her questioner's directly. "I didn't from the start believe such a shocking thing. I was *always* convinced there was some other explanation which—which would remove the blame and—and—the *stigma* from them. And then, when I got these letters the day before yesterday, I *knew* they had been murdered."

"You *knew?*" Lecky echoed. Stupidly, she told herself.

Miss Tidy bent her head omnisciently. It was unwise to be too repetitive with one's effects.

"Well, that's clear," the superintendent said almost briskly. "You knew they'd been murdered." He had, she noticed, a trick of dismissing the next moment what he had been at pains to elicit just before. He went on, "You were, you say, on intimate terms with Mrs. Livingston-Bole?"

She flushed, more at the sudden nature of the remark than because she objected to it. "Yes—that is, I didn't see a great deal of her. She was a—a contemporary of mine—a little older than I, of course," she added hastily. "At one time she underwent a course of massage with me. She often dropped in for advice, minor treatment, and so on. A very beautiful woman, as you will remember."

And entirely the credit of the Minerva, they expected her to add.

"Yes indeed," Lecky said absently. "And because, shall we say, you knew her better than you knew the others, you're emphatic that the verdict was a mistaken one?"

"A *cruel* one," Miss Tidy amended in her sharpest voice. "For one thing she was a deeply religious woman, and *devoted* to the poor old colonel."

The dark man leaned forward, ingratiatingly.

"You base your conclusions—*this* conclusion—Miss Tidy, on character?"

"Why not?" Miss Tidy demanded with spirit.

"No reason whatever," he agreed warmly. "It's a very sound basis."

"Deaths by drowning, you know," said Lecky in a confidential under-tone, "admittedly carry a margin of doubt, though accident's a readier alternative than murder. But when we come to Colonel Livingston-Bole's death four weeks later, in his case there can be little reason to question the verdict, do you think? Especially considering his deep attachment to his wife."

"Oh, I know shooting's a different matter!" Miss Tidy cried. "And with the gun there on the spot too ... such a *horrid* masculine way of finishing things!" Ignoring the sergeant's smothered grin, she concluded by sticking, metaphorically at least, to her guns. "But if, as I am *quite* sure, dear Mrs. Livingston-Bole met her death at another's hands, why shouldn't the same person have killed her husband?"

"Do you know," said the dark man irrelevantly, "if Long Greeting Place is still unoccupied?"

"It's not," Miss Tidy said, prompt to be informative. "The colonel's sister has come there to live. I don't know her."

They nodded pleasantly. They *were* so agreeable, whatever suggestion, hint, opinion, or statement she made. It was all so easy she was fast learning not to falter, to discard the necessity for looking before she leapt.

"And that," Lecky said cozily, leaving Colonel Livingston-Bole's murderer at large, "brings us to Miss Edith Drake's death. She was the third person to go in tragic circumstances in the past few weeks, but leaving, we think, no doubt as to suicide."

"But why, why, *why?*" Miss Tidy reiterated recklessly.

They looked at her in some surprise.

The dark man broke the silence. "That's something one prefers to answer—if one can. One hasn't got to, you know, in order to determine suicide. The human heart's *always* inexplicable." He looked at her gravely. "Sometimes the dead themselves leave explanations, for us to make of what we will—what we can. Sometimes they're clearly the wrong ones, and we have to reject them. When they're right, they only tell part of the story."

"The balance of his—of her mind," the superintendent said, as if that simplified it.

"Tush," said Miss Tidy, emboldened by all the indulgence she had received, and with the feminine aptitude for turning the general into the particular, "the balance of Edith Drake's mind was *never* disturbed!"

"You knew her quite well?" Lecky enquired sweetly.

"Everybody did," she said. "And she made it her business to know people too, running the Ravenchurch Dramatic and what not. She was a young woman of forcible character. People thought she was rather wasted as headmistress of so obscure a village school as Haydock's End."

"But she enjoyed her work there," Lecky said, more as a statement than anything else.

"She must have."

Something in her voice constrained him to ask why.

"Because," Miss Tidy said patiently, "as everyone knows, she carried on with the work when she could comfortably have left off."

"Oh yes," said the superintendent, "you mean her luck in the Irish Sweep?"

"Of course. It's years ago, but nobody's ever forgotten. A little schoolmistress at Haydock's End winning *twelve thousand pounds* in one swoop!"

"Sweep," murmured Sergeant Hassall, contributing his solitary mite.

"And then, still more surprising," went on Miss Tidy, who had not heard him, "she continued with her sickening old routine job as if nothing had happened! It was the talk of the place."

"Dear me," Lecky said jocularly, "is teaching as bad as all that?"

"I taught once. Believe me." She sounded grim.

He looked at her flushed cheeks and said nothing.

"The balance of her mind," Miss Tidy repeated with quiet scorn. "Forgive me, superintendent," she added on a more winning note, "but to anyone who knew her it is really absurd. If her mind wasn't disturbed by a prize ticket in the Irish Sweep, what else could do it?"

As this was apparently judged unanswerable, both men left it alone.

"Hanging, however," said Lecky mildly, "is a rare choice for a murderer. It's only what's in store for himself, scarcely ever for his victim. And Miss Drake was found hanged."

Miss Tidy did not dispute it. But her mouth was stubborn, and with a disregard for logic and an anxiety for the last word wholly worthy of her sex she concluded, "Miss Drake simply couldn't have taken her own life."

"And you hold the same views for Miss Graves and Miss Kane?" the superintendent encouraged her.

"Certainly." But her voice sounded irresolute. "Beatrice Graves had a very good job. As dress designer at Fripp and Saltmarsh she was practically her own mistress, and she'd been enjoying the position for almost a year, long enough to be thoroughly established, but not *too* long—that is, she was still excited at having secured the post."

The stranger was looking at Miss Tidy with admiration.

"Your psychological judgments are pretty shrewd, you know," he said. "Those *are* arguments against suicide."

Miss Tidy glowed. "I felt so all along."

"But they don't," Lecky objected, "tell the whole story. We admitted as much just now. Behind the successful facade there's something else, something darker and sadder. Else suicide would never be in question at all. In short, we have to consider the arguments *for*, when suicide it so clearly is, and however obscure they remain for us we may be sure they were cogent enough to the victim."

Miss Tidy reddened angrily. This was being merely obstructive. The interview wasn't going as she wanted it to go. She decided to snatch the initiative of the discussion before this damp line of thought could be pursued in more dangerous directions, and addressed herself exclusively to the appreciative young man on the superintendent's left.

"And as for poor little Iris Kane's case," she babbled quickly, "why, a stronger argument against suicide couldn't be found! She was engaged to be married to a man *far* above her in station, who was clearly head over heels in love with her—well, he was really being a bit ridiculous and ostentatious about it, showering so many expensive presents on her. A very pretty girl, with the world at her feet, one might say. If anything was calculated to turn her head it was all the attention she was receiving, I admit, but I don't think any of us would be prepared to say she'd drown herself for having too devoted a fiancé!"

"No, I don't think we would, Miss Tidy," the superintendent agreed.

Something in the noncommittal remark pulled her up short. She remembered with sudden discomfort that Iris was said to have left a letter. She waited for Lecky to broach it. He said nothing, and, to fortify herself against the silence, she again spoke first.

"I do know what I'm talking about in this instance. Iris was a Long Greeting girl. So, of course, were the Livingston-Boles—from the village, I mean. And Edith Drake was on the doorstep, so to speak, and came to our church because Haydock's End is in the parish. Only Miss Graves was a Ravenchurch person."

To her listeners Miss Tidy's claim for Long Greeting struck a jealous note. If murders they were, she grudged them to Ravenchurch. The parochial view with a literal vengeance, thought Lecky.

"You don't," he said tentatively, "suggest accident as an alternative in all or any of these cases?"

Miss Tidy stared as if he had hinted at a device like a conjuring trick.

"Accident?" she exclaimed incredulously, with an unconcealed distaste that seemed to amuse the dark man. "No such thing."

The superintendent sighed. He tapped the letters, which to her disappointment had been read without comment.

"These—er—these anonymous threats—the recipient, as you probably know, is sometimes a pretty shrewd judge of their source. Can you give a guess as to their origin, Miss Tidy?"

She turned this over in silence, while he mistook her lack of response for reluctance.

"You're privileged, you know," he persuaded, "to say anything you like at a—discussion of this kind. Indeed, if you know anything whatever that is likely to help the police trace the writer of these letters it's not only in your own interest I ask you to be explicit."

"I don't *know* anything," Miss Tidy said carefully, giving her disclaimer a delicate emphasis. "But it would be unnatural if I didn't *suspect* something or other—wouldn't it?"

"Exactly. Suppose you tell us what you suspect."

Under this encouragement Miss Tidy looked arch. "I might indicate *suspicion* best by telling you the conclusions I drew from the letters themselves. I suppose they're written by two different people, though it's funny they should arrive by the same post. It makes me think the writers are in some sort of collusion. Then, anonymous letters are commonly *not* the work of men, are they? Men are just not subtle enough, and"—she gave a deprecatory little laugh—"perhaps not sufficiently spiteful either! Assuming it's a woman, or women, since I got two of them—I fancy they're each written by a more or less educated person, with—with a taste for *mystery*, who knows me well enough to refer accurately to one or two rather intimate points about my home, who certainly bears me ill will, who lives in Long Greeting, and who knows *very* much more than she would care to say about the local tragedies."

"In short," said the dark man bluntly, "you'd say she knew who was responsible for the deaths, assuming they're not suicides?"

Miss Tidy put out a small protesting hand. "Please. I've said nothing of the sort. But her mention of—of them in writing shows that she too must have her mind on them, and of course by the very words she uses judges them to be no suicides!"

"But so," the dark man gently reminded her, "did you judge them too. That doesn't mean—or does it?—that you yourself know very much more than you'd care to say about the deaths."

Lecky shot him a swift glance which Miss Tidy did not intercept.

"No—no, of course," she said, confusion struggling with indignation. "I've told you all I know—or rather, all I think. She—this woman may simply be taking unpleasant advantage of the situation. Poison-pen writers do, don't they?"

"Yes indeed," Lecky said heartily, anxious to allay any irritation his colleague had provoked.

"But then, why *me?*" she asked, still appealingly.

The superintendent shrugged. "Don't worry overmuch about that side of it." He smiled rather ponderously. "It's two-edged—there's a bit of flattery in it, unintentional, I admit. These poison-pen effusions are hardly ever sent to obscure folk. *You* get them because you're one of the more—shall we say, important, and therefore conspicuous, residents of Long Greeting."

"Well," said Miss Tidy, looking not at all displeased, however, "it's cold comfort when one becomes a target of *that* sort!"

"Never mind," said the stranger, making smooth amends, "perhaps you're not the only one so favored. Maybe one or two other of your Long Greeting neighbors have received the same sort of letter."

"As a matter of fact"—Miss Tidy rushed the words in a low voice, her eyes narrowed—"there was—I mean, did you get—did she …?" The unfinished question trailed off to confusion. She made small, fussy movements indicative of departure. Her visit, apparently so well received, was getting, she felt, just the least bit out of hand. She wanted now to go home where she could reflect to advantage on its more successful features.

Lecky made no attempt to detain her. Neither man pressed her to make clear what she had begun to say.

The superintendent picked up the letters. "I'll hold onto these for the present, Miss Tidy," he said. "They shall be examined in the proper quarter, I promise you, and I've no doubt they'll be a help to us—perhaps a very great help."

Both men rose as she got up too. Lecky came round the table and slowly accompanied her to the door.

"Meantime," he said amiably, "don't fret, and don't give way to *needless* fears. But you're a lady of sound sense, I know, and can keep your head, so all I'll say is, please regard your visit here as the best of all possible safeguards against whatever bogeys your unknown correspondent wants to raise. These things are worth usually no more than the paper they're written on. You were prompt to put the matter in our hands, and we'll see you come to no harm."

He could not then tell that he was to recall those easy words with acute discomfort twenty-four hours later.

2

Detective Inspector Raikes of New Scotland Yard, his dark face alight with controlled pleasure, met the equally eloquent gaze of Superintendent Lecky.

"They give themselves away, eh?" Lecky observed quietly.

"With a little inducement." Raikes smiled. "Well, it wouldn't be the first time they'd written 'em to themselves."

"Nor the last." But the superintendent shook his head slowly. "Can't be sure—yet," he went on cautiously. "But she's got it pretty well fixed, who she means us to think the writer is."

"The novelist?"

"Huh-huh. Assumed it might be two women writing, and straightway dropped the idea in favor of one. How did it go? A woman, educated—living in Long Greeting—more or less intimate with the Keepsake. And then that damning touch—'with a taste for mystery.' The answer—*her* answer's—Miss Beaton, of course."

"Of course," Raikes echoed absently. His voice brightened, took on a puzzled edge. "Why else should she say 'educated'? I don't remember a particularly erudite touch about those letters. In fact … But I only skimmed 'em. Let's have another look."

Superficially, they bore little resemblance to one another. For that very reason, Raikes surmised, the same hand, resolute to point differences, had penned both.

Penned was hardly the word; for one of them had been laboriously built up from letters cut out of newspapers—the various types side by side were obvious even before expert examination could determine their sources—and even the address had been executed in similar fashion, though with a neatness far more marked than that with which the message inside had been pasted, perhaps, suggested Lecky, with the idea of disarming the postman's curiosity.

The piece of coarse postwar writing paper, which Raikes indelicately pronounced toilet roll, was stiffened still further by the amount of glue inexpertly applied. The unpunctuated words ran:

YOU THINK YOU GET AWAY WITH THE CRIME WAIT SEE THE EYE OF GOD IT IS ON YOU DEATH MAY BE NEXT FOR YOU WHO KNOW.

"A few full stops wouldn't come amiss," Lecky observed. "Here, let's see what it looks like then."

"When I was a kid," Raikes said, watching the reflective hovering and jab of the superintendent's pencil, "we used to play a nice little parlor game called 'Unpunctuated Passages.' You wrote a story or an anecdote, what you will, innocent of the breath-saving comma, stop, and so on. A bit of ingenuity made it amusing. We, of course, robbed it of *gentility* by introducing a tough thread of ribaldry. ..." He looked more closely. "Well, that's a shade less incoherent."

YOU THINK YOU GET AWAY WITH THE CRIME. WAIT. SEE THE EYE OF GOD. IT IS ON YOU. DEATH MAY BE NEXT FOR YOU. WHO KNOW?

Lecky frowned. "It's right—but it's *wrong*. Here, take it."

Raikes spread the paper flat on the table and bent over it.

"What about our old friend, the mark of interrogation? He wouldn't do badly after 'crime,' else why the rather curious use of 'you think you get away'? 'You won't get away with the crime' would have saved our penman's time and glue."

"Maybe the other letters came to hand first."

"Maybe," said Raikes. "There's something phony though. Something that *rings* wrong, and may yet ring a bell for us presently. What about 'Wait see'? It sounds more like Mr. Asquith to me than your version, sir. Like this. 'Wait. See.' Though I'd have liked the conjunction too."

Lecky looked doubtful. "That's all right. You can't have everything. But with that coupled you've got 'the eye of God' as a phrase to itself—and it looks peculiar that way, to me."

"Looks peculiar any way," Raikes agreed. "The end of it's funnier than the rest. Is 'who' a relative qualifying 'you,' or is it as you've put it? Now I'd read it: 'Death may be next for you who know.' "

"Know what?" enquired the superintendent.

"Everything," said Raikes largely. "Why and how the quintet died, for example."

"Could be." Lecky nodded, without enthusiasm. "Such knowledge being dangerous to its possessor?"

Raikes made no reply, only remarked irritably, "If it's not what I say, why's the terminal *s* missing from 'know'? After all that messy labor, sticking on one more letter wouldn't have got the lady down, surely."

"You never can tell." Lecky picked up the sheet and read aloud the twice-amended message.

"YOU THINK YOU GET AWAY WITH THE CRIME? WAIT. SEE. THE EYE OF GOD. IT IS ON YOU. DEATH MAY BE NEXT FOR YOU WHO KNOW."

Lecky looked sideways at the inspector. "Not so good?"

"Wrong—all wrong," Raikes said decisively. "It's my ear it offends, not my eye. What about the other one?"

Lecky pulled out a thin sheet of folded paper from the second envelope. Both envelope and paper were of a slightly superior quality to those they had just handled. Here were no pasted words, but block letters in pale ink and a spidery, backward-sloping hand.

They read:

When you sit in your drawing room and watch. When you sleep in your soft bed. When you eat the good food prepared, and look sometimes it may be at the photograph in the locker by the bed, tell me, do you not fear? Five have died. But six may die. Think well. It may be now that you think too late.

"Educated?" Lecky remarked.

"Stilted," said Raikes. "There's a hint—dammit, what do I mean? It's not *merely* spiteful—well, it isn't actually spiteful at all—it's sinister, all right, but it's sensitive too, somehow simple and sincere; it hasn't precisely the qualities one associates with poison pens."

"Definite, but not brutal," said Lecky. "Yes. Educated, no, I agree. Punctuation still undisciplined, and a puzzling oddity of style. That 'tell me' and the creakiness of the final sentence, so like the stiff jerks of the other screed."

"I'd say at once the same body sent 'em."

"So'd I," the superintendent said firmly. "But why do we?"

"For one thing," Raikes said, "they're complementary rather than imitative, which is what a simple writer trying to be artful might contrive. Then of course the obvious contrast of scrawly manuscript with painfully glued-down type: she wasn't risking features of her script being identified in both letters."

Lecky nodded. "And I'd say the written piece was done first. Let's call it number one."

"Right. But why first?" Raikes asked.

"Because it's a warning rather than a threat; it's got a reproachful flavor. By the time the second came to be put together our scribe was warming up. Number two's a threat."

"Agreed," Raikes said, "but they were posted on the same day. So the warming up was a fast process. And why two letters anyway? Number two doesn't really get us any forrader."

Lecky looked nonplussed, and Raikes added quickly, "I know. She—our writer—wanted Tidy to feel the pressure of more than one opinion. Threats from two quarters, she'd argue, are clearly more frightening than when they come singly. Hence another letter, different paper, apparently different hand. But she wasn't sufficiently subtle, or patient enough it may have been, to post 'em on different dates. She bunged 'em off in one, and stressed their *un*likeness too heavily."

Lecky, who privately judged this a little fanciful, was off on a tack of his own.

"One thing that pretty well sticks out," he said, "is Miss Beaton's innocence. None of this—this style is hers."

"No?"

"It couldn't be, not if she tried, it couldn't."

"Ah, that's another pair of shoes. Not if she tried, eh?"

"What you getting at?" Lecky sounded suspicious.

"Why, that perhaps that's just what she did do—tried to write something which in style and sentiment would be judged quite out of character."

"I don't believe it."

"It wouldn't," Raikes persisted, "be difficult for a novelist."

"I don't believe it," Lecky repeated stubbornly. "You may know her as a skilful contriver of improbable plots. You don't know *her*."

"Meaning?"

"She's a plain, curt, take-it-or-leave-it body. She's often ill-mannered enough, and for that reason, I'd say, doesn't cherish inhibitions of this sort. She wouldn't *think* about an anonymous letter—not outside the pages of a yarn—much less write one."

Raikes sighed. "You sound sure enough. But it has been done, you know. And after the kinds of argument you're using have been used, too. However, I only do it because I know it teases. I think Bertha Tidy wrote the letters."

"I'm inclined to. Though it's a bit of a shock, even for me. But why?"

"For one of two reasons. Major and serious one, the letters are the age-old device for diverting suspicion. Things are getting a bit hot with Iris

Kane's death, so she decides to go all out and voluntarily attract our undivided attention to herself."

"Mm. And t'other?"

"Minor, and more common reason for all poison-pen productions—working off a private spleen. Miss Tidy's jealous of Miss Beaton. There's Greatorex to take into account, and probably any number of things we know nothing about. So Miss Tidy writes the letters and by hint and implication sees to it that Miss Beaton's the bull's-eye for our suspicions."

"I'd like to believe it was just that," Lecky said heavily, "but there's something more to it, old man. You can work off a private grudge even in an anonymous letter without reference to a string of local suicides."

Raikes grinned happily. "Never say die." He grimaced quickly at the word. "I mean, 'Wait. See!' "

He shoved the letters back into their envelopes and picked up the scrap of paper on which Lecky had been idly scribbling while Miss Tidy told her fears.

"What's this?"

The superintendent looked grim all at once. "A spider in its web—I think."

3

Whether or not the spider's parlor was to be located at Ravenchurch police station, Kate Beaton walked into it, a thoroughly forthright fly, a couple of hours after Miss Tidy had left.

She waited a little before being admitted to the superintendent's office. Lecky she knew quite well, and was astonished at the faint aura of embarrassment that hung about him during her visit. The dark man in well-groomed civvies, quietly shuffling papers at a corner desk, with an agreeably amused face, was not entirely unfamiliar to her either. Her sharp eyes took him in, all the more shrewdly since he apparently took no notice whatever of herself.

"I thought so," she said below her breath, and nodded with some satisfaction, recalling where she had seen him before and what she had thought of him then.

"I beg your pardon," Lecky said in some surprise.

"I was talking to myself," Miss Beaton disconcertingly assured him. "But not about the business that fetched me here."

She pulled up the chair Miss Tidy had occupied and took possession of it with a resolutely unceremonious air.

"Now look—I've not come to waste your time and make mountains out of molehills. I fancy the best way to scotch these silly doings is to bring 'em to you—and as it happens I come with the express permission, if not the blessings, of the individual most concerned."

She tossed a letter on the table.

"Our hoary acquaintance, the anonymous letter," she said. "At least, it's hoary to me, gives a nice little waspish touch to the story, don't you know. But this, believe it or not, is the first *I* ever saw written by someone else!"

She eyed Lecky's gingerly approach to it with a gleam of derision.

"But not the first you've seen, Mr. Lecky, I guess," she added, and was surprised at the unaccountable glance he shot her. "Please read it."

The superintendent drew the flimsy sheet from its envelope with exaggerated care. His slowness was the outcome of a mind rapidly working along another line. He was not, however, so abstracted as to fail to note that the feel of the paper and the weak toppling characters appeared to be those of Miss Tidy's correspondent. The badly spaced lines ran from edge to edge of the paper.

How often have you wondered [he read] when all will be known about the deaths in Long Greting. Ask Miss Tidy. Tell her she is not safe. One more will repay what has been PAYED.

Besides being misspelled, "payed" was twice underlined with scoring so heavy it had raked the paper.

Kate Beaton gave the baffled superintendent stare for stare.

"Funny business, eh?" She sounded casual. "After all, why not warn Miss Tidy direct? You'll ask it—I asked it at once. Besides which, *I'm* not the happiest choice of a go-between, seeing the good lady's opinion of me's what it is."

"And have you," Lecky asked with the rather labored humor he thought the situation called for, "been wondering when all will be known about the deaths in Long Greeting? By the way, your correspondent can't spell it."

"No, I've not. One has all one can do with wondering about death in fiction—disposal of bodies and what not. 'Fraid I leave fact to you people."

"I wish everybody did," Lecky said gloomily. "Then we shouldn't get this sort of thing."

"It came," Miss Beaton continued, "yesterday morning—Ravenchurch postmark, as you see, but of course that doesn't mean it wasn't popped into a Long Greeting pillar box. My first idea was for throwing it on the fire. Then one or two others stuck out their heads, notably Miss Tidy's well-known objections to me, which I didn't want encouraged by suppressing this. One letter, if you ignore it, probably means two or three others later on. Besides, hush-hush in a village isn't a good policy, I've found."

So Lecky would have imagined, judging by reports of Miss Beaton's candid tongue.

"So you decided to come to us?"

"Not right away. I took it first to the Keepsake. After all, Miss Tidy, not I was the accused, so to speak. She ought not, I argued, to be left in the dark about it."

"And how did she take it?" Lecky asked, with more interest than he cared to show.

"She didn't," said Kate Beaton, obstinately literal. "Refused to touch with a bargepole a letter about me. When I explained it was about her she read it."

"And then?"

"She was furious. Seemed to hold me responsible for it. Though writing it to myself and then hawking it round for her to read would be too crazy even for me! However, women don't know how to be logical—and that goes for both of us. But she wasn't only angry. She was horribly upset, and she urged me, practically *ordered* me, to hand it over to the police."

"When you say 'upset,' does that mean clearly taken by surprise at sight of the letter?"

"Absolutely." But she gave him a guarded look. "Queer you should say that. You see, *I* didn't think it was going to be any surprise to her."

"Why not?" Lecky, who knew the answer, asked.

"Frankly, I thought Miss Tidy had written it."

He calmly accepted this statement. "Actually you wanted to confront her with it?"

"Yes. If she wasn't the author—well, I still thought it only fair she should know somebody was using her name in vain."

"Then you no longer think Miss Tidy wrote it?"

"I don't—know," Kate Beaton said slowly. "The shock she had—and she undoubtedly was stunned at reading it—was *after* she'd looked at it. When I first told her about it and she refused to touch the thing, she didn't seem to me in the least perturbed. That looks as if the contents *were* a surprise to her, and that therefore she didn't write it. On the other hand ..."

"Yes?"

"I was going to say, when I first mentioned that I'd received an anonymous letter, her attitude appeared to mean quite the other thing."

"Can you explain that, Miss Beaton?"

"I mean, it was as if she were *expecting* me to mention it."

"I see. Interesting, but doesn't get us anywhere," Lecky said. "Now, working on your first assumption that Miss Tidy had written it, don't you agree it's a *very* odd letter for her to write herself?"

"We-ll, yes, I do," she admitted honestly. "While it doesn't really suggest any harm to me, it *is* quite hostile to her. But you can't analyze these things properly. I mean, the mind of the anonymous scribe is anyway a perverted one, and who can say how oblique will be the approach made if it's thought the end in view can be achieved that way? I haven't taken it to pieces anyway. The misspelled words could be spotted at once, of course, but nine times out of ten those would be deliberate."

Lecky nodded. "Anyhow, you obeyed instructions," he said cheerfully. "The writer advises you to tell Miss Tidy she's not safe, and you discharge the duty promptly." He added carelessly, "Do you know if any of these documents have been received elsewhere in the village?"

"If they have, I haven't been told."

In the short silence that followed, Kate Beaton, her eyes clear as water in her brick-red face, studied what she could see of Raikes. It wasn't much, for he had slewed round now and was presenting a back view, strong fingers thrust deeply into his wiry hair, the other hand turning over from time to time the papers he was studying with apparent diligence.

"Since you got this letter, Miss Beaton," the superintendent was saying, "have you wondered anything about the deaths it mentions?"

"I haven't changed my mind, if that's what you mean. I agree with you people they were suicides. That being so, it's pretty hopeless trying to say why."

"Yes. But people won't be sensible. So we get all this buzz."

"Don't I know? It's only a very ordinary human failing in evidence, after all, you know." She chuckled ghoulishly. "How much more satisfying is a nice juicy murder than your veriest suicide! The poor beggar who takes himself off closes the chapter all right—puts, shall we say, p-a-y-e-d to it, as our orthographically inaccurate friend would write—but *murder*, dear sir— why, somebody gets hanged for that!"

Miss Beaton was anticipating. Two people, alive that evening, had yet to die.

CHAPTER 4

Brickbats and tiles,
Say the bells of St. Giles'.

Jane pushed the door with renewed effort but no result. She turned the handle; nothing happened. It was clearly bolted too. She frowned, vaguely annoyed. There was no reason, of course, to see anything odd in the circumstance. Even though you'd worked two years and more at a place where your employer had invariably had the door unlocked every morning of your arrival, it was perhaps too much to expect no exception to the rule. A cyclist from Long Greeting couldn't, for example, always be expected to outstrip the bus. Tidy wasn't getting any younger; she might oversleep; she might not feel up to the mark.

Jane pulled herself up short. Funny, she'd been wrestling with the door a couple of minutes and had not remembered till now something overheard last night. Silly, really, to call it last night, for no teas were served after five, and she and Marion had always left by six, sometimes earlier, when the washing up was done.

She had come down from the upstairs cubbyhole that served for staff cloakroom, intending to leave by the door in Flute Lane till, entering the teashop, she saw that Miss Tidy had got it open and was standing there talking to Mrs. Weaver, the bookseller. She changed her mind then and went out through hats, but not before she had heard Miss Tidy say, "I shall be here all night if you like to show it me then."

So the old girl had slept here *again?* It was true, what Titus had said. But in that case she must be inside now, and it might be here at the Minerva she was doing her oversleeping. Yes, that must be it: going to bed in an unusual place might have changed her waking hour. But according to Titus, who seemed well informed on the point, it wasn't an unusual place. Oh, hang it all! Well, if she *was* inside she could jolly well come forward and let her in too.

Jane pulled the old-fashioned bell embedded in the post, a little astonished herself to know she had applied as much vigor as the clanging inside indicated. Tidy wouldn't like that.

She waited another half minute, expecting the door to open to an icy disapproval unsparingly expressed. When nothing happened she suddenly thought of the teashop and ran round into Flute Lane. But it too was locked. Returning, she could see Mrs. Emmie Weaver at work in the back of her window. She seemed to be unrolling some old colored maps ready for display. Jane, catching her eye, made signs she believed eloquent of her dilemma, but the gaunt old lady, used to not interpreting the extravagant gestures of youth, only smiled and nodded. While Jane was making up her mind to enter the bookshop, Samela and her bicycle came round the corner.

"Kicked out, darling?" Sammy asked, lifting a brow at sight of Jane in the Slip, by which the lane was known to the undignified.

"No, shut out," Jane said briefly, and explained.

Sammy wrinkled her nose. "It's too early for her to have gone out for a quick one. How *odd*—though I don't suppose it is, really. If she did doss here last night she may be snoring now, as you say—or perhaps only in the vest and step-in stage when you pulled the bell." She twisted her cycle round into the alley behind the bookshop and put her arm in Jane's. "Let's see what allied operations will do."

But instead of approaching the front door, Samela stopped short at the window, dragging Jane to a standstill beside her while she peered through into hats.

"Jane, look—it isn't only the sun, is it? There's a light burning in the teashop."

There was, or appeared to be. With the full sunlight playing tricks with the shop window, and reflected on the glass-paneled partition that divided hatshop from café, it was hard to say at first. But after some shading of eyes and a few contortions they decided that the teashop lights were on.

"Couldn't you see when you were at the window in the Slip just now?" Samela asked.

"No. The curtain was across. It always is lately because Titus or I have to pull it back in the mornings before we can see a thing inside."

"Funny for summer," Samela said reflectively. "Because on the nights Bertha doesn't sleep here—and surely there's a few still—she can't need to light up, even though she goes later than we do."

Jane was thinking. She measured Samela with a critical eye. "Sammy, you know the kitchen window at the back where the bins are? I'd get stuck in the middle if I tried—but *you*, if I gave you a leg up, do you think?"

"Do I not?" cried Sammy, delighted with the unorthodox vision presented to her. "I always felt it would be fun to see the Minerva from a new angle. And this makes a perfectly legitimate excuse for putting on the Bill Sikes act!"

There was no yard at the back, only a dingy enclosed strip of broken flags bounded by the high walls of other people's backs, and with an un-locked iron gate at a right angle to the cul-de-sac end of Flute Lane. Samela picked a catlike but rapid way to the grey, discouraged-looking window whose only view was a couple of dustbins, one marked "Kitchen Waste," and a damp brick wall. She put her finger tips on the sill and turned to Jane.

"Isn't this locked too?"

"Yes," Jane said simply. "We'll have to break it to turn the latch."

"Tut, tut, what a lawless child it is," said Sammy. "You didn't say that before."

"I forgot. Look, before we smash a way in let's try knocking on the kitchen door."

" 'Wake Duncan with thy——' "

"Sh-h," Jane said. "That's awfully unlucky."

They pounded in turn, then together. Jane put her eye to the keyhole to Samela's scornful demands of what she expected to see. Samela herself called "Miss Tidy!" in a rising key.

"Here," she said, suddenly serious, "we must get in."

She picked up a half brick and glanced, with a grimace, at Jane.

"Pray it doesn't bring the neighborhood on our heels—else, if Bertha's only sleeping it off, my days in the kingdom of Minerva will be short!"

"Sammy, wait a minute! Suppose she's still in Long Greeting? Oughtn't we to ring up the Keepsake?"

"And you said *she* said she'd be here all night!"

"Yes, I know. But she might have changed her mind."

"Shucks! And with the light on too? It *is*, you know. Here goes!"

"And here's Crystal," Jane said with a measure of relief as the brick, inexpertly aimed, broke the window too far down for getting at the latch. With a speed and vigor that made the other two stare, Jane, who had started elucidating matters to Crystal, finished off the job.

"Gosh, our Strong, if not Silent, Woman," Samela breathed, eyeing with alarm such of the mess as had fallen outside. "Never know what you can do till you try."

She brushed away wicked fragments of glass and, unlatching the frames, pushed up the lower window to the accompaniment of fresh tinkles.

"Well," Crystal said solemnly, watching Jane preparing to hoist the already mounted Sammy, "if she's sleeping the sleep of the just in there—"

"She'll be most unjustly wakened by now!" Jane giggled nervously.

Tittering was so uncharacteristic of Jane that Crystal eyed her doubtfully. She had a white, strained look Crystal had never seen before. Neither spoke, each listening acutely to the silence which had shut down on the first hollow sounds of Samela's entry.

But when nearly five minutes had gone by Crystal shifted irritably.

"What's Sammy up to?" she complained. "I thought she was going to let us in straight off anyway, but I suppose she was too inquisitive to think of it."

"Come to that," Jane said, "though you're tall, that window would take you, Chrissy. It's only me—"

But there was no further need for unconventional entry. The bolt of the kitchen door rattled, and then the door was open and Samela's small, shrinking figure came into view.

"Oh, Sammy, you might have—" Crystal began, but was struck silent by the sick, white face.

Samela tried to say something. She said nothing, but smiled weakly at them both.

"Sam," Jane said. That was all. They went inside, not speaking, not even exchanging glances, each carrying with her the unvoiced fear of some enormity.

Beyond the chill dark kitchen, that Jane called her "six-by-four," the tearoom lay with that twilit air of desertion it bore morning and evening. The drawn curtain on the Flute Lane window added to the gloom that was always there, imparting an odd spatial unfamiliarity to well-known holes and corners. The brushed and polished tables, somberly bare, reflected points of light from daylight piercing the chinky curtain and the glass partition of the hatshop.

"There's no light burning," Jane whispered.

"I turned it off, mechanically, you know," Samela said in the same tone, and switched it on again.

The room came to view but without animation. Jane, if she could have defined the feeling she got then, would have said it was not the same place as that where the Ravenchurch elite gathered to sip tea and coffee and nibble cucumber sandwiches and gulp their gossip.

The divan against the end wall was neatly made up for a sleeper who had not used it. On the floor a foot or two away, clear of the tables, her head towards the kitchen door, her feet to the hatshop, Miss Tidy was lying on her face. She was fully dressed. Nothing of her features was visible. The back of her head had been crushed in and where her matted hair was swept horribly off her neck something thick was tied about it with unbelievable tightness.

The silence was only a prelude, Samela knew, to sound perhaps so dreadful that she had at all costs to prevent it. She looked at Jane, to see her crushing both hands against her lovely mouth to stem nobody could say what gusts of hysteria. She saw Crystal, stiffly erect, with an inexplicably stern look of judgment on her face, eyes unseeing. She herself, more shaken just now than either, moved and felt strength return. She took Jane's elbow firmly, steering her with pushes to the divan. When she sat huddled there obediently, Samela walked over to the telephone standing on the small table that served for pay desk.

"Marion will be here any minute," Crystal said, mouthing the syllables.

They both stared at her in silence as if she had given voice to an utterance that changed everything. Then Samela dialed the police.

2

"Where's the weapon?" Dr. Hare demanded for the second time.

They had placed Bertha Tidy on the divan, beneath the shattered skull an old mackintosh Crystal had rummaged for. The girls, joined by Marion Oates, who had accepted the situation with a phlegm worthy of a case-hardened police doctor, had been dispatched upstairs by the raffish-looking man with the comehithery eye, as Samela described him afterwards. He had introduced himself as Detective Inspector Raikes—not, they judged quickly, of the local force—and had sent a bashful constable to take charge of them and the coffee he'd suggested Marion, the least dithery, might prepare.

In the teashop Sergeant Brook, a stout, tactful, deservedly popular figure in Ravenchurch, assisted by P. C. Miller, who privately thanked his stars he hadn't been selected for the apparently less onerous job abovestairs, moved unobtrusively about his work, hiding the excitement he felt at being for the first time in double harness with Scotland Yard. They'd dusted everything likely for prints, noted that on the face of it nothing seemed missing, and set the photographers to work. When they, racing silently through their job on the room and the corpse it held, had gone away, it was the police surgeon's turn.

Raikes, with the admiration he always had for economy of labor, watched the doctor's neat, unfussy examination of the body. Hare was a little man with a tightly stretched red skin and clever, steely eyes flush with his face, who looked at you with a detachment that missed nothing.

"Cause of death—strangulation," he pronounced in an expressionless voice, "with this—knotted at the back." He pointed to the blue and white woolen scarf they had unwound from the dead woman's neck.

"And what about the head blows, sir?" Brook asked when he could see the inspector wasn't going to comment.

"Use your brains, man," Hare snapped. He talked to everyone as he pleased and rarely roused resentment. "Nothing strike you about the floor and so on?"

"It's all pretty clean," Brook confessed.

"And clear—like it or lump it, the blows were struck after death. Nothing else accounts for amazin' absence of blood—only an unwilling, localized flow, so to speak, as you see. But dammit, I ask you, where's the bludgeon that did it? Looks like the murderer cleared out with it."

"What sort of an instrument d'you suggest?" Raikes murmured, frowning as he bent more closely over a wound above the ear.

The doctor did not answer directly. Instead he traced with his finger the outer rim of the wound Raikes peered at.

"Look at this," he said, "and this—and then this bruise. What 'ud *you* say? Something curved—something with a blunt, but mighty nasty, edge."

The inspector nodded. "We've got it, I think," he said quietly.

"Where?" Hare sounded testy. "Don't hold out on me."

P. C. Miller's eyes followed those of the Scotland Yard man. He began to walk towards the fireplace, an antique grate with a simply carved overmantel that stood in the wall dividing kitchen from café.

"Don't touch it, son," Raikes said in the same quiet voice, moving across too. "It *may* carry some useful evidence."

He pulled a large handkerchief from his pocket, shook it out, and wrapped it round the handle of an old copper vessel standing in the hearth. It was about a foot in height, broad-based, round of body, tapering rather abruptly from the lower bulge to a narrow neck and shallow head with a blunt spout like a jug. Raikes held it up, the bottom thrust like a shield in the face of his expectant audience. The condition of the rim told them all they needed to know.

"And the hearthstone's the same—see," Raikes said as they came over. "It's an old corn measure, George IV stamp, used last night to batter a dead woman, and then replaced—I take it. The murderer would hardly bring anything so unhandy with him."

"The girls will be able to say," Brook remarked. He found it something of an effort to say anything at all. Ravenchurch didn't treat itself to murders. And bashing a corpse was something worse, if you asked him.

"It's a formidable thing," Raikes went on, "in the hands of—" He broke off to give the doctor a quizzical look. "Man or woman, Doc?"

Hare was disgusted. "Be your age. She was a very small body—tiny. And sex doesn't play so much of a part in crimes of violence as you might suppose. Given a greater height—very probable gift here—and physical superiority, you can have he, she, or neuter for this business."

"You're accommodating, aren't you?" Raikes sighed. "How long dead?"

The doctor flicked his wrist watch round. "It's all but ten-thirty now— say, not more than twelve hours—not less than ten. Somewhere between ten pip emma and midnight—but I won't be accommodating there either."

"Good enough," the inspector said.

Miller, who had been keeping an eye on the hatshop, turned round. "The ambulance is here, sir."

"All right. Let 'em in."

While the constable went through to unfasten the front door, locked again to order after the official incursion, Sergeant Brook caught the inspector's eye.

"Well, no *suicide* here," he said. "That's something."

Hare gave him a sharp look. "What you talking about? What damn fool suggested a woman first choked herself, then stove her own head in?"

Raikes smiled. "Nobody. He doesn't mean that. He's talking of your five suicides since last April—that rumor says were not so but far otherwise."

"And by rumor you mean a flock of clacking hens," the doctor said ferociously.

"The dead lady among 'em then," the inspector pointed out.

"What d'you mean?"

"Only that Miss Tidy came yesterday afternoon to tell the superintendent that his suicides were murders."

Hare's grim little mouth twisted skeptically. "*Women,*" he said in a low voice, and again, "Women! Well, I was her doctor. I'll say she talked to me from time to time about pretty well everything that went on in this little burg, but she never threw water on the suicide theory—not to *me*. No *sir*. But I believe you—oh yes. Women aren't content with suicides. Nothing short of murder for them. And we call 'em the gentle sex!"

When the ambulance men came in he directed the removal of the body with the same quiet dispatch as before, leaving the scarf behind on the divan for Raikes.

The teashop, less horrid, looked at once forlorn.

"Bring the girls down," Raikes said briefly to Miller. "One at a time—beginning with the one who got here first this morning."

CHAPTER 5

Half-pence and farthings,
Say the bells of St. Martin's.

Avoiding the divan, Jane sat uncomfortably twisted round at one of the teashop tables, her brown arms along the back of the chair, her eyes on Raikes at another table, but her thoughts elsewhere.

There was something pressing, urgent, clamoring for expression. But it wasn't to this man she wanted to say it first. How desperately she'd longed upstairs for a word in private with Samela; for a word with Crystal! And how effectually that redeared, uncommunicative constable had blocked the way. What she couldn't believe, however, was that only she had noticed *it*. The others must have seen it too; it was there, naked to everyone's eyes. If they had—and they included this detective and Sergeant Brook as well as the girls upstairs—what conclusions had they drawn? As ugly as her own?

"But why," Raikes was asking, "did you break the window *before* telephoning Miss Tidy's cottage? Rather a desperate measure, eh?"

Jane licked her dry lips. "The lights were on in here."

"Yes, I know you've said so." He noticed how large her eyes were, how drained of warmth her skin beneath the sunburn. "But even before you and your friend saw that the teashop was lit, your one anxiety was to get inside, wasn't it?"

"Yes—oh yes," Jane murmured, to fill a gap her distrait air was creating.

"Why, Miss Kingsley? Wasn't the quickest, most natural course to ring up Long Greeting when you found you were locked out and could make nobody hear?"

"Well, no, it wasn't," said Jane, making palpable effort to attend to the question. "You see, I'd heard Miss Tidy say the evening before that she would be staying the night at Minerva."

Why couldn't he leave her alone, to resolve the implications of what she knew—of what, perhaps, they *all* knew, but for one reason or another were keeping up their respective sleeves? She caught the eye of Sergeant Brook, who sat apart on the end of the divan, apparently absorbed in a large and, so far as she could see, virgin notebook. He returned her look owlishly, then gave his attention to another page.

"Was that an unusual proceeding?" asked the inspector, who by the presence of the divan had guessed that it couldn't be.

Jane explained, a little haltingly, Miss Tidy's intermittent reluctance for night cycling. "But," she added, "we didn't think she minded so much on light summer evenings."

"No. When you say you heard her announce her intention of stopping the night, do you mean she said it to you?"

"No, I was just ready to leave after clearing away teas. She was standing in the doorway—there. She said it to Mrs. Weaver. She's the bookseller in the Slip."

"The Slip?"

"She means Flute Lane," Brook rumbled. "Local name for the alley."

"I see. Can you recall her exact words?"

"I—think so. I didn't catch what Mrs. Weaver said first, but I heard Miss Tidy's reply. She said, 'I shall be here all night, so you can show it to me then.' "

"Show what?"

"I wouldn't know. I didn't know."

"Did anybody else hear her say it?"

"I don't know that either. We were all there, of course."

"Why 'of course'?"

"Because I always go first. I live farthest off. I've a bus to catch."

"Didn't you say anything to the other girls about what she'd said?"

"But why should I?"

Raikes smiled. "My dear child, I'm not asking you to account for what you may have discussed among yourselves. I say, did you report Miss Tidy's remark to anybody in the Minerva, or did anybody report it to you?"

"No—no to both," Jane said in a breath. "There wasn't time. I went straight out. Besides, when we all knew she did that sort of thing on and off there was nothing much to talk about."

Raikes glanced at his scribbling pad. "You live at Stoneacre. Alone?"

"With my brother and his wife. He's a smallholder. My parents are dead."

"Any friends out there? Girls? Young men?"

Jane flushed. This man was stupid—and impudent. "Not in Stoneacre. My friends are here—Sammy—Mrs. Wild, and Mrs. Bates."

"Not Miss Oates?" He seemed to be quizzing her.

"Of course," Jane said quickly. "Friendly, I mean. She's much younger than the rest of us."

"Much?" Then he dropped his banter. "But you see what I'm driving at—your contacts outside business. You see, you *could* have mentioned Miss Tidy's whereabouts last night to others besides Mrs. Wild and Mrs. Bates."

"But I didn't," Jane declared. "Really, I didn't. Ralph and Elsie wouldn't have been interested," she explained with studied patience. "They've neither of them ever been inside the Minerva in their lives, I know, and I don't suppose they'd have recognized Tidy—Miss Tidy—in the street if they'd seen her. My brother wouldn't, I know."

"So you don't talk shop at home?"

Jane broke into sudden warmth. "You'd know if you were one of us that the only people you care to talk shop to are those you work with!"

"But I do know," the inspector agreed. "A quite profound truth—universally applicable. The only folk I ever talk shop with are cops like me."

"And if," Jane went on heatedly, ignoring this confidence, "you are looking for people who knew Miss Tidy was spending last night here, why should you look no further than the Minerva staff? Others could have gossiped about it. What about her maid at home? What about Mrs. Weaver herself? And people in Long Greeting who must have known her habits by now?"

"I stand corrected," Raikes said solemnly, and Brook, unappreciative of ambiguous humor, frowned. "Miss Kingsley, here's something that comes under direct personal observation. Have you noticed a change in Miss Tidy lately, any change? Was she worried, frightened, *anything*, indeed, that seemed to you unusual?"

But Jane, feverishly busy again with her own thoughts, showed a mulish indisposition to helpfulness. Direct personal observation indeed! Very well, he should have it for the negative thing it was. Hearsay, after all, wasn't admissible, was it? She'd heard something of the sort. So *she* wouldn't air Sammy's and Crystal's views, nor give old Titus away to this fellow who had clearly missed the most important point of all, from under his very nose. Well, he must have, or he would have questioned her about it.

"Have I noticed anything unusual?" she repeated, with so innocent an emphasis on the pronoun she was persuaded it had escaped the police. "Why, no. She was much as ever—to me. And anything odd at any time—well, it was in character. She was like that, you know."

"I see," Raikes said. "Are you able to throw any light at all on the circumstances of her death?"

Jane breathed deeply. It was now or never. She looked at the absorbed, uninspired features of Sergeant Brook, at the glint of sardonic humor on the inspector's face. It was never.

"No," she said with an ease that surprised herself. "I'm sorry, I can't."

After all, she argued in defensive silence as, Raikes holding the door for her, she went out—after all, each of them had had the same opportunity as herself of observation and inference. If they hadn't taken it, it wasn't her fault. If they failed to question her about it specifically, she wasn't *obliged*, was she, to proffer the information?

She wouldn't speak first now. Not to Sammy, or Crystal—or Titus, of course. What she'd got was probably the clue of clues. And though at the moment she couldn't quite see where it led, she had an idea that it indicated, if not the murderer, then the most important witness.

She would see what she could do with it, playing a lone hand.

It was really rather a good thing that the young clodhopper of a policeman who had frustrated all attempts at conversation had prevented her from sharing it—with Sam and Crystal—and, of course, Marion.

2

"You shouldn't badger Jane," Samela remarked in calm reproof. Beneath the popeyed gaze of their unvocal police guard she had turned the not-so-shining hour to account by liberal application of lipstick and was prepared for any emergency. "She's not built for it. Now I'm tough."

"In short," Raikes said, eyeing Mrs. Wild's miniature charms, "fight a chap your own size. Why do you think I badgered Miss Kingsley?"

Samela, smiling, decided to be in no hurry to sum up the inspector. You never knew with the public school type. But if he *was* all at sea, she had the game in her own hands.

So she changed, "She looked upset," which might have reacted unfavorably for Jane, to, "You kept her too long. After all, it was I who found the body."

Raikes, who had not met her sick and shaken at the door she'd opened to Crystal and Jane, detected a callous note in the early use of the phrase.

"I hadn't forgotten, Mrs. Wild. You did rather more, if you remember. You noticed the lights burning in here before climbing in through the back window. How was it then that the place was in darkness when you admitted your friends?"

Samela checked in time an involuntary movement. She looked at him meltingly and lifted an eyebrow.

"I turned them out," she said in a small-girl voice.

"Why?"

She hesitated. That was all right, surely. Hesitation wasn't necessarily a mark of guilt. "It—it—somehow—seemed more decent."

"Decent?" Raikes echoed, with mock incredulity.

"With—with Miss Tidy lying there, like that."

"But you knew the lights would have to go on again."

"But it had been daylight for hours by then."

"Of course. Only in that case why didn't you draw the curtain from the window?"

Samela frowned. What was he getting at? She looked at the window, only to catch a glimpse of a solid, uniformed back outside. "Didn't I?" she asked.

"When we arrived in answer to your telephone call you three girls were in here with the café lighted up and the blinds down still."

"How forgetful of us!" Sammy breathed.

Something in the tone made him look at her sharply, to see the touch of watchful scorn in the long-lashed, too intent gaze.

"What does darkness suggest to you?" he shot at her.

Samela gave this a delicate split-second consideration. "Peace and quiet."

"It has other functions."

She acquiesced in a polite little gesture. "I've told you what it means to me."

He leaned forward. "Mrs. Wild, darkness has the quality of concealment. It hides from us, from others, what we don't care shall be seen."

Brook looked up in plain disapproval. A local man wouldn't be handling the little lady like this.

Samela looked down into her lap, withdrawing her eyes without confusion or defeat.

"I think you ought to have warned me, don't you?" she said in a conspicuously good-tempered voice. "I mean, about the possibility of what I say being used in evidence. Otherwise I might be—*persuaded* to say something as—as picturesque as what you've just said about a dark room."

When Raikes did not answer she looked up at him again. Though his mouth was smiling, there was a glint of something else in his eyes.

"You mustn't look for traps where there are none," he said quietly.

"There are none only because I don't fall into them," Sammy returned with angelic ease.

He ignored that. "Dark or light, Mrs. Wild, the room was entered first by you. Can you explain why the door over there"—he nodded at the Flute Lane entrance—"should be locked, but no key found?"

"I found it."

"Where?"

"On the floor."

"Where is it now?"

Samela opened her handbag and held out the key in silence.

"What d'you do these things for?" Raikes asked testily. "Plunging a room into darkness as soon as you've discovered a murder, concealing a key? It's plain silly. Did the others see you pick it up?"

"No. I took it before I let them in."

"There you go. Sillier still. Why not have left it where it was?"

"I did it automatically, like touching the light switch. It was more or less reflex action, because I knew it ought not to be on the floor. Does it matter?"

"It could matter a great deal," the inspector said sternly. "You've no witness to the fact that the key was lying on the floor. By the way, where was it exactly? Show me."

He handed her the key. Samela got up and, after a moment's reflection, placed it four or five inches from the door.

"Just about there," she said. "I noticed it at once, because I've never seen it out of the inner keyhole. Miss Tidy leaves last every night—when she does leave, I mean. And she goes out by the front door, this being already locked and bolted."

She stopped short, bending down to look at the door.

"It's not bolted," she said, "but—"

"But nobody's used it since we came because it couldn't be unlocked, you were going to say?" Raikes put in. "Therefore it hasn't been bolted. Exactly. Which may indicate to you the importance of the key." He held out his hand for it as Samela returned to her chair. "It's pretty clear, Mrs. Wild, that Miss Tidy's murderer left by that door, and, having locked it, chucked the key through the letter box. However, since murder was obvious from the first glance, the murderer might just as well have thrown the key away in the street as deposit it neatly on the floor. But that's not the point. The point is, the key was on the floor *according to your evidence alone*. Nobody else saw it there, you say. So it may have been elsewhere."

"But it wasn't," Samela protested.

"I said it might have been."

"Where—might it have been?"

"In the murderer's possession. On the murderer's person. Even, perhaps, in the murderer's handbag."

There was a short, heavy silence which Brook cracked by an ostentatious clearing of his throat.

"You have a wonderful imagination," Samela said, but her voice was tight.

"And you," Raikes replied, "a wonderful propensity for injudicious action." He switched suddenly. "How long have you worked here, Mrs. Wild?"

"Through the war, and after—till now," Samela said. "About seven years hard, I suppose."

"Longer than the others?"

"Oh yes. Jane about four, Crystal nearly the same, I think, and Titus—that's Marion Oates, you know—under a year. She hasn't long left school."

"Seven years," Raikes mused. "Long enough to notice things. For instance, has Miss Tidy changed much since you knew her first? If so, how? Take your time."

What surprise Samela felt at the direction the enquiry was taking, she did not show. She thought for a minute, then said, "Yes—she did change. Yes, she certainly did. She got more mistrustful as time went on. It wasn't only I who noticed it. When you work with somebody in a fairly small establishment like this, you expect the association to mean there's more understanding, more confidence, the longer you're there. But it turned out to be the other thing with Tidy. The more you knew her, the less you knew her. I don't know how to put it more clearly. Bit by bit she grew very—aloof. It didn't make work easier, of course. And there was another thing." She stopped.

"Go on."

"We got busier, much busier—made more and wider connections, not only with millinery, but through the beauty culture which had just been started when I came here. Yet—in the days when things were duller and the Minerva had a comparatively little-known name, more people were employed here than now. *And* they were given a free hand. There used actually to be *three* girls as beauty specialists—*now* Tidy runs that department by herself—oh, you know what I mean—she—she did, till now."

"When did she begin looking after it alone?"

"Early spring. The last girl went then. Another had been sacked at Christmas. No, I don't think she had anything at all against them. If she did, I'm pretty sure they didn't know of it."

"No trumped-up charge?"

"Good gracious, no. Tidy just told them she had other plans. On the surface she always kept up good relations with the staff."

"What do you mean, 'on the surface'?" Raikes pounced.

Samela flushed. "I shouldn't have said that. You're bound to read into it a sinister meaning I didn't intend. I suppose all I meant was she wasn't on intimate terms with any of us."

"You mean you didn't like her?"

"I didn't say that."

"But it's true?"

"You'd have to know sooner or later. None of us *liked* her."

"Why not?"

Samela sighed and leveled at Raikes a look that was almost compassionate. "Inspector, *you* don't analyze, or do you, every like and dislike you have for people you rub up against? I expect we were all mildly allergic to her, or she to us."

"*All* of you?"

"Yes," Samela said, suddenly defiant. "Each one of us, without exception. Miss Tidy didn't inspire affection. I don't mean that that's necessarily against her. There's no reason why she shouldn't have been cold and detached if she was made that way. I'm only suggesting it breeds a sort of mutual indifference. That's why, though we're all shocked at what's happened—and I admit I'm frightened too—you don't see any of us really distressed."

"What have you got to be frightened about, Mrs. Wild?" Raikes quizzed.

Samela's eyes widened. "Isn't it obvious? It's a—a particularly horrid way to die, isn't it? And nobody being able to see why makes it horrider. And then it comes so soon after the suicides which are the talk of the town. I'm not a so-as-you'd-notice-it jittery person, but it makes me shiver a bit, and ask, who next?"

"Nonsense," Raikes said, the more robustly perhaps since Bertha Tidy's murder had jolted the police into asking the same thing. "Why, in any case, do you suggest a connection between a number of *suicides* and a death that's clearly—"

"Homicide," Samela finished, and shrugged. "If I do suggest a link I'm only anticipating what everybody else is going to say."

"But *why* should they say it?"

"Why, why, *why*," Samela, losing control, repeated, thumping a small fist into the palm of the other hand. "Forgive me for saying so, Inspector—though most likely you won't—I do think outsiders coming into a town are obtuse! This isn't a big place, nor a bad one, as civic reputations go, yet six people in two months or so have come to violent ends here! How *can* the rest of us see them all as unrelated—sheer coincidence, in fact? *Bunk!*"

"All right, all right," soothed Raikes, more gratified than otherwise at the outburst he had provoked. "I agree it's understandable those impressions should get around, but I think *you* ought to agree they're not worth much unless they can be substantiated—to a degree, at least. Merely *saying*, however emphatically, that one event's related to another won't disprove the factor of coincidence. You must go further than that and show at any rate a glimpse of the common denominator that rumor's suggesting for these deaths."

"We're not detectives," Samela said.

"You're wrong there," Raikes took her up. "Everybody who speculates about an unexplained event is setting up to be a detective. You mean, you don't want the responsibilities of detection. Unscientific poking about and baseless rumor and furtive hints in unsigned letters is more in Ravenchurch's line, isn't it?"

"I don't know what you mean," Samela said. She was breathing quickly.

"Don't you? Do you think the rest of the Minerva staff might?"

"You had better ask them yourself."

"I will," he said. "That's all for now, Mrs. Wild."

Samela stood up. She was pale and dry-lipped. "Before I go I would like to say I don't know who killed Miss Tidy, nor why. *I* didn't. If you want to know where I was at the time she died, you have my address—ask my husband."

"How do you know," Raikes asked quietly, "*when* Miss Tidy died?"

Samela, knowing she couldn't grow whiter, stood her ground. "It was in the night, wasn't it?"

"There were quite a few morning hours unaccounted for before Miss Kingsley arrived, you know."

"But she must have been—dead, while the lights were still burning."

He opened the door for her without reply.

3

Crystal Bates was enjoying herself. To say that she looked more distressed than either Jane or Sammy was still true; it did not blunt the edge of her pleasure. Though unaware herself of events giving rise to the resemblance, she was experiencing precisely Miss Tidy's own satisfaction on her visit to the police station the day before yesterday. Instead of getting involved in a discussion of what was Going On, in an argument in which she could never hold her own, she had secured an attentive and, therefore to her, sympathetic audience which questioned comparatively little and then only, it seemed, to accelerate her own powers of narration.

Raikes, who liked them tall and queenly and with *that* sort of hair, was indisposed to provoke the antagonism he had roused in Sammy. Crystal, slow on the uptake only where the issue was impersonal, sensed the cooperative spirit and gushed response.

"Why, nobody talks about anything else!" she repeated. "*Five* suicides? It just isn't believable—only," she broke off, "isn't it funny, now this awful thing has happened *they* don't seem half so important as they did—not to me, I mean. But of course, up to yesterday—well, it was different. And choosing hats and trying on, and beauty treatment, and teas—they're all exactly the things to start people talking, and as I say, that's *all* they ever talked about here, as far as I could tell. But not Miss Tidy. *She* wouldn't say a word. Not ever. And that set me thinking."

"Yes?"

"Well, wouldn't it you? People didn't like it, her not joining in, I mean. It was plain snubbing. Everyone else so het up with the inquests and everything, and Tidy shutting up like a trap whenever they tried it on her."

"And what was it you thought?"

"Me? There was only one thing anybody could think." Crystal stopped dramatically.

"And that was?"

"Why, that Miss Tidy knew a good deal more than she cared to say about the deaths. After all, if she *knew* things she wouldn't want to join a hen party that was just guessing, would she?"

"You're right there, I expect," Raikes said. "Everyone else putting forward theories as to how and why and so forth, and Miss Tidy contributing nothing because *you* think she was in possession of the facts of the matter?"

"Yes, and this proves I'm right, doesn't it?" Crystal urged.

"Remains to be seen," Raikes answered. He had an indulgent air. "Anything else occur to you?"

"What?"

"Well, I wouldn't know, would I? About the suicides, for instance—did *you* put forward any pet theory of your own?"

"To Miss Tidy, do you mean?"

"To anybody."

"When I saw how unpopular the chatter was I didn't mention the subject in her hearing. Not even when Iris Kane drowned herself. And *that* made more talk than all the rest—seeing she was so soon going to be married. Or because it came last, perhaps. But I did say one or two things to other people. After all, we're expected to talk to customers, and if people will keep flogging the same subject—"

"Having to ignore it cramps your style," the inspector finished briefly. "Yes. And what were the one or two things you said?"

Crystal was not at her best after interruption. She looked at him dreamily. "Oh, *things*," she said with a large, vague gesture. "Well, of course, I've *always* said they weren't suicides—not real ones."

"Indeed?" Raikes said, with the bright air of one receiving an original suggestion. "And why not, Mrs. Bates?"

"People don't *do* it," Crystal said simply. "Not one after another, like that." She spoke with a touch of resentment at the bad taste which disregarded the necessity for well-spaced timing in these affairs.

"But don't you think," Raikes probed, "that five *murders* following each other so fast are hardly more credible?"

Crystal turned this over to make sure she'd got the hang of it.

"I hadn't got as far as thinking about it that way," she said with patent sincerity. "Anyway, the five would be only a coverup."

"To cover up what?"

"Why, the sixth murder—Miss Tidy's murder!"

"Explain what you mean, please."

Crystal stared at him in pained, though lovely, amazement. "But—but it's *easy*," she stammered, then, spreading the wings of imagination in the loftiest flight she was ever to attain, exclaimed, "I think there's somebody with a *motive* for killing one person pretending that there's somebody killing a lot of people *without* a motive! Kenneth—that's my husband—thinks so too."

"And what," asked Raikes when he had sufficiently recovered, "is your husband's occupation, Mrs. Bates?"

"Who—Ken? Oh, he's a black-and-white artist on the *Daily Screed*, and other papers. He says it's probably a Jack the Ripper thug staging a senseless massacre so as to get at one person under cover of it. *I* don't think anybody else will be murdered now that Miss Tidy's dead."

But she was wrong there.

4

At twelve-thirty Marion Oates reached her home in Thistle Street, and a few minutes afterwards sat down to her lunch. She ate with the adolescent's usual morose concentration, while Aunts Hilda and Win, who had heard hours before of the dreadful affair at the Minerva, waited in trepidation for hysteria, panic, loss of appetite, anything in fact but the calculating introspection they got.

"You know, Win," their niece said at last in a comfortably replete voice, "this cheese isn't so good as what we got last week."

"No—no, dear," said Aunt Win, feeling sudden exhaustion at this atomic destruction of her own and her sister's efforts to turn an extraordinary situation into an ordinary one.

And, "I believe it used to be nicer when the ration was smaller," the deflated Hilda agreed.

"Funny, don't you think," Marion went on, dismissing the cheese, "that the Scotland Yard man didn't want to see me. He kept Jane and Samela quite a time, and even Crystal long enough."

"Oh, my dear," said Win, "don't *think* about it. Why should he want to see you?"

Marion gave her a long look. "Why *shouldn't* he, you mean. There's a fair amount I could say. But there, he's got my address, so I suppose he'll roll along pretty soon."

"How *can* you, Marie?" Aunt Hilda said. "Be thankful you're out of this horrible, *horrible* business. Of course he wouldn't need to question you. The others were inside the shop and had found—it all, long before you arrived."

"You don't understand, Auntie," Marion said with cool indulgence. "And I'm not out of it. The only thing I'm out of is the teashop—no more teas this afternoon, or tomorrow afternoon, or *any* afternoon. It's too good to be true!"

"*Marion!*" cried both ladies together. "How heartless!" Aunt Hilda added.

"She's upset," Win said hurriedly.

Marion caught in the words the faint plea for her to be upset. She smiled. It was the smile of a headmistress for two favorite, though temporarily foolish, pupils. She went to the door, preparatory to going up to her room.

"Oh, Aunt Win," she said slowly, "if anything *is* said to you, you'll know to say that we always took our night walks *together*. I never went alone."

<h1 style="text-align:center">5</h1>

Jane sat brushing with methodical strokes the hair so artfully tangled by day. Midsummer though it was, it was late enough for a light upstairs, and heavy moths, displaying the only activity apparent in Stoneacre at this hour, bumped her window where a lick of night wind moved the curtains.

Somebody tapped at the door. It was Elsie.

"You all right?" she enquired perfunctorily. Tired after the usual day's grind among the milkers and poultry, she could only feel as remote unreality a five-mile-away murder. But her young sister-in-law, she recollected, was uncomfortably closer to things.

"Sure," Jane said, smiling as she turned. "I'm over it now. The worst bits, I mean. And however you see it, Sammy was really the one to take it between the eyes, poor lass. She got in first. Elsie?" Her voice brightened.

"What?"

"If—if the police don't *ask* you something, you're not—not holding out on them, are you, if you don't say anything about it?"

Elsie frowned. "I don't know what you mean, Jane. Who's holding out on the police? That wouldn't do."

"Nobody," Jane said impatiently. "That's just what I'm saying. You're *not* doing anything wrong if you don't tell them what they haven't asked for."

"I'm sure I don't know," Elsie said, unable to determine so nice a point unrelated to hens and milk, "not at this time of night. I'll ask Ralph."

"Oh, don't *bother*," Jane cried, as nearly cross as she ever got. They were always the same. Their own lives were too circumscribed to make interesting discussion, especially on academic points, ever possible. So their advice was felt to be without authority. That was why Sammy ... dear, nimble-witted Sam ... was always the person you turned to in the last resort. But she hadn't come to the last resort yet.

Ralph, hearing his name as a tailpiece, came out of the other bedroom. Now and then it crossed his mind that he should, perhaps, acquaint himself a little more conscientiously with the possible doubts and difficulties of the sister, twelve years his junior, for whom he had a staunch affection. Not, he argued, that any personal blame was attaching to him for this rotten business at the Minerva. But now that he came to think about it, there was precious little he did know about Janey's private life.

He scrutinized her from the doorway as Elsie muddled the question.

"But, good lor', girl," he grumbled when he had disentangled the point, "you don't *wait* for this question and that where murder's concerned. If you know something, you out with it!"

"If you only know part of a thing?" Jane innocently enquired.

"Anything," Ralph said with pontifical finality. "It doesn't take a lot, remember, to make you in their eyes an accessory after the fact."

"Oh, bother the fact," his sister returned. "*I'd* rather have a few more facts myself before I get talking to Mr. Raikes again!"

By the time she got to sleep that night she had made up her mind and fully determined her course of action.

6

In the peace and quiet of her darkness, with George's uneasy length stretched beside her, Samela fixed her gaze upon a glittering point of light in the strip of sky topping her window.

"Aldebaran," she murmured, not knowing why. "Perhaps it's Aldebaran. ... Nice name for a star."

"Uh?" said George restlessly.

"I didn't know you were awake," Sammy whispered. "Darling, I don't think Inspector Raikes likes me much."

George grunted ambiguously.

"What did you say, George?"

"I said, 'sall right by me."

Samela, unhampered by the dark, neatly bit the tip of his ear. "Listen ... if he says anything to you about it, swear I was here all last night, won't you?"

" 'Course," Mr. Wild muttered serenely. "Though you were a ruddy little fool not to be, an' I said so."

He pulled Sammy into his arms and closed his eyes. That he could do this, with an English night in June lapping the walls that held them, was to him still so much a rediscovery that it held all the quality of a dream.

7

Raikes, thought Superintendent Lecky, had a despondent, if not chastened, air when he returned at lunchtime. He himself had perhaps not been mistaken in reckoning him the wrong man for the bucolic and urban mixture of self-possession that was Ravenchurch. Well, it was the inspector who had set the pace, and the inspector who would have to make the running.

"I'll see the old lady this afternoon," Raikes said. "The maid at Long Greeting too. With a chap posted in Flute Lane there's not likely to be much hanky-panky before two o'clock."

Lecky raised his eyebrows coldly. "None, if I know Mrs. Weaver," he said with a curtness not lost on Raikes, who retorted, "Perhaps you don't."

"You think you know these people, but do you?" Raikes went on. "Perhaps you do—perhaps it's all hunky-dory because they've grown up with the place, and maybe we've got to go outside for our murderer and give Ravenchurch and Long Greeting and Stoneacre a clean bill of health. But I don't think so. There's a crack, you know, about the guy who sees most of the game, and I fancy it holds water when it comes to crime in a country town. You can know people too well."

"What exactly you driving at?" asked Lecky, with what geniality he could muster.

"Oh, no offense—I'm only stating what's inevitable when you live cheek by jowl with folk. Don't tell me somebody hasn't been pulling the wool over your eyes with devilish neatness ever since Mrs. Livingston-Bole drowned herself."

"You're sure," Lecky inquired with heavy sarcasm, "she did drown herself?"

"Practically," Raikes, unperturbed, agreed. "It's not the fact of suicide I question. The alternative would be homicidal mania—more. Homicidal mania rarely, I believe, produces genius, and nobody inferior to a genius could have rigged up five murders to look like incontestable suicides!"

"Then what's biting you?"

"The link-up between the five—and between them and number six, which happens to be incontestable murder. I'll stake my last dime it's there, and why? Because Miss Tidy and Miss Beaton both thought it worthwhile to interest the police in certain aspects of the case—and twenty-four hours later the first of 'em is disposed of, with no chance of a comeback."

"What about Bertha Tidy now as the author of those letters? D'you still think she wrote 'em?"

"I—don't—know," Raikes said slowly. "I think perhaps they're not *frightfully* important. But they made the *occasion* for a visit to the local police. And—I say it without the veriest shadow of offensiveness—I think she came along to talk about 'em to you—neither she nor Miss Beaton knew I'd be there—because she and the locals'd been mutually acquainted for years, her visit being just part of the wool pulling I'm trying to get at. Nothing like voluntarily coming out into the limelight to draw off the chase."

"Nobody," Lecky said with unconscious humor, "was chasing Miss Tidy."

"I believe you," Raikes returned. "Metaphorically speaking, though, I think somebody, or something, was. She was clearly plagued mentally, and saw herself as the next victim. We, with a handful of *suicides* behind us, flouted the idea of possible murder. But she was right."

Lecky did not reply. For many a day to come the parting assurance he had given to Miss Tidy was going to be a bitter pill for repetitive dosage.

"As for those girls," Raikes continued, "I'm not putting it past one of 'em—the murder, I mean. Oh yes, after due consideration of the physical factors too. She was a sparrow of a woman, remember—as small as Mrs. Wild, and a great deal older. *Much* smaller than Mrs. Bates and the fighting-fit Kingsley. And she was strangled: not too hard a job for a woman. There's that jiggery-pokery with the teashop lights—who's to say they ever were burning, except as an excuse for breaking in? There's the very odd point about failing to ring up the Keepsake before smashing the window—yes, I know Jane Kingsley says she overheard her talking about being there that night, but it seems to have taken very little to convince Mrs. Wild that she wasn't still in Long Greeting. After all, she was the senior member of the staff and should have tried every legitimate means of getting in touch with her employer before butting in the way they did—*unless she knew she was already dead.* As for the business of the key—it's phony, if you like. Why not in her handbag all the time?"

"Silly place for a murderer to pop it," Lecky said drily, "who was going to hand it over so easily."

"Besides," Raikes added, ignoring him, "what's to say the staff didn't have duplicate keys to the front door? In which case the café key on the floor or not, need never have come into the story."

The superintendent sighed. "When you've got the why, you'll have the who."

"On the contrary," Raikes said obstinately, "when I've got the who in this case I'll have the why."

"Did you see the little girl?"

"Which one?"

"Oates is the name."

"Not yet. Sixteen, isn't she? Brook already thinks me a nasty piece of imported third degree. So I'll see her at her home, nicely bolstered up with witnesses. Anyway, she got there this morning later than we did."

"If she's nothing more material to say than the others," Lecky remarked ruefully, "we shan't be a lot better off."

"Bits an' pieces," Raikes admitted. "Ha'pence and farthings. But added up, they may one day make a hefty bill for somebody to foot."

CHAPTER 6

Pancakes and fritters,
Say the bells of St. Peter's.

The frying pan sputtered, and Emmie Weaver, stooping over the gas cooker, drew it back hastily. Meals with her were always chancy affairs, for the most part untimed, and lunch today was a late, slapdash business of reconditioned eggs that seemed to be taking unkindly to the metamorphosis. She didn't pretend to be a cook; life and the bookshop held things so much more interesting than were to be found in saucepan and baking dish, which, while living alone and liking it were her governing conditions, she could not entirely ignore. And eating was still necessary, though next door Miss Tidy had been knocked on the head.

She flicked a blue-and-white checked cloth over the table, took a knife and fork from the drawer, a cruet from the dresser and a plate from the shelf, upsetting upon its cold surface the rather unsavory dollop out of the pan. It had neither the symmetry nor the melting appeal of a pancake; it was dark, fretful, unshapely, with edge indignantly burned, but Mrs. Weaver regarded it with a benign, unseeing eye and sat down to meditate upon death in the midst of life.

One good thing, now she had left the shop for the kitchen, was her change of view. She had never supposed she would find satisfaction in eyeing the dingy alley where the hatshop girls kept their bicycles, but after a morning darkened by the passage of the constabulary in Flute Lane and along the front, this mean vista was astonishingly agreeable. She wondered why policemen had to cast a more substantial shadow than other folk.

The electric floor bell, one of her few concessions to modernity, jangled insistently, and she went into the shop. The hatless stranger, standing there almost as umbrageously as her police guards, stepped off the mat as though it was biting him. She recognized him for the man who had spent the morning at the Minerva.

"Mrs. Weaver, I think?" he said, coming forward, "I'm Inspector Raikes of New Scotland Yard. Some nice stock you have here."

She beamed at that. He approved of her books. They were her children, the only children she had ever had; a fierce maternal pride burned in her. The man who admired them stepped at once into a place in her estimation from which it would be difficult to dislodge him.

Ostensibly, Raikes gave his attention to the imposing shelves of vellum and calf and golden, tooled spines; but while he was reviewing the ranks of folio and quarto, and running his eye over a nice contemporary set of Clarendon, his appraisal was all for the gaunt figure of the shopkeeper.

Close on six foot, he told himself, and muscular. Thinness here doesn't denote debility. Long, scraggy arms, very useful reach. About Tidy's age. Or younger, though looking older, but doesn't prink herself. All mental drive. Disregard of the physical. Touch of the fanatic? Perhaps.

Aloud he said, "I'm down here, you know, about this bad business next door. You can help me a good deal."

Her reply found him off his guard a little. "But you were in Ravenchurch some time before Miss Tidy was killed."

He smiled faintly. "Of course. I came down on other business. Now we

think there may be some connection between that and the murder last night."
He shot her a jesting glance. "You're officially well informed, Mrs. Weaver.
But it's all right—I got my orders this morning to carry on!"

She smiled and nodded, not quite sure of the drift of his remarks. It
seemed that she had not meant precisely what he meant, but her mind moved
ahead too rapidly to debate the point.

"I'm having my lunch," she said, "but you won't mind that. And look—
we'll have no customers interrupting." She strode past Raikes down the
center alley between the towering cases of books and, at the front door,
turned round on its string a card bearing the word "Closed."

"I do that on and off, you know, living by myself as I do. *My* business
doesn't suffer as some might," she added proudly. "Books are like people—
they're always there, and my sort aren't to be had for the picking up."

She took him into the odorous kitchen and, drawing a chair out on the
other side of the table, motioned him to it. Then she filled the kettle at the
sink and, lighting the ring, put it on to boil.

"I'll make you a cup of tea in a minute," she said and, seating herself at
the table, calmly resumed her meal. "When this gets quite cold and stuck to
the plate, I don't fancy it, so I'd better finish now. What is it you want to
know?"

"Just a few things you can tell me better than anyone else," Raikes said,
sighing with relief at having for once the pace set for him. "First, you live
here at the shop, don't you? I mean you sleep here?"

"Oh yes," Mrs. Weaver said, lovingly retrieving a burnt forkful and conveying it to her mouth. "This is my house. But home's really only the kitchen,
you know. The attics are stock rooms, and the books overflow into my
bedroom. I've some delightful Bewicks up there—in lately—if you——"

"Indeed I would," Raikes put in gravely, "later on. Now to take last things
first, as we usually have to do in a case of murder, did you know where
Miss Tidy was spending last night?"

"Of course," the bookseller said in a prompt, high voice, tucking away a
strand of grayhair and fixing sharp brown eyes on the inspector. "She told
me herself she would be sleeping at the café. Nothing unusual in that—she
did, you see, quite often."

"And was it also usual for her to tell you beforehand of her intention?"

It wasn't. But there was a special reason yesterday. She had had some
seventeenth-century color maps come in, including one of Ravenchurch
and environs which she thought might interest Miss Tidy. No, Miss Tidy
didn't as a rule care about old books, or anything of the sort; a regrettably
defective taste which really made a barrier to their better acquaintance. But
she was always hoping to catch her eye with something out of the common
run, a hope based on the presence in the Minerva of that charming sampler
which she had made tentative efforts at buying, but which Miss Tidy refused to sell.

"But it made me think she might not be averse to pairing it with a nice old map of purely local interest, which would have a more than decorative appeal if hung in the teashop. She *used* to be very careful to cherish the period attractions of the café."

Raikes echoed, "Used to be?"

"I mean she seemed lately to have lost interest in the business."

He nodded, but would not deflect her from her story.

"So I took the maps over in the afternoon," Mrs. Weaver went on. "It sounds quite a journey put like that, but the Slip is so narrow that it's really like living with the Minerva folk, with only a passage between rooms. Miss Tidy would hardly spare a glance for the maps. I fear I must bore her sadly at times. Enthusiasm runs away with one, and it's not always easy to remember that others don't share it. She was preoccupied—she often is nowadays. She suggested I might show them to her later as she wasn't returning home. At least," she amended, "I don't mean she said just that—her words were she'd be at the Minerva all night."

"And do you know," Raikes asked, "if anybody could have overheard her tell you that?"

Mrs. Weaver stared, looking as if she had been caught out saying something she should not. "I—don't know—oh yes, I should *think* so. Most of the girls seemed about still. But, you know, it couldn't have made any difference either way. I think it was common knowledge that Miss Tidy frequently slept here and not at Long Greeting. Arrangements, bed and so on, for her to do so, were permanent. I've thought it must have been a bit lonely for old Léonie—her maid at the cottage—being left like that any night Miss Tidy took a fancy not to go back."

"No doubt it may have been," said Raikes. "Your kettle's getting noisy," he added.

Mrs. Weaver gave it an admonitory glance over her shoulder, then got up to make the tea. While she was chinking cups and hospitably pushing oatmeal biscuits under his nose, Raikes reflected on her apparent disregard of the crux they were approaching. For if she had responded to Miss Tidy's invitation she was probably the last person, bar the murderer, to have seen her alive. And so long as the murderer figured as X, the last person to have seen Miss Tidy before her death was in no comfortable position.

He put the question to her over tea.

Mrs. Weaver clasped her bony fingers round the hot cup and looked at him without excitement. "Funny to be warming myself on a June day as good as this one," she said, "but my hands are always cold. Books, you know. And then, I'm so stringy. Oh yes, I went in there last night. Just after I'd had my supper—nine o'clock, to be exact, because the cathedral clock was striking, I remember, as I opened my door on the lane. Miss Tidy answered my knock."

"One moment, Mrs. Weaver. This is important. When Miss Tidy let you in, do you remember if she merely opened the door or unlocked it first?"

"Unlocked it," was the firm reply. "*And* drew back the bolt. You see, Miss Tidy always locked and bolted the teashop door—the one that gives onto the Slip—as soon as her staff had gone. She did that whether or not she was going home any evening."

"That's clear. Now tell me please, as carefully as possible, just what happened while you were with Miss Tidy, and anything you may have noticed, *anything*—even if to you it seems too trivial for mention. By the way, when you were inside did Miss Tidy fasten the door again?"

"She locked it," Mrs. Weaver said. "I don't remember about the bolt."

For the rest, the account held no highlights, though there were some significant points worth examining. The teashop was bare and tidy, the lights at that hour in midsummer not burning yet. The divan, she thought, was not then made up for sleeping, but she could not be quite sure. Because her attention hadn't been drawn to it, however, she supposed it had probably had its usual daytime appearance. Miss Tidy, fully dressed, had apparently been writing at a table farthest from the Flute Lane window. A chair was pushed back, and a piece of pink blotting paper drawn so neatly over whatever it had been that she was busy at that Mrs. Weaver had been quite unable to glimpse more than an edge of white paper, a fountain pen beside it. Her handbag was lying there too.

Raikes frowned. Miss Tidy's handbag had not been recovered. Nor had there been any sign of writing materials. He said nothing, and the bookseller continued.

"I unrolled the maps—three of them, they're in my window now—and she admired them, with the perfunctory sort of appreciation she had for such things. I knew her thoughts were not on them. No—oh no, I didn't *at all* get the impression she wanted to be rid of me. She had no use for the maps; she didn't want to talk about them, but I felt—yes, rather strongly— that she was glad to have me there. She wanted to make me coffee, but I had just had my supper and was disinclined. Indeed, it was I who must have seemed more anxious to be gone than Miss Tidy was for me to go—and as it was unusual for her to dissemble her impatience I think I must be right in believing that this time she was sincerely pleased I came in. No, I don't know why."

She had stayed hardly longer than ten minutes. Long enough, though, to detect a change of mood in Miss Tidy before she left.

"She seemed," said Mrs. Weaver, "to get a little more excited. She was not at all an excitable person, as you may have gathered, but self-contained and *very* uncommunicative; and I think it was only someone coming in as I did, rather late, after she'd been some hours alone and was feeling—who can say?—ready for company, that made her relax at all."

Her excitement, as Mrs. Weaver was doubtful if she ought to term it, expressed itself in fidgetiness and random talk. She walked about restlessly, which her visitor had not seen her do before, made unpurposive movements and irrelevant remarks, and finally, on seeing Mrs. Weaver out, had said something which, in the light of after events, struck her hearer as significant. Mrs. Weaver herself had provoked the remark by mentioning a collection of books she hoped to secure at a sale next week.

"You don't let *your* business get you down," Miss Tidy had observed, a bitter note in her voice, "though you run it alone. Mine is getting the upper hand of me. I am thinking of giving it up."

Then she had laughed, so unpleasantly that Mrs. Weaver had carried the echo of it indoors but, speculating about it afterwards, could find no satisfactory explanation. For it was the first she had heard of any intention on Miss Tidy's part to retire from her flourishing hatshop, café, and beauty parlor.

Raikes received this without comment, though with frank interest. This was a not inopportune moment to bring home to Mrs. Weaver a realization of her position in the case.

"And so you left her," he rounded off noncommittally. "Mrs. Weaver, has it struck you that you are the last person to have seen Miss Tidy alive?"

Mrs. Weaver reached for the inspector's empty cup and poured some milk into it.

"But I wasn't," she said calmly. "The murderer saw her after I did."

"Eh?" Raikes was jolted into surprise. "Oh, quite. But unfortunately we're not at the moment in a position to discuss with the murderer what hour that was."

"I think I can tell you," Mrs. Weaver said.

"What?" Raikes almost shouted, leaning forward and jeopardizing his steaming cup. "What evidence have you got relating to the murder?"

"I don't *know*," Mrs. Weaver said quietly, "that it's connected with the murder. But I certainly heard someone leaving the Minerva last night—oh, long after I'd left."

"Go on," Raikes urged. "Tell me all you can remember."

Mrs. Weaver had gone to bed early and, reckoning by the cathedral chimes, had fallen asleep before half past ten.

"I woke up suddenly," she explained, "and quite completely. I mean, one minute I was asleep and the next I was wide awake and knowing at once what had roused me. My bedroom window overlooks the Slip and, as the way is with these very old houses, if I were to lean out with a stick in my hand I'd be able to touch the window of the beauty parlor across the way. Not that I've tried, but that's how it is. There wasn't anything going on up there, I don't mean that—but I tell you this to show how close we are and how easily sound penetrates, especially as I keep my rather small window open summer nights."

"And the sound you heard?" Raikes almost groaned with impatience, yearning to take the old lady by the shoulders and shake it out of her.

"I heard," she said, "the teashop door being locked. But whoever was doing it was fumbling it a good deal first. I'd never heard that noise before. Whenever Miss Tidy turned the key, it was just a quiet click. Then all at once there was a muffled, sort of scrabbling sound, and then a little thud. I lay still, listening. I heard a chuckle, a quite horrid chuckle, and then a few soft steps, and then everything was silent." Mrs. Weaver sighed. "And, do you know, it never occurred to me till it was too late?"

"What didn't?"

"Why, that the door wasn't being locked from the *inside*, as always before, but by somebody in Flute Lane, who then dropped the key through the letter slit. And even last night when I had no reason to suspect anything, that struck me as so *unusual* that I would certainly have gone to the window to look if I had been in time. But whoever had locked the door had had time to disappear. So I came to the only conclusion I could."

"Which was?"

"I supposed Miss Tidy had done whatever it was she had wanted to do and decided to go home after all. I turned on the light and looked at my watch. It was five minutes to midnight. I must say I never knew her do such a thing before. She was nervous of the dark."

Raikes groaned outright this time. So near and yet so far. Feminine curiosity for once lagging behind the event sufficiently to miss what, for the police, would undoubtedly have been the catch of the season.

"These footsteps," he said, snatching at straws, "man's or woman's— which would you say?"

Mrs. Weaver thought. "I'm *so* sorry," she said at last, discerning something of official disappointment, "but I can't even say *that*. I'm quite sure they were rubber soles, you know, but I'd only be guessing if I went further."

"That's all right." Raikes made an effort to cheer up. "A scrap of knowledge in our work is more valuable than a whole heap of imagination. Just one thing—why did you say just now that you didn't know whether this evidence of yours had any connection with the murder? You *do* know now that it couldn't have been Miss Tidy returning to Long Greeting. So, unless somebody else left the café *after* your unknown—"

"That's just it," Mrs. Weaver said quickly. "Suppose someone else did? I slept again without waking till nearly seven, so I wouldn't know. You see, it wasn't at *all* out of the ordinary."

"What wasn't?"

"For people to leave the teashop at odd hours on the nights Miss Tidy stayed there."

Raikes nearly bounded out of his chair. This was better. This was something to get one's teeth in.

It appeared that in all seasons in the past couple of years, but more frequently during this spring and summer, Mrs. Weaver had heard various night visitors to the Minerva, it might be on arrival, or else in departure. Often it was the only indication she had had that Miss Tidy was still there. It was certainly her experience in the matter which had enabled her to distinguish between the sounds of locking the door from inside and outside. Always, before last night, Miss Tidy herself had locked the door after her guests.

"It's been going on such a long while," she admitted with almost an air of apology, "that I never think about it at all now. I'm always in bed when I happen to hear these sounds, and I'm not nearly inquisitive enough to get out and look. Once, a long time ago when I wasn't so used to it—sometime last year—I did peep out of the window and noticed a woman leaving. But she was very quick, and I scarcely caught a glimpse of her. It was winter, and blackout."

"Nothing you can recall about her?" Raikes, hungry for morsels, asked.

Mrs. Weaver shook her head. "I remember she was tall—but that's not very helpful, is it? You see, it's a good while ago, and I never thought twice about it."

"Not even to wonder why Miss Tidy was receiving visitors at her place of business in the middle of a winter night?" Raikes made no effort to hide incredulity.

"Well, no," Mrs. Weaver said, resigned to the impossibility of explaining to those who did not lead it themselves just what were the implications of a self-contained life. "I've never bothered about neighbors' activities. Perhaps not enough. Not that I didn't make a guess or two, you know. And I thought these people who came and went odd hours after the Minerva was closed were perhaps receiving beauty treatment of some sort by special appointment."

"In the night?" the bewildered Raikes reminded her.

"You never know," Mrs. Weaver defended her astonishing theory. "Women do queer things, especially at middle age, or when they've passed it. It isn't impossible some of Miss Tidy's clients were too sensitive to have facial buildups, and so on, by day. I don't know much about these things, but I do know a little about women, Inspector."

Raikes, who at the moment was feeling rather severely his own limitations in this respect, agreed that she might be right.

"But Miss Tidy herself," he asked, "didn't she ever let fall a word about these nights at the Minerva?"

"Never. She probably waited for me to bring the matter up first."

She probably had, thought Raikes. If Bertha Tidy had had something to conceal—and it looked uncommonly like it—how lucky, how infernally lucky she had been in the only near neighbor who could have poked a nose to some effect in the business! Lucky? There were two sides to that. A show of healthy inquisitiveness on the part of the bookseller, and it was on the cards that the course of events might have been less hideous.

There was little more he was able to elicit. On her own admissions Mrs.

Weaver had neither known nor cared to know her business neighbor outside the boundary of Flute Lane. The character of each precluded an exchange of confidence, and Mrs. Weaver confessed that she had never called at the cottage, nor had she received an invitation to do so. She knew Léonie by sight, on the rare occasions the old maid had looked in at the Minerva when she was, perhaps, shopping in Ravenchurch, and believed her the usual devoted, industrious example of her class and generation. But she was entirely unfamiliar with Miss Tidy's menage in Long Greeting; nor did she know any of the villagers except the only two who were interested in her books.

"Miss Beaton comes in sometimes, and doesn't stay long," she explained. "And Mr. Greatorex comes often, and usually lingers here reading this and that."

No, she held no heretical views about the tragedies in Ravenchurch during the spring. She took them for the suicides they were pronounced to be, a high proportion for so quiet a neighborhood, it was true, but there was no accounting for these things; none of the deceased, except the schoolteacher, Edith Drake, had been inside her shop, so far as she recalled.

Raikes gathered that even the feverish gossip had failed to reach Mrs. Weaver except as the lightest backwash. She knew, she said, that Miss Tidy never wanted to speak of the deaths, and put it down to the friendship she had had for Mrs. Livingston-Bole, who had drowned herself a couple of months ago.

"I believe she was a very charming person," Mrs. Weaver said sadly. "Some six months to a year ago she used to come frequently to the Minerva and have tea there. I didn't notice her about here for some time before her death. People said, though, she hadn't been well a long while."

It was evident that Mrs. Weaver, who had contributed nothing to the buzz about the fatal events in Ravenchurch, saw no relation between them and last night's murder. The manner of Bertha Tidy's death she received with horror, the fact she accepted with equanimity.

Raikes when he left her, unsentimental fellow that he was, felt a little chilled at the thought that he had still to meet the person genuinely sorry Miss Tidy was dead.

2

Nor, when he got to the Keepsake, did he think he had found her.

The sunny, bee-thronged, innocuous-looking little house, with its suggestion of floral retirement, predisposed him to milder judgments; and as he walked up the path, with the afternoon somnolence quelling even suspicion, he heard the same pleasant clatter of dishes as had greeted Miss Tidy two evenings before.

Léonie was washing up. "One must eat," she said somberly, wiping her large hands in a drying cloth as she opened the door to him. "Not," she added, "with an air so punctual as one did, but still, it is necessary to cook, to eat, to wash the dishes, *n'est-ce pas?*"

Raikes concurred with this philosophy in a solemn gesture that seemed to satisfy her. She began leading the way along the short, cool passage to the kitchen. The inspector, however, surfeited with cookers and sinks, paused by the sitting-room door.

"Why not in here?" he asked.

Léonie stopped, shrugged, came back, and, opening the door, drew to one side for him to enter.

"It is not usual, you understand—not usual for *me*. My visitors, they are in the kitchen. Miss Bert'a's in here."

"Well, nothing's usual at the moment," Raikes replied. "Maybe it will be a little more comfortable to talk in here. I am sure you must have had a very great shock."

After a swift glance at the enchanting view from the window, he looked more closely at the maid as she seated herself with stiff dignity on a narrow-backed chair, the light falling on her profile. With her hands folded on her apron and the scrubbed, lined look of her, she was like a Chardin painting with the cheerfulness washed out of it. A large woman, he saw, strong, at one time probably not uncomely. There were no marks of weeping on her face; high on the prominent cheekbones two red spots burned brightly.

She gave him look for look, with the habitually hooded gaze of the older type of domestic servant.

"Yes and no," she said with deliberation. "I am not thinking Miss Bert'a is going to die just *when* she die, but I 'ave told her so often, oh, so often, that she will be murdered one day, you understand, that—shock, you say? No."

Raikes applauded the uncompromising opening that looked like making things easier for himself, while feeling a little quelled at having the wind taken so effectually out of the sails of his condolence.

Asked to amplify this blunt disavowal of alarm, she merely pointed out that her mistress's habit of sleeping alone at her place of business was an invitation to the wicked, who abounded, to enter and slay her, Raikes forbearing to observe that murder without motive, even among an abundance of sinners, was extremely rare.

He wrote down her name, Léonie Blanchard; her age, sixty-two; her years of service with Miss Tidy, close on twenty-one.

He drew from her an unemotional recital of yesterday's simple facts. Miss Tidy had left the cottage as usual in the morning, wheeling her bicycle down the path at half past eight, as she did every day—that is, every day after a night spent at the Keepsake. She was extremely punctual and methodical in all her habits. At breakfast she had informed Léonie that she would not be home that night. Yes, it was true that she sometimes did not make her mind up on the point until she had arrived in Ravenchurch; when that happened she always rang up to say that she was staying till the following day. But this was not so yesterday; she had told her in advance. No, it had never happened that Mam'selle had slept at the teashop *without* letting her know. In matters of that sort she was a lady very punctilious, oh, the most considerate. Not loving, not, perhaps, conspicuous for her *bonté*, but, *vous comprenez*, of the most considerate, in the fashion of the methodical and orderly.

Raikes recognized the portrait at once. For him it served merely to intensify the aura of coldness that clung like an icy shroud to every fresh report he got of the dead woman. People seemed anxious to stress her unloving qualities. Was it because each new witness wanted to suggest that murder was not after all so unthinkable when associated with Bertha Tidy? He heard Samela: "None of us *liked* her. She didn't inspire affection."

"How was Miss Tidy dressed yesterday morning?" he asked abruptly.

Léonie thought. She gave a slow, accurate description tallying with the police record of the murdered woman's clothes.

"What about a scarf?" Raikes added lightly. "Do you remember if she wore one?"

Léonie was silent long enough for him to wonder whether she had heard. Then she said, carefully, "She has scarves—several. This weather, it is not the weather when one wears them."

"I know," Raikes said, feeling his way, "but we found one."

"Then," the old servant agreed, "she had one, yes?"

"But what I'd like to know," Raikes repeated patiently, "is, was she *wearing* this scarf when she left the house yesterday? It was a hot day, a blazing hot day—it seems a little out of place."

"*Mais certainement*," Léonie murmured. "She was not wearing it."

Raikes saw himself in the position of Hamlet pointing out the cloud to Polonius. If he had suggested Miss Tidy wore it as a turban or pinned it, a train, to her frock, he felt that the old woman would have agreed.

"Did you *see* it on her?" he persisted.

"No," Léonie said, shaking her head. Then, sensing by now that something more was expected of her, she added, "But if she do not wear it she may, perhaps, take it with her. I do not know what she carry."

"You haven't checked her wardrobe?" Raikes asked.

"But *why?*" Léonie showed not unreasonable surprise. "I do not know until you tell me that Miss Tidy, she wear a scarf yesterday. I hear only from *les gendarmes* that she has been killed, and that it is for me to stay *à la maison* till one comes to question. I do not know about scarves. How is it then that I should examine the clothes?"

She had worked herself up to a measure of excitement which Raikes tried to allay.

"All right, all right," he said quietly. "There was no reason for you to have thought of such a thing in so short a time. It will be something we can do together. Now what exactly did Miss Tidy take with her when she left here intending to spend the night at the Minerva?"

"But nothing," Léonie said firmly. "There is not the necessity. All she want, it is there, at the café."

"But wasn't there a suitcase, or something smaller—a lunch case, say— she carried on these occasions?"

"Nev-*aire*," said Léonie with finality.

"Not a bicycle basket?" Raikes pressed hopefully.

Léonie looked enquiry. He enlarged on what he meant, sketching with his fingers this adjunct to the handlebars.

"But the bicycle, you see it for yourself?" she replied. "There is on it no object such as you say."

Raikes had to agree, but was left frankly puzzled. For, if she were right in saying that Miss Tidy had worn no scarf yesterday, evidence corroborated by the weather, where had she concealed it, and why? Unless, indeed, it had been for some obscure reason kept permanently at the teashop, in which case a strangler intent on business had had few obstacles in his way.

He suggested they go upstairs and examine the scarves. Noting her hesitation, and remembering how she had first proposed to receive him for the interview in the kitchen, he explained the position.

"The police are in charge now," he told her. "It is murder, Mlle. Blanchard, and a thorough investigation has to be made, without permission or hindrance. You understand?"

"It is so," Léonie acquiesced. "*Mais* the house, *le ménage*, these duties, who takes them? The bills, who pay them?"

Raikes suppressed a smile. How neatly Léonie expressed the acquisitive instinct, the practical grasp of the French peasant.

"Miss Tidy's brother has been sent for," he said shortly. "He will be coming down from Yorkshire soon—at once. Perhaps you know him?"

Léonie pursed her lips indifferently. "He stay here one week—six, ten year ago," she said. "Miss Bert'a, she has no other relatives."

"No. So you see you won't be offending anyone by having me run an eye over her belongings. In fact you will be materially assisting the police to track down her murderer."

He thought that a commendable flight and was a little damped at the old woman's unenthusiastic reception of it. She made no reply, but led the way up the crooked oak stairs, with their worn, finely polished treads, and thence to Miss Tidy's bedroom.

It looked to him, with its pastel tints and expensive furnishings, the bed made up and no speck of dust visible, exquisitely trim in the *soignée* fashion of its late occupant. His eye went at once to the small buff-painted bedside locker. He thought of the anonymous letter Miss Tidy had had, hinting at a photograph it contained. When he stooped to look more closely an odd feature came to view: this little portable had been made without a lock, as one might have expected, but a lock there was now. It was unmistakably a late addition, not part of the original structure. He did not touch it, but turned to Léonie.

"Is this locked?"

She gave the locker, then himself, a hard, resentful look. "*Mais oui*. There is nothing that is not locked."

Raikes glanced round at that, to note that there certainly were keyholes to most of the doors and drawers, and that all, including wardrobe and tallboy, were neatly closed.

"Where are the keys?" he asked.

"They are with Mam'selle."

"You mean Miss Tidy has—had them on her?"

"*Oui, monsieur.*"

She was showing all at once, he saw, deference without docility. Since entering the room she had stood in precisely the same spot, shifting no inch of ground, attentive apparently to whatever his next remark or wish might be.

"Her handbag," he said abruptly, "where is it?"

She turned her head slowly and gave him a long, puzzled look.

"The 'andbag, monsieur? But the bag, it is always with Mam'selle, *mais toujours*. Miss Bert'a, she do not ever forget to take it where she go."

"It's possible she forgot this time," Raikes said. "The handbag has not been found."

Léonie made an eloquent gesture with brows and hands. "Then for the po-leece, it is *difficile, n'est-ce pas?*" she commiserated. "While it is quite certain that Miss Bert'a take it with her to Ravenchurch, it must be that the thief have it now."

"The thief?"

"*Mais oui.* The murderer, he kill Mam'selle to possess the bag."

"Oh," Raikes said, "you're supplying the motive, eh? Well, snatch and grab on the fairly lonely road between here and the town would have suited his book equally well, you know, and not, what's more, have landed him with a halter—as this will." He studied her forbidding expression. "Unless—of course—Miss Tidy carried something extremely valuable in her handbag?"

His shot in the dark did not find its target. Léonie shrugged. "That I do not know, monsieur. I am not Mam'selle's *confidante*."

Raikes refused to accept the snub. "Well, perhaps everything's not under lock and key after all," he said. "Let's see."

He gripped as he spoke the chromium handle of the locker. The door swung open. Raikes lifted his eyebrows sharply. But he neither looked at Léonie nor addressed her while she stood, watchful, behind; instead he squatted on his haunches to examine the interior, divided into two compartments by a shelf. It was empty, except for a small bottle of iodine and a glass eye bath at the bottom. On both was a fine sheen of dust. He looked more closely at the vacant top shelf where the same film of dust appeared. It did not look quite uniform, however. Taking a torch from his pocket, he shone it inside, then gently tilted the locker towards the window. There sprang to view, free of dust, a rectangle of the shelf, formed by the right-hand corner at the back. About four inches wide by six or seven inches long, it was almost the length of the depth of the shelf. Something had recently been removed from the locker. He clicked the door shut and stood up.

"First time lucky," he addressed the dour Léonie with geniality. "Not locked, you see—so perhaps there are other open doors. Where would the scarves be?"

Not waiting for an answer, he tried first one drawer, then another. One or two were locked, but the majority opened without difficulty; so did the wardrobe doors.

"Here," said Léonie quietly, making her first cooperative movement by placing on the dressing table a handful of colored silk objects she had lifted from a drawer containing handkerchiefs.

There were four silk scarves of various hues and a short one closely knitted in brown wool. Raikes looked them over.

"Are these all?" he asked significantly.

"But no, monsieur," Léonie said frankly. "A scarf Miss Bert'a wear in the winter, it is not here. It may be, if we look, it is elsewhere in the room."

"What is it like?" Raikes asked. "Describe it to me."

"Monsieur say the po-leece find one at the café, *n'est-ce pas?*" She spoke with a deliberate courtesy that Raikes found more offensive than downright rudeness. "It is doubtless the scarf that we do not find here. *Mais oui*—I will tell you what it look like. It is of the wool. It is long. It is white, with blue bands on the ends."

"And when did you last see it?"

"But, in the winter, monsieur. March, it may be, February? April perhaps. I do not think it necessary to remember when Mam'selle wear this or that."

But Raikes, unconvinced, pressed the point. "Have you seen it at all, whether or not worn by Miss Tidy, in the past week?"

Léonie licked her lips and eyed him with hostility. "I have told you, monsieur. No."

A quiet knock, once repeated, reached their ears from downstairs. Raikes glanced involuntarily at the window, then, realizing it was not possible to catch sight of a caller under that deep porch, turned away, to be struck to silence by the appearance of the maid. She stood as if frozen, her eyeballs glittering, her mouth half open and distorted, like, he thought with a chilly pang, an inaudible screamer. Such was the quality of her terror that something of it was imparted to himself. For a few seconds he too stood foolishly rooted there.

As the knock came again he brusquely told her to stay where she was and went downstairs. At the front door, his mind preoccupied less with the identity of the visitor than with the maid's alarm, he was confronted by a tall, elderly man, with abundant silver hair, hatless, in comfortable tweeds, a heavy walking stick in his hand. Raikes felt at once that a gun and a couple of dogs were oddly missing from the picture.

The stranger looked sideways at him with a quiet, inscrutable air.

"Police?" he queried politely.

"Correct," Raikes said. "Anything I can do, sir?"

The man had not moved, he noticed, since he had opened the door to him. He presented his right side to the inspector, and in addressing him turned his head so slightly that he was obliged to look at him out of the corners of his eyes, a demeanor which impressed one, perhaps spuriously, Raikes conceded, as extraordinarily sly. He was handsome in a polished, not particularly individual style, and as he waited for a reply the inspector got the unmistakable feeling that he had seen him somewhere before in a wholly different setting.

"Yes," he said in the same affable voice, "I think there may be something you can do. My name is Owen Greatorex. I live at Mile House, only a stone's throw from here. You, I think, have been with us a week or two?"

"I was here before Miss Tidy's murder, yes," Raikes answered shortly. He wasn't at all sure he was taking to Mr. Greatorex, and in any case had no mind to respond to catechism. "My name's Raikes—Inspector—New Scotland Yard." Owen Greatorex—of course, the big shot in fiction, but getting to be less and less the diet of the critics who appreciated caviar; he'd seen press photographs of him looking exactly like this. "Come inside, Mr. Greatorex."

He had to turn then, stooping his leonine head in what looked like majestic acquiescence, but actually to avoid brushing the tangled strands of honeysuckle slipping from the porch.

Raikes drew him to the threshold of the sitting-room door, calling, "All right," to Léonie, whom he sensed rather than saw at the top of the stairs.

Greatorex threw an appraising glance round the room. Raikes saw it rest for a moment on a closely stacked bookcase to the left of the hearth.

"I have been here before," he said, smiling self-consciously as he felt the inspector's eyes on him. "Though *very* infrequently. Social gadding's out of my line. Shocking business, eh?"

He threw it out with such an air of afterthought that it was not at once Raikes decided he was referring to Miss Tidy's death and not to social intercourse.

"It was Mrs. Phail suggested it," Greatorex went on with rather surprising inconsequence. "Don't think of these things myself. She's my excellent housekeeper. She's an idea the old maid here may in the circumstances be nervous of staying on alone. So, coming back from my afternoon tramp, I was to leave a message that she should come on to us—yourselves permitting, of course—until a more permanent arrangement could be made."

"Very good of you, I'm sure," Raikes murmured, a trifle sketchily, for he was well aware that, whatever Mrs. Phail's compunction in the matter, Greatorex himself was unmoved. "Mr. Arthur Tidy, the brother, will be down here shortly, I believe. But meantime an elderly woman won't exactly be at her ease in the cottage, I dare say."

He was pretty sure that none of this was lost on Léonie, who was probably by now engaged in full-time eavesdropping, but thought it as well to add, "Will you put it to her yourself?"

He called her down, and while Greatorex addressed her in the hall, himself pushed open a door on the other side. Here was a small, oak-beamed dining room, lightened by cream wash, with leaded panes looking on a tiny fruit garden in the rear of the house. There were one or two good pictures on the walls, a great shallow bowl of veronica on the wide sill. Outside a blackbird in the laden raspberry bushes chinked his metallic warning of a cat's approach. A pleasant spot, Raikes thought. One would not lightly relinquish it. He saw again the battered body in the Minerva teashop.

A roll-top desk, the kneehole flanked by three drawers a side, caught his eye in the window corner. The cover was down, but it was unlocked and ran back easily. Nothing but a desk blotter and a bottle of ink came to light. The pigeonholes at the back yawned vacantly, and even the top sheet of the blotter was virgin blank. Five of the drawers were empty, the sixth locked. The wastepaper basket was innocent of the merest fragment. It was too good to be true or rather, from his own standpoint, too bad. Had the woman left nothing on which evidence of personal activity and interest had been imprinted? Suicides, he knew, did sometimes before the act rid themselves of betraying material. But in the case of violent, unexpected death at someone else's hands there was no chance of prefatory spring cleaning on this scale. Unexpected? Miss Tidy had, after all, been warned.

He lifted his eyes from gloomy consideration of the desk as a shadow darkened the open door.

"Thank you, Inspector," Greatorex said, putting his head round discreetly. "The old lady's assented, grudgingly. Says she'll have to look in by day. By the way"—he came into the room, pushing the door to behind him—"I wonder—would you dine with me tonight? There's one or two things I'd like to talk about, and this ..." He included the scope of the cottage and the ears of its occupant in an eloquent gesture. "Seven's the hour—but it can be what you like, if you *do* like."

"Thanks," Raikes said coolly, tempted to denounce social gadding as out of his line. "I'll come and talk with pleasure. But it will have to be early—too early for dinner, I'm afraid. We're hard at it, you understand, and I've one or two jobs in hand tonight."

Greatorex made no protest. "Strictly business, then," he said urbanely. "And when you please."

Raikes, making no further move to detain him, watched him go, then himself went to the sitting room, where he had noticed the telephone. Though Léonie was in the kitchen at the moment, he closed the door pointedly and, lifting the receiver, dialed the Ravenchurch police. He was through at once, and explaining to Lecky what he wanted. "No—no exceptions," he said. "Let the prints wallah work on 'em all. Well, this is no time for being thin-skinned. Tidy's we've got—but I want the girls' too, and Mrs. Weaver's. *She*'ll be amenable, I guess. I'll take Blanchard's while I'm here, though she won't know it."

Nor did she. Foreseeing obstruction or, at the least, a tiresome stupidity that might or might not be assumed, Raikes determined to obtain the old woman's fingerprints by a less direct but more pacific method. He joined her in the kitchen for a few words on her proposed move to Mile House that night and contrived, before returning to the bedroom to take, as he said, a last look round, to leave on the table a pocket diary in a shiny leather loose cover.

His survey upstairs, after he had slipped the inner bolt of the bedroom door, consisted of a quick powdering of all polished surfaces adjacent to the keyholes of drawers and doors that were unlocked. The locker received special attention, mainly outside, though he did not neglect some smears round the dust-free portion of the top shelf.

Half an hour went by before he let himself out of the room. In the last few minutes his ear had been caught by indistinct sounds close at hand, and these were explained when, on the landing, he saw the door of Léonie's small room ajar and a glimpse of herself filling an antiquated Gladstone bag.

Absorbed in her task, she looked at him dully when he addressed her.

"Keys of the 'ouse?" she repeated exasperatingly. "*Oui*. There are t'ree of them. Miss Bert'a, she 'ave one, in the bunch with the others. There is another for me. And one—it 'ang on a nail in the kitchen."

"Splendid," said Raikes, who had noticed the cottage was fitted with a latch. "I'll take that one. Then you can keep yours and come in if you want to during the day. Meantime, we'll have Miss Tidy's room locked for a little while."

He turned, as he spoke, the key in question, and dropped it into a pocket. Léonie said nothing. When he went downstairs she followed and, as he reached the hall, walked into the kitchen, returning with the key and his diary.

"The book, you leave it be'ind," she said without interest.

He thanked her and, as soon as he had reached his car, gave it the safe disposal it warranted. On the way back something nagged at him. It was nothing he had seen. Rather was it like the echo of something heard at another time, the precise sense of which just eludes capture.

CHAPTER 7

Two sticks and an apple,
Say the bells of Whitechapel.

A quarter of an hour later he was sitting in the superintendent's office, turning things over and inside out with Lecky, and inviting suggestions from Brook, who, though still doubtful that the inspector was a man of good will, was expanding visibly under his newly acquired importance.

"About those prints," Lecky was saying. "I don't know just what you've in mind, but so far as the teashop is concerned they're not going to be very useful. Forbisher's report says the corn measure's innocent of a mark, dang it. Whoever grabbed it either wore gloves in time-honored fashion, or else wrapped the handle up pretty effectually—"

"Or wiped it afterwards," Raikes interrupted. "It's not exactly that I'm after, though. But go on."

"I was going to say that most of the tables were wiped clean, probably by Miss Kingsley or Miss Oates before leaving yesterday. And only on one of them was there a number of blurred marks, and a few sharply imposed enough to be identified as Miss Tidy's."

"An' the hatshop counter, an'—an' accessories, sir," the sergeant put in, "are pretty well plastered, an' they're not the deceased lady's."

"No," Lecky said impatiently, "but as they're more than likely to turn out to be Mrs. Wild's and her colleague's we shall be as wise as ever. A murderer careful not to mark the scene of the crime would hardly stroll into the hatshop and oblige with his prints on that generous scale."

Brooks subsided into squashed reflection, while Raikes explained that he was less concerned with the prints at the Minerva, whose infertility in this respect held no surprise for him, than with a possible crop at the Keepsake; and went on to describe the unlocked and apparently evacuated bedside cupboard, and the number of drawers and closet doors which, though closed, had yielded at once to opening.

"Now before I tried 'em the old woman suggested the bedroom furniture was locked. Implied Tidy habitually turned the key on all and sundry. But, put to the test, it wasn't so. The funny part of the business is the locker, which is the article Poison Pen writes about, with special reference to the photograph inside. But the locker's in a Mother Hubbard condition—except for a couple of medicine-chest items of no account. What's more, the top shelf is dusty, all but a space at one end which must have been covered by an object six inches or so long and not quite so wide—about the size and shape, in fact, of some photograph mounts."

"Which Bertha Tidy," Lecky pointed out, "could have removed herself after getting that letter."

"Of course," Raikes agreed, "and which, equally, could have been taken by somebody else, since the cupboard's open and the lock—a recent addition, by the way—undamaged. Pretty suggestive, that, with Tidy's handbag, said to contain her keys, missing too. Look at it this way: if Tidy took the photograph away, either she destroyed it or else it's vanished since her death. It's not at the Minerva, that's certain. If we see her hand in this, and not a third party's, then it seems we ought to agree she obligingly left nearly everything at the Keepsake unlocked before she went away yesterday morning with the keys which haven't been seen since. Dammit, I can't see why. It's out of character."

But Lecky could not forbear pointing out that in consideration of the anonymous letter no one was so likely to have removed the alleged photograph as Miss Tidy herself. Raikes shook his head.

"I don't see it that way," he said. "Granted, she came to us in the belief her life was threatened—she *can't* possibly have anticipated an attack at the precise hour it was made, because had she done so she'd never have stayed alone at the Minerva last night, nor have herself admitted her murderer, as we know she must have done. In that case why meddle at all with the contents of a cupboard which she's lately gone to the trouble to have fitted with an excellent lock? She expected to return to the Keepsake, so why not leave anything important where she was used to concealing it?"

"How far," Lecky said, "did she conceal it? I wonder. Poison Pen knew about it, eh? And we're not now prepared to see Miss Tidy in the role of Anon."

This objection coming from the superintendent encouraged Sergeant Brook to put a question that had been bothering him.

"What's the Minerva staff got to do with the bedroom at the cottage, sir? I mean, *their* fingerprints won't be any help with the stuff that end."

"How do we know?" the inspector returned quickly. "There's no evidence so far connecting the girls with the Keepsake, but on the other hand we don't know that they've not been there lately. I'm not probing Léonie for this, because the fewer people put on their guard just now the better. But there's nobody can be eliminated at this stage. There's that handbag not accounted for. Put beside it Mrs. Wild's suspicious behavior—fiddling with the lights, her very questionable story of what she did with the teashop key, she and Jane Kingsley smashing a window *before* taking a dozen steps to a call box and ringing Long Greeting. Oh yes, I know they *said* they saw lights and that they'd overheard Tidy's remark to Mrs. Weaver the evening before. But people don't normally smash windows in circumstances like those without more urgent grounds for doing so than theirs. And if any of 'em do cut up rough about having their prints taken it's going to look still more phony."

"Not necessarily," murmured the superintendent, who had welcomed Brook's question. He was finding the charge of ubiquity against Samela and the rest hard to swallow. "More innocent they are, rougher they cut up—often."

As a psychologist Raikes did not impress him. Look at it himself what way he would, Samela's acquisition of the key, her switching off the light and bringing the others into a dark room, were convincing *because* they were illogical. Even the sense of something wrong impelling her to break into the café rather than waste precious minutes on the telephone commended itself to him. Reflex action and apparently meaningless behavior in a crisis were to him far more explicable than the kind of purposive conduct so unimpeachable as not to require explanation. Besides, whatever the inspector's disparagement of a police force too closely acquainted with the *dramatis personae*, there was a good deal to be said, Lecky maintained, for knowing your people well. Time and temper were alike saved when suspicion could be concentrated rather than dispersed.

"Well," he finished on an optimistic note, "if we've no reason to be grateful to Mrs. Weaver's eyes, thanks to her ears we're pretty sure of the time of the murder."

2

As Raikes had had reason to observe on a good many other occasions, men frequently presented against their own backgrounds facets of themselves entirely different from what one had remarked elsewhere.

Owen Greatorex was no exception. At five-thirty in his study at Mile House he lost for Raikes that touch of the poseur that had irritated the inspector earlier in the afternoon. Now he seemed wholly at ease, simple, forthright, patently sincere with, at the same time, a restraint that gave him now and again an air of austerity Raikes did not dislike. Rather a dry old stick, really, he caught himself thinking, probably the type that needs his own material environment to give him the necessary self-confidence.

"Look here," Greatorex said almost at once, "I've not brought you over because I can be helpful about this murder. I don't know anything about it. But that there's been something beastly afoot for some time is pretty clear. This murder's more than likely part and parcel of it." He stopped abruptly, as if he had said his piece. But Raikes waited for the more he knew was coming. When it came, however, it was the unexpected. "You see," Greatorex went on simply, "Colonel and Mrs. Livingston-Bole were my good friends."

Raikes let a moment or two slip before he spoke. Then, "I understand," he said untruthfully and, feeling his way, added, "You can throw some light for us on their tragedy?"

"I don't—know, Inspector. All I can do is something which perhaps I ought to have done at the time. I did not do so then because, as I thought, I should have been publicizing a fact which could only give rise to a spate of snowball chatter."

"Which actually," Raikes said, "has been going on in any case, ever since."

"Yes—but that was something I could not have foreseen at the date of the inquest."

"Quite, sir. You gave evidence then to the effect that you were one of the last persons to see Mrs. Livingston-Bole alive, and that she had appeared normal during the conversation she'd had with you."

"That is so," Greatorex said. "It wasn't the whole truth. I had better tell it you just as it happened. Colonel Livingston-Bole, who, as you will know, was some years older than his wife, suffered a good deal from malaria. March was always a pretty bad month for him, and this year he'd got in addition a bout of influenza, and between one and the other had been thoroughly ill. After about three weeks in bed, or rather on and off there—for he was a difficult patient to keep within bounds—he was convalescing a little when April came in, but was still kept to his room. On the afternoon of April 2—it was a Tuesday—I called to see him."

"The afternoon," Raikes put in, "on which Mrs. Livingston-Bole disappeared."

"Yes. I talked to him for a few minutes, but he was clearly inattentive and drowsy, and not wanting to bother him, I left his room in under a quarter of an hour."

"You were alone with him, I think?"

"I was. The housekeeper, who'd told me Mrs. Livingston-Bole was resting—she nursed the colonel, you know, practically single-handed—had taken me to his room and then left us. The same housekeeper is at present with Miss Clara Livingston-Bole, the colonel's sister, who's come to live at Long Greeting Place."

"And the colonel's parting remark to you was the occasion of your seeing his wife before you left the house?" Raikes reminded him.

Greatorex gave a melancholy smile. "While you're so well informed, Inspector, I must not stray from the facts. Yes, the colonel roused himself a little in the last minute or two to speak of Phoebe—his wife."

"Will you," Raikes said, "repeat his actual words so far as you recall them?"

"You have them, you know, in the report of the inquest. But of course. He said, 'I wish you'd have a word with Phoebe as you go out. I'm worried about her. I think she's feeling the strain of nursing me, and she won't bring in anybody else to give a hand.' "

"That was all he said?"

"That was all. He seemed at once to be settling down for a nap, and I went out. Except at the funeral, where he avoided everyone, I never saw him again. You'll know that in the few weeks that elapsed between his wife's death and his own he shut himself up indoors and refused admittance to everyone except his doctor. I made three or four efforts to see him, but it was of no use. I wrote to him once after Phoebe's death. He did not reply. To thrust myself upon him forcibly was out of the question. And yet I cannot help wondering over and over again if he would ever have turned that gun on himself had I been able to get him to talk to me. Another man, you know—an old friend—the opportunity to disburden oneself, to rid the bosom of 'much perilous stuff.' "

"I know," Raikes said. "But the fact remains he *had* the opportunity and did not take it. Dr. Hare seems not to have been denied access on any occasion. But the colonel was completely reticent with him."

"Yes," Greatorex agreed heavily. He made as if to say more, then checked himself.

"But," said Raikes, "it was about Mrs. Livingston-Bole you were going to tell me."

"She had a small private study on the first floor," Greatorex said quickly. "It was there, I had been told, and not in her bedroom, that she was resting. So as I came down from the colonel I tapped on her door. I should not have done so if it hadn't been for his last remarks." He paused, then went on hurriedly. "What happened then was due to a mistake I made. As soon as I knocked I heard her voice, saying, I thought, what my mind was prepared to hear it say: 'Come in.' But when I'd opened the door and shown myself I knew, with the sense of infallibility that comes with one's own momentary intuitions, that though she'd indeed been talking she hadn't spoken to me. I felt that I should not have gone in and, simultaneously with the startled look she gave me, I was making my apologies and withdrawing."

"She was not alone after all?" Raikes said.

"But she was. She had been talking to herself, in the rather high voice of a woman whose nerve is cracking, and a remark she'd made—I don't know what—was coincident with my tap at the door. That was all. But directly I was inside I knew something was wrong. Inspector, Mrs. Livingston-Bole was a very beautiful woman, with the kind of serenity that is at once imparted to other people. That afternoon she had lost it. She was pale and rigid, but not with the rigor of self-control. As I made to go out again she said to me—no, *cried* to me, in a sharp voice, 'No, *don't* go, Owen! Come in, come in!' And when, of course, I came in and closed the door and asked her if anything was the matter, she made a valiant, almost successful effort at taking herself in hand and told me she was very worried about her husband."

Raikes looked closely at him. "Which you didn't believe?"

"I believed it, yes. But I did *not* believe her worry about Henry had anything at all to do with her present agitation."

"Why not?"

Greatorex showed a mild surprise. "But *why?* The colonel was clearly so much better that many things might have been felt for and about him—relief, for the most part, fatigue too, with tension relaxing. But hardly worry in that excited, *frightened* manner. Yes," he reflected, "she was frightened. And I'd not seen Phoebe afraid before. Besides, there was the oddness about the room."

"What was that?" Raikes asked, aware that nothing of this nature had been divulged at the inquest.

"The hearth," Greatorex said. "It was cold just then, if you remember. Snow in Ravenchurch at the end of March, and we'd all fires when April came in. She had one burning in the study. It was still alight, though choked. For heaped up on the coals, lifting and shivering in the chimney draft, was a mass of charred and glowing papers, just burned."

"And did you find out what they were?"

"Yes—and no. Partly from Mrs. Livingston-Bole's next remark, a voluntary one, since I should myself have made no reference to the condition of the grate. But she said to me, again in the overwrought voice in which she'd begged me to enter, 'Never, never, *never* keep letters!' She cut the words short. All at once she seemed desperately resolute to appear ordinary. She wanted me to sit down, and herself took a chair."

"And there was nothing further abnormal about her behavior?"

"No-o. She spoke of this and that, but now, instead of fear and excitement, there was merely indifference. She spoke dully, *she*—she'd always sparkled in the simplest of exchanges. I stayed perhaps ten minutes. We spoke of Henry, and I tried to get her to tell me what was worrying her now that he was markedly better. She could only say that he wasn't getting well quickly enough—that *he* was depressed. Her replies weren't convincing. I remembered the colonel's anxiety for *her*. I didn't speak of it to her, but I did suggest that long and tireless attendance on him had exhausted her, and advised a doctor. She said that was all right, she was already seeing Hare."

"True only in the narrowest sense," Raikes said, "as it turned out afterwards. She had not consulted him about herself, and all that had been done was that the doctor himself on a visit about a week before yours had prescribed a tonic on noticing how tired she looked."

"I know. She was of course meeting every remark of mine with the sort of response calculated to head off enquiry. I think—one *knows* her mind was then made up for what she did only a few hours later."

"We don't know," Raikes objected. "The final act, following however quickly, may still have been one of impulse."

Greatorex shook his head. "You would not think so if you remembered her as I do that afternoon at Long Greeting Place."

"Yet when you were called upon to give evidence," Raikes could not forbear pointing out, "you reported her manner as normal while you were with her."

"Except for those first moments off her guard, it was," Greatorex maintained. "An *assumed* normality."

"And so—abnormal," Raikes argued.

"Have it your own way, Inspector—but look at it mine. What does the suppressed evidence amount to? Handfuls of burnt paper, reduced to indecipherable carbon, a few remarks never elucidated. For I made no reply or reference to what she'd said about the letters—I wish now that I had. No—there was Henry to think of too. What could—what *would* a coroner's jury have made of such insubstantial, unsubstantiated evidence as I had to offer? It would have been pawed and mauled over in court, and out, and turned into fodder for rumor. I fancied too that a servant would have come upon the stuff destroyed in the grate, and might take from me the responsibility for mentioning it. But the matter was never introduced."

"No. And within half an hour of your having left the house—"

"She'd gone out, not to come back again," Greatorex finished somberly. "When they took her out of the water the next afternoon, my first impulse was to admit that I'd at any rate glimpsed something of her despair the day before. But there was always the old man to think of. He should be the first to be told of it. I couldn't know then that he was going to refuse to see me, or that, so little was life without her, there were only three weeks of it left to him."

"Of course not. If the future—"

"Was obliging enough to reveal itself," Greatorex took him up quickly, "we should all behave differently. Or should we? I question if more wisely. However, that was why I wanted to talk to you."

"Why?" Raikes echoed.

"To try," said Owen Greatorex with a smile, "to anticipate this same future, and head off perhaps its more fearful activities. For we don't know that this is the end of the business."

"I take it," Raikes said quietly, "you're not now referring to the Livingston-Bole tragedy?"

"I'm talking about Miss Tidy's murder."

"Yes?"

"She was," said Greatorex, "an intimate friend of Phoebe's—Mrs. Livingston-Bole. I rather recall hearing once that they were at school together."

"Nevertheless," Raikes replied, "the suicide of one and murder of the other separated in time by nearly three months aren't necessarily linked."

Greatorex gave him a shrewd look. "I'm thinking," he said, "of the letters."

Raikes studied him thoughtfully. "Have *you* had them too?"

"No. Not yet—that is. But I know that Kate Beaton has. And I can't forget Phoebe's urgency that last afternoon about the letters she had burned."

"But *that*," Raikes reminded him, "was a plea for letters not to be *kept*."

Owen Greatorex shrugged. "No matter. As long as we don't know the nature of the letters she'd destroyed, the poison-pen species can't be ruled out of court."

3

Arthur Tidy made it quite clear that, in spite of Léonie's sketchy preparations, he had no intention of putting up at the Keepsake. What was more, he turned his back squarely on the Loggerheads with a hint that proximity made it equally distasteful, and took a room at the Whitehouse Temperance Hotel in Ravenchurch itself.

He was a small bleak man who bore a superficial resemblance to his sister. But what in Bertha had been at best a rather forbidding, at worst an odious, charm was, Raikes decided, wholly revolting in this North Country solicitor. His professional caution was emphasized by the natural wariness of a man who does not mean to allow events of however intimate a character to assault his security or impair a cherished reputation. Sister or no sister, the inspector thought with a touch of contempt, Mr. Arthur Tidy has made up his mind to keep out of deep waters.

He was amused to note that the solicitor plainly thought it necessary to defend his repudiation of Léonie's hospitality.

"I have never," he said with mingled precision and asperity, "endorsed my sister's choice of a housekeeper, or rather housekeeper-companion, for the relationship was, I believe, more than ordinarily intimate. Without, I hope, an undue display of insularity, I may say that in my opinion a British-born domestic would have served her better."

"In what way?" asked Raikes, disposed to think every line worth pursuing.

Mr. Tidy lifted his left eyebrow and slithered at him a glance charged with meaning.

"The Gallic temperament, my dear sir—the Gallic temperament," he minced through pursed lips. "It will out, don't you know."

Raikes didn't. But if the old humbug permitted himself to unbend so far he'd be tittering now, he thought; and if the insinuation was what he took it for, it was a bit of a shock to associate the grim Léonie with what he mentally dubbed "that sort of thing."

"The Blanchard woman," Tidy went on, with less personal bias than he would have used in reference to a legal technicality, "entered my sister's service some few years after the end of the 1914 war, with—I was going to say—dubious references, but that would be incorrect. Bertha, then headmistress of a Yorkshire village church school, took her without references at all. The woman had left her previous post of lady's maid in disgrace. She was then about forty, I suppose, but not too old to have made a fool of herself. There was a child—father," he shrugged, "possibly unknown, at any rate keeping in the background, oh, *very* unpaternally in the background!"

"Indeed?" said Raikes, and made it a quelling word. "And when this happened you mean Miss Tidy took her into her employment knowing the facts?"

"Knowing such facts as there were, as there ever are in these cases. But not at once. Blanchard had been dismissed from her previous post before the birth of the child. She'd been in service not in Rise Pitchley, my sister's village, but in an adjacent hamlet, and Bertha, as a matter of fact, knew nothing about her. Nothing, that is, until a certain notoriety began to attach to her after she'd lodged her child with a woman of the village. She herself was clearly in need of work, and the upshot was that, in spite of all my advice to the contrary, Bertha engaged her."

"Out of goodness of heart?" The words were wrung from Raikes, nor did he try to keep the bite out of them.

Arthur Tidy flicked him a shrewd glance. "Oh, I hardly think so," he said solemnly, as if, thought Raikes, renouncing goodness of heart on behalf of the entire Tidy clan. "I don't think so at all. Bertha wanted a maid. She naturally wanted one who wouldn't leave her lightly. And—and she enjoyed as much as all women the feeling that she'd made another person grateful to her, you see."

Raikes saw. Indeed, it was his turn to eye a little more closely Mr. Tidy, who had also, it appeared, seen to some purpose. He could not help wondering how deeply fraternal experience of Miss Tidy's want of heart had barbed the remark. Anyway, it etched with yet more acid the unkind portrait of the murdered woman.

As if to underline his last words, Tidy went on in the same dry voice, "I must say that though Bertha was headstrong enough to give a position of trust to a woman without character, she made it plain from the outset that she would make no concessions in any direction. And she let Blanchard know at once that conditions of her employment included the removal of the child from Rise Pitchley."

"Why?" Raikes asked bluntly.

Mr. Tidy gave him a testy look. "My dear Inspector, isn't it obvious? Apart from the fact that the buzz of gossip in a village might give an unrespectable character to my sister's ménage, you must know that Blanchard was at that time making a ridiculous spectacle of her maternal responsibilities. Having boarded the child out, she couldn't let well—or, in this case, ill—alone, but must needs go on lavishing attentions on it as well as asserting that she would never be separated from it. I believe such behavior isn't uncommon in middle-aged women, though one might have hoped that the circumstances of Blanchard's case would have damped her enthusiasm in some measure. However, Bertha very properly put an end to such nonsense."

And Léonie, Raikes added to himself, had had to toe the line. Without the work Tidy offered her she'd have been faced with the problem of how to support the child she adored. To her fundamentally practical mind that had proved the ultimate consideration, separation the lesser sacrifice. It was damnable, all the same.

"Where did the child go?"

"And *that*," returned the solicitor with an air of enjoying denial, "I really do not know, I am afraid. So far as I was concerned in the matter at all, that aspect of it was—well, less than subsidiary. The *disposal* of the child wasn't relevant to my objections to Blanchard's being employed. And what I tell you of it are merely such facts as were told me by Bertha. I know she refused so much as to see the infant."

"She did, did she?" Raikes murmured with interest. That might not be without point.

It did not look as if he were likely to extract any further details of Léonie's history. Well, he'd got more than he'd supposed would be forthcoming in this quarter. He switched abruptly to the murder, and immediately came up against a stone wall.

"No light whatever, I fear," the solicitor said with the same hint of relishing his own unhelpfulness. "I can't shed a gleam on the sorry business. No, I don't know of any enemies Bertha may have had. Wise folk avoid making them, you know, just as they are careful to evade friendship. She had neither, so far as I am aware. But the extent of my knowledge, of course, may not cover the case. Though we corresponded, as frequently as once a month, I saw her only once in the last twelve years. That was when, at her invitation, I came to Long Greeting, ostensibly for a brief holiday, actually for the purpose of a business discussion."

"And the nature of it?"

"We-ell," Arthur Tidy said, "in view of the character of this investigation I can hardly object to answering your question—though I'm bound to add it's entirely irrelevant to the very pressing one of who killed my sister, and why. When I visited her in the summer preceding the outbreak of war—1939, I mean—it was to talk over a scheme she had for expanding her business."

"Here in Ravenchurch, I take it?"

"Certainly. She wanted to acquire additional premises for what I thought a very fanciful project in beauty culture. She lacked capital. I was opposed to the plan."

Raikes sized it up. "She was anxious for a loan?"

"Which I did not make. Like many others of her sex, my sister's faith in her financial acumen was not justified in practice by the size of her purse. In any case I failed to see why *I* should gamble on a scheme which, even if it succeeded, would merely perpetuate the follies of women."

"Quite," said Raikes seriously.

"And then," the solicitor went on quickly with a little air of personal triumph, "the war came. Commercial expansion was put out of court. She had, then, to wait until hostilities were over." He shrugged. "What she may have been going to do in the next year or so I have no idea."

Raikes was thinking hard. Whatever Brother Arthur's opinion of Bertha Tidy's deficiencies as a businesswoman, hearsay credited her with having done very well indeed out of the Minerva since its opening.

"We've not gone into the question of Miss Tidy's finances," he said, "but I doubt, when we do, that we shall find she lacked capital nowadays."

Mr. Tidy directed a rather queer look at him. "My dear sir, *I* haven't a doubt that my sister is—was a rich woman. She's always made a point of emphasizing in her letters the lucrative nature of her business."

"Why do you think she did that, sir?"

The solicitor cocked an eyebrow again. "Why do any of us boast, Inspector? She was," he added simply, "very fond of money. Not, I mean, just as a medium of exchange. She loved money for itself."

"Yes, I see," said Raikes, deciding it was possibly a family weakness. "That brings me to a point which may prove important: did your sister leave a will?"

"If she did," was the curt reply, "it must have been made very recently indeed. I have not been informed of it. On the contrary, Bertha shared a peculiarly common feminine antipathy to putting her affairs in order. It was quite useless for me to point out to her over and over again that to do so would not necessarily shorten her life."

But may not a will after all, thought Raikes, have done just that? He had a note that her local solicitors were Bannerman, Bannerman, and Waite; and was reminded of something else.

"Assuming your sister died intestate, sir, who gets the estate?"

Mr. Tidy answered without hesitation. "Myself, of course, as next of kin. Neither of us has any other near relative."

Raikes made no comment but, handing him a piece of paper on which a short list had been scribbled, enquired: "Is any name down there familiar to you?"

The lawyer quickly pinched his nose with a pair of pince-nez and, eyeing the sheet with a sidelong quirk that gave him a sudden extraordinary resemblance to his dead sister, scanned it with greedy curiosity. He mumbled the names half audibly:

"Colonel Livingston-Bole
Mrs. Livingston-Bole
Miss Edith Drake
Miss Beatrice Graves
Miss Iris Kane"

He scrutinized the inspector over the rim of his glasses.

"What little game is this, may I ask? A variant of the identification parade? I'm disinclined, you know, to commit myself to a statement while still in the dark."

"That's all right," Raikes said easily, though he felt irritable. "They're five people about whom we've made, and are making, enquiry, and anybody, like yourself, possibly claiming acquaintance, however slight, might be able to give us a helpful line."

"But why," Mr. Tidy persisted almost stupidly, "should you imagine *me* to be acquainted with any of them?"

"Routine enquiry," Raikes said negligently. "No stone unturned, nor avenue unexplored, and all the rest of it, y'know. There's always the chance. They're all Ravenchurch people, and perhaps even a casual mention in your sister's letters—"

The solicitor, who did not appear to be listening, stared again at the list. He suddenly snatched it up, tut-tutted, and uttered an irrelevant "Dear me!"

"There *is* one name down here belonging to a person I knew better under another name. The other four," he dismissed them in a rapid aside, "I know nothing whatever about. Yes, yes, of course it is she."

"Which one would that be?" Raikes asked in a painfully incurious voice.

Mr. Tidy tapped the second on the list with a wrinkled finger. "Here—Mrs. Livingston-Bole."

"And when you knew her?"

"She was Phoebe Ballantyne, and before that Phoebe Young. She was a friend of Bertha's from their schooldays. She took her life last April."

"Yes," Raikes said. Ballantyne … Young … "She was married twice, I take it?"

"Oh yes. I don't know Colonel Livingston-Bole. When I remember her best she was Mrs. Ballantyne, wife of a handsome scamp of an army captain, 1914 commission. He played for some years a rather dubious game of wife desertion and reconciliation, and again desertion, and finally died abroad, I believe, of tumor of the brain—which had no doubt influenced his unmatrimonial conduct." He mused. "He was quite mad, I'm told. Bertha had a lucky escape."

"How?" Raikes asked, with visions of an earlier, and unsuccessful, homicidal attack upon Miss Tidy.

To his astonishment Mr. Tidy giggled. It struck Raikes as odd how a man could titter without amusement felt or recollected.

"It was touch and go, Inspector. Whether he married Phoebe or Bertha. Phoebe it was, poor lady. But, yes—you might say it was touch and go."

4

Kate Beaton, not for the first time in her life, was finding it hard to decide how expedient it might be to lay all your cards on the table. Was expediency the issue, though? Not really. What she didn't like about this ugly business— or rather, one of the things that she especially loathed—was that it was getting morally imperative to put the police in possession of every known fact. She had hesitated long enough, since long before Bertha Tidy's murder, because it had seemed to her that such evidence would be merely contributory tattle. When she remembered that she really shrank less from contributing than from being known as a contributor of tattle, she made at once a wry face and a mental note that the observation might look well introduced into fiction.

Anyway, she thought, a second visit to the police station was uncalled for; it might point things too uncomfortably. Since the letters were already claiming attention, the police were the more likely to pay her a visit. So she waited in the crepuscular gloom of the cold stone house that more than one visitor had found at variance with Miss Beaton's own red-faced, loud-voiced cheerfulness.

When Raikes turned up, on the afternoon of the day he had talked with Arthur Tidy, she was washing one of the Airedales in a flagged outhouse that had once been the laundry. She came into the old, murky drawing room, damp of hands, about her the odor of dog, her cheeks shining like scrubbed apples, and, sighing hopelessly, asked Raikes to sit down.

He glanced at her in some surprise. She met his eye humorously, seating herself on a chesterfield which, like the rest of the spare suite, bore a faintly mangled air.

"I knew you'd come," she said. "I'd been rather hoping the moment could be put off indefinitely."

As this frankness, he suspected, was designed to take him aback, he remained unmoved.

"We won't be too hard on you," he said lightly. "I needn't in fact keep you long on the matter I've come about today."

"Why *have* you come?" she said with undisguised eagerness.

Funny sort of question, thought Raikes, seeing we were approached first about the letters and their authorship. Aloud he said: "It's these earlier cases we're investigating, Miss Beaton, tied up, as we think, with the murder of Miss Tidy—the Ravenchurch suicides. You know the names of the five who died in the spring and early summer, but just in case a refresher's necessary I've got them down here on this slip of paper. All I want you to say is whether you knew any of them other than by name or sight—in any degree of intimacy, in fact?"

He noticed her eyes widen and a duskier color in her cheeks.

"Well, well," she said below her breath, fixing him with her hard gaze. "A shade telepathic, what? It's that very point I've been thrashing out solo— arguing whether I ought to tell you, deciding I must, and waiting for you to open the ball. Which you've done."

"I see," said Raikes. "So they *were* more than names and sights to you?"

"Hardly 'they.' I didn't know Miss Graves at all, though I believe I can recall seeing her at Fripp and Saltmarsh. Colonel and Mrs. Livingston-Bole I knew slightly, and we'd exchange greetings in the woods and so on when I was exercising the dogs. Little Iris Kane, of course, all the village knew, and she and it were thrilled about her coming wedding to Sir Dan Froggatt's son from the other side of the county. Some of us were kind enough to say it was putting her on the financial map, whatever else." Her mouth gave a cynical twist. "But that's neither here nor there." She suddenly caught her words back and, ignoring Raikes, said softly, "I—wonder, though."

Before he could speak she went straight on in the old blunt tone: "I used to chat and nod with the kid. But it's none of them I've anything to say about. It was Edith Drake I knew."

"How well?" Raikes asked quietly.

"Well enough to visit and be visited. Oh yes, I know what you're going to say—everybody does that as a matter of course in these country nests. But it wasn't that way at all. I'm no hand at the social round. Solitude—unmisanthropic, one hopes, but solitude anyway—is my long suit. My work won't stand for gadding and frittering. But Edith Drake was different. If you want the sentimental touch, the homely phrase, the cliché—well, she was a kindred soul. I liked her enormously. It's because of that—because I liked her as I did for her drive and vigor and sincerity *and*, if you like, an unconciliatory touch for which Ravenchurch is always unprepared—it's because of all that I'm going to tell you what I know. Because I want her murderer found."

"Her murderer?" Raikes repeated carefully. "Then you *don't* believe Miss Drake's death was suicide?"

She moved a hand impatiently. "Of course she hanged herself," she said baldly. "I'm not questioning who adjusted the rope. But somebody drove her to it. Somebody hounded her to die. Somebody who knew."

"Knew what?"

"What Edith was taking great pains should never be known. What she told me. What I've kept to myself till now."

Raikes, who thought he detected a melodramatic monkeying with the story instead of any noticeable desire to embark on a simple narration of fact, intimated that he was tired of this song and dance about the bush.

"Well, let's get down to brass tacks, Miss Beaton. How long did you know Edith Drake?"

"Soon after I came to this corner of the world—about three years ago." Taking the plunge steadied her. The defiant edge wore off her voice. "I can't remember whether I ran across her first among Ma Weaver's books, or else at the Dramatic, where I poked my nose in at an early date. Both about the same time, I fancy. She was more than the life and soul of Ravenchurch Dramatic Society. She was its blood and bones. She *was* the Dramatic. Anyway, after those early bookshop and clubroom meetings she came over here, and we shared books and talks and got, I like to think and remember, a whole heap of mutual stimulation. At least I know I did."

Raikes put a word in: "About that sweepstake prize she won?"

"Yes, what about it?"

Raikes, who took her to be in a jumpy condition, was unduly mild. "I was wondering," he said, "if she ever confided to you her reasons for continuing to teach at Haydock's End after suddenly annexing a fortune."

"But why *shouldn't* she?" She leaned forward a little, attitude and voice emphatic. "I mean, why shouldn't she go on teaching? Edith happened to be one of those, perhaps not so few, happy people who was doing the work she most wanted to do. She loved kids. She loved teaching. She loved the school. She made a big thing of Haydock's End—a good thing. She's left her mark on it. Why *should* she have flung it all up when she suddenly came into a whole wallop of money she'd never given a second thought to when she bought the ticket?"

Raikes felt himself unfairly called upon to refute an opinion he hadn't held.

"No reason in the world," he conceded. "Strangely enough people *do* like their jobs. I do—believe it or not. So, that's granted—Miss Drake gained a fortune and elected to stay on as headmistress of Haydock's End village school because her work was also her pleasure."

"It was more," Kate Beaton said quietly. "It was a—a sort of fulfilment of personality. Haydock's End School was an extension of herself."

Raikes nodded. "Same thing."

"And *that*," she went on as if he had not spoken, "is another reason why I hope you catch her murderer and—and hang the brute, as high as Haman."

She drew in her breath. "What does that remind me of?" she asked, shooting a half-guilty glance at the inspector.

Raikes could not tell her. "A biblical—episode," he offered vaguely. "But that's the end of the story. We hang a murderer—as high as you please—after we've caught him. Now to the catching. What is it makes you suppose somebody drove Miss Drake to take her own life?"

She was silent a full minute. "Look here, I can't assure myself that I'm not betraying her even now by giving away the story."

"The only person you're helping to betray," Raikes, leashing impatience, replied, "is the individual you suggest hounded Miss Drake to suicide. If such there is—well, I don't need to point out that anything you know, important or apparently trivial, about your friend, is likely to prove material in running down the guilty party."

"All right," Kate Beaton said, and after a pause, "Here you are then. Edith Drake was a quiet, self-contained, unfrivolous creature. Any enquiry you may have been conducting will have disclosed that, though. Seemingly she had no life at all in which men figured other than in the easy, superficial friendships bodies such as the Ravenchurch Dramatic encouraged. Don't think I mean she wasn't the marrying kind. She *was*. But she was too the one-man type of woman that wouldn't previously be experimental."

She pulled a wry mouth. "Hang it all, if I am going to trumpet her story, I won't represent her other than the girl she was."

Raikes said nothing, and she went on: "In the last Easter holiday before the war she spent three weeks in Switzerland in April. I saw her soon after she came back, and though she said nothing to me at that time I noticed she was changed. More self-contained, even more reticent—but with it all more *alive*. I don't know how to make you understand that—unless, perhaps, I say that she seemed to be living to the full an inner life that had nothing at all to do with any of us who made other points of contact with her. An absent, sometimes dreaming, but always real life. This, of course," she added hastily, "is a personal impression only and factual evidence of nothing. But I give it to let you know that I sensed the difference in Edith four months before she broke the ice and told me about those few weeks abroad."

"And what made her tell you then?"

"Illness. She had been very seedy all that summer term, and as soon as they broke up in July she went away without a word to me or anybody else."

"Where to?"

"I didn't know at the time. Only later. To London. She came back for the September reopening, looking like a ghost—and a devilish new term it was for not feeling up to the mark. War had started, the evacuee kiddies were poured down on Ravenchurch and the villages round, and Haydock's End got its quota, and Edith's school. And there were the other jobs, ARP and the rest. As head teacher she had double the work to contend with, and none of the physical toughness to meet it. Before the end of September she collapsed. She was away till half term, and ought to have stayed away the other half and the January term too, but she was afraid all the time of rousing suspicion by prolonged absence."

"Suspicion of what?" Raikes asked, guessing anyway.

"The truth," Kate Beaton said with blunt ambiguity. "In town she'd been to a doctor—one of the unregistered gentry, you know. She told me all about it in those wretched weeks in the early autumn when she did what she could to discourage sick visitors. But she couldn't keep me out." She added, grimly, he thought: "Not me."

Raikes scrutinized her thoughtfully under cover of mere listening. The idea Lecky had turned down stuck up a shadowy head again, grew monstrous and chilly. Suppose, after all, Kate Beaton were the author of those letters? That might not be the end of it. Suppose it was she who—what had been her own words? "I'm not questioning who adjusted the rope. But somebody drove her to it. Somebody hounded her to die. Somebody who knew." It would not be the first time the accuser had become identifiable with accused in the dangerous employment of a defense mechanism prompted by overweening vanity, or else despair.

While his mind played with its notion his ears registered what her voice went on recording in staccato, perhaps even defiant phrases.

In Switzerland there had been a man. She knew nothing about him, name, occupation, origin, nothing. She had never sought to know. He was married and had apparently not concealed the fact from Edith. Edith had walked into things with her eyes open. When, back in England a month or so later, she was faced with the truth, she saw too that she was faced with the loss of Haydock's End if she left things to take their course and the truth were known.

"It was the school she wanted to keep. She was fierce about that, in the possessive, it's-part-of-me way that won't let go." She gave a bleak smile. "It was *that* was her passion. A sort of reversal of roles, you know, with Haydock's End School her real lover and the Swiss adventure, by comparison, almost on the academic plane. And that's precisely what somebody else got to know. Knew they could put the screw on—threatening to smash the one by exposing the other. Oh, it wasn't social stigma and what not that bothered Edith. It was the knowledge she'd lose the school."

"Put the screw on," Raikes repeated after her.

"She was very rich," Kate Beaton said simply.

"Blackmail?"

"That's about it."

"And you're suggesting the Swiss episode was discovered and put to use by somebody seven years afterwards?"

"As a matter of fact," she said slowly, "I don't mean exactly that— though it comes to the same thing. Sorry I didn't make myself clear. I don't think anybody, bar me, got wise to what she did with herself on that holiday. It was the London end of it they got hold of, that visit in August, the operation that precipitated the illness that made her absent from school in the autumn."

"Look here, Miss Beaton," Raikes said, "how much of this part is supposition and imagination? Perhaps I ought to say, how little? Have you anything whatever to offer in corroboration of your statement that Edith Drake was being blackmailed?"

"Her own word."

"When?"

"A fortnight before she died."

Raikes stared. "But you brought nothing up at the inquest."

"Of course not. Edith never used the term blackmail to me. It was only later—only when I'd time to think about it—only when others had died too, and her name kept recurring in connection with theirs, that I thought at all clearly about it."

"Then what had she said to you?"

"She was highly strung, jumpy, for long periods unnaturally taciturn in the weeks before her death. One evening she came in to see me. She didn't often come those last months. She didn't stay long, and all the time she seemed on the verge of something that never got said. But in a suddenly expansive moment she burst out with, 'Katy, it's no good thinking one has secrets. There's always a leakage.' I said, 'What do you mean?' She said, 'The London op. Somebody's onto it.' 'Fiddlesticks,' I said, 'all that time ago.' But she shook her head. She was looking white. No tears, but worse than if there had been. 'It's no good,' she said. It was the flattest voice you ever heard. 'They've even got the man's name.' "

He stopped her. "Her lover? Then the facts of the Swiss holiday—"

"No, no," she broke in. "You're taking that out of its context. She was talking about the quack she'd seen in town."

"Who put her onto him?"

"I—don't know." She gave him an interested look. "That might be worth finding out. Edith, I swear, was the complete innocent in that direction. So she must have approached somebody in however roundabout a way. It's perfectly true—there's always a leakage when there has to be a measure of dependence on others—and, living hugger-mugger as we do, life doesn't offer many opportunities of playing solitaire."

"Except to the blackmailer," Raikes finished smoothly.

On that note he took thoughtful leave of her.

CHAPTER 8

Pokers and tongs,
Say the bells of St. John's.

Jane Kingsley walked along the road beyond the Loggerheads in the shimmering afternoon dust, behind her the Greatorex and Beaton houses, ahead the winding tape of highway that led back to Ravenchurch. It was marked as far as eye could see only by the Bus Stop sign where she might pick up a home-going bus. On her right the river ran its glittering, deadly course, presently on her left the woods behind Long Greeting Place smudged and made somber the tender summer country.

But tenderness was absent from this hour. Even the dreaming warmth of sky above had for her a brassy, relentless stare. There was no shade on this uncompassionate road. Dust clogged her shoes. She was tired, horribly, unaccountably tired. Her mouth was dry. Her hands were too large. She felt intolerably conspicuous. She was experiencing all at once a passionate longing for company which, because of her generation and upbringing, she would have repudiated as self-pity but that fatigue left her now a prey to its hunger.

For she had failed. She had planned and made this visit with some sort of vague belief that she was thereby furthering the ends of social justice while not betraying the humanitarian impulse that was always a dearer, more intimate motive. She could, she knew, have imparted to the police the special piece of observation that had driven her out on this desperate road; justice might then indeed have been reached by a shorter cut, although she was not sure that the skeptical inspector would have acted promptly on her report.

What would have been certain, however, was that a police handling of the case would have deprived Jane's suspect of the very warning she meant to convey. Jane admitted ruefully that she was not at heart a good citizen; rather did she cherish ideas, judged sloppy by many, that gave the individual, not society, the initial break. After all, she argued, the hunter gets all the breaks in the end, the hunted none. The police would catch up anyway.

She shuddered. She had come to Long Greeting in the hope of persuading a reluctant, but perhaps guiltless, witness to give testimony of the first importance. By no direct plea, only by the frank disclosure of the knowledge she herself had acquired, would persuasion be effected. But it hadn't worked out that way. She had not encountered an innocent, if material, witness. With terrifying distinctness of vision not commonly hers she had recognized a murderer. She knew now who had killed Miss Tidy. That she still did not know the why of the murder seemed to her to matter little.

She had bungled things badly. For there was something else too. Because she had taken the murderer off guard her own guard had slipped at the first impact of the shock. So it was not what she alone knew that mattered. If only in those first moments she had been able to dissemble, so that it might have been believed she was still ignorant of the killer's identity! But she had rushed her fences; there had been self-betrayal on both sides. Each knew that the other knew. And so the margin of time in which she could safely act had shrunk to negligible proportions.

Besides, her mind was shaken, chilly, no longer functioning in any undivided direction. She thought all at once of Ralph and Elsie with such astonishing clarity that, out there in the silent afternoon where no bird whistled and the very leaves held each a rigid pose as in that motionless game of "statues" one had played as a child, the grim phrase came to mind: "They say drowning people see all their past rise up before them." Sammy, Crystal, Marion, the teashop, the Slip, Mrs. Weaver, the fussing, talking, unpredictable police, Ravenchurch with its come-day-go-day respectabilities, and Stoneacre and the hens at the other end of the dusty road laced with dog roses and wild parsley ... They were all there, only a kind of objective vision now, withholding the composite help their familiarity suggested.

She glanced at the watch on her wrist. The bus for Stoneacre wouldn't be along for more than half an hour. It was there she must go, and tell Ralph what she should have told him the other night. Meantime, she couldn't hang aimlessly about this unsheltered highway. There was a telephone at the Loggerheads, she knew, but the thought of ringing up Ravenchurch police station in her present uncollected state, with none of her wits come home to roost, made her shiver.

Close by and in a line with the bus stop was the stile that took you over a field track directly behind Long Greeting Place to the fringes of the woods. There, among the foxgloves and hazels and felled logs, only five minutes away, was an old wooden seat where you could sit down and watch for the flash of red as the Ravenchurch bus came round the bend before its descent into the village. That was a good way off, giving you time to return behind the big house and across the field and climb the stile again before it lumbered to a stop practically at your feet. Sitting there for twenty minutes in that unwatchful solitude, she might control her fears and resolve some new, constructive pattern out of the beastly evidence she had stumbled upon.

The road was still empty. A step across the nettle-bound ditch, and she was over the stile used daily by Kate Beaton and her Airedales. The meadow, patched here and there with shining yellow bedstraw, was less stifling than the road, and in a minute the chimneys and trees of the Place promised a still deeper coolness.

As she came into the wood something slipped with a thin rustle through last year's beech leaves. An adder, perhaps, she thought indifferently, her fears now less than ever embracing the inoffensive creatures of wood and field.

When she sat down in the shade of the trees themselves on a little wooden bench scarred with dozens of initials, she knew how exhausted she was. Body and mind were alike drained of vitality by the mental assault just made upon her; she was frightened too at the utter lack of coordination in her present thinking. Precious minutes were dribbling away while she sat in this windless refuge in the apparent apathy of defeatism, whispering to herself the murderer's name, seeing dangle before her horrified mind's eye the murderer's face in that moment when they had both known. Beyond this drumming repetition of the shock she had sustained, she was incapable of visualizing anything, any future action she knew must be taken, anything at all, except—a flash of red she must look out for on the distant crown of the road. A gleam of red ... among the trees.

That brought her up with a jerk. A splash of red. Red, in green surroundings. What did that make her think of? She had seen it, just now. A post office letter box it was, of course, set in the wall that bounded the grounds at the back of Long Greeting Place. There would be an afternoon or early evening collection. Sammy ... she could write to Sammy. She must get in touch with her. Sammy knew better than anyone else the things that ought to be done, the approaches that had to be made. With the Minerva closed, and neither Samela nor herself on the telephone, there could be no quicker way of getting in touch with her than by scribbling a note at once and posting it before she went home to Stoneacre. That would ensure Sammy's being at home at the earliest possible hour she could get to her in the morning.

She explored her bag clumsily, not for the paper and envelope that wouldn't be there anyway, but for the franked postcard she was pretty sure she was carrying. Here it was, grubby and dog-eared but serviceable, and a pencil for writing down the message which, necessarily public, must combine discretion with urgency.

Characteristically, the very thought of Samela lifted for a moment the cloud of inertia threatening to swamp her. And a moment was all she needed. Habit prevailing, she began to write the address first:

> Mrs. George Wild
> 4a Fletcher Mansions
> Moat Street
> Ravenchurch

As she wrote the last word part of her mind registered the fact that somewhere close by the adder was still active.

But she was not distracted by its quiet rustling. That was why she knew nothing more until in one appalling second sky and trees crashed to meet the wavering earth and crumpled together in the blackness that engulfed her.

2

To their mutual displeasure Sergeant Brook it was who had been detailed to "have a chat with little Miss Oates." Discomfort was perhaps a more accurate term to describe the sergeant's feelings, for he was ill at ease in the company of very young girls, especially those of the "off" school age, and would any day have preferred handling a boy. Marion, on the other hand, was frankly disgusted at having failed to net Scotland Yard for the interview for which she had done the equivalent of praying earnestly. And Brook, that tiresomely familiar figure, benign and conciliatory in the face of no matter what provocation, or so the legend ran, was no kind of answer to a maiden's prayer.

At first she retired into monosyllabic sulks which Aunts Hilda and Win, encouraged by the sergeant to hover together or by turn about their chicken, interpreted nervously as the shock they had always predicted; delayed, certainly, as such manifestation often was, but becomingly there all right.

"I really don't think," said Aunt Win with what firmness she could summon, "that Marion can add anything useful to what the others have told you."

"You're wrong," Marion said loudly, before Brook could reply. He saw that the girl was still sitting in the stiff, unbending pose she had assumed at once, her lips purposefully compressed, her mournful eyes set high on the window she faced.

Setting the usual preposterous value on her evidence—such as it may be, Brook thought, amused. But it was only faint amusement; experience in even so humdrum a place as Ravenchurch had taught him that the unknown, the unheard, could never be safely prejudged or discounted, and that occasionally from the mouths of babes and sucklings …

"We understood," he said genially, determined not to rush her, "that Miss

Oates, besides helping in the tearoom, sometimes gave a hand in tidying up the cubicles upstairs where ladies received—er—beauty treatment, and as none of the other staff seems to have been admitted to that department since Miss Tidy took it over singlehanded, we were wondering—that is to say, there may have been little things which came to your notice, Miss Marion, which your colleagues would be bound to miss anyway." He glanced deprecatingly at Aunt Hilda. "That's the only reason I'm here."

"Good enough," Marion commended curtly. She began to wake up. After all, it was one thing to hold out on the police on *infra dig* grounds, but the nose-cutting policy was always face-spiting, and that was another matter. If she stayed morose and wordless and looked plain stupid—and nobody knew better how to do that—it was true there was nothing officialdom could do about it, but on the other hand she would be flinging away her own chances of for once holding the spotlight.

"I'll tell you what I know," she said graciously. "I've not told anybody up to now." She eyed the reproachful glances of the aunts.

"Not Mrs. Wild or Mrs. Bates—or Miss Kingsley?" the sergeant asked.

"No—I couldn't."

"Why not?"

"It was one of those things that was in my own thoughts, you see. It made me feel—well, sickish, if it meant what I thought it meant. I would have made it real by talking about it. And even if I had an inclination to let the others in on it something always choked the words down. They take life easily, you know. They make a jest of things. But I—I would have made it real by telling it."

"Yes, I see," Brook agreed gravely. Watching the taut face, he thought how earnest, how even elderly, life was before twenty. "Tell me. We will deal with the reality."

She shrugged. "She's dead. I don't mind talking now."

Her unemotional young voice turned the simplest fact sinister, Brook thought. But this tale was the nastier for being unadorned. And it fitted. It dovetailed neatly with official theory and evidence.

Marion, on her own resentful admission, had been a Jack-of-all-trades at the Minerva. Beyond washing up, there was little enough of the teashop business she had learned; she was expected to run errands, do what dusting and polishing the hatshop might require, and in this ubiquitous capacity had been charged with what she described as the "mucky business" of cleaning the cubicles after beauty treatment. On heavy days, when, she explained, appointments followed one another closely, the same cubicle—there were four of them—might have to be put in order several times, but during recent months there had been a marked decline in the number of clients and a corresponding slackening of her work upstairs.

"How would you account for that?" Brook asked. "I mean, fewer clients." He had to check the inclination to call her "Missy," instinct advising that a productive interview was to be looked for only if he treated her as an adult.

"Because the qualified assistants were all gone by the New Year," Marion said promptly. "And even if she'd had the job at her finger ends, which she hadn't, Miss Tidy could never have carried on alone and given the same sort of satisfaction as when she had a staff. She got bothered and absentminded, and it made her rude to people—and she wasn't really polite at the best of times—and clients didn't like having their appointments forgotten without apology, or else being treated for the wrong thing."

"I'd say they didn't," Brook agreed. This brought him to the question of why precisely Miss Tidy had chosen to kill a flourishing and lucrative business by so arbitrary an evacuation of its staff. But he did not ask it yet. Let the girl develop her story in her own way. His restraint was rewarded almost at once by what seemed a display of mind reading on Marion's part.

"Seems on the face of it a silly sort of thing to do, sack your people just when everything's going okay. We all had a bit of a shock and thought it odd, you know, because there wasn't any explanation good enough. Not till I began to think about it, and take notice. Even being frightfully arrogant and—and bossy, as Tidy was, wouldn't altogether account for taking into your own hands a show you didn't know the ABC of. But it wasn't that at all, of course."

She paused, her curtain beautifully timed, tasting lingeringly the sweet triumph of Aunt Win's and Aunt Hilda's deferential attention.

"No?" Brook encouraged.

"No," Marion echoed firmly. "It wasn't that, not just her mag—meg-a-lo-mania that made her do it. It was because she was out to use the beauty-culture stuff as a cover for other—other things. Other activities," she corrected, with the touch of importance due her subject.

"And they were?" the sergeant prompted.

She flung him a shrewd glance. "Something to interest the police, I'm sure." She went on jerkily: "I don't know. I can only guess, and then guess. She had some hold over them. I thought at first it was gambling. On the big scale, you know," she said with the air of a disillusioned rake, "like women enjoy. But it couldn't have been."

"Why not?"

"Because *nobody* enjoyed it. Far from it." Excitement warmed her voice, and something, Brook judged, that was remembered fear. "They were miserable. I tell you they were *miserable*."

Brook's quiet interest and the fluttered chirrups of the aunts drew from her a coherent account. There was no doubt, the sergeant congratulated himself, that sharpness, practiced observation, and, it had to be admitted, personal loathing of Miss Tidy herself, made Marion Oates a valuable witness.

Something had first struck her as wrong when she had been given a cubicle to clean which had clearly not been in use—not, that is, Marion added, used for its recognized purpose. The washbasin was clean, the floor unstained, all accessories in place.

"And I was just going to exclaim, 'But there's nothing at all to do here,' when I caught sight of Miss Tidy in the mirror over the basin. She was in the doorway, watching. And all in a flash I saw that she'd spotted her mistake the moment *I* had noticed the state of the cubicle, and I never said what I had been going to say."

"You could have, all the same," Brook remarked, though he knew, with approval, why she hadn't. "What kept you silent?"

"Knowing that to have spoken then would have been the end of my work upstairs," Marion said. "Oh yes, I was sick of the filthy business, right enough. But, you see, it had just begun to look as if it might be interesting. Anything to relieve the general monotony, I thought. So I made my face blank and stupid enough to take Tidy in—she wasn't all *that* sharp, you know, about people she wasn't interested in, people like me; she was too much wrapped up in herself for that—up to the last she believed I was as stupid as I meant she should. So, till she moved away, I fiddled with this and straightened that, and rinsed the spotless basin, and poked about for the things clients often leave behind, and so on."

"Good for you," Brook said heartily, beaming on this subtlety of the serpent. "Now tell me, how did you know that the cubicle *had* been occupied at all that time? Mightn't you have been directed to it by mistake?"

"Well, I was, of course," Marion said contemptuously. "But not the way you mean. Somebody had been there all right. You see, there were two other cubicles where work had really gone on, steamy holes they were too—and *three* clients had kept their appointments that afternoon. I saw them leave— besides, I looked in the appointments book afterwards, and after that I always ran an eye over it."

"Nice work," the sergeant chuckled. Aunt Hilda looked pained.

"Wasn't it rather like spying, dear?" she asked in a valiant effort to temper the approbation.

"Snooping?" Marion said unashamedly. "It was in intention but, funnily enough, not in practice. Of course when I sensed there was something queer going on I was all out to unearth it. But the book wasn't a secret—any of us could have looked at it. Sam and Crystal wrote down the entries, and they were just what they seemed. But if Mrs. So-and-so was down for a mud pack, it didn't always mean she got it, not on my theory."

Aunt Win sighed. "So secretive, dear, to have kept all this to yourself."

"That's all right," Brook put in hastily. "Look here, Miss Marion, can you date this incident?"

"Yes. January—about the middle. It's been going on ever since."

He nodded. "And do you remember who those three clients were?"

"Why, ra-ther. Old Mrs. Wardle-Phlox, who is rheumaticky and makes very regular visits, and a girl named Marlow, who isn't exactly local but one of the country gentry—and the other was Mrs. Livingston-Bole."

She finished on a note of hesitation. Brook took her up.

"Yes? There was something else you were going to say?"

"Only," said Marion, "that I sort of guessed you were going to ask me if I knew which of them used which cubicle—and I do know."

"How?" Brook asked. This girl, he reminded himself, was the imaginative type, and he must be on guard against swallowing rashly the bait of what might well prove to be mingled fact and fiction. "Did you see each one leave her respective cubicle?"

"Oh no. I used not to go upstairs until after they'd all gone. I saw them going when I was in the teashop, as usual. But it really wasn't hard to tell who had been where."

She gave indeed a convincing enough explanation, confirming Brook's opinion of her reliability and aptitude for immediate observation. Mrs. Wardle-Phlox had required massage and was always allotted the same cubicle on each visit. Miss Marlow, who came infrequently, was in the habit of buying of such cosmetics as the Minerva could offer, and there were nearly always things to put away after she'd made her selection; on this occasion, however, there had been an additional clue which identified beyond doubt the cubicle she had used. Miss Tidy had provided a brush and comb for each client. Miss Marlow had used hers freely.

"And she had auburn hair," Marion said. "Very conspicuous, it was. Not so good as Crystal's—well, not the same, darker stuff. I took it out of the comb."

Brook was satisfied. "So the orderly cubicle …?"

"Was Mrs. Livingston-Bole's—yes."

"And did you keep track of her future appointments in the book?"

"She never came again," Marion said simply.

The sergeant allowed the first look of surprise to light up his face, then recalled that this fitted Mrs. Weaver's statement to the inspector.

"You know," Marion said, "when I knew it was Mrs. Livingston-Bole who hadn't received beauty culture that day, my mystery got a bit flat. Just for a little while. Everybody knew she was a great friend of Tidy's anyway, and so it seemed feasible she'd paid her just a social visit. Only it seemed queer for them to choose a stuffy cubicle to sit in. And then, when she didn't come any more, *that* was mysterious too."

Brook nodded. Things were moving all right. He handed her a slip of paper.

"Miss Marion, did any of the people down there attend for beauty treatment between January and the early summer?"

She took the copy of the list Arthur Tidy had examined, except that this one omitted the name of Colonel Livingston-Bole.

As she bent over the paper she nodded with the only undisguised excitement she had yet shown, then looked up at the waiting sergeant.

"So far as I can tell you," she said, "Miss Drake was never at the Minerva. Mrs. Weaver's books were more in her line. Miss Graves? She managed gowns, didn't she, at Fripp and Saltmarsh? And committed suicide. I remember her. And yes, she did have an appointment for something or other—removing sunburn, I think—but it isn't going to help much, because it was a long time ago, in the days when Tidy still had her upstairs staff. She didn't come afterwards, I'm pretty sure. Quite a lot of people dropped the beauty culture when they knew Miss Tidy was carrying on alone."

"And Miss Kane?"

"I was coming to her. She came always. Quite regularly, up to the time she died. And it was she—she—more than any of them—"

"What?"

"That made me think something was going on, something unprofessional and secret, something *bad.*"

"Why?"

"For one thing, in March and April she came *too* often. I mean she came oftener than the appointments booked to her, and not only that, but it was too many times for anybody to need beautifying," Marion added gravely.

"And the cubicles?"

"In the last month or two, far too tidy and clean. I noticed sometimes that Tidy created a bit of artificial disorder with the intention of hoodwinking me. When things looked messy they didn't look natural-messy, you see."

If this were all, it might not add up to anything necessarily sinister. But there was more, of a nature which carried conviction even to Brook, no authority on femininity. Iris Kane, Marion divulged, had twice left the Minerva weeping, after protracted sessions.

"Once, when I spoke to her at the bottom of the stairs—I knew her well—I could see her eyes and nose were very red, and the other time she didn't want to notice me, because she didn't want *me* to notice her, but hurried by crying quite badly—I mean, so that you could hear her crying."

Brook nodded. "Just how well did you know her?" he asked.

"Mainly because she came so often to the Minerva," Marion replied. She suddenly became enthusiastic and irrelevant. "She was lovely to look at, you know. She had been three times beauty queen in Ravenchurch. In the war she worked in the munitions factory by Stoneacre, and then she met Chris Froggatt—and *he's* on the way to being a millionaire—and it was love at first sight, and they were to be married this month." She pulled herself up, breathing deeply. "About me knowing her? She was older than I was, about twenty-two, but she was an old girl of my school, and we had the same youth club, and she was nice to everybody."

Brook thought she looked whiter, and shaken, and decided to close the interview.

"And nothing more this time, I suppose," he said lightly, getting up.

"I don't know," Marion said in a flat voice. She went back to Iris. "She didn't always live in Long Greeting—she came there when she was ten."

"We know," Brook said.

"Oh. And do you know about her name?"

"Her name?"

"She wasn't christened Iris, she said. She said her real name was Fleur, and she could remember being called it when she was about three or four. But afterwards they changed it, she didn't know why. She had a film test, you know—that was before she got engaged to be married—and she said if she got a job she should change the name back again."

"Marion," Aunt Hilda said, "you're tired, dear. Having to remember all these things which can't matter about poor little Iris. It isn't of much interest to Sergeant Brook for you to run on like this."

"All grist to the mill, ma'am," Brook said with a curt note. He looked at the child's pale, intent face, he made to pat her shoulder, changed his mind, and, instead, shook her hand.

"Thank you very much, Miss Oates," he said warmly. "You've helped as much as anyone."

When he had gone there was an uncomfortable silence which Aunt Win broke.

"He seems a very nice man," she said vaguely, though with an air of apology.

Aunt Hilda made one of her rare snaps. "He's *not!* Hammering away at the whole thing, and what's the use—"

"Oh, be *quiet*," Marion said, her voice a stormy whisper. She stood up suddenly, and with a movement as abrupt sat down again. Her palms hard against her cheeks, she burst into tears.

The aunts held their breath in a mingling of consternation and relief.

"I *knew*—" Aunt Hilda began, and Win broke in, "*There*, Marie—now, dear—"

Their niece lifted a fierce, twisted face. "It's not, it's not, it's *not!*" she cried, replying to their unspoken remarks. "You're all *wrong*—it's not the *police!* It's that—that night, the night I went out without Win, the night she was killed!" She dropped her head in anguish. "It was *Samela* I saw that night—Sam, *slinking* away!"

3

Kate Beaton stood by the body of Jane Kingsley, waiting for the police. She wondered if she had done the best thing, especially the best thing for herself, in sending the weedy, ineffectual youth who was Owen Greatorex's gardener, to the Loggerheads to telephone Superintendent Lecky. When she had run down the meadow towards the road and had caught sight of him shambling by, there had indeed seemed no alternative; none, that was, if she intended herself mounting guard over the dead girl. And she had felt no doubt as to the expediency of that.

They were a long while coming. Not really, but it was bound to seem so. At this hour of the afternoon even the fringes of the wood seemed sucked dry of air and movement. She shuddered a little to see that the only visible motion came from the gnats and flies that, in so short a time, would have become predatory monsters for the thing lying at her feet.

She shifted her position a few inches, but even the indeterminate sound of her own feet in the undergrowth brought a fresh pang of disquiet. She peered more closely, though, and was glad to be able to remind herself that she had touched nothing. Touching in this case had been unnecessary for ascertaining death. So far as she could see there were no signs of a struggle. The surrounding grass, of the dry, discouraged variety growing beneath trees, was apparently little bloodstained. It even looked, though she could not be sure without the closer examination she was reluctant to make, as if a pen or pencil were clutched still in the fearfully tightened fingers of the right hand. Then her eyes moved furtively to the sickening head and hair of the girl she remembered as beautiful. Kate Beaton, her ruddy apple skin paled almost beyond recognition, began to look as well as feel unwholesome herself.

Murder in fact was disgracefully unlike its fictional cousin. Even "cousin" seemed to rate too closely the blood relationship—"blood relationship" drew a pawky smile to her lips—for while the one was a trimly rounded affair in which the author at least could derive unbounded pleasure from his own callousness, the real thing was a matter of mess, of improvisation, of unco-ordinated thinking and a reversion to the unspecific terrors of infancy, of choking indignations and a realization of unguessed-at scruples within one-self, and, above all, the knowledge, freezing intention and execution alike, of horribly ramified consequences, unlimited in time and extent, utterly unpredictable in detail.

When at last the police arrived she noticed with some displeasure that Owen Greatorex was among them. He was chatting to a rather unresponsive Inspector Raikes, but broke off to greet her solemnly as soon as he had come within tactful hailing distance. That was all, however, for Raikes shepherded him off at once and left him backed against the towering wall of Long Greeting Place, an isolated and not unimpressive figure looking as if he were due to be shot at dawn.

So it's to be segregation for me, Kate Beaton thought with a wry mouth; till, reason asserting itself, she decided they were merely adopting normal routine. It wasn't to be expected that the first approach made to her would be from other than the police. She saw, as Raikes drew nearer, that Sergeant Brook was not in the group, his place being taken by another local sergeant she found oddly unfamiliar in plain clothes. He was followed by a uniformed constable, another carrying a camera, and, breathing truculently in the rear, Dr. Hare.

The inspector, who had motioned her away a yard or so, gave his attention to the body for a few minutes before leaving the others to carry on. Then he crossed to her side.

"Now, Miss Beaton." He was briskly quiet. She was glad he beat about no bush, and responded by giving him in a few sentences her account of the discovery.

He glanced at his wrist. "It's now four-forty. At four-twelve we got Pemberton's telephone message. Can you say how long before that it was you came upon the body?"

"Yes. Because I looked at my watch. It was between ten and five minutes to four when I reached the seat and—saw her. I suppose I was going on for five minutes in a state of stupefaction and horror, trying to get a grip on myself and eyeing what was left of the poor girl. By the way, I touched nothing. I'm too squeamish for that, believe it or not. And she was clearly dead. Then I came to life because I knew I must, ran back down the meadow to contact somebody, anybody. Knowing that, if I didn't, I'd have to go to the Loggerheads and ring up Ravenchurch myself."

"You didn't want to?"

"I didn't want to leave the—the girl."

"Why? The first step was calling the police."

"I know. I just felt I ought not to leave her alone."

For Raikes this rang psychologically true. At the first douche of shock so cruel the living can admit only without realization that the sudden and violently dead are indeed dead. The obligations of tenderness and service are still imperative. He said nothing of this, however; he was trained to suspect, anyway, and had already asked himself the question: what if Kate Beaton had had personal reasons for lingering by the body, for the purpose, perhaps, of removing or faking evidence? She had, after all, gone out of her way to deny handling anything.

He said mildly, "What time did you leave the house for your walk?"

"At twenty to four."

"Corroboration?"

She shrugged. "None you'd accept. I haven't a resident staff, thank God. My morning woman's off by two. But people often twig me sallying forth, you know. There's not much else to do in villages, except watch other folk's front doors opening and shutting."

He had heard these strictures before and, if they were true, wondered why on earth anybody intelligent ever lived in a village. Yet they continued to do so.

In a moment his expression had sharpened. "Where are the dogs?"

"What? Which dogs?" She looked frankly taken aback.

"*Which?* Why, yours. You exercise them daily, don't you?"

To his surprise she flushed heavily. There was an appreciable pause before she spoke.

"Boris isn't feeling too good," she explained in a sullen voice. "I've starved and dosed him, poor fellow, and left him quiet. Jock is staying behind to keep him company." She added with a hint of temper, "*Does* it matter?"

"Does it?" Raikes returned carelessly. Before he could say anything else he was hailed by the police surgeon, who came towards them with a red, resentful face he kept for the more noisome part of his work.

"What you say just now killed her?" he asked the inspector in an aggressive tone.

"I didn't commit myself," said Raikes. "Heavy—very heavy instrument, of course. Like a poker, was my suggestion."

"Come over here," Hare rasped.

He led him in an opposite direction to the wall of the big house, to where about ten yards from the spot where Jane Kingsley had been attacked a ditch ran, separating the glade in which they stood from the denser wood beyond. Kate Beaton, receiving no contrary instruction, followed and looked down with the inspector at that portion of the hemlock-grown trench Hare and the plainclothes sergeant were indicating. In the wet seasons it was a watercourse; now it was smothered in coarse grass and weeds that were crushed into a hollow in one place.

The sergeant drew out a wicked-looking wooden object shaped like a mallet, holding it by the middle. The striking end was sticky with blood and hair.

"Know what it is?" the doctor snapped.

"Of course," Kate Beaton replied at once. "It's a beetle. Non-entomological, naturally. A hedge beetle, used as a sort of rammer."

"Or hammer," Hare amended. "And every bit as effective as the woppiest poker that ever was."

When they were taking it away, with particular if unhopeful attention for the handle, the ambulance men arrived.

4

In Samela's flat Raikes faced an indignant trio. George Wild, it was true, slung along the arm of his wife's chair, was keeping his indignation well leashed, but the ladies had given a fine display. Anger, moreover, was doing them good; temporarily, at least, it burned up grief. It was later that all thoughts would end in the one thought, that Jane was dead.

Wrath was not to be wondered at, perhaps. There had been little that was veiled about the inspector's suggestion regarding the postcard found underneath Jane's body.

"But you must be crazy!" Samela cried again, with reckless deliberation, in spite of the hot incredulity that choked her. "*I* kill Jane! And if I *could*, if I did, how would she have the chance to put my name and address so neatly on a postcard so as to let you know? I've heard some fantastic theories aired in the last few days, but this beats them all!"

Raikes gave her a bitter little smile, edged with triumph. "You've heard nothing aired suggesting you killed Miss Kingsley, Mrs. Wild. The remarks are your own."

Samela, who could have sworn they were the inspector's, subsided momentarily like a landed fish. George took time by the forelock.

"Don't be a fool, Sam," he said in a voice of quiet authority, and to Raikes, "It's like this, Inspector. My wife's giving tactless expression to what we're all, perhaps, more or less feeling, namely, that by imputation, at least, you do regard her as an object of suspicion because her name appears on the card you found—"

"Oh, not only because of *that!*" Sammy, irrepressible, interrupted, fanning her own flames and near to tears. "*I* was suspected straight off when Miss Tidy was killed, because I didn't ring up the Keepsake, and *because* I was the first to see the lights burning though the sun was shining, and *because* I wanted the window broken, and—because—because of *hundreds* of other sins of commission and omission!"

"*Will* you shut up?" her husband growled with good-natured ferocity. He shot a wary look at Raikes. "Don't want to sound brutal or—or indifferent, you know, but this business of young Jane has hit us all harder than the old girl's affair, ghastly as it was. That's why Samela is giving us the works."

"Giving me, you mean," the inspector said smoothly. "Mrs. Wild is inclined—if I may say so without calling down more brimstone—to a hypersensitivity which, in fairness you should admit, is in itself suspicious. She *will* anticipate, forestall, make cutting little remarks that at least *sound* self-condemnatory, and from the beginning of this enquiry continually takes the words out of my mouth—"

"Then they are there to take," Sammy muttered, quelled but unquenched.

"Hush," Crystal said loudly. She was unashamedly frightened and took no pains to conceal the fact that she had been crying her eyes out. "All this—this *quarrelling* isn't decent, truly it isn't, with Jane gone."

"Agreed," Raikes said heartily. "As friends of Jane Kingsley you can't want to place yourselves in an opposite camp to me. We're all in this investigation together, and frayed tempers are only obstructive—"

"And," George put in, with a shadow of the first grin they had seen, "Scotland Yard's given you a treat of a character reading, my girl. Better than anything you'd get out of a slot machine. Hypersensitive, self-condemnatory, *always* interrupting—she's all that, Inspector, but there's no harm in Sammy. At least," he added hastily, "not to a homicidal degree."

After that they got down to business. It was Crystal, wide-eyed and

desperately anxious to clear the innocent of unwarranted charges, who remembered Jane's habit of writing the address before the message. "So you
see," she finished on a note of certainty, "she was meaning to write to
Samela."

"But why?" Raikes persisted, as much to himself as to them.

George Wild frowned. "We're not on the phone in this benighted shack.
She must have wanted to contact Sam with some urgency."

"Then why not come in person? The postcard couldn't reach you till
next day."

"Next morning," George corrected. "And the Stoneacre bus service
is antediluvian. She could have cycled in, that afternoon or evening. But
maybe the poor lass had other fish to fry those times. Besides, she'd be
anything but sure of finding us at home. A postcard was a sensible way
of keeping us in."

This was plausible enough, Raikes had to admit. But what had the girl
been doing in Long Greeting? Brook was looking after the Stoneacre end
and was probably now making his report of what the Kingsleys had had to
tell him. Precious little, was Raikes's guess. Girls nowadays made a great
show of frankness, but it was to conceal the fact that they were all as
secretive as oysters. It was unlikely Jane had wanted tabs kept on her movements anywhere. And relations were notoriously the last persons to know
anything. Something of this he voiced, till Samela, mollified though still cold,
said, "She probably called on somebody in Long Greeting."

"That had occurred," Raikes said without sarcasm. "But so far no Long
Greeting householder admits so much, nor to having seen her at all. Bar the
murderer, those known to have last seen her alive are the conductor of the
bus which took her into the village and one or two passengers who remember her alighting at the Loggerheads. She was put down at the stop there at
one-ten. After that her movements are a mystery. We'd particularly like to
know why she was in the wood just then."

"A rendezvous?" George suggested.

"With Death," breathed Crystal, who went more often to the pictures
than the others.

"We don't think so," Raikes explained patiently. "You see, it's pretty evident she addressed the card to Mrs. Wild *before* the attack was made on her.
She was still grasping her fountain pen when we found her. Yet to have
written a message at all so as to be in time to catch the last village post—by
the way, it would be collected at four forty-five if, as we suppose, she was
going to drop it in the box in the wall of the big house—to have been writing
it at all, I repeat, warrants us in attaching urgency to it. So if there *was* a
rendezvous, which is doubtful, we feel that the purport of the message was
something that happened earlier."

"But," persisted George, who, with Samela and Crystal, knew nothing of
the possibility of watching for the Ravenchurch bus from the seat in the

wood, "all this doesn't actually preclude such a meeting, does it?"

"I rather think it does," the inspector, all sweet reasonableness, replied. "She left the bus at one-ten. Miss Beaton found her body just before four o'clock—sorry, I *have* to go over this—and when the police surgeon saw it at twenty to five he said she had been dead hardly over the hour. So you see, we're left with the question: what did she do with herself between one-ten and three-thirty or thereabouts? Because in any case, if there had been an appointment to meet someone in the wood about the fatal hour, she could have left Stoneacre on a later bus, on the three-five, in fact."

Sammy frowned. "But suppose the meeting *was* for an early hour, after all. Suppose—oh, it's quite horrible—suppose they stayed talking for about two hours, and things went badly, from bad to worse—and then—and then—"

Raikes regarded her with an air of indulgent sympathy. "Only, you see, Mrs. Wild, when Jane Kingsley stepped out of the Stoneacre bus just after one o'clock she was seen to walk *not* in the direction of the wood, which is reached by crossing the field stile, but up the road past the Loggerheads, in the same direction, in fact, as the bus was going, and where all the Long Greeting houses are situated."

"Except the Place and the vicarage," said George, who liked being accurate.

"Yes. So we can take it her objective in the first place was not the wood."

In the unhelpful silence which followed, communal thinking was almost noisy. You can all but hear us, Sammy decided, counting on our mental fingers possible ports of call in Greeting, from the Keepsake itself (or was it shut up now?) to Mile House where Mr. Greatorex lived, and Kate Beaton's chilly barn, or maybe Iris Kane's cottage by the river—*the* river—and oh, lots of others, of course.

Everybody clamping his and her real thoughts down, George said politely, as if remarking on the weather, "I suppose it was Miss Beaton's dogs found Jane?"

"Miss Beaton hadn't her dogs with her," Raikes said shortly.

The moment itself was openmouthed.

"*Well*," Crystal cried, "I've *never* seen her without them!"

There was another busy silence. Then, "Dogs can be a nuisance at times as well as helpful," Samela said in a small, considering voice.

Nobody took up the challenge. George's face was impassive and had got to look, somehow, disquietingly older. Crystal, who liked notice of most statements as well as questions, had to turn the remark about in her head and knead it a little before it meant anything at all to her. She remembered that she had had to do that with Sammy's observations other times too.

The inspector saved them from further embarrassment by breaking out at a tangent.

"Any of you been blackmailed any time, anywhere?" he asked cheerfully enough.

Miss Beaton's canine aberrations abruptly shelved, they stared at him with wholehearted attention.

"Are you just being offensive again?" Sammy asked.

"Don't be daft," George said. "I mean you, Sam. Matter of fact, it 'ud be quite a distinction if we had. But in the interests of truth, no sir. Sammy's and my joint income wouldn't be worth the most unambitious blackmailer's while."

"Nor mine," Crystal echoed. "Besides," she went on regretfully, "you'd have to be a sort of adventuress, wouldn't you, to tempt one to try it on? And except for marrying Kenneth, I've had an awfully dull life."

They laughed, and Raikes said, "That's conclusive, then, isn't it? Next best thing: know anybody else who's been?"

"What *is* all this?" Samela said. It dawned on her that he was in earnest.

"So that's what it was, eh?" George said quietly, half to himself.

"I used to think black *market* was perhaps the answer," Samela added.

"To what?" Raikes asked quickly.

"To the night visitors," she said at once.

"You know?"

She shrugged. "One isn't indoors every night and all night."

"So I gather." Raikes looked grim. "Where were you, Mrs. Wild, on the night Miss Tidy was killed?"

"I've told you. In bed, with my husband," Samela said chastely and with such promptitude as to cut the ground from under the feet of George, who had been looking, frowningly, on the brink of revelations.

The inspector apparently accepted this, and when he did not challenge it Crystal piped up.

"That goes for everyone, I'll say. We must all have been in bed at the hour of the murder. There's never anything to *do* in Ravenchurch."

"And how," asked Raikes, making his now familiar pounce, "do you know the hour of the murder?"

Crystal flushed. "Well, everyone knows," she said defensively. "It was near the longest day it happened, with nights not properly dark at all, but the light was burning when we got in next morning, so she must have been killed after dark."

Raikes merely looked cryptic and therefore annoying. Samela, remembering his earlier insinuations about the teashop lights, yearned to hit him.

There was not much else he wanted with them. But, night callers at the Minerva having been mooted, he did a little necessary probing for more specific information. Sammy, with the reluctance he was now prepared for, confessed to having seen Mrs. Livingston-Bole on two occasions, both in the winter, and, to everyone's surprise, though they could hardly have said why, Beatrice Graves in the early spring.

"I wasn't snooping in those days either," she said, "because in the dark seasons it was the understood thing for Bertha to sleep at the shop. I just happened to be out and saw these people arriving or leaving. It was later, in the light, warm days, the same goings on got to seem odd."

When the door had finally closed behind Raikes, Sammy relaxed limply.

"That man," she said with controlled viciousness, "he leads you on with the most horrible suggestions, and then makes hay of what you think he's been saying. He never leaves behind him a feeling of reassurance."

"You don't deserve it," George retorted irritably. "Why, if you must let on you've watched the Minerva after closing hours, couldn't you come clean and say you were hanging around the night she was killed? They'll probably jump to it sooner or later. I'd half a mind to split on you myself, only you headed me off like that."

"Oh, but it would never do," Crystal protested.

Samela was gazing at George with a practiced look of affectionate contempt.

"Darling, you know why I'm keeping quiet."

"I know what you told me," George said sulkily, as if they were two distinct things. "You girls make me sick. All this lying doggo, all this thick-an'-thin loyalty business to one another at a time when you must see equivocation's only a sort of boomerang for yourselves—and yet obviously you don't trust one another an inch."

"That's not fair," Crystal said stoutly.

"Of course it is. It's you and Sam that haven't an ounce of logic between you."

"Let him run on," Sammy said with a sort of tired indulgence. "Now and then he has to get off his chest what he feels about feminine inferiority. But I *did* see old Titus that night, looking like Lady Macbeth, and I'm *not* going to say I was there!"

CHAPTER 9

Kettles and pans,
Say the bells of St. Ann's.

Mrs. Phail, the housekeeper at Mile House, was a lady who knew her own position and everyone else's with disconcerting clarity. In appearance and manner she was not unlike Queen Victoria, though lacking the royal individuality. Her figure, walk, mode of speech—each was a carryover from a period of outlines, both physical and social, far less blurred than the present; and because her efficiency in its own limited sphere reposed on self-confidence and went for the most part unchallenged Owen Greatorex found her services unquestionably to his taste.

It had not been charity that had moved her to offer hospitality to Léonie

Blanchard after Miss Tidy's murder, although she preferred to think that it was. Her sense of the impropriety, always some reflection on the neighborhood which tolerated it, of a single woman living alone in a house already disgraced by crime, had urged her in the first place to the only course of action possible. It was characteristic of her to be seldom, if ever, faced with an alternative in conduct. So she remained untroubled in the midst of distress and complexity. But an obscurer motive, exercising an even greater compulsion, which nothing but painstaking psychiatry was likely to unearth, sprang from the fact that Léonie was noted for the range and taste of her cooking, and Mile House had recently lost its cook. Mrs. Phail's sharply defined grading in domesticity did not recognize practical work in the kitchen among the duties of a housekeeper, though loyalty to Mr. Greatorex permitted it as a temporary concession; and as it seemed improbable they would secure the services of a cook from beyond the boundary of Long Greeting while all this slaughter and self-slaughter abounded, it might be said to be a further dispensation of Providence which had liberated at such a time the culinary skill of Léonie.

Not that Mrs. Phail approved of foreigners, or even acknowledged their existence except from a discreetly distant mind's eye. The physical one was trained to occlude them. By her they were grouped and classified with, for example, people who lived by their wits, artists who were not royal academicians, and unknighted actors. She felt their inferiority called for compassion rather than patronage, and took their resentment at these evidences of kindliness for one of their more offensive traits.

Now that Léonie was in the house she had little impermanent waves of unease, more on Mr. Greatorex's behalf than her own. True, the woman was quiet and as industrious as she had always been led to suppose, in spite of a certain air of truculence and sarcasm she carried about with her bony frame (how odd to be so delicately discriminative in the matter of food and *so* blunt and prickly in human approach!) but was her presence going to be a magnet for the police? To be quite just, and Mrs. Phail was always acutely conscious of the efforts she made towards fair-mindedness, the earlier visit today by members of the local force had been ostensibly to discover if the unfortunate girl Kingsley had called at Mile House on the afternoon she met her death. What an idea! Only policemen would get such a notion. She herself had never on any occasion seen the young person, and she was sure neither had Mr. Greatorex. Now, when she believed they had dismissed with courtesy and firmness the inquisitors of the morning, here they were back again, or rather one of them was, representing himself to be a Scotland Yard inspector and clearly bent on the same errand. She was finding it hard to realize that a blameless establishment like Mile House should attract in a single day so many of these tiresome gentry, who treated you to a display of obtuseness when you wanted them to take your meaning, and were so uncomfortably alert when deaf ear and blind eye would have been more acceptable. And how difficult from the social standpoint to pigeonhole them! She had even heard tell that some of the new police had been to Eton and Harrow.

"I had been wondering, Léonie," she remarked after the first departure, "if this story of the young girl having called on a resident here may not itself be a cover, or rather an excuse, for the police to pay us a visit for some other reason. Superintendent Lecky, at least, is a very nice man, I believe. It may be he is anxious about *your* welfare, in view of the—the trouble which has overtaken you. They may have come here to keep a—a so-called eye upon you."

This struck, she felt, the precise note of solicitude desirable in the circumstances, while conveying a faint undertone of warning that Mrs. Phail was convinced it was neither Mr. Greatorex nor herself who could possibly interest the police. She was totally unprepared for the ferocity that met her in Léonie's eye.

"The po-leece, they 'ave not'ing on *me*," the woman said in her harsh, uncompromising voice. She made an appreciable pause for the implication to sink in, then added, "You 'ave a gardener, *n'est-ce pas?* Yesterday, he is so r-ready, so—on the spot, *n'est-ce pas?* What then is *he* doing in those minutes before Mam'selle Beaton find 'im so quick, *hein?*"

Mrs. Phail, used to the circumlocution of the English upper servant, did not at once comprehend what was being said. When she did she was aghast. It was outrageous, unanswerable. Then the pity she made a point of reserving for aliens melted her indignation. She drew in her lips, refraining from reply, but observing mentally: They are all barbarians at heart.

That was why, when Raikes arrived, he remarked some tension between the two. He remarked it without suspicion. There was always tension between women, even when they were plastering one another with reciprocal smiles. And, he supposed, the really remarkable thing at a time like this would have been absence of it.

He started off, as he put it, on the wrong foot with Mrs. Phail, by approaching the kitchen premises first and then refusing to be drawn into the housekeeper's room for the interview. Mrs. Phail, not entirely stupid, ascribed this unconventional behavior to the presence in the kitchen of Léonie, who was shelling peas with the frightening indifference of a robot. Since she was seated, and had clearly no intention of moving, it was more than ever patent to Mrs. Phail that it was she and none other who was exciting these attentions.

The inspector found the kitchen a barnlike place of farmhouse proportions, which nevertheless wore an inadequately modernized air as though contriving with difficulty to subdue its more formidable aspects to what Mrs. Phail expected from it. A highly polished but not very efficient-looking range occupied almost all the space on one side and formed a vast funereal backcloth to the gauntly striped cat which sat aloof from the ladies and at once exchanged with Raikes, if not a wink, a secret glance of complete understanding.

At a deal table, scrubbed out of countenance, Léonie sat with her vegetables, so immobile that, with a basket of golden dessert gooseberries at her elbow, she seemed only to enforce the quality of "still life." It was obvious that Mrs. Phail had been talking to her at the moment that the inspector, a wolf in sheep's clothing, had tapped with his knuckles at the outside door. It was she who had opened to him, as soon as she had seen his badge (Mrs. Phail disapproved emphatically of *plainclothes* policemen), the unladylike thought flashing through her head: So you thought to catch Blanchard alone.

"We were very careful," she said with reproof, "to tell your—your men this morning"—this was presumably a superior—"all that we knew. That included nothing about the young person who met her death yesterday, *nothing* whatever."

"You were," said the inspector, "admirably clear." He walked over to the hearth to stroke the unresponsive brindled cat, a gesture which aroused the displeasure and contempt of Mrs. Phail, who noticed he was paying very little attention to her and none at all to Léonie. That would be mere camouflage of course. She watched him, hands in pockets, teeter on toes and heels, his head tilted back, to examine the rafters.

"Nice old place," he said reflectively.

Mrs. Phail bridled at the patronage. "A very fine house," she agreed coldly. "Mr. Greatorex has a taste for fine things."

"You're telling me," said the insufferable policeman. "Is he at home now?"

"Mr. Greatorex is taking his evening walk."

Without which the sun wouldn't set, he finished for her. Aloud, he said, "I thought he might be. It doesn't matter." He broke off, wheeling in the direction of Léonie's back. "By Jove, a fine garden as well as house! What gooseberries!"

Mrs. Phail, trained to veracity for all occasions when the truth hurt nobody, felt paradoxically annoyed at this compliment, and began, "Our own garden doesn't—"

An appalling din shattered her words. Even Raikes jumped, while Mrs. Phail gave a timid shriek which she translated too late into an exclamation of disgust. Her experience did not embrace such violence. Only the cat, after a baleful contraction of its pupils, stuck to its guns, sitting up tautly and washing in furious protest the fur it took to be disordered by so much noise.

Léonie got up and retrieved the enormous jam kettle together with the colander carried along in its fall.

"These beeg vessels," she said with scorn, ignoring Mrs. Phail's faint expostulations. "No good—no good at all."

"It will be chipped after such a dreadful bang," Mrs. Phail said, taking it from Léonie's untrustworthy grasp as fiercely as dignity allowed. "And so hard, so *impossible* to replace these days."

She was stung by the inspector's unconcealed amusement. Her annoyance indeed was swelling visibly, for this man's disregard of the proprieties in declining to talk to her in the correct room had made it awkward to suggest he should be seated or to sit anywhere herself in comfort.

Raikes suddenly solved the problem by lugging forward a severe-looking wheelback known as "Cook's chair" and saying, "Do sit down, Mrs. Phail. We're provoking the tame poltergeist by hopping about like this."

Taking compliance for granted, he perched himself on the table, securing a view of Léonie's face instead of her back. The Breton, seated again, her large hands idle among the pods, challenged him with a grim, sardonic gaze that managed somehow to exclude the housekeeper in much the same way as the cat had done.

Mrs. Phail, accepting the situation, sat down in Edwardian composure. She did so the more readily since she had learned that her stumpy figure gained surprisingly from that posture.

"When were you last at the Keepsake?" Raikes said to Léonie almost casually.

She puckered her strong brows. "The morning—of yesterday, yes. But I do not go in."

"Did you want to?"

She shrugged. "It was her birthday. A few flowers in the room, p'raps—one has the sentiment, you understand."

"Miss Tidy's birthday, eh?" The inspector sounded mild surprise. "You could have gone in, you know. The constable has orders to let you."

Léonie twisted on him furiously. "You—you do not say to me, ever, that there is a po-leeceman at the 'ouse. He want to come in with me. I stay outside." This dramatic outburst appeased her at once, it seemed. She threw out her hands meekly and, eyes cast down, added in a quiet voice: "It does not signify, *naturellement*. One must not yield to the sentiment."

"It was a pretty intention at least," Mrs. Phail said largely. However unforgiving she might feel about the jam kettle, she disapproved still more strongly of Raikes.

Prettiness and Léonie were for him so absolutely divorced that the inspector caught himself staring thoughtfully at Mrs. Phail to see if she were real or not.

"You were all most helpful this morning," he said at last, with the touch of deference he knew would appeal, "and my presence here now casts no doubt on anything said then. But my colleague concentrated on the matter of whether or not Miss Kingsley had called here yesterday. It's other details I'd like to clear up—relative to that point, of course."

Mrs. Phail bent her head for him to proceed.

"Will you be good enough to say where you were between one o'clock and three-thirty yesterday afternoon?"

"But," said Mrs. Phail with studied patience, "I told the sergeant without his asking. We were *all* indoors. Had anyone rung or knocked at the front or back of the house it's impossible but—"

"I know." Raikes stopped her. "But, you see, here are just the missing details I mean. Indoors isn't enough. I'd much prefer to be told how exactly the household was employed in those two and a half hours."

Léonie all at once flattened her palms on the table and prepared to speak. Before she could begin Mrs. Phail waved haughty silence at her. Léonie tightened her mouth and watched her with narrow eyes.

"That is very easily disclosed—er—Inspector. Meals here are of course particularly regular, otherwise they would disorganize Mr. Greatorex's work. Lunch was as usual at twelve-thirty. We finished by one-fifteen, when the morning maid cleared away."

"Her name, please?"

Mrs. Phail, who hated interruption, raised her brows in rebuke. "She is of no possible importance to your enquiry. However, the name is Peggy Fisk."

"And what time does she leave?" Raikes asked.

"When the washing up is done, at about two o'clock each day. It's a deplorable state of affairs that a house like this should have to tolerate part-time domestic—"

"Yes," said the inspector. "Now about yourself, Mrs. Phail—where were you after lunch was over?"

Mrs. Phail judged that the only way to keep her dignity unimpaired beneath assaults of this kind was to let an appreciable pause fall before satisfying curiosity.

"I supervise here in the kitchen until the girl has left," she said at last. "Then from shortly after two o'clock until a quarter to four precisely I rest in my room. I was there today. I was there yesterday."

(And will be tomorrow.) Raikes studied her. "Such remarkable precision of habit makes for longevity," was his assurance. "And Mr. Greatorex? Is his practice as regular?"

"Of course. That is the foundation of his success. He has a great respect for Anthony Trollope, who, he tells me, was very careful to observe a time-table of work and relaxation. Yes, Mr. Greatorex too rests after lunch, and no one disturbs him until the tea bell is struck at four-fifteen."

"In his room?"

"In the dining room. An afternoon—nap. Gentlemen," added Mrs. Phail, coyly indulgent, "don't care for the trouble of moving from one room to another. They take their repose where they are."

Raikes considered this interesting sidelight, then said, "By the way, when you retire to your room, Mrs. Phail, do you mean the housekeeper's room?"

She looked affronted. "Oh no. I rest in my bedroom."

He nodded, turning quickly to the silent Léonie. "And you, Mam'selle Blanchard—where were you?"

"But where?" echoed Léonie, with the undertone of contempt tinging all her remarks. "What does one say? When in Rome, behave as a Roman. The trouble, it is thus saved, *n'est-ce pas?* I, I too rest in my room."

"Your bedroom?"

"I have no other."

"Quite so. Stupid of me," Raikes confessed. He swung his legs down. "Mrs. Phail, I'll ask you to be so kind as to let me see the lie of the house— your bedroom, the room occupied by Mam'selle, and the dining room."

Mrs. Phail rose, motioning Léonie, who showed no other inclination, to stay where she was. In spite of the fact that she felt genteel protest obligatory, the itch of detective fever was beginning to bother her own cool blood. She would have died rather than admit it. Without another word she led the inspector out of the kitchen, where he had never had any right to be, of course.

The dining room, on the ground floor, was the first to be examined. Though furnished with conventionality and some opulence, Turkey carpet, somber crimson flock paper on the walls, it was pleasant enough in its solid way. Raikes put this down in the main to the French windows which poured a generous flood of light on the dark scene. They opened onto a modest lawn, with a gleam of flowerbeds in the gap between well-kept hedges of Chinese honeysuckle. Raikes noted that as he stood at the windows the front door was only a few yards to his right. Anybody approaching it could be at the windows in a second or two.

Upstairs the outlook was different. Mrs. Phail's delicately encumbered abode looked down on a sidewalk blocked by untrimmed shrubs. Cut off from the ordinary traffic of the indoor and outdoor staff, with its drawn curtains and half-canopied bed, the room provided, it was clear, exactly the type of rest its present occupant would enjoy.

The inspector made no comment, rather, he felt, to Mrs. Phail's disappointment, and they repaired to the room Léonie had been given. A passage running the breadth of the house, then a short turn right, separated it from the bedroom they had just left. It was narrow, with walls that seemed disproportionately high and an attenuated window from which Raikes obtained an excellent view of the kitchen garden. He could see Pemberton nonchalantly regarding some coming-on broad beans, and stood there so long that Mrs. Phail grew impatient.

"Is there anything further you would wish to see?" she asked with a mild sarcasm that missed its target.

Raikes thanked her but intimated he was now prepared to go. No, he did not want to speak with Léonie again.

Though he had been unexpectedly dumb during their tour of the house, the inspector's Parthian shot provided a pretty enough puzzle for Mrs. Phail's now thoroughly engaged wits. For why should he ask for Peggy Fisk's home address, and insist, with official firmness, on getting it? The girl would be here again in the morning.

Add to this an inexplicable reluctance to leave the kitchen garden where

Mrs. Phail, posted at Léonie's window, could see him chatting to the unloquacious Pemberton, and here was a problem to enliven bedtime thought. That particular portion of the grounds Mrs. Phail had always considered the most poorly equipped and least attractive feature of Mile House.

2

Superintendent Lecky sent, somewhat dubiously, for Police Constable Jordan. Jordan had been on duty at the Keepsake yesterday morning. During his absence in the afternoon Jane Kingsley had been murdered a mile away.

"Why," Raikes had asked, "was the guard withdrawn instead of being, in the usual way, relieved?"

"Because," Lecky replied, "we've been enjoying a hell of a kickup with Mr. Arthur Tidy. Apparently it's not enough for him that a constable should accompany Miss Blanchard on any visit she should pay to the cottage. He was as unpleasant as he could be about our letting her have a key—"

"The very best concession we could make. You don't," said Raikes frankly, "catch your man—or woman—by shutting 'em carefully off from the object of temptation. Surely a wily old North Country lawyer didn't need that pointed out to him."

Lecky sighed. "He's got a pretty stiff hatred of Léonie. Maybe his sister's reluctance to talk about a will all these years put it into his head the maid would net the lot. I don't know. All I know is, he stuck out for a padlock, with the key of that for the police only. Magnanimously waived his own claim to one. Said *he* didn't want to get into the house, and if he did would be perfectly satisfied for the constable on duty to lead him in by the hand, so to say."

"So padlock it was," Raikes said with resignation.

"From 1 P.M. yesterday. Chap came along in the morning to do it. And Jordan left happily as soon as the job was finished. After all, there didn't seem much harm the woman could do, prowling about outside, if that was her idea. That is," the superintendent added, "there seemed nothing could come of it until you got hold of your gooseberry story. And even that may have an innocent explanation."

"I'm not denying it," Raikes said. "Though, if innocent, as you suggest, why should Blanchard lie about what she was doing in the afternoon? Not to mention hurling pots and pans about to stop Mrs. Phail spilling the beans— or rather, gooseberries."

It was then that P. C. Jordan came in, an earnest, pink-faced young man, looking a shade doubtful of his reception, but clearly possessed of a lurking sense of humor.

"Yes sir, I suppose I may say I know as much as anybody about those gooseberries. I *did* sample a few of 'em, not having come across that sort before, being used to the green uns. Thirst quenchers, I'd call 'em. But as for pinching 'em to take away, or anything like that, all I can say is—well, I *never*, not to say as how I didn't have anything to carry 'em home in, *if* I was so minded, which I wasn't—"

"That's all right, Jordan." Lecky cut short the protestations. "The point is, were those gooseberries on the bushes, or were they not, when you went away at one o'clock?"

"Every one on 'em, sir, except," Jordan, reddening, added with meticulous honesty, "the couple of dozen I'd popped in me mouth beforehand. Thirst quenchers, that's what they was. There was four trees altogether, and I'd noticed they were all unpicked, and ready for the picking."

Raikes put in, "When Miss Blanchard turned up that morning did she make any request to pick the gooseberries?"

"Not she, sir. All her request, which she dinned at me good and proper, was to go inside the house alone. I couldn't let her do that, and I said so. But she kept worrying the matter like it was a rat, for all it was only to put a handful of flowers in the lady's room. If that's all, I told her, what harm I come along with you? It isn't a graveyard, like, nor a church altar, I tell her. But heathenish, if you ask me. But she was in a fair tear. And took herself off in the same."

"With no covetous glance for the gooseberries?"

"Never a look at 'em, sir. She didn't go round to the back at all."

"Was this before or after the locksmith came?"

"Before, sir. Well before. She turned up soon after breakfast, an hour after I'd taken over from the night constable."

"All right, Jordan. And when you looked in at the place this morning what about your nice thirst quenchers?"

Jordan let an abashed grin escape him. "All gone, sir. Every bush stripped."

"Tut-tut," Raikes said, and Lecky dismissed the constable.

"That's watertight," said the inspector. "And Peggy Fisk clinches it. She says there were no gooseberries in the kitchen when she left at 2 P.M. yesterday. But when she turned up this morning—she comes at eight-thirty—they were the first thing she noticed. Moreover, she knows all about Miss Tidy producing these luscious monsters, and said a big basket of them went every summer to the local hospital."

The superintendent pulled a sour face. "Uncookable. And not too good in the raw state, I'd say, for the sick and convalescent."

"Isn't that what you'd expect from the lady?" Raikes asked. "Anyway, our third corroboration is the kitchen garden at Mile House, a sound enough witness, you'll agree. If it's ever admitted a gooseberry to its unfertile bosom, I'll eat my—my boots. Pemberton, I'll wager, hardly knows what one looks like."

"Well," Lecky said after a pause, "it's clear enough Léonie gathered the fruit at the Keepsake sometime after 1 P.M.."

"After 2 P.M.," Raikes corrected, "Peggy—and Mrs. Phail, no doubt—
can testify she was in the house up to two o'clock."

"Yes. Granted, but picking ripe fruit in your own garden's a guiltless
enough proceeding."

"Quite. But not so guiltless when you take the trouble to conceal it."

"That's so. Only I'd point out there's still a big step from that to murder."

"We've caught up with longer in our stride," Raikes said hopefully.

3

Emmie Weaver was a little surprised that it was Edith Drake the inspector
wanted to talk to her about, and not that poor girl from the Minerva. True,
her acquaintance with Jane was only a slight one, but she had seen her daily
when the business was open, and spoken to her sometimes, and she knew
that now the police and, for that matter, all Ravenchurch, were agog with
this new murder, while Edith Drake, unhappy woman, had been dead a
month or two.

Blunted sensibility, the result of age, she thought, must be the reason for
her comparative indifference as the catalogue of untimely deaths mounted.
She was not, she realized not without a pang of shame, feeling Jane's murder so acutely as she had received news of, say, the drowning of Mrs.
Livingston-Bole and that little Iris Kane who had been so excited about her
forthcoming wedding. It seemed that time and repetition could dull the stab
even of murder and sudden death, but it was nonetheless a horrid realization.

She received the inspector with the easy, quizzical air of their first meeting, and, having this time removed the more conspicuous traces of domesticity, sat facing him in her quiet living room behind the shop. Portions of
that ubiquitous establishment, however, had found their way in here too, for,
newly unpacked and piled on a spread-out newspaper was a complete set of
Ouida. Mrs. Weaver flapped an introductory hand at her.

"She's rather under a cloud these days," she said apologetically. "You
know, readers are shy of *flamboyant* writing, and very unforgiving towards
factual inaccuracy, but she had her good points, and I'm hoping," she finished with a wistful eye on her perilously tilted tower of flamboyancy, "there
may still be one or two hero-worshippers who like reading about her masculine characters."

Raikes gave her a humorous look. "Cheer up, there's always somebody
yearning for the good old days. We men are a poor lot at present, or so
Ravenchurch must be thinking, running to and fro and poking our noses
everywhere and not getting anybody arrested."

"You do your best," said Mrs. Weaver magnanimously.

Perhaps it was that which gave her the idea he had come about Jane
Kingsley. When, instead, he spoke at once of the schoolteacher she thought

for a moment Edith Drake's name was a slip of the tongue.

"Miss Drake?" she repeated. "But she passed away some weeks ago. She—she hanged herself."

"I know. It's she I want you to tell me about."

"I don't think she knew anyone from the Minerva," Mrs. Weaver persisted, her mind still on Jane.

He looked at her sharply. "Perhaps not. But *you* knew her. It seems that few people did, intimately. Oh yes, I know you'll say she played a pretty active part in the social life of Ravenchurch, but that's not the same thing as sharing your troubles with somebody."

"I know," Mrs. Weaver said. "Dear me, people are very indifferent, though I don't suppose they mean to be. 'Laugh, and the world laughs with you.' I am myself, if it comes to that—seemingly indifferent, you know, though not callous. It comes not so much from not caring as from being unobservant. I just can't see what goes on under my nose. Books segregate one a good deal, I'm afraid. So I don't know that I can help much. Edith Drake spent a long time with my books, but she didn't confide in me. Her best friend, I think, was Miss Beaton."

"Miss Beaton has been helpful." Raikes nodded. "But here and there we find ourselves up against a blank wall. You notice I have to attempt peeps over it at odd points of vantage."

"One of them into my shop," she said almost merrily.

"Exactly."

He saw that, having recovered from her initial surprise, she was showing no curiosity about his line of approach. The police were, after all, ostensibly concentrating their efforts on enquiry into the murders of Bertha Tidy and Jane Kingsley. To all intents and purposes the suicide of Edith Drake was, with the inquest verdict, a closed affair. But here was Mrs. Weaver accepting without more ado the introduction of this apparently alien subject. Comes of living in an ivory tower, Raikes decided. She's grown the inevitably incurious skin. Well, it may be a thought inhuman, but give me her sort every time for easy questioning.

It was then he put to her the medical query.

He was sure at once that he had again drawn blank. Mrs. Weaver frowned. She shook her head, slowly, but with an air of great confidence.

"Miss Drake never showed any interest whatever in such books," she declared, and Raikes breathed again, for he had not meant anything like that. "She liked drama of the seventeenth and eighteenth centuries, old travel books—"

"Ah," the inspector said, "I didn't make myself clear. It wasn't the literature of medicine I was suggesting she might be interested in—"

"Then," Mrs. Weaver interrupted firmly, "that's all right. For beyond a few herbalists' tomes now and again, if you call *them* medical, I don't have any. So what might it be you were meaning?"

With a delicacy he rarely employed, Raikes explained. She listened unmoved, with complete attention, her gaunt face so expressionless as to inspire him with neither hope nor despair. When he had done she said nothing for a time. Raikes, recognizing the expediency of patience, waited.

"You are asking me to hark back a long time ago," she said at last. "To the summer before the war? That was another world. And my memory isn't all it was. Not being much interested in other people's private affairs stops one's mental register from functioning efficiently. But I'll try."

Raikes wondered a little at her constant disclaimer of interest in her fellows. When she spoke she surprised him by saying, "You have, I suppose, the best of reasons for wishing to know? Yes—yes, of course you have. And if you are going to remove an iron curtain—that's what they say nowadays, isn't it?—from much unguessed evil in Ravenchurch, then it *should* be all for the best. Here is what I can recall."

It was brief, sketchy even—and damnable. But if ever a man felt his spirits heartened, Raikes did. It was the first clean break he had had, the first lifting of the fog of hypothesis and the conflict of evidence they had groped in up to now.

"Yes, there was one week—an uneasy week in that terribly uneasy summer. So far away and long ago. She came, I remember, more often to the shop, but less purposefully, if you can understand me. People are always coming in for idle browsing—she did, a great deal. But this was different. She picked up books she didn't open at all, she didn't talk to me. Not till the end of the week, that is. If I hadn't known her for the cheerful, forthright woman she was I'd have said she was moping. And then, after behaving like this two or three days, she began to take herself in hand and talk again."

Emmie Weaver hesitated, in an earnest search for exactitude of recollection of that day gone with the wind. What Edith Drake had talked about had made too light an impression, as did the confidences of everyone when they happened to penetrate her book-embattled fortress.

"I've got it now," she said solemnly. "But I must be clear about one thing because it shows, after all, that what I remember is likely to be of little use to you. It's this—Edith wasn't seeking information for *herself*, as you seem to think, but for her young sister."

"Please go on."

"There isn't much. She said her sister—these were her actual words—had got herself into a mess. She said it was quite impossible for the man to marry her. She said she was looking for a doctor who would help her out without asking questions."

"I thought," Raikes said, "it would be something of the sort. But why come to you with the problem?"

"She didn't, exactly. I mean she suddenly burst out to me what was worrying her with no thought that I could help her or direct her to the doctor in question. I am sure of that. She was right too—I couldn't have. And then she apologized for bothering me, as she said, with family troubles, but admitted that she felt better for having spoken."

"And did you do anything at all about it?" Raikes asked quietly. On her answer everything depended.

She looked suddenly rueful. "I was hoping you wouldn't ask me that. I ought *not* to have done anything about it, I know. And what I did wasn't, I assure you, prompted by gossip. Which doesn't titillate me." She gestured haltingly. "It just came from taking things—too lightly, from seeing only the academic interest in neighbors' difficulties."

"Yes. What was it you did?"

"I told Miss Tidy."

Raikes breathed a sigh of pure satisfaction.

Mrs. Weaver went on: "She was very much a woman of the world. I'm not. She might well have been helpful, while I could never have been. And, please remember, Miss Drake hadn't requested secrecy. All I knew was that she was most anxious to get hold of information I couldn't give. So I told Bertha Tidy about the young sister."

"And then?" Raikes encouraged.

"She—Miss Tidy—was interested. She asked lots of questions *I* couldn't possibly answer, seeing I knew very little really. She was like that, you know—interested acutely in people, I nearly said indecently, but without warmth and sympathy. Almost, one would say—if it weren't like maligning the dead—*malevolently* interested."

Raikes rubbed his hands in open glee. "Mrs. Weaver, you're great woman," he told the astonished bookseller. "Now one further question: what, if anything, was Miss Tidy prepared to do about it?"

"Well, I never knew her admit to being unable to do anything, and she suggested I should ask Edith Drake to look in at the Minerva. Which I believe she did. Miss Tidy said she was pretty sure she could help her sister without involving illegality."

Raikes got up. "Thank you—thank you very much."

She followed him to the door, half puzzled at, half indulgent for his lighthearted departure. She herself took too detached a view of life to feel resentment or shock at sight of a policeman extracting consolation from death and disaster.

"Why are you so pleased?" she asked.

He smiled. "Day's breaking. That's why." He did not think it necessary to add that they knew beyond all doubt that Edith Drake had had no sister.

4

His luck was in. At Long Greeting Place he was shown straight into the presence of Miss Clara Livingston-Bole, a small, neat woman of sixty-odd,

Raikes judged, with a poise that put her companion of the moment at once at ease, and a pair of remarkably penetrating but by no means unfriendly eyes.

"Your visit isn't altogether a surprise, Inspector," she said when they were seated. "I've lived here in my dead brother's house for six or seven weeks, and expect to be gone again before summer's out, but even in so short a time one or two things have happened which, interpreted properly, will, I am sure, throw a good deal of light on these—deaths."

Her hesitation before the final word was so marked that Raikes cocked an enquiring eye. She nodded intelligently.

"I was going to say murders. But what I really meant was Bertha Tidy's murder and the succession of other deaths, including my brother's and his wife's, which preceded it. About Miss Kingsley's end I know, and can guess, nothing. The only two domestic staff who live in the house besides myself have already told the police that so far as they are aware she did not call here on the fatal afternoon."

The brisk confidence of her manner and frank response to a visit that, looked at from any angle, must almost certainly be disagreeable won the inspector's regard.

"You are making things easy for me," he told her. "I've not called on you in connection with Miss Kingsley's murder. And I did want to see you about your sister-in-law. So, to save painful and perhaps off-the-point questions at the start, please tell me what has been happening since you came to live here, which you think may help to clear things up."

Miss Livingston-Bole smiled mirthlessly. "Nothing could be more painful. But I remind myself that the people who would feel the wound most sharply— one of them did—have passed beyond hurt." She braced herself and returned his look squarely. "The fact is, I've discovered in the past month that my brother's wife was not legally his wife at all."

Raikes let a moment pass before replying quietly, "I think I understand. Captain Ballantyne is still living?"

She scrutinized him, frowning. "You are either more than usually well informed or quick to catch a meaning. Yes, unfortunately Cyril Ballantyne is alive. I have a very recent and quite authentic letter of his in my possession."

"Addressed to yourself?"

"Not the first one that came. I should explain that I am sole executor of my late brother's will. Correspondence delivered at the house since his death has passed through my hands. This letter to Phoebe was among it, more than three weeks ago, postmarked London."

"Has it been followed by others?"

"By one other. I had better give you the facts in some order. And, first, let me say that if I were not convinced that poor Phoebe's death was the direct result of this affair I should have suppressed all knowledge of it so far as lay in my power. As it is, I am anxious for you to know all there is to know. I have told no one, and it will be a load off my mind to speak of it now."

She stopped as if to arrange her thoughts, and then went on, her eyes no longer on Raikes: "More than forty years ago, when Phoebe was a young girl, she was intending to adopt a teaching career and was studying at a training college in the north of England. Bertha Tidy was there too. Bertha became a schoolteacher. Phoebe didn't. Instead she married Cyril Ballantyne, a young infantry lieutenant stationed in the town where the college was."

"Forgive the interruption," Raikes said. "Wasn't Mrs. Livingston-Bole older than her friend Miss Tidy?"

She looked at him then. "A year perhaps. Perhaps rather less. It was merely one of Bertha's innumerable petty vanities to spread the idea of Phoebe's seniority."

"Please go on."

"Cyril Ballantyne—whom I, of course, never knew—was reputed to possess an extraordinary superficial charm which required very little rubbing to expose the sadist and indeed, I believe, maniac actually beneath. Phoebe had a hideous life with him, and ample grounds for a divorce which she never sought. She belonged to a period and upbringing which conceived it one's duty to stick to marriage whatever the circumstances, often with disastrous results.

"Fortunately for her he deserted her again and again, but unfortunately never seems to have failed to return. Then, again happily, he was caught up in the 1914 war when she had for a time a certain respite, but, again unhappily, he wasn't killed. Instead a wound he received towards the close of the 1917 campaign seems to have aggravated his mental malady, and soon after the Armistice his family—who apparently spared no expense in the matter— had him confined in what was then an extremely up-to-date home for the insane needing special psychiatric treatment, in Switzerland."

She drew a sharp breath and went on in a more concerned tone: "I want to be as fair as I can to Cyril Ballantyne, Inspector. Perhaps the most truthful thing to say of him is that he suffered from a profound maladjustment to life and society and should long ago have been looked after where he could harm neither himself nor others—long, that is, before 1919. He *was* the villain of the piece in Phoebe's life up to nearly thirty years ago when he ceased to trouble anyone. To say he's the villain of this piece would be wrong, I think. He's been serving unwittingly as the instrument of another's villainy, and if he's the occasion of Phoebe's death, as I know him now to be, the cause of it lies at someone else's door."

Before Raikes could comment she continued quickly: "But I'm speaking out of time. In 1929 news of his death reached us. Actually Phoebe, who, I should add, had been a friend of ours for the past three years, saw it in the *Times* obituary. She wrote to the family—they'd virtually broken with her years before—and received a reply couched in the briefest, coldest terms. It confirmed the news. A year later she married Henry.

"So far as we all were concerned the wretched Ballantyne chapter seemed closed forever. And now—these letters."

"Just now," Raikes said, "you mentioned another as having followed the one which disclosed to you the fact of Cyril Ballantyne being alive. Was that one too addressed to your sister-in-law?"

"No. To me. You see, after reading the first letter I gathered that Ballantyne had been in correspondence with Phoebe for some time and met with little response. He urges her to write explicitly—I shall pass the letters on to you—refers to earlier requests for a meeting, and states that he doesn't want to make trouble—*very* uncharacteristic of Cyril, I'm bound to say—but that he does feel a meeting is imperative. He suggests lunch in London and asks her to give him a date.

"It was only after a great deal of consideration that I composed a reply to this letter. At that stage I did not wish to consult anybody, not even a lawyer. It seemed to me, in the shock that I'd had, that to seek advice would involve unthinkable betrayal of both Phoebe and Henry. Still less did I want Cyril Ballantyne arriving here in person, as, by the urgency of this last letter, I was half inclined to think might happen. Finally I wrote very shortly, stating the fact of my brother's and his wife's deaths, with dates, and expressing astonishment at hearing from him. I added that Phoebe had for sixteen years believed herself happily married to another man, and that nothing now could be gained by pulling to pieces the memory of their lives."

"And then he wrote to you?"

"He wrote to me. By return. A long and, I think, a highly important letter. It appears that he was discharged from the nursing home in 1929, evidently, I feel, as unfit as when he entered it, for the first thing his warped mind conceived was to hoax his unsympathetic family, who, he says, never corresponded with him or attempted to see him, into believing he had died. He said he did it by means of a fake cable and letter purporting to come from a friend who had kept in touch with him in Switzerland and met him on his discharge. The friend, I take it, was also fictitious. You notice he was crafty enough not to send the news as from the nursing home, which might have been approached by the family for particulars and would promptly have denied knowledge of his supposed death. It's feasible, I think, that his people, who would have been vastly relieved to hear of his death years earlier, cheerfully accepted the announcement without further enquiry. Perhaps they did communicate with the friend and, getting no reply, didn't bother further. How exactly he thought to profit by this deception I don't know, and I don't suppose he knew either—I dare say his motives, for even his more beastly behavior, were always obscure."

"It doesn't look," Raikes remarked, "as if he wanted at that time to bother your sister-in-law. On the contrary, one would say. For she was almost bound to learn through the Ballantynes of his death."

"Oh yes. It wasn't for years, he writes, that he had any hankering for picking up the old threads of his life. He didn't even come back to England.

What he did with himself in the next ten years is matter for conjecture—he doesn't touch on it—garnered an unscrupulous living, one imagines, in and out the less savory corners of Europe in those dark years before the war. By 1939, he says, he saw that Switzerland, which had given him refuge before, might well prove the most comfortable asylum. And there he stayed, snugly nested, with plenty of time for reflection and to plan a course of action which he embarked on as soon as he reached England last autumn."

Raikes frowned. "Did he explain how he'd learned of your sister-in-law's new marriage? Because it appears he must have kept himself pretty well informed during those buried years if he was able to contact her under her present name directly he landed."

"He didn't," Miss Livingston-Bole said firmly. "Contact her, I mean. I'm coming to that. In my opinion his first move was the most important of all and has given rise to the whole tragedy. No, he hadn't kept himself in touch at all while in exile and admits in the letter to me that he had no idea whether Phoebe were alive or dead, nor where he could find her. But most unfortunately he had remembered one thing."

"What was that?"

"Bertha Tidy's old Yorkshire address. I ought to explain—so many interpolations when one goes over an old story. Phoebe has told me that when they first met him in those salad days he was, quite definitely, attracted most to Bertha. Why, it is hard to imagine. That's a quite uncharitable remark, I know—but in spite of her retained prettiness she was the most repellent woman I ever met, and that is understatement." She made a gesture reproving herself. "It's neither here nor there *now*. And you are waiting ... He remembered the home address of the Tidy family, which had accorded him long ago some cap-setting hospitality, and wrote to Bertha—to *Bertha*, of *all* people—asking for news of Phoebe."

"Miss Tidy, of course, had lived in Long Greeting for years when that letter reached her."

"Yes. To be near Phoebe, she'd said. In spite of unconcealed anger and disappointment at the time of Cyril Ballantyne's marriage. Her brother was still at the Yorkshire address, though. It was Arthur Tidy who forwarded the letter."

Things were falling into place, thought Raikes, becoming shipshape like a jigsaw, for long meaningless and discordant till at last a coherent picture begins to appear.

She was watching him. "You can guess, Inspector, can't you, with sufficient certainty, the outcome of that misjudged, perhaps wilfully misjudged, letter? After all, they were an unscrupulous pair, and who knows whether Cyril Ballantyne had it in mind to seek Bertha's cooperation for the pressure he was going to apply to Phoebe?"

"I can guess," Raikes replied, ignoring her last remark, "what is in your own mind about it. All the same, I would rather you told me."

"Certainly I will. Bertha Tidy used her knowledge to blackmail my sister-in-law. She drove Phoebe to take her own life."

Raikes leaned forward eagerly. "Yes, yes—I know that's what you think. But the proof, Miss Livingston-Bole, the proof—"

"Is here," she said calmly. She got up and walked a few paces away to a small satinwood cabinet. Unlocking a drawer, she returned at once with a large square envelope, sealed but undirected.

"This is for you," she said, handing it over. "Don't open it now. It contains four letters. Two of them are those of which you've just heard, written by Cyril Ballantyne to this house after Phoebe's death. But there are two others besides, very brief ones written by Bertha to my sister-in-law in the spring, apparently at a time when personal meetings between them were getting infrequent. Your eyes, Inspector, should be more than twice as sharp as mine in the interpretative sense, so when you've read them you'll know them for what they are."

"Thank you. Now as to the letters you say Ballantyne was writing to Mrs. Livingston-Bole?"

"I found none. But it's made clear from his letter to her after her death, and then by what he writes to me, that there were such letters. She would have destroyed them either as received, or else when she'd resolved to end her life."

"That," said Raikes, remembering the charred paper Greatorex had described, "agrees to some extent with evidence we already have."

"You know, I'm convinced she kept this disaster from my brother. Henry died because he could not live without her, not because he'd learned her secret. That's why she would have been extremely careful to burn Cyril's letters. So that he should not know through any oversight on her part. But Bertha Tidy, even in that case, was as responsible for his death as she was for hers."

When he rose to go there was something still she had to say.

"A moment ago I suggested that Captain Ballantyne and Bertha Tidy might have been hand in glove in this vile persecution. I don't really think so. She was a woman who, so far as I knew her, played a lone hand, always. Besides, anyone as unstable as Phoebe's first husband would have made a very poor collaborator in a dangerous undertaking."

Raikes nodded. "Was Mrs. Livingston-Bole a wealthy woman in her own right?"

"Not wealthy. Comfortably well off, maybe. And my brother was very openhanded."

"Do you know if Ballantyne was pressing her for money?"

"I don't. But when you read his letter to me you'll note he's not backward in pushing what he's pleased to regard as his present claim. I'd told him, you see, of Henry's death too, and you'll mark how anxious he is to learn which of them predeceased the other. He points out more than once that he is Phoebe's next of kin. It is true that she died intestate *but* she died before Henry, so even if he could establish his preposterous and impudent claim it's not Henry's estate will enrich him."

"Well, I fancy a good lawyer will soon dispose of Mr. Cyril Ballantyne. And what of Mrs. Livingston-Bole's own capital on which he may try to lay hands? Will he find it worth the effort?"

She looked at him strangely. "That, Inspector, has dwindled out of all reason within the last *six or seven months*."

CHAPTER 10

Old Father Baldpate,
Say the slow bells of Aldgate.

The glacial atmosphere into which Raikes stepped at Messrs. Fripp and Saltmarsh was not entirely unexpected. Distaste into enquiry beyond a severely imposed limit had been rather forcibly expressed by the firm at the inquest on Miss Graves, who, it was felt, should in her capacity as manageress of the gown department have shown enough consideration for the untarnished reputation of her employers not to place both them and herself in so dubious a light.

"Untarnished" was the word, Raikes thought, blinking amid the glitter, and a darned sight too much of it. Chromium and concealed lighting, and the pile on unending roads of carpet that subdued the tread of proletarian feet, could be overdone to the point of fatigue, and Fripp and Saltmarsh had not been modest about it. In that pastel glow even Utility frocks on green-faced ladies without any arms, challenging you like Wingless Victories from this side and that, wore a patrician air.

When he was shown into the manager's office Raikes was thankful for its relatively small dimensions, though he saw at once that it was as impeccably furnished as the outer regions of this modern Purgatory. This establishment, considered as a whole or sectionally, subordinated the human element to the extent that what you were really alive to was the material layout, what you neglected to see were the men and women who served it. So when he had given his secondary attention to Mr. Trumpington himself Raikes observed without surprise that Fripp and Saltmarsh had selected their general manager with an eye to the prevailing tone of the place. He blended without discernible flaw.

He was a tall man with a small body of well-controlled rotundity, a polished face looking as if it had just received an austerity shave or perhaps never required one, and the baldest crown Raikes had ever seen. From a pair of hardly perceptible brows it retreated in a masterly arc to meet the unwrinkled neck behind. Unfretted by a single hair, in gloss and luminosity it fell nothing short of the firm's standard.

"We had assumed that—er—distressing affair closed," Mr. Trumpington pronounced when Raikes, accepting a chair, had broached the matter of Beatrice Graves. It was a tribute to his person that the inspector took the pronoun in its royal sense and not in reference to Fripp and Saltmarsh.

He explained patiently how independent investigation into the recent murders had led them to reconsider the earlier deaths. Mr. Trumpington tapped his fingers on the sparely appointed desk in front of him and gave skeptical attention to the official suggestion. He said he did not really see what help Fripp and Saltmarsh could give additional to their evidence at the inquest. And that, thought Raikes, had been about as niggardly as could be.

Banking on the good fortune which had just enriched his interviews with Mrs. Weaver and Miss Livingston-Bole, he crossed his legs and looked genially upon the far from genial Mr. Trumpington.

"The inquest on Miss Graves," he said, "took place early in May. We're now nearly into July. There's always the possibility that in the interval a certain amount of discussion has gone on in the more relaxed atmosphere one gets when a court case is ended. Customers, for instance—people who knew her in business life—"

Mr. Trumpington, deploring the term customers, interrupted frigidly, "Neither our patrons nor our staff are encouraged to indulge in gossip of the nature you imply. We could hardly maintain our unbroken reputation for courtesy and discretion in services rendered if we allowed any department to become a vehicle for mere home chat."

Raikes, unchastened if a little knocked back by this noble reputation, replied, "People are human beings, you know—and women rather more so, that's all. And discretion, courtesy, good taste, and what have you do sometimes take back seats. However, you'll know better than I to what extent your staff has lost the human touch. No matter. There's one thing you can tell me, though. Was Miss Bertha Tidy a regular —patron of your store?"

Store was something to shudder at, if you liked, but Mr. Trumpington, scenting the incorrigible, let it pass.

"She was," he said. "A lady of sound taste and excellent grooming, and therefore satisfied with only the best."

"And in the course of her visits she would encounter Miss Graves?"

"Certainly." The manager lifted his gaze from contemplation of his nails and allowed a glimmer of surprise to appear through his rimless glasses. "But as they were both residents of Ravenchurch—or rather, Miss Tidy was in a sense—they might well have met off these premises."

"Quite so," Raikes agreed, being sure they had done so. "Now, to cover old ground, I'm afraid: Miss Graves wasn't a native, was she? Her home wasn't here?"

"No, she was a Londoner." He clipped his reply short as if there were something he had meant to add.

The inspector, fishing, remarked, "And had a furnished flat here in Ravenchurch. Was she, do you know, living at the same address throughout the period of her employment by Fripp and Saltmarsh?"

"I believe so," Mr. Trumpington said, amending it to, "Yes, she was."

He had taken on a peculiarly guarded air which Raikes found intriguing. It was worth probing.

"I ask," he went on in a man-to-man undertone he had found productive before, "because, in fact, it was a line rather neglected at the inquest. I mean Miss Graves's life outside business hours. When a suicide takes place at the victim's own address, searching questions relating to the place and inmates are expected, and usually put. But Miss Graves drowned herself, she left no letter, indeed nothing but an orderly flat behind her, and there was very little evidence of any sort her landlady could offer."

Mr. Trumpington was listening with close attention. He was silent for a moment or two, though not exactly inactive, for he seemed to be bracing himself for something disagreeable. Whatever it was, Raikes noticed with relief that the temperature had risen perceptibly, if only to a slight degree. Mr. Trumpington, worried, was prepared to relax his hauteur.

"I don't know where this is leading," he said at last. "Unless, of course, you are hedging and know more than you claim to know. In any case I think you'll probably get at the facts eventually, and as I much prefer you should have them here and now from me than waste a great deal of time exciting the curiosity of my staff, who are ignorant of them, I will tell you what came to light a week or two after the inquest was over."

"It was pretty clear that something had," said Raikes, hoping that Mr. Trumpington wouldn't call his bluff. "Please carry on."

The manager hesitated. "I would like you to know that this was not brought to the notice of the police. For that I am prepared to take the blame. How much Mrs. Parragon, the landlady, may have talked, or even how much she guessed, I don't know. She was certainly tardy in coming to me after the discovery had been made. I did not bring the matter to the notice of the board, so that as far as Fripp and Saltmarsh are concerned I am the only member of the firm who knows. The woman had died in tragic and—er— conspicuous circumstances, and to have divulged this business could only have meant more and wholly unprofitable mud raking, as well, of course, as involving a number of other persons."

"Serious then?"

"Serious enough. It appears that Miss Graves, for some time before her death, had been engaged in the illegal buying and selling of clothing coupons on a fairly extensive scale."

The inspector lifted his eyebrows. "And the proofs?" he asked quietly.

Mr. Trumpington, it might be said, had by now dissolved. Having decided to liberate his tongue after more than a month's incarceration, he became almost voluble and, without relinquishing his defensive attitude, rather suspiciously conciliatory.

His story hinged on the house-proud and inquisitive qualities displayed by Mrs. Parragon, Miss Graves's landlady. She was of the type which, letting furnished rooms only, views with instant mistrust the entry of every new tenant. On her own showing she had so enslaved herself to the furniture and appointments of her cherished dwelling that even impermanent separation from any part of them was incalculable torment. No sooner had she handed a room over to the temporary care of another woman than she was hankering to get inside it and enjoy the sensuous pleasure of touching her own possessions and examining them for evidences of the neglect she was certain they suffered from the very first day. For these reasons it could never be said that she was on amicable terms with any of her "lets," who failed to recognize a necessity for entertaining Mrs. Parragon in the rooms for which they paid a stiff enough rental. Tenancies were, in consequence, usually characterized by brevity. Mrs. Parragon, clinging to hope, liked new faces.

Miss Graves had stayed much longer than most, though, oddly enough, even less accommodating. But Mrs. Parragon, while maddened at her lack of hospitality, had hesitated about making a change during the war years for fear of having billeted upon her somebody she herself would be unable to turn out. Miss Graves was at any rate a tolerably conscientious lodger, though her housewifery fell lamentably short of Mrs. Parragon's standards, and a self-effacing one—too self-effacing, of course—who was absent from the house for quite considerable periods.

"When of course," Raikes put in, "the master key became operative."

"Probably," said Mr. Trumpington. "She wouldn't be able to resist it, would she? Well, I gathered this state of affairs went on for the best part of four years—that is, for the time Miss Graves was in our employ." He threw a quick, half-despairing look at the inspector. "I—I can't—*understand* how she came to do these things, how she brought herself to that pass. Why, it was only last autumn we promoted her to the position she held at the time of her death—at, I need not say, a substantial increase of salary." He named it at the inspector's request. Raikes made a note of it.

Mr. Trumpington mused a moment, smoothing imagined wrinkles from his plump fingers.

"You will recall that her body was taken from the river on a Wednesday evening. Later that night a police officer called on Mrs. Parragon. He did not go into the house and did not, she says, ask at that hour to see the flat. He said that they would communicate with her further in the morning. Having recovered from the first shock, the landlady's feelings about the abandoned flat seem to have got the better of her."

"Police or no police, she meant to be one move ahead," Raikes murmured. "I know 'em."

"Yes. Well, she admits entering—I suppose she *had* a right to?—and says she neither moved nor removed anything, with the exception of one object."

"Ha-ha," cried Raikes, "we grow warm!"

"It seems," Mr. Trumpington continued, ignoring this pleasantry, "that some time previously she had lent Miss Graves a small leather lunch case in place of one with a damaged handle which was undergoing repair. This had not been returned to her up to the time of her tenant's death, and she said that when she caught sight of it in a corner of the room she appropriated it—naturally enough, perhaps, if not quite in order. She then, it appears, left and relocked the room, satisfied that its condition was not going to disgrace her when the police entered next day."

"Dust and an unmade bed ranking higher," Raikes remarked, "than the torment which drives to suicide. What a woman! Well, I suppose the next step was the Pandora act?"

"If you mean," said Mr. Trumpington after a moment's reflection, "did she open the case?—no, not at first. Because she couldn't. She told me that she had never possessed a key to it. If there ever had been one she did not know what had become of it. But now it was locked. So Miss Graves had apparently found, or had had made, a key that fitted. That seems to have at once provoked all Mrs. Parragon's curiosity."

"You're telling me. So what?"

"Eventually she forced the lock, a trifling matter with those small cases. According to her, when she first picked it up she judged it empty, but on taking it to her rooms she felt something slide from one end to the other. She said her idea was to take out whatever it was, replace it in Miss Graves's flat, while retaining her own property, the empty case."

Raikes looked skeptical. "Quite. 'Assume a virtue, if you have it not.' Especially after the event when explanations are overdue."

Mr. Trumpington looked a little less assured. "I can only report what she has told me. In the case were some thirty books of current clothing coupons, in addition to a number of covers only—covers of the books, I mean, with the sheets of coupons removed."

"You saw these things for yourself?" Raikes asked.

"Yes. She brought them to me nearly a fortnight after the close of the inquest. She said she was frightened. She said she had not known what to do about it, what she *ought* to do about it. She dreads nothing so much as getting what she calls 'mixed up with the police,' and defended her action in approaching me in the matter by saying—not very intelligently, I'm afraid—that she thought that after all they *might* be the property of Fripp and Saltmarsh."

"Funny," said Raikes, "how women go out of their way to proclaim their stupidity. Yet there's the devil to pay when you charge them with being plain silly. But you too, Mr. Trumpington—why haven't you handed these books over to the police?"

The manager, looking thoroughly miserable, began to flounder. "I—I couldn't make up my mind to bring this shocking matter to the notice of the board—"

"I'm not concerned with the board," Raikes retorted. "This is a police matter. By hanging onto these coupons you put yourself in the wrong, in the light of an accessory even. Where are they?"

"Locked up here," said the unhappy Mr. Trumpington. "Under my hand."

He took a bunch of keys from his pocket and fumbled a little confusedly until he had selected a small one. Then he unlocked a shallow drawer in the kneehole desk at which he sat, and, taking out with both hands a quantity of clothing books, pushed them across to Raikes.

"Um," the inspector grunted, running through them, "no names and addresses, no registration numbers. In the condition, in fact, in which they left the Food Office. Well, the owners are easily traceable through the serial numbers which coincide with those on their ration books. The office codes vary, I see—so they're not all belonging to Ravenchurch and district."

"No," Mr. Trumpington groaned. "Not even a localized scandal."

"And these empty covers. Careless of her not to burn *them*. Look at the metal binders—gone altogether here and there, for the rest, sticking out like pins. The pages of coupons have been neatly unhooked, to be refastened in the new owners' books." He looked hard at the manager, who in turn was fixing the coupons with the gaze of a rabbit mesmerized by a stoat. "Have you got anything else to offer in support of the assumption that Miss Graves was *trading* in these? Between you and me, it's one of those certain guesses, I'd say—but mere possession of this incriminating bundle doesn't imply she was profiting financially by her game." His skeptical smile, however, robbed the words of any conviction.

"There *is*, unfortunately, something else." Mr. Trumpington made a hasty movement repudiating further hidden contraband. "Oh, nothing I can show you. Miss Graves had been too careful for that, and, as you know, the police search of her flat brought nothing to light."

"Mrs. Parragon having gone ahead with a toothcomb."

Mr. Trumpington doubled his chin in acknowledgment. "It happened before Mrs. Parragon brought the books to me. And on that account was the more bewildering. Miss Capper, our lingerie saleswoman, came to me one day hardly a week after the funeral, in some distress because, she said, she could not get rid of an undesirable person who did not wish to purchase anything, persisted in airing some real or fancied grievance against the late Miss Graves, and would not leave. The woman was attracting some attention from the assistants, and Miss Capper felt that it might be expedient to let her state her case in a less public atmosphere.

"When I entered the department I saw at once that the troublemaker was not, and never could have been, one of *our* patrons. She was an unclean creature, looking even at that hour as if laboring under the influence of drink. I got her quickly to the office and, in the presence of Miss Capper, listened to her outpourings. Nothing, I am sorry to say, would induce her to be explicit. All I could gather was that Miss Graves owed her two pounds—'That's the price of 'em,' she kept on repeating, and added over and over again, '*She* got a fiver apiece off them as could pay, the rich uns she met in business.'

"She was a quarter of an hour in the office, rambling in this ugly way but becoming at once evasive when I wanted to pin her to specific statements. She would *not* name what merchandise it was she had sold for two pounds. At last I told her that if she had any legitimate claim on the estate of the late Miss Graves she had better consult a solicitor about it, and that if she paid another such visit to Fripp and Saltmarsh I should call in the police to remove her. She turned on me in a flash and said brazenly, 'You wouldn't dare, mister! I know a sight too much for that.' It was only with difficulty we got rid of her, but she must, I think, have been apprehensive of her own position, because we were not troubled with her again."

"Did you get hold of her name?"

"I asked her to leave name and address. She immediately looked crafty and in unrepeatable language declined to do anything of the sort. Then Miss Capper, who should have reported the matter earlier, told me that a sales assistant in Miss Graves's own department had been approached on two occasions by unknown women before the funeral. They had not, as in this last instance, attempted to create a disturbance, but had departed early after letting fall some significant remarks. One of them had asked if Miss Graves had left a message for her—'It might be in an envelope, miss'—and the other had whispered even more tellingly, 'Do you know how I stand now Miss Graves is gone?' They both seemed, said Miss Atkins, the assistant in question, wholly unfamiliar with the establishment, and very timid about opening their case at all."

"Which looks," Raikes said, "as if Miss Graves didn't actually *purchase* the things during business hours."

"Oh *no*," Mr. Trumpington groaned agreement. "That would be unthinkable."

"But," the unmerciful inspector pointed out, "she may well have *sold* them to the—how did it go?—'rich uns' over the counter. That would be easy enough."

The mental vision thus presented robbed Mr. Trumpington of further speech, which was not restored by Raikes's parting words.

"I'll take charge of this little lot. And I can by no means promise you that you've heard the last of it."

2

Tangles of any sort were a vexation and a challenge to Raikes, who spent perforce the greater part of his time unraveling such as came his way. Yet he

could not help admitting there was something altogether homely and agreeable in the unkempt condition of the rectory at Long Greeting, as he saw it
for the first time next morning.

He had left Superintendent Lecky and his staff in complacent contemplation of last night's Case of the Confiscated Coupons, so much more in the
Ravenchurch tradition than the sanguinary matters of the past week or two.
Of course it involved these, but it had its own separate and soluble problem
smacking more familiarly of the "Now then, you can't do that there 'ere"
than the odor of blood these Scotland Yard blokes carried about with them.

The Scotland Yard bloke in question was enjoying this morning the double
promise of a cooler day and a happy issue out of all his afflictions. Perhaps
"happy" wasn't the right word, but that was how you felt about it, anyway.
A strong breeze that flicked into changing shapes small clouds which had
appeared overnight was exciting the undisciplined shrubs in the Rev. Daniel
Buskin's garden and sighing through the grasses of the adjacent churchyard. When the old rector himself greeted his visitor in the porch, it lifted his
thin white hairs and made him look like a Lear in clerical garb being driven
out into the wilderness.

He was, Raikes saw, a very old man, whom the years and the conflicts he
had never hesitated to engage in had fined down to little more than spiritual
force. Though he was tall, his physical frailty had to be seen to be believed.
No, on second thoughts, hardly frailty; fragile, transparent even in the large
delicate hands and stretched skin at the temples, but lithe enough for all that,
and suffering from no apparent disability.

Raikes had made it his business beforehand to learn that he had been
rector of Long Greeting for more than forty years. In the whole of that time
he had won the respect of all his parishioners and the love of a handful.
Those were the few who were sensible that into the come-day-go-day existence of the physical world their rector brought daily, without incongruity,
the values of another world; that a childlike capacity for imparting equality
to all, all things and all people at all times, was not to be identified with an
infantile outlook; that, in short, Daniel Buskin had the pure, sometimes terrible attributes of saintliness.

"I've known for some time there must be something I could do to help
you," he said simply when he had taken Raikes into a small room crowded
with books at the bottom of the hall. "I have been waiting for you to tell me
what it is."

The inspector took the sagging leather chair offered him and met the
most guileless and at the same time searching gaze he had encountered in
Ravenchurch. It would be of little use pitting any sort of duplicity against
candor of this degree. Raikes had reason to know single-mindedness when
he saw it. Holy men and murderers alike had, he reminded himself, been
qualified by it.

"I think there is, sir," he said, and explained that it was now certain that the deaths in the spring which had so distressed the life of Ravenchurch and Long Greeting were linked with the recent murders of Miss Tidy and Jane Kingsley. "Now four of the people concerned were your parishioners and, we believe, regularly attended church here—namely, Colonel and Mrs. Livingston-Bole, Miss Edith Drake from Haydock's End, and Miss Iris Kane, the last to die by her own hand. Their graves are in the churchyard, and here, in and about this village, the most significant year of their lives, from the standpoint of ourselves who are examining it, was spent."

"They were my friends," said Mr. Buskin. "In that measure I failed them. Yes, I failed them. For I know only too little of the dark roads their minds and spirits wandered in."

"Things are getting clearer," Raikes assured him, "even while the story grows darker. But though I've mentioned these four as a group it's not about all of them that I've come to you for help. It's about Iris Kane."

The rector showed no surprise. It was, Raikes thought, as if he had been expecting her name.

"I did not christen her," he said with the ingenuous abruptness for which Raikes was prepared. "I confirmed her. I was to have married her. Instead I buried her." A curious warmth lit the shining gaze with which he scrutinized the inspector. "What do you want me to tell you?"

"You say you didn't christen her, sir. We understand she came first to live in Long Greeting when a schoolchild, from Yorkshire where a sister-in-law of Mr. Kane had charge of her. I don't want to reopen for the Kanes the wound the inquest made—not, at least, until I may be bound to. Can you add anything to this early background for Iris?"

"Why, yes. But not very much. You are right in your conclusion that Mr. and Mrs. Kane were her foster parents only. Indeed, I don't know who were her actual father and mother. She had been adopted as a baby by Mr. Kane's brother and his wife, who, as you say, lived in the north. Then thirteen or fourteen years ago the Yorkshire Mrs. Kane died suddenly, and the widower, who was employed as a groom on a local estate, did not feel he would be doing the right thing by the little girl—then about eight years old, I suppose—by depriving her of a woman's care. So the arrangement was made with his childless brother and wife, who had not been living long here in Greeting."

"Not long before adopting Iris?"

"Yes."

"Mr. Kane—*this* Mr. Kane, I mean—was employed by Colonel Livingston-Bole, wasn't he?"

"Yes. He is a gamekeeper at the Place. That is to say, his actual employer was Mrs. Livingston-Bole, who was one of the Yorkshire Youngs, you know. On her marriage, about fifteen years ago, when she took up residence here, the Kanes joined their staff. Mr. Kane's brother, in whose home Iris lived as a baby, still works for that branch of Mrs. Livingston-Bole's family which keeps on the Yorkshire home."

"I see," Raikes murmured, seeing, he believed, a great deal more than Mr. Buskin. "Do you know, sir, if it was legal adoption by the Kanes?"

"Oh, I think not. Not by the Long Greeting ones, that is to say. What the original agreement may have been I don't know, but this seemed an informal one between relatives—something, you know, on the lines of evacuee and foster parent during the war."

"Yes. Iris didn't look upon them as mother and father."

"She always called them aunt and uncle. Her 'daddy,' of whom she sometimes spoke to me, was the Yorkshire Kane."

"And when she first turned up in Greeting was she known as Iris or by another name?"

Mr. Buskin was silent a moment, though not, Raikes thought, because he had to reflect on the question.

"She had—or perhaps it was only the 'let's pretend' of an imaginative child—the alternative name of Fleur. She was entered in the school register as Iris Kane, but now and again some imp would enter into her when she was asked her name to answer with Fleur. The child was endowed with great physical beauty, and," the old man added fiercely, "goodness—goodness. And at one time she wished very ardently to act for the screen. 'When that happens,' she told me, 'I shall once again be Fleur-de-Lys. That was what I was christened, you know.' She added that she would have to drop Kane then, as too awkward a handle for the other." He sighed. "There was to be no such future for her."

"And now," said Raikes, "I get onto what you will possibly think ground too intimate. But policemen are always doing that. They've little or no choice. It's like this, sir. At the inquest the matter of her approaching marriage was touched on, and both Mr. and Mrs. Kane testified very firmly that Iris's whole attitude towards it was one of supremely happy anticipation—that is, until within a couple of months of her death. Mr. Froggatt, too, her fiancé, volunteered information as to the state of her mind, and of his own complete ignorance of anything seriously wrong during those last weeks. He gave every evidence of being moved by overwhelming grief."

He paused, while Mr. Buskin watched him with compassion in his eyes, though Raikes knew that the compassion was not for him.

"Yes?" was all the rector said.

"Well, to put it bluntly, was all this so much plain eyewash? A mere facade? Had something, in fact, gone gravely amiss with the marriage plans, something which the parties I have mentioned knew but would not admit? It's on that account I'm seeking your help rather than theirs. You know—everyone knows—Iris left a letter for Mrs. Kane before going down to the river that morning. Did you see it?"

"No. I knew there was such a letter."

Raikes took from a breast pocket an elastic-bound book and, slipping off the band, drew out a folded sheet of unlined note paper. He held it out to Mr. Buskin.

"Please read it."

The rector took the paper and, with no change of posture, only the withdrawal of his eyes from the inspector's, read the few lines written in pencil in a clear sloping hand that had not faltered.

DEAR AUNTIE,

This is the end. There is no way out but this. I cannot face things knowing how Chris's money would have to go. All my own has gone to pay for silence about the old foolishness. It must not be his as well. We have been too happy for that. Remember I loved you all. Try to forgive.

IRIS

Mr. Buskin gave it back to Raikes. "And you, of course," he said, "have asked the Kanes about the old foolishness?"

The inspector shook his head. "Not I, but the local police at the time of the inquest. The Kanes said that they did not know what it meant. They admitted, however, it was true that Iris's own small capital, acquired through earnings in the munitions factory, had disappeared, and produced her Post Office Savings book in evidence."

"They said they did not know what it meant," the old man repeated gently. "Is it necessary for you to learn it in order to bring to light the sin against the child?"

"It would help," Raikes said.

The rector nodded slowly. "It would help. Yes. *I* can help. I failed Iris when she told me those things. I will help you now. It is told in few words." He stopped, looking, it seemed, closely at Raikes without seeing him. " 'The old foolishness.' She called it that. She was right. It was only foolishness. Iris was young, gay, high-spirited, beautiful. She was also good. I know. The homage that went to her head never spoiled her heart. The hollow little prizes showered on charm and a lovely face gratified her, but they did not sully the charm nor make the face a mask for the unlovely."

He knotted his sinuous old hands in a loose clasp, frowning a little. "I tell you this in case, not having known the child, you should mistake foolishness for something more serious. When Iris was fifteen or thereabouts she left school and was for a little while without occupation. Unwise perhaps, but I think her foster parents were anxious to find something more congenial and worth while than Ravenchurch offered before the war, and Iris herself has told me that as she was not really their daughter she got the impression they thought they weren't entirely free to make decisions about her future."

"They had to consult someone else?"

"It may have been so. There was a time, at any rate, when she was doing nothing in particular except excite admiration. At that time there was a boy in

Long Greeting, a couple of years older than Iris. His background and family don't matter to this tale—he was killed on the Anzio beaches. He was then a garage hand in Ravenchurch, a lively, intelligent youngster, very good-hearted and equally high-spirited. Iris and he—his first name was Ray—were attracted to one another. One week end they both disappeared. There was consternation in two homes and, before it was realized that they had perhaps gone together, too much idle babble. But not from the Kanes. They, perhaps because Iris was in their care and not their own, were curiously silent. They did not take the matter to the police—"

"The Kanes only grudgingly conceded the law's right of intervention even at her death," Raikes said.

"I know. They have always, I think, been considering the feelings of a third party. So they did not ask the police to help to find her, nor did Ray's parents on his account. They said he was old enough to look after himself."

"The truth being, sir," Raikes said, "that they all thought making a police matter of it wasn't respectable. That's why we hit so many cold trails."

"You are probably right," Mr. Buskin said calmly. "Respectability is too often put first, with tragic results sometimes. Not in this case, however. Ray returned to his work, a little late, on the Monday morning, and Iris to her home. It was then it transpired that they had been away together. They made no bones about it. At least Iris didn't. She included me at once in her confidence, expressed penitence at all the anxieties felt, and said quite innocently that she hadn't asked permission because she had known it would be refused.

"They had gone on a fishing weekend—Ray was an enthusiastic angler—to Channinglea, a place on the river about twelve miles away. There they had put up at the Pied Bull, a picturesque old inn they thought highly romantic. They were a couple of children. The proprietor had seen no reason to doubt their assertion that they were brother and sister on holiday. Those were not the days of identity cards and detailed registration. They were thoroughly nice children with a joint air of great candor. I mean candor was real, not assumed."

"Yet," Raikes pointed out, "Iris must deliberately have given Ray's surname."

Mr. Buskin spread patient hands. "Of course. Of course she did. It was a lie. But it doesn't weaken the truth of what I am saying. It helps indeed to establish the nature of that weekend, to confirm its innocence. Ray and Iris passed themselves off as brother and sister. They behaved as brother and sister."

"You believe that?" The words, weighted with skepticism, escaped Raikes, the man of the world, before Inspector Raikes could check them.

"I know it. I knew Iris and Ray, you see."

Raikes was in no position to dispute it. He made an effort to recover with,

"The very fact, though, that this was, as you admit, a romantic affair in their eyes—"

The rector confidently interrupted. "What you mean by romance is merely sexual, isn't it? What Iris and Ray meant was something else."

Nor could the unbelieving Raikes deny that either.

The old man continued as if he had stopped to flick only a gnat off his sleeve.

"When they returned silence closed at once on the subject of their absence. But of course there had already been overmuch unguarded talk. Iris, being innocent, was too frank. Ray's people I didn't know, so I cannot tell you his side of it, except that almost directly after his return a post away was obtained for the lad. He wasn't much seen in Ravenchurch again, and after that—the war came.

"But Iris stayed on. The first happy excitement over stolen pleasure, and exultation even, which the young must often enjoy from their own wilfulness, was followed by a few months of what is called 'living it down.' A difficult, heartless, *silly* business, brought about in small communities as much by want of occupation as want of charity. If women had more to do they would have fewer unkind things to say."

Raikes smiled broadly. "An economic question, sir, which sensible women have long been alive to."

"I know. I blame no one. But for Iris it ends like this." He drummed a clenched hand on the table. His eyes blazed. "It—it brings home to me the measure of my own failures. It is a great lesson in humility."

Raikes watched him thoughtfully while the old man continued.

"She—the child—changed a little after that. But she was always the same good child. Now she grew quieter, more sophisticated perhaps. She *appeared* more sure of herself, but," he added wisely, "she was less sure. Somebody—oh, not one person but a cumulative somebody had steeped what she had done in a sense of sin, though she had known there was no sin. And though they never convinced her, they shook her faith in herself. They did not destroy it, but it was an adolescent self, ripe for doubts, and the doubts took root.

"Employment was found for her as counter hand in one of the chain stores in Ravenchurch. She mixed with other girls. Her beauty was so much part of her goodness it made her loved there, not envied. I do not know to what source you will trace this persecution, but it will not be to her contemporaries."

"Can you suggest," Raikes said quickly, "where it will be?"

"No."

"I ask because when you read Iris's letter just now you said you had failed her when *she told you these things*. What things, sir?"

"She told me a few months ago that the old tongue wagging had started again. She was worried about it because she was engaged to be married to

Christopher Froggatt. He, poor lad, is a very personable young man, with a character for goodness and simplicity unspoiled by material possessions. I took her troubles too lightly—I mean I saw them in the mind's eye too lightly disposed of. I advised her to give Christopher a full account of what had happened with Ray. She was horrified. She said he would never understand. I think she was wrong. I did not know then that blackmail had already begun. I tried to comfort, to advise. But I was not inquisitive enough. I should have probed deeper."

"How could you have known?"

"It was my business, my responsibility, to have found out. But we have had nothing like this before, nothing that went beyond the misuse of tongues. This is a more terrible poison. But how is it that you believe murder too has sprung from the same root?"

Raikes evaded direct reply by asking, "You knew the late Miss Tidy well, sir?"

"Not well," Mr. Buskin said gravely. "Few did, you know. She attended church with fair regularity until the New Year, but I have wondered sometimes why she came at all. You see, I visited her from time to time, and—how can I describe these things without uncharitableness? It was not that she was ever skeptical or argumentative or even derisive. Such attitudes are often evidence of much spiritual strength. No, she was, in her very reception of one stepping over her threshold, *negative*. Negative and cold in—in an unearthly sense. Perhaps," he added in some confusion, "I mean unworldly. These things—things of the spirit—are hard to translate into speech. But it seemed to me, always, that she was closing ears and vision to everything but some inner thought, unsatisfying while absorbing—something that for all her attention was only sterile."

Raikes felt himself caught up involuntarily in the other's sincerity. There was something that chilled the blood in the picture of that inturned eye, appraising—what? He brought himself down with a bump. What the old chap means, he thought, is simply the worship of Mammon. Why doesn't he say so? He found himself speaking of Léonie.

"The maid," Mr. Buskin said. All at once he sounded tired out. The fire in voice and eye had burned down. He was trembling a little from exhaustion. "Ah, she is different. Not negative or cold—a spirit which might indeed be a furnace." He passed a hand across his hair and for the first time looked vaguely at Raikes. "Forgive me. I am muddled. Léonie is a member of the Roman community in Ravenchurch. My old friend, Father Connolly, knows her better than I."

He was old, inattentive, drained of interest. Raikes, with a spark of compunction for a fatigue he himself had caused, saw that there was no more to be had and took leave of him. He would not let him come to the door.

As he came into the hall he turned his head for a parting look at the rector slumped in his chair. It seemed to him as if the Rev. Daniel Buskin were himself employing that inward gaze in reluctant contemplation of something he had never seen before.

CHAPTER 11

You owe me ten shillings,
Say the bells of St. Helen's.

Raikes was driving to Ravenchurch to call on a number of banks there, but that was not the business he gave his mind to on the way. The further behind he left Long Greeting the more fruitful appeared his interview with the rector. Now that he had no longer to listen, question, and contribute to the give and take of discussion, he could submit what he had learned to a detached examination.

While he did not discount outright Mr. Buskin's faith in the innocence of Ray and Iris, experience had bred in him the skepticism which suggested it was more than likely to have been misplaced. Then he saw that it made no difference either way. Whatever those two children might have done, feminine criticism would have inferred the worst. Women were made that way. Nor was their particular form of gratification necessarily achieved by tooth-and-claw methods. A note of pseudo compassion here, a hint of tolerance for youthful peccadilloes, and the job was done.

The village, putting its own interpretation on that weekend truancy, had made it easy for a blackmailer at a later date to stir up the settled mud. He considered the facts relating to Iris's brief life, how few, how important, how linked to what at first had seemed entirely independent problems. Paths, once remote in their several courses, were converging. The deeper you got into this case the more clearly you saw that everyone's tragedy was the tragedy of all, that calamity had not dealt isolated blows.

Bertha Tidy and Phoebe Young, the Kanes who worked for the Livingston-Boles, the child Léonie had borne, all derived in one way or another from the same county. Regionally, Yorkshire was their common denominator.

It was at that point that he decided to engage as soon as might be the help of the Yorkshire police in an examination of Iris's registration of birth.

Once in Ravenchurch he drove to the Bull Ring, where was the bank Bertha Tidy had used as well as the offices of her solicitors, Bannerman, Bannerman, and Waite. Stumbling on their stairs, midnight at noon, snuffing the dust of antiquity, Raikes thought that if age and dilapidation in the trappings of the law stood for integrity, then Messrs. Bannerman must be Bayards indeed. The only representative he saw, however, resembled Humpty Dumpty rather than the chevalier. When the inspector enquired about a will he buttoned his little mouth tightly and shook his head.

"So far as we know," he said mournfully, "intestate. A regrettable—over-sight," giving an edge to the euphemism he knew he had employed, "but one common in our experience of lady clients. I indicated, emphasized, *urged* the importance of a will, the last time as recently as the spring. But Miss Tidy was obdurate on the subject, or else committed to a policy of more or less permanent procrastination."

Raikes, enjoying the term, laughed, and Mr. Bannerman permitted him-self a prim smile.

"Believe me, Inspector, that's not so fanciful as it sounds. Ladies—those at any rate who make a success of business—are curiously unbusinesslike in regard to the eventual disposition of their property. It comes, I dare say, from an undeveloped sense of mortality."

Raikes, thanking him, left with the impression that Mr. Bannerman at least possessed a by no means undeveloped sense of humor.

This vein seemed not to have been worked in the bank manager to whom he was talking ten minutes later, or perhaps to have evaporated in the odor of finance. Gravity, however, did not impair the efficiency with which he dealt with the inspector's enquiry. It only deepened as Raikes outlined his case.

"This is a fearful allegation," he said, "against a dead woman. And a woman of such standing. But you, I know, are suggesting she wouldn't be dead in such circumstances if it were not so? Well, it's for you to substan-tiate your charges. I can let you have a schedule of investments in a very short time, and a detailed statement of account for—the past eight or nine months? Yes. You must give us a little longer for that, but it will be ready today." He frowned. "I seem to be treating the matter like an automaton. But the shock's pretty severe. First the murder—now this. Oh yes, she made weekly cash payment to her account—no, never by messenger, always in person. They were increasingly substantial since about Christmas. Checks? Comparatively few. In spite of the social standing she seems to have de-manded of her patrons, she was averse to accepting checks and did not mind saying so. They grumbled, and paid."

Raikes jotted a few notes and switched to the subject of Edith Drake, who had banked here too. The manager drew down the corners of his mouth as he listened.

"That there was something very wrong there for some months before Miss Drake's death was pretty obvious," he admitted. "But you must see that there are limits to the degree of inquisitiveness we can show in the matter, or to the advice we can give. In spite of continual and very heavy withdrawals, always on checks drawn to self, and such an incursion to her share holdings and account generally that there was a quite inconsiderable amount remaining at her death, she was always on the right side as regards balance—never once an overdraft. But then, she had at one time a large capital to play about with."

"Which," said Raikes, "melted away as Miss Tidy's swelled correspondingly?"

The manager's solemn face took on a more than ever pained expression. "Really—I mean, is this the stage to put quite so bad an interpretation upon it? Well, fortunately for me, I have to leave that to you. Yes, the fact is these frequent payments to self, always large, coupled with the marked depression which seemed to cloud even Miss Drake's professional relationships, *were* a source of anxiety. There's no doubt about it. But what was I to do? She was acting within her rights, and if she chose to be reticent about it— well, my hands were tied. But yes, the mystery darkened when I remembered her as having once been, in spite of her wealth, an entirely unmercenary person who seemed content to live on her teaching salary and dispense the unearned increment, so to say, largely in charitable directions."

He promised, with a discouraging air and a barely suppressed groan, to furnish Raikes with a complete statement of Edith Drake's account for a year before her death, and to send it in together with the disclosures relating to Miss Tidy.

The inspector, in clamorous need of his lunch, decided to leave the financial affairs of Mrs. Livingston-Bole and Beatrice Graves until after he had eaten. He dived into a restaurant which displayed an appetizing exterior without, alas, interior fulfilment. Everything, it appeared, which had been on a half hour ago was now irrecoverably off, and he caught himself regarding a dubious "cheese omelette" with the wonder that he had ever derided spam.

2

A few hours later he was marshaling the facts before Lecky.

"Taken singly," he said, "they'd be suspicious. Collectively, they're damning. And when the forthcoming bank statements supply details, the inference should be incontestable."

The superintendent wore the look of resignation this horrible affair had stamped upon him. Sergeant Brook, new from his coupon chase, wondered yet again what the world, as represented by Ravenchurch, was coming to.

"No good," he said aloud.

Raikes, misunderstanding, replied at once, "Plenty good, old man. Cold evidence in black and white, that's what those balance sheets will be. Figures too, more incorruptible than words, which lend themselves to ambiguity. I grant you, though, they're not going to be so useful in the case of Beatrice Graves."

"No," said Lecky. "She was carrying on a piece of shady business herself, and there won't be any record, as such, of the transactions."

"Exactly. The buying and selling of clothing coupons rules out payments by cheque. She would certainly pay for them in notes, and it's pretty clear she insisted on receiving only notes for them from her own buyers. Her account shows very few withdrawals to self since last autumn—surprisingly few, for she was paying in throughout the period pretty large sums. The significant point is, as the paying-in book indicates, these were always in currency notes, for the most part one-pounds."

"And the suggestion is she was well furnished with ready money for the payment of blackmail, without having recourse to her banking account?"

"Of course. Say she made the alleged three pounds' profit on each book—two pounds to the seller, and five pounds down, at least, when *she* made a sale—there'd be money to hand all the time, and the necessary rake-off for Tidy."

Lecky sighed. "Look here, we've got to take into consideration that there are only two issues of clothing books in a year. If this has been going on since the winter it looks on the face of it as if she'd soon exhaust her sources of supply."

Raikes shook his head. "You're forgetting these weren't merely local."

Brook nodded. "That's right. We're on to half a dozen places besides Ravenchurch already. And no knowing how many we shall end up with."

"Well," Lecky summed up, "I must say the Fripp and Saltmarsh end of it doesn't look too healthy. Mean to say an affair on this scale's been going on for months while they were in the dark about it?"

Raikes shrugged. "Feasible, I think. Remember, Miss Graves was in a trusted position. That's what made Tidy put the pressure on too smartly—increased prestige as well as a higher salary. I grant this hush-hush on Trumpington's part has queered their pitch, but there's no reason at this stage for disbelieving him when he admits it was a purely personal decision. It's fifty-fifty he'll lose his job over it when we've pried and prodded a bit more, and really got the firm's hackles up."

"So he should," Lecky said with unusual vehemence. "These lah-di-dah gents won't see a scandal that's handed to them on a plate—it's not that they *can't*. Peace at any price—only in this case it's reputation—so hide it up, push it under the counter, go on playing ostrich. Never mind if somebody dies because of it. Let's keep our own lily-white hands clean. Till Nosy Parkers like you and me come and drag it all out."

Sergeant Brook as well as the inspector listened with some surprise to the mild superintendent. Then Raikes reminded himself that the cumulative beastliness of this case must be strain enough on the nerves of the locals; and Brook remembered that Lecky loved Ravenchurch.

It was Raikes who, without preamble, changed the subject. "Cast an eye over these letters Miss Livingston-Bole handed over, will you? They're the ones Tidy wrote to the late Mrs. Livingston-Bole in the spring when she wasn't seeing enough of her friend to satisfy her—or, shall we say, to satisfy her banking account." He sensed rather than saw Lecky's expression, and added, "We're facing facts now, not airing hypotheses. And that's how it is."

He slid the letters across to Lecky, who selected the one with the earlier date and read:

DEAR PHOEBE,

Such a long time since we had a chat. Rather *overdue*, don't you think? I telephoned you twice, but you weren't available, hence this. Remembering poor Cyril and all the past I feel sure you'd *count the cost* before consigning to oblivion,

Your ever attentive
BERTHA

Lecky passed it to Brook without a word and picked up its companion, written nine days later.

DEAR PHOEBE,

Don't you think this has gone on long enough? I do very much want to see you, and am positive that when you think it over you will want to see me too. Our interests are mutual, oh, so mutual. I know you're probably much preoccupied, as usual, with Henry's happiness, but I have shown you so clearly how that can be maintained. *You owe me* at least some measure of your devoted time. Full as mine is, I called on you the other afternoon, but was told (with suspicious promptitude) that you were out. Well, do come in—to the Minerva. *You owe me* that much, don't you?

Your friend, unrelaxingly,
BERTHA

Nobody spoke till Brook had finished reading the second letter. Then the superintendent, busy only with his thoughts, laid both slowly on the table, fitting edge to edge with almost fussy precision.

"The woman was mad," he said at last with the exasperated finality of the man who habitually employs understatement. "Look at the phrases she's underlined—heavy scoring too: 'overdue,' 'count the cost,' 'you owe me,' and that twice."

"Megalomania, yes," Raikes agreed. "Blackmailers who score initial success grow megalomaniac in the later stages. Inevitable, when you come to think of it. Poisoners likewise—let 'em get away with the first job, and the habit not only grows, it breeds recklessness. Same with the Bertha Tidy brand, who are spiritual poisoners if ever there were any."

The sergeant was swallowing hard. "To think," he said in hushed tones, "that it was only just before the war she was offering herself as a candidate for the Ravenchurch municipal elections."

"And did she get in?" Raikes asked, amused.

"No," Lecky answered crisply. "The truth is, the place never took to Miss Tidy."

The inspector, detecting a gentlemanly hint that the judgment of Ravenchurch had not, after all, been let down, smiled.

"Local government, eh? Well, if she couldn't get it by hook, she took it by crook, seeing she's misgoverned a good many of the local lives for some time past."

3

At the Loggerheads a letter was awaiting Raikes. Left by a lady, he was told in sinister undertones, for the inn's pride in his sojourn had a lugubrious tinge.

The large, square white envelope, stiffened by its contents, clearly held more than a letter. Raikes opened it with hasty neatness and drew out a piece of brown cardboard against which was flattened a slightly cracked and aged photograph. Pinned to a corner of the improvised mount was a small sheet of note paper on which the following lines were written in scholarly hand:

The enclosed photograph may possibly be of interest. It shows my sister-in-law before her first marriage on the left of Cyril Ballantyne. On his right is Bertha Tidy.

C. LIVINGSTON-BOLE

Raikes looked down at the still shiny sepia, out of which three white faces glimmered strangely up at him. The two girls, in Edwardian garb, were seated, one on each side of what looked like a little rickety garden table, behind which stood a uniformed figure. All three were properly focussing a starchy gaze upon the camera, but Raikes noted at once that while the figure on the left sat with hands demurely in lap, the smaller girl on Ballantyne's right had placed her left hand on the edge of the table, where the gallant lieutenant's had closed over it. The entire picture, in spite of its dissolving hues, carried the comically self-conscious air photographs acquire in the passage of time.

Raikes looked thoughtful, then excited. He took from his pocket a measuring tape and stretched it over the length and breadth of the picture. Roughly, seven and three eighths by four and a half—the size of the dust-free rectangular portion of the shelf in Miss Tidy's bedside locker. So far, so good. He pushed photograph, cardboard, and letter back into their envelope, and let a sudden spate of liberated recollections range over that visit to Léonie at the Keepsake the other day.

Something that had bothered him that day, something like an echo, an uncatchable remembrance he couldn't pin down, returned with the patience of a mosquito. It had bothered him from the moment he had set foot in the Keepsake; it hadn't entirely submitted to being shoved away all the time he was questioning Léonie and examining the rooms; it had returned with new vigor to the assault after Greatorex had gone away, and when he himself had left the cottage.

An echo ... vocal? Something vocal, that was it ... but connected with ... what they'd been doing just now in Lecky's room? Rubbish! He'd given his thoughts carte blanche, and they'd stampeded. There could be *no* connection, and yet ... what *had* they been up to an hour or so ago? Letters ... reading letters ... *That* was it—letters. But not the same letters. That couldn't be, seeing he'd only now come into possession of Bertha Tidy's to Phoebe Livingston-Bole. The letters uppermost in his mind when he had called at the Keepsake were the anonymous couple Tidy had brought to the police, and the other Kate Beaton had produced the same evening. Those were the letters which had started that echo whispering and babbling at him from the four walls of the Keepsake. All at once he thought of something practical he could do about it.

Five minutes later the watch that seemed always kept nowadays at one or other of the Loggerheads windows noted that their Inspector Raikes had left the house and was making his way down the road with a thoroughly jaunty air.

4

At Kate Beaton's house a rush and slither of paws on parquet and a tumult of barks answered his knock. A voice at the ground-floor window a foot or two away called with familiar brusqueness, "Come right in, will you, Inspector? Like me, they don't bite—or seldom. And please shut the door after you, else I'll lose one or t'other under the bus."

When he had obeyed instructions he found the Airedales, their zeal spent, slunk to the bottom of the hall and intent on a flea hunt, from which, as a less interesting proposition, he was excluded. A door on the right stood open, and a lady caller appeared to be taking leave of Miss Beaton.

Seeing his hesitation, Kate Beaton said, "Do come in. Mrs. Wardle-Phlox was just going anyway. Let me introduce you."

Raikes found himself rumbling the usual nothings to a flushed elderly woman who examined him a little anxiously.

"You and your work," she exclaimed below her breath. "How dreadful! How wonderful!"

When, panting a little, she had rustled past in an odor of Parma violet, Raikes was left wondering which epithet he was to apply to himself.

"Not a friend," Kate Beaton said unnecessarily on her return. She looked at him, he thought, with peculiar directness. "Ostensibly she's called on a gold-digging survey—wants me to contribute to a canine club called Your Pal and Mine. But as the four-legged members are the Peke and French Butterfly breeds which my own ruffians would make mincemeat of, I feel a bit two-faced in the matter. However," she added, with mock cheerfulness indicating the table by the window, "we've had tea in a spirit of sisterly amity, and now I believe all that's left in the pot for you is stone cold."

"I've had tea," Raikes said briefly. In a changed tone he added, "I say, why 'ostensibly'?"

"What?"

"You said Mrs.—Mrs. What's-her-name—called 'ostensibly' for a subscription. What did she really come about?"

"Sakes!" Kate Beaton exclaimed. "Your thirst for knowledge is a bottomless well. She really came for a spot of gossip. She was an earnest patron of the Minerva, to which she looked for rejuvenation. There, I knew that would brighten you. She's steeped in morbidity, like all us women, so she came to me for the lowdown, seeing it was I—I who— —"

"Yes?" he said as she stumbled.

"I who found Jane's body," she finished quietly. "Mrs. W.-P. came to angle for gory details she didn't get. Your arrival was a beautiful climax, like the Demon King's."

"I thought she looked a bit stricken," Raikes said. He had seated himself at the disheveled tea table, disregarding the scones and fluid she was steering across to him.

"Look here." He leaned forward. A confidential air rarely failed with women, even with the hardest-boiled. "I shouldn't bother you with this. But, if you don't mind my saying so, you strike me as a sport. And you *were* in on this anyway—"

He got no further. Kate Beaton, eyes and voice like flint, rapped out, "What do you mean?"

"Good lor'," the genuinely astonished Raikes replied, "*nothing*. Cross my heart. That is, nothing you can object to or deny. I simply meant that you were in on the anonymous letter business, since you brought us one yourself urging you to warn Miss Tidy."

She sighed, leaning back and pressing her weight into the creaky basket chair.

"That all? Sorry I flew off the handle. I resent imputations that haven't the honesty of a direct charge—and there's a whole pack of 'em flying about this village in the last few days. All right. What can I do for you about Poison Pen?"

When Raikes replied, his thoughts were on another tack. (What did you think I meant? Something about Jane Kingsley? Something perhaps about Edith Drake? Or Tidy herself?) "I want the letters read aloud to me, the two Miss Tidy received as well as the one addressed to you. Oh yes, I've lots of bobbies who'd oblige, but I'm fuddled about something I can't explain even to myself, and I want to hear them in a *feminine* voice. Will you play?"

"Why, yes." But her eyes were still hard, and seemed loth to let his go. She breathed like a runner. "I never saw Tidy's anyway. What fun!"

She stretched a hand for the letters he passed to her. He watched closely for her first reactions at sight of the pasted capitals on the one, the block characters on the other of Bertha Tidy's communications, but could detect nothing amiss—unless she was perhaps unnaturally still?

After about half a minute she began to read, without lifting her head, quietly but with some expression of the menace the writer had intended to convey.

" 'You think you get away with the crime. Wait. See. The eye of God is on you. Death may be next for you. Who know?' "

Raikes made as if to speak, then, seeing her take up the second letter, waited in silence.

" 'When you sit in your drawing room and watch,' " Kate Beaton read. " 'When you sleep in your soft bed. When you eat the good food prepared, and look sometimes it may be at the photograph in the locker by the bed, tell me, do you not fear? Five have died. But six may die. Think well. It may be now that you think too late.' "

She said nothing for a moment. Then, "Cheerful little pen friend, eh?" she murmured. She picked up the letter she herself had received.

" 'How often have you wondered when all will be known about the deaths in Long Greting. Ask Miss Tidy. Tell her she is not safe. One more will repay what has been payed.' "

She stared suddenly at Raikes and said with a kind of nervous irrelevance, "Last word's spelt p-a-y-e-d, you'll remember. And it's I that put in the interrogative accents. They're not here. Our scribe can handle only full stops."

"Yes," Raikes said at once, "and you've put in a whole lot more that's of value too. In that first letter, I mean. The gummed cutouts. They're unpunctuated, and you supplied a new punctuation, better than ours, I think. D'you mind running over it again while I take it down at dictation?"

Kate Beaton gave him a suspicious glance and licked her lips. "Funny, that. I gave it the only punctuation that seemed possible. Well, here goes—but I warn you, I mayn't do exactly the same this time."

She did, however, and Raikes got it down as read. He caught her looking at him with a smile hard to interpret.

"Thank you," he said, stuffing the papers away and getting up to go. "You've been a tremendous help—laid one bogey for me, even if you've raised another. I know now what was bothering me."

"Good," Kate Beaton remarked without enthusiasm. She thought he seemed in a hurry to go. At the door she remembered the handful of policewomen in the Ravenchurch force and said, "Flattering of you to select *my* old croak as a feminine voice—seeing what a large field you had to pick from."

And with that ambiguity in his ears, Raikes thankfully left her.

CHAPTER 12

When will you pay me?
Say the bells of Old Bailey.

The inquest on Jane Kingsley that opened with the fanfare of a crowded and expectant court had, within the half hour, closed disappointingly for Ravenchurch. The public, first dulled by a succession of suicides which only now appeared to be of far less dreary interest than it had supposed, had been forced onto its toes by the murders of the past week. Exploiting the modern weakness for detecting a Ripper at work as soon as the killing became plural, it was beginning to huddle, herd, move about in parties, and whip its bored blood to the heat of condemning police methods it had never taken the trouble to understand, and longing for the opportunity to exercise lynch law.

A manhunt, that was what was needed. Poor old Lecky—getting past his work, he was. And these boosted Scotland Yard fellows no better. It was time people took matters into their own hands, what with charming old ladies getting strangled and innocent girls bashed on the head.

The dry-lipped coroner, with his veiled eyes and deceptive air of inattention, gave them less than satisfaction. Dr. Hare submitted brief and almost inaudible evidence, acceptable, it seemed, to everyone but the hungry public, who felt no real compensation in the ringing replies of Miss Beaton, who testified to finding the body in tones suggesting she was addressing a latently hostile open-air meeting. After that everybody was cleared out in less than no time, the police getting the fortnight's adjournment they had asked for, and Raikes, from an obscure point of vantage, listened to the swelling undercurrent of grumbles as the court emptied. Somebody was for it. Somebody must pay. Nor did they care who.

"First mutterings on the horizon," said the inspector. "Looks like a tempest is going to burst in this well-behaved city."

"We shan't let it reach the zenith," Lecky said, waxing in turn metaphorical. But he looked disquieted.

"Well-behaved, eh?" Hare snapped. "Like to know what you call real misconduct. Driving without a license, perhaps. Two murders a week are a bit indigestible even for me. But you London chaps no doubt can toss 'em off without turning a hair."

"Or Hare?" Raikes enquired.

The doctor spluttered disgust.

2

Midafternoon sunshine shone through the foliage screening the bench where Jane had died. The present occupant of the seat was caught in its shifting dapple of light and shade, and his own shadow on the grass looked extraordinarily like that of Silenus lurking in the thicket with undefined intentions. That is, the resemblance might have been noted if the necessary spectator had been there. And was there such a presence?

Owen Greatorex did not think so, else he would not have sat there so quietly in a pose which even solitude did not persuade him to discard. The nobility of his hatless head, round which the sun, conscious of its duty, played a delicate nimbus, was, it is true, wasted on the desert air, but it stayed noble nevertheless.

He had been thinking about Henry James. Would posterity, did even his contemporaries perhaps, accord him a similar pedestal? He was interested in pedestals and statuary and the more material emblems of man's fame. Maybe it was a symptom of what Mr. Bannerman would have called an undeveloped sense of mortality. The world was very much with Mr. Greatorex. He decided, not without pride, that he had become in his later period a little too florid to carry James's tortuous halo with entire success. In the creative sense only, it went without saying; not at all florid physically, he could still reassure himself he was undeservedly blessed with an aura of austerity he did not need to practice.

He prodded the grass in front of him with the ferrule of his handsome stick and thought again of present miseries. Why he had allowed himself to agree with Mrs. Phail's suggestion that Léonie Blanchard should be admitted to the house he couldn't imagine. Mrs. Phail herself was, he was sure, unable by now to imagine it too. Pity there was of course (he knew little of compassion), a quality one could not afford to dispense with while hoping to maintain a public in England; but there were limits surely. Her cooking might be excellent, but the degree of interest focused upon her was, to say the least of it, highly disconcerting. What were they expecting? That she would be the third victim? He could not help chuckling at that—really, when you came to think of it, it was funny. He laughed aloud, shaking himself into a still nearer resemblance of a satyr in the brakes. He stopped abruptly. Not altogether amusing, for to tell the truth (which might always be told in a solitude of this sort) the Amazonian Breton was making him nervous. She wasn't exactly nice to have about the house.

He liked his women small and pretty and submissive, the authentic Dresden. He liked them to have lives dedicated to him. He thought of Bertha Tidy and shuddered. It was a thought which could make even the sun-steeped glade chilly. Really, how she had run after him! And how—*how* she had paid for it. He swelled a little, bracing his shoulders. You heard a lot of talk about masculine vanity, but wasn't it usually pardonable? All his days he had of course been used to the homage of women and had invariably found it acceptable when they were willing to become instrumental to the furtherance of his literary career. But he had not sought it. Nobody could say so. And in Ravenchurch adulation had assumed an unprofitable character. Not one of the female disciples here had shown the least inclination to undertake the role of Milton's daughters, or even the less arduous typewriting other girls had done for love instead of money. No—their only strong suit was tooth-and-claw rivalry among themselves, and if contention was flattering in its early stages the bone of it soon experienced an immense fatigue. Perpetual running away was an unenviable activity. And what a lot of it he had done! Never faint, and always pursuing, the pack led by Bertha Tidy and Kate Beaton had stayed the course.

Death had seemed the only release. Not for himself, of course. He didn't intend ever dying for a woman. Women were mortal, weren't they? So one of *them* had died. Even a worm will turn. And Bertha's murderer could scarcely be called a worm. He chuckled again, but mirth had gone out of him. He believed it had really gone out of him years and years ago, and remembered with a drowning wave of nostalgia a hungry young man in love with his pen who had not begun to think about pedestals. But it wouldn't do. Going over one's past, remote or near, was only demoralizing in the conditions in which he found himself now.

He squared his shoulders again—they were good ones still—and took pride in the thought that he had never betrayed Bertha's nymphomania to the police. Of course, he reminded himself with a kind of hasty bow to the honesty which never dared too close an approach nowadays, if he had told the inspector *that* he'd have been involved in a measure of self-betrayal too. So his lips had been sealed. And he felt congratulations were due him for behaving like a gentleman in provocative circumstances.

Kate Beaton too. He shivered again. Different tactics certainly, but another distressing example of frustrated womanhood making a nuisance of itself. Nor did the weakness sit so prettily on her as it had done on Bertha. To him privately, she was the Shrew—Katharine the Shrew. A pity really it was Bertha who had had to die. But what was going to happen next? He didn't like the look of things at all. And *wasn't* it a funny thing—wasn't it odd that Kate should go out the other day *without* the dogs? Why, those brutes were her satellites, but—*but satellites and dogs alike might be very awkward customers if one was on a life-and-death errand, might they not? How easily they might give one away.*

There was a crashing, a snuffling, a slobbering in the undergrowth, and a whistle farther off. He got to his feet with a speed and agility which would not have discredited the young man of years gone by. She was coming. But not my own, my sweet. He had let the time run on. It was Kate Beaton and the dogs. Spied upon by the police out of doors, by Blanchard in, he preferred either to the Shrew's pursuit, especially with the memory of Jane at this very spot.

As he loped down the path into the brightness of the meadow he felt like Acteon … running, running, always cutting and running …

As he came out onto the open grass a stone struck him hard between the shoulders. He grew suddenly white, though not at the hurt. The meadow was empty. He hurried on.

That evening Kate Beaton's dining-room window was smashed by half a brick.

Ugly words were scratched with a knife on the lintel of the Loggerheads.

Messrs. Fripp and Saltmarsh, sorely tried, discovered in the morning a nasty crack that not only destroyed the impeccability of their plate glass, but quite marred the beauty of the green-faced lady in a petunia frock who stood behind it.

The storm had left the horizon and, in spite of Lecky, was darkening the Ravenchurch sky. Pay, pay, pay—for the sins you never committed too. How else obtain the scapegoat necessary to us all?

Owen Greatorex sat in comparative safety inside Mile House.

But there was always Léonie, even there.

3

The Slip, thought Mrs. Weaver, was uncommonly quiet these days. She put it down to the fact that it had become a regular beat for one or another policeman, for though the guard had been withdrawn from the locked and silent Minerva, the guardians of the law continued to take an unflagging interest in the little passage. At first they had been dogged at a discreet distance by groups of small boys and sometimes hooligans, till interest in so severely localized a spot had waned; and now, though there was a dangerous air of unrest, she was told, in Ravenchurch itself, Flute Lane was silent—as the grave.

Not a nice simile at all, Emmie, Mrs. Weaver rebuked herself. But it popped up all the same. Her thoughts seemed less manageable in the last day or two. Since Jane's death, and the frightening review of the Edith Drake tragedy, she had found it difficult to remain the disinterested party she had always been. Books were no longer a bulwark, or at least not an impregnable one.

She was finding it out now as she sat in the dark and rather frowsty back corner of the shop which she called her office, behind the last stack of books and close to the kitchen door. There she had a little table littered with pens and ink and catalogues and invoices, and there in winter burned a smelly stove. Even now it was airless, and shut in and very private, and she loved it. She would sit there with a book and a bun and a cold cup of tea, and indulge in a child's gloating at her unseen presence in that poky nook. Customers and bookworms and people who only wanted to read and forget the outside streets and not to buy were invisible while they roamed all but her own retreat. She couldn't see a feather of them, nor they of her, only hear the shuffle and scrape and tap of their feet perambulating the cases, and now and again the slide of a book leaving or returning to its shelf, or else the bump when one slipped to the floor. Come to think of it, that way suited her best. She didn't care in the least about people's faces; she only liked books.

And when at length they rounded the rear-guard stack and peered into the hole where she was, the females among them would sometimes exclaim, "Oh, Mrs. Weaver, what a start you gave me!" And the gentlemen would nod to her with widened eyes and a rather self-conscious air. And she enjoyed both encounters.

This evening she sat thumbing with for once awkward fingers a queer duodecimo on New England witchcraft, worth a great deal of money. At any other time it would have exercised upon Mrs. Weaver a suitably unholy fascination; perhaps it did even now, for though she looked at the text with unseeing eyes she was thinking of murderers. Not precisely. What she thought of was one murderer.

From the body of the shop came the faint sounds of a book hunter on the trail. She knew who it was. She had seen her come in and spoken to her, getting a gruff response and turned shoulder which, because she demanded nothing from others, left her entirely without resentment. It was the youngest of the girls who used to work at the Minerva, the gawky Oates child, poor lonely little thing, she'd always thought. Possibly, though, she had a taste for solitude, a predilection Mrs. Weaver shared to the point of complete understanding. Indeed, she could go further and say that some there were who would call her a fanatic if they knew everything, for she was beginning to love the solitary condition with a passion which could only inspire approval of the elimination of everyone else. ... Not, of course, by atomic bombs and suchlike, nor, *if it could be helped*, by scarves and blunt instruments. Better really if they might dissolve away like the dew and so leave the world to Emmie Weaver ...

She went on thinking about a murderer.

The floor bell tinkled madly, and a cool draft flowed in. Some well-planted steps crossed the center gangway and, instead of halting in the usual way at a nearby shelf, came straight on to the office.

Mrs. Weaver, not unlike a basilisk in that ill-lighted angle, lifted only her eyes and saw Kate Beaton, hatless, tweedy, tousled, importing to these academic precincts the bucolic spirit its proprietor loathed.

"I was sure you'd be right here," Miss Beaton announced with a gusto that took credit even for that. "When I'd had tea after my walk I remembered something I ought to ask you, so I hopped on the bus forthwith. By the way, in the woods this afternoon I came upon the Portrait of the Artist as an Old Man. Can you riddle me *that* ree?"

She edged the words with an abrupt laugh. She was flushed and rather loud. Evidently Marion Oates had been hidden behind one of the cases when she came in, and she believed them to be alone. Mrs. Weaver, who cared nothing about the duty of enlightening her on the matter, decided to say nothing.

"I expect you saw Mr. Greatorex," she said calmly. "I always think he's very well preserved myself."

Kate Beaton laughed again. "Pickled in self-esteem, eh? Like a fly in amber. Or poor Jim Jay. You know what happened to him, don't you?"

Mrs. Weaver looked at her politely. The gentleman was possibly another Ravenchurch suicide that had passed her by.

" 'Got stuck fast in the middle of yesterday,' " her informant supplied with hearty pity.

She sat down suddenly on the end of the already burdened table, squashing into a much darkened blotting pad the remains of Mrs. Weaver's tea. She slapped her knee, as if closing one chapter and opening the next, and screwed round towards the bookseller, shutting out for good and all the last filter of daylight to the office.

"I've been horribly worried for some time," she said. Nobody, Mrs. Weaver reflected, could look less worried. She continued to give courteous attention.

"These police," Miss Beaton went on truculently, as if Mrs. Weaver had summoned them, "they're everywhere except in the right place—"

"But where's that?" Mrs. Weaver asked innocently.

"Oh, I'm not hinting at specific guilt here, there, or anywhere," the novelist said, swinging her leg with a nervous violence Mrs. Weaver deprecated from every point of view. "What I mean is, they ought to be getting on with Jane Kingsley's murder instead of this continual hunting into the past, don't you think? Going over all these suicides, for instance. Pretty painful for the relatives, I'd say."

"Most of them didn't seem to have any," Mrs. Weaver pointed out. "Except, of course, poor Miss Drake's young sister."

There was a heavy silence. Mrs. Weaver sat with demurely hooded eyes, considering a morsel of foxing on the New England witches which might detract from their monetary value. She was very honest where books were concerned.

Kate Beaton's leg stopped swinging. She snorted, with the indignation of one woman against another who had outstripped her in the race for gossip.

"Sister?" she said. "What sister?"

Mrs. Weaver shook her head in a melancholy that disguised extreme pleasure. For once, just for once in her backwater life, she was a move ahead of the highlights and gadabouts.

"I never learned her name," she said with studious indifference. "Just a sister, you know. Poor Miss Drake, how she felt the responsibility!"

This was too much. "I don't know what you're talking about!" Kate Beaton burst out. (What the heck was the matter with the old dame? Was it a trap?) "There was *no* sister. Edith was an orphan, and alone in the world."

"You are mistaken," said Emmie Weaver sweetly. Never, outside the realm of her library, had she been able to indicate that to anyone before. "Though I always said you knew more about Miss Drake than any of the rest of us. However, her sister was an important person in her life, as I was able to assure the inspector. But what did you come to ask me?"

"You've stolen it. With all this talk of a sister. I knew Miss Drake came here as often as she could. I thought you may have picked up something, that's all."

"I did."

"What?"

Mrs. Weaver, basely deserting the traditions of anonymity and reticence in which she and her books had so long dwelled, and flushed with her triumph over the knowledgeable Miss Beaton, told her.

Kate Beaton's eyes shone. *The credulous old fool.* "But, Mrs. Weaver, my dear, don't you see? She wasn't being anxious about her sister at all. There *was* no sister. It was for *herself* she was asking advice."

"Deary me now, was it?" said the bookseller with the right touch of mild irony. That was the tone calculated to spoil this madam's hastily snatched victory. Did she think Emmie Weaver cared in the very least? "The poor girl's gone, so I dare say it makes very little difference either way."

Kate Beaton, suitably daunted by this undefeated air, resigned herself to the inferior role of inquisitor.

"How did she get the information she wanted?"

"From the Minerva."

The shop was very quiet. Outside Ravenchurch rumbled and rode.

"*That* old——"

"She's dead," Mrs. Weaver said with unusual haste. Even if people had to be eliminated, it should be a disinterested, not an abusive operation. "I didn't say who supplied it. How can I? There were young people there too—and it's the young these days, isn't it, who tell us all we need to know?"

From somewhere in front came an "Oh!" of mingled grief and despair. A book banged. A second bang, after a delirious tinkle of the bell, announced precipitate exit.

Kate Beaton stared at Mrs. Weaver, who had the grace to look slightly ashamed. "I—I forgot. There was—a browser," she said.

"Oh well, it can't be helped. No names, no pack drill. Anyway, the town's agog with every rumor under the sun. Do you know, when I got down from the bus just now some unseen well-wisher 'booed' me—*me?*"

"Tut-tut," said Mrs. Weaver, silently commending the booer.

She wished Miss Beaton good evening at the door, looked out for a moment on the apparently pacific street, then, returning, cast an uncommonly observant eye round the now vacated shop before repairing to her corner.

What sympathies one could have for the miller in one of Mary Webb's tales, wasn't he, who, drowning successive litters of kittens, had wished all the world were a kit-cat, that he might drown it too. ...

"I do *not* like its Silly Face," said Mrs. Weaver aloud to the Human Race, settling down once more to her violated solitude.

4

Samela Wild had had a cup of tea with Crystal and Kenneth Bates. By frank agreement they had kept off the subject dominating them all, with the result that it had been a strained and unnatural party from which Sammy had been glad to release herself. How stupid evasion is, she thought, with a grim little rider for the more particular one she was herself practicing. How abysmally stupid and useless! Coming clean with everything, even with your thoughts at a tea party, was the only course after all.

The late afternoon was bright and shining after the cooling breeze of the last day and night. Moat Street was off the main bus route, and to reach her flat she would have to change twice. Not worth it. Dependence on the buses was as much a habit as tea drinking, her legs were young and nimble, and there was high summer in the streets.

She walked briskly, with conscious grace, in an old linen frock fresh as a daisy, conscious too of the foolishness of rejecting thoughts she was still at pains to quash. At a by-street corner she stopped at a greengrocer's to buy a little chip of luscious, too expensive strawberries. George had more than the common weakness for strawberries. She carried them with fitting solicitude.

When she came to the middle of the town, there, passing the Eagle and Child, next door to Fripp and Saltmarsh's, was George himself limping towards her.

She smiled up at his grave face, always grave now.

"Home?"

"That's about it."

"Me too."

"Hey," said George, peering, "what have we here? What was it the old chappie said? 'Doubtless God could have made a better berry, but doubtless He never did.' "

He popped one into his mouth while Samela, eyes on Fripp and Saltmarsh, plucked his sleeve.

"Oh, George," she sighed, the tip of her nose blunted on the glass, "I'll swear that wasn't in this morning. It's *wizard!* No, silly, not the petunia, the little S W behind—I don't know what they call that divine shade, rose caramel, I think—"

"We haven't the coupons," said her practical husband, "so there's no need to break your neck trying to read the price ticket. And, if you ask me, it's a sort of Argentine beef color—"

That was as far as the Philistine got. Less than a minute earlier the thoroughfare had suddenly sprouted a press of picture-goers on their way home. Somebody jostled Samela's back. Up went her elbow at a second shove, and the strawberries cascaded in all directions as a hoarse voice shot into her ear, "Minerva *murderers!*"

Things happened so fast nobody could say afterwards what came first. George dived into the melting crowd at a burst of laughter from a flying group of hobbledehoys who dived into an arcade close at hand. In less than a minute, with the speed of water rushing down a drain, the crowd had disappeared. A little girl had propped her bicycle against the curb and was helping Samela in silence to pick up the fruit that had not been trampled on. The child looked frightened. When they had done Sammy pushed the chip into her hands.

"For you," she whispered, turning her head to see George in conversation with a police constable. She joined them.

"We know about the gang, Mrs. Wild," said the man. "What we want is to get an individual member on a specific charge. They'll scatter now, mark my words, and butter won't melt in A's mouth as he says he don't know what B's been up to."

"He'd know if he'd got my knuckles under his nose," George said.

The policeman sighed. "There's been a nasty spot of trouble, breaking out like pimples, since this morning's inquest, that's what it is—a couple of stones at the police station, and dirty words like chalked up here and there. They wanted a circus, you see, and they got a mere formality and an adjournment."

George nodded. "Epitaph on the public spirit of Ravenchurch. Well, I'm thinking we'd best roll along to Moat Street and see if we've got a couple of stones there too."

The constable looked sympathetic and a shade embarrassed.

"I was going to suggest, sir—if you get my meaning—seeing your wife's from the Minerva—"

"I know," said George quickly. "Stop indoors, and don't tempt the swine. That's it, isn't it?"

"Well," the man said, sensing the advice was unacceptable, "it won't be for long. Take my word for that. Meantime we'll have our hands full. It was twilight, and after, I was thinking of most."

"All right," George muttered. "Good of you. S'long."

As they mutually turned away the constable suddenly stepped back to them.

"Are you hurt, Mrs. Wild? Your frock!"

Sammy twisted, in a vain attempt to see. It was George who told her that the linen had been slashed open from waist almost to neckline.

"It'll have to be the rose caramel now, darling," was all she said on a weakly hysterical note.

They went home a circuitous way, George's arm screening her back. They walked in silence. But to Samela it was like conversation, of the comforting kind she could remember holding so often with George.

They crossed the close under the soaring spire of the cathedral and came out into Thistle Square. Already it was a well of shadow, uncommercial, deserted. George, his eyes on nowhere, felt his wife, who had been walking like a marionette, twist again.

"Old thing, you can't see it," he murmured. "And there's nobody here to stare."

But he stopped, because she did.

"It's not that—not that at all. Didn't you see? Oh, George, it was Marion hurrying home over there. I turned, but that was to smile at her."

"Yes, I *know*," George said patiently. "At least *I* didn't see her, but I can hear what you're telling me. Don't be so earnest—don't *worry*. The kid's got to go home sometime, and you've got to meet her. Keep your sense of proportion, Sam."

"I've kept it—I've kept it too long," said Samela. "George, will you never understand? Marion was looking at me. She saw me smile. She cut me dead—as mutton."

George pulled her on, but he made no answer. The suspicion polluting Ravenchurch had got him too. At last he was disposed to think Sammy might have got hold of the right end of a hideously wrong stick. He remembered her words the other day, "old Titus, looking like Lady Macbeth." *Did* schoolgirls commit murders? He tried to think of a classical case; there was Constance Kent, of course, but she didn't seem to fit the bill exactly, though she might have looked a little like the repressed Oates child.

He wouldn't put it past the girl; if old Bertha had had a hand in that repression—and what more likely?—she might have paid all right for it.

CHAPTER 13

When I grow rich,
Say the bells of Shoreditch.

By day Léonie sat for hours in her room at Mile House, undisturbed, as in a cell. By night, if summer's halfhearted drawing of the curtains could be called night, she wandered till late in the byways she knew by heart in Long Greeting, in the woods behind the Place, in the Keepsake garden, from which no padlock could exclude her, and among the tall grasses of the churchyard.

They—by which pronoun Mrs. Phail might be understood—hadn't liked it at first; and she had been granted no key to facilitate a midnight return. But it was wonderful what compromises might be reached and concessions made in the endeavor to keep a good cook. Léonie knew it, Mrs. Phail knew it, and, in the recesses of his study, Mr. Greatorex presumably knew it too. But when she was curtly informed that the bolt of the scullery door would be left slipped against her reentry, not one of them was so tactless as to mention her cooking. Miss Tidy's proficiency in the cruder forms of blackmail was, perhaps, shared to some extent, and in a sense more subtle, by her servant.

Nor was there any demur about her shutting herself up for so long in her bedroom. Actually Mrs. Phail was thankful for the respite; almost at once she had discovered Léonie to be one of those extremely able and intolerant cooks who insist on monopoly of the kitchen while infecting the whole house with an air of tension until the meal has been served. After that climax it was a real consolation to find her exiling herself voluntarily to the little room upstairs. What she did there nobody could say precisely. Owen Greatorex, several degrees more imaginative than Mrs. Phail, suspected that she prayed. Prayer was, after all, a very proper exercise for a woman. But the housekeeper, curtailing her rest one afternoon to creep with ungenteel stealth to Blanchard's door, had heard the rustle of paper and an unmistakable chink, and then a low voice apparently addressing itself in rapid French, and now and again in passages of surprising tenderness. In Mrs. Phail's limited vocabulary it was all very weird; she had not stayed long and had said nothing to Mr. Greatorex, who in any case had for some time now been eyeing their guest in what Mrs. Phail's generation would have termed an old-fashioned way.

So by night Léonie roamed, by day—reflected. She thought, with an objectivity Mrs. Phail would have considered shocking though characteristically foreign, of her late employer's life, death, and probable abode at present. She was assailed by few doubts and no misgivings. When she recalled the absence of a will, the failure to recognize her service of a score of years, she did not spend herself in disappointment and recrimination. Had she not, with the penetrative vision of one who lives cheek by jowl with another and sees behind the facade, provided for just such a contingency? Her personal wants becoming more and more frugal with the years, she had been able of course to hoard without much sacrifice her slender monthly wage. But in the past year another source had opened. Miss Bertha had surrendered so unconditionally to an absorbing interest of her own that she no longer had eye and ear for that domestic life which one takes for granted anyway. And Léonie was an expert manager in more ways than one. Out of very little schooling and an adolescence which to the English would have spelled bitter maturity, she had developed a hard clarity of intelligence that knew how to manipulate figures to the best personal advantage. She was, in fact, contemptuous of values, wilfully conscious of prices, and altogether without scruple.

For nearly twelve months she had consistently cooked the housekeeping account as successfully as the delightful meals which Miss Tidy, blind to all menial responsibilities (was she not a Power in Ravenchurch?), never suspected cost less than half the price she paid for them. In ethical debate Léonie might have argued that she was only receiving sub rosa what her salary should justly have been worth.

So the nest egg grew. That the purpose to which it had been dedicated was now ashes in the mouth was neither here nor there. She had it, crackling, chinking; and she had deprived Miss Tidy of it, who for twenty years had deprived her of a number of things that made life worth while.

In the blue twilight of her room she put the last coin back lovingly into the Gladstone bag, stroking it with hard-tipped fingers; then locked the bag and spent an elaborate couple of minutes concealing it beneath a pile of voluminously unattractive clothing.

The tin clock with silly round face on the mantelpiece pointed to ten o'clock. She took down from a peg a rusty black coat and put it on; rummaged in a drawer for a wide woolen scarf of purple which she wound deftly round head and throat. Then she went downstairs and let herself out through the deserted scullery.

The garden was cool and moon-white. The moon was nearly full, the few stars pallid in its light, and the night she longed for quenched in unkind brilliance. She moved down the alley without hesitation, making for the plot where Mr. Greatorex's roses gleamed mysteriously in all their comeliness. With the calm in which she had forged receipted bills, she took from her pocket a thick penknife and cut a dozen of them far down the stem. Buds and all? It was better perhaps that buds should perish young, but the manner of their perishing …

She let herself out of the garden gate and crossed the main road at a resolute pace.

2

The financial documentary Raikes had wrung from the banks had shaken Lecky's last prejudice. Exposing as it did the respective depletions and fattening of the incomes under survey, it might be termed a study in comparative economy which left no doubt that systematic blackmail in the person of Bertha Tidy had functioned and flourished for a considerable time.

"Probably well before the period for which all this is evidence," the inspector said wearily, tapping the statements under his hand. Their perusal had been one of those prolonged grinds which, highly profitable as to result, end in an immediate exhaustion for which nothing seems compensation.

"And the grounds for that?" Lecky questioned. Raikes might have pulled out a plum, but it was as well not to let him forget that he had been full of assumptions from the beginning.

"Several. Blackmailers in a large way—you're not now denying the scale of this, I suppose?—are apt, like other business folk, to start in a small way. If Tidy's earliest victims didn't feel the pinch sufficiently to take their own lives, and that *en masse*, there's no reason why any limelight at all should have been shed on the proceedings. Again—here's the first Yorkshire report. She left her school, where she was head teacher, mark you, suddenly and under a cloud which, the authorities—it was a church school—being anxious to avoid scandal and the onus of bringing a charge, was never dissolved. But it has a nasty taste, even after all these years."

"A man, perhaps?" Lecky observed hopefully.

"That's not suggested. What *is* uncovered is the fact that for some time she'd been on markedly bad terms with her assistant teacher, who seems to have been dominated and even cowed by Tidy. When things eventually blew up there was vague talk about money being involved and the head teacher having held her tongue for a consideration. They both left, it's true, but in the circumstances it would hardly have been Tidy who'd have got the sack unless her conduct too had been questionable. Besides, don't you remember that day she brought us the anonymous letters how, talking of Edith Drake, she suddenly flared out that she too had taught once and needed not to be told anything about the teaching profession?"

"Um-um," Lecky reflected. "Sour grapes? Hitting back? But it doesn't get us anywhere, not like the activities of the past year."

"I don't know. It sheds light on character. What's more, it bears indirectly on her planned vengeance on Phoebe Livingston-Bole, whom she undoubtedly followed to this part of the world. As I see it, Tidy turned sour after Ballantyne married Phoebe Young, having led Bertha up the path. Gosh, it was about as safe as pushing a doodlebug up same path. The school episode postdates the jilting, and I haven't a doubt it was then that misanthropy began to turn to something worse. It wouldn't be the first time blackmail's been tried as a gratifying means of getting one's own back from an unappreciative world—or sex."

Brook, all ears, fastened on the last word. "Funny all her victims were women."

"All the known ones," Lecky amended.

"Yes," Raikes said. "A man had thrown her over, but vanity as well, maybe, as some lingering, malicious hope in that direction stopped her exacting damages from men. A *woman* had profited by her loss, or so she supposed, so, as far as we know, it was women she took it out on. Though, mind you, indirectly again she was prepared to make inroads on Colonel Livingston-Bole's capital which his wife, having exhausted her own, might obtain from him—and much less indirectly was she aiming to get her clutch on Mr. Froggatt's fortune. Iris Kane's own resources would hardly have been worth a single effort. But Iris married was a potential gold mine."

"Well," Lecky sighed, "we're still shy of the real issue: which is, who killed her?"

"Brave man," Raikes said, "all set for a showdown."

"Whoever killed her," Brook growled, "murdered Miss Kingsley too."

The inspector shot him a quick look that was at the same time expressionless. "Not if it was Jane who killed her."

Lecky was audibly contemptuous. "What for? And if Jane Kingsley was Miss Tidy's murderer who'd be found to revenge Tidy?"

Raikes shrugged. "Léonie? Still, one at a time, please. Motive for Jane? Not so wobbly as you seem to think. Haven't Kingsley and his wife turned up an odd story of the girl hugging some secret in which she clearly took enough pride to withhold it? And that *after* the murder. Remember those girls seem to've been pretty hot on nocturnal prowls round the Minerva."

"Not Jane," Lecky put in quickly. "She lived at Stoneacre."

"We don't know," Raikes pointed out. "If, in fact, she had a motive for getting rid of her employer, the distance between Stoneacre and Ravenchurch wouldn't have been much obstacle. And we needn't put it past the ingenuity of a healthy, determined girl to absent herself at any hour without her relatives' knowledge. They've pulled the wool over their people's eyes before now."

"Granted," said the superintendent, in the tone of one who grants nothing of the sort. "But given the opportunity to hop over to Ravenchurch by night doesn't explain *why* she killed Tidy."

"Knowing Tidy by now, we shouldn't have far to look," Raikes returned with some acerbity. Ever since he had set foot in the place Lecky, jealous of the good name of his precious Ravenchurch, had tried to cramp his style. "Persecution of some sort, you can bet your life. Either in the petty, particularly hellish sense of employer to employed, or, if you want bigger stuff, why not blackmail in this instance too?"

"Because," Lecky said patiently, with the silent endorsement of the sergeant, "Jane Kingsley was poor by Miss Tidy's standards."

"*Touché.*" Raikes nodded. "I agree she attacked the wealthy or, at any rate, those, like Iris, with Great Expectations."

"And there," Lecky said, anxious to leave the subject of Jane, "a new line's opened up. Other wealthy people are still, presumably, in the land of the living, even in these days, and may well have been blackmailed by Tidy. What d'you say to one of tougher fiber than the suicides being the murderer?"

"Nothing against it," Raikes replied, "though I don't quite see that it opens up your new line. For the obvious notion all along was surely that she was killed by a victim of blackmail who preferred taking her life to his own?"

"Of course," the superintendent agreed. "I put it like that, I suppose, to wean you of the idea that Mrs. Wild, Mrs. Bates, Miss Oates, or the late Miss Kingsley might be responsible. Apart from other considerations, not one of her staff would measure up financially to Miss Tidy's blackmailing yardstick."

Raikes groaned. "I know, I know. But you go on overlooking the possibility that she wasn't after all murdered on account of being a blackmailer, but for some quite other reason, for which the blackmailing motive would prove an excellent cover. Disagreeable relations with one or another of the girls perhaps, creating an intolerable situation."

"People go on sticking intolerable situations of that sort," Lecky answered obstinately. "Or else they quit. They don't commit murder."

Raikes stared. "*Don't* they indeed? It's the crime which has been prompted again and again by more apparently trivial reasons than any other. Remember Wainwright and his victim's thick ankles? However, I'm going on to what you say about the chances of a tougher—perhaps still more desperate—victim of blackmail having killed her. And that brings us at once to two people, either of whom can be said to be sufficiently wealthy to have tempted Tidy to try it on."

"And they?" Lecky asked, knowing whom he meant.

"Kate Beaton and Owen Greatorex. Take the gentleman first. Although he's probably congratulating himself on how little he's given away, you and I and the sergeant here know what Ravenchurch knows—that he was well and truly run after by said Bertha Tidy."

"You suggest that's motive enough?"

"Don't you? *Ad nauseam*, I'd say. With or without blackmail too. Though if at any time there'd been indiscretion on the part of Greatorex—perhaps not misconduct but, say, letters, which might be more up a literary gent's tree—well, a little judicious pressure may have seemed just the thing to Tidy. Injudicious in the circumstances, as it proved—on the assumption that it was Greatorex who afterwards strangled her."

"So you think he'd have been let into the Minerva that night?"

"Why not? It's not a dead cert that those after-dark callers were *all* women, and Mrs. Weaver's testimony leaves the sex of the departing visitor on the night of the murder a moot question."

"What a risk for a man with his reputation to run!"

"Murderers are prepared to run greater yet. As for reputation, 'O Iago,' how can we tell in what worse peril it stood from Tidy if she were blackmailing him? It may well have been a case of balancing one risk against another and finding murder the minor one."

Lecky and Brook, to whom this hypothetical charge against Mr. Greatorex appeared about as substantial as one against the Albert Memorial, remained silent, and the inspector, caring little for unvocal opposition, continued.

"Not such a flimsy case, eh? He's got the requisites, you won't deny— wealth, standing, reputation, a way with the ladies he likes to keep quiet about. Isn't that what it takes? *And* the will and opportunity to defend jealously the wealth and reputation he intends holding onto. In short, shall we say, the very potential blackmail-ee of tougher fiber you hinted at just now?"

"I think you're wrong," Lecky said. "But go on."

"To another tack, then," Raikes said. "What about Miss Beaton? The lady doth protest too much, don't you think? Remember how I picked her for Poison Pen in the beginning, and how you crushed me, of course—but more of that later. Let's see now how she shapes for the other job—that of murder."

"She wasn't," Lecky observed, "in any sense a client of the Minerva—not for hats, tea, or beauty."

"Man alive! It's neither here nor there. Where Tidy was concerned the teashop wasn't the sole point of contact. It was the rendezvous for the Ravenchurch end of the business, but Miss Beaton's a resident of Long Greeting, Bertha Tidy's village too, and *that* end might prove even more sinister because less public."

"You never know," the experienced Brook agreed, "what's going on in those quiet spots."

"Well, as a matter of fact, you usually do, because the other villagers make it their business to know too. So the participants in any goings on have to be particularly cautious and clever where others make it their job to broadcast the precise hour of your bedtime, whether or not you turn the key in your back door, and what you told the postman the Friday before last. None of which weakens my case, since Misses Tidy and Beaton can both qualify as particularly clever women and may have hoodwinked even the Greetingites."

"What about?"

"Plenty. A superfluous question, really, where women are concerned. Their towers of mutual jealousy want no foundations. Anyway, the rivalry of those two need *not*, as it happens, have been in the least baseless. Wasn't Greatorex there to occasion it, not to say the usual power politics—who was to be chatelaine of Long Greeting?"

"That," Lecky said, quick on the mark, "was Mrs. Livingston-Bole's office."

"She, poor lady, was out of the running, I gather, some months before her death. And seeing how modestly she must at all times have fulfilled those functions, both Tidy and Miss Beaton would have considered her negligible."

"You don't mind my saying, do you," Lecky remarked after a pause, "that you're the most plausible beggar I ever struck?"

"Not in the least," Raikes replied. "But it's you would have it so—I'm only prosecuting counsel in the case of Rex v. your tough-fibered victim."

"All right," the superintendent admitted. "Only I must say I'm rather surprised at one thing in both the cases you've outlined."

"And that?"

"Why either of them, Mr. Greatorex or Miss Beaton, should go to Ravenchurch at night to kill Miss Tidy when they all three lived at Greeting and she could have been caught one night at the Keepsake. Why not?"

"Easy to answer on all counts," Raikes said. "Murdering Bertha Tidy at home where she received no mysterious callers would certainly limit the number of suspects. It meant, too, killing her, in a place where she always had company. Léonie was always there. So only Léonie could have killed her with comparative safety at the cottage. But doing the deed in Ravenchurch, in the teashop where she sat and slept alone at night, was a different matter—more trouble, perhaps, in one way, but just consider the baffling number of people it placed instantly under a cloud of suspicion."

Brook nodded. That was sound enough not to be plausible.

Lecky said, "That's true. That's why it's the very devil, all those people who'd have the opportunity for doing it at the Minerva, seeing she issued a sort of 'Walk into my parlor' invite by night, and the comparative few who could have committed the murder at the Keepsake." He sighed. "Well, if you're now pinning it on somebody alive-o that clears Jane Kingsley."

"If Jane didn't murder Tidy," Raikes said gravely, "whoever killed Tidy killed Jane. As the sergeant pointed out. In that case the confidence the brother says Jane started to make that night and then closed down on would in all probability be a piece of material evidence that made her a danger to the murderer."

"She was wanting, wasn't she," Lecky said, "to get quite clear what made one an accessory to murder? That being so, it hardly looks as though the secret you said just now she was hugging was the murder of Miss Tidy by herself."

"Old man," Raikes said with a weary smile, "I know it can be made to look absurd. What can't? I'm simply 'exploring every avenue.' *I* don't personally plump for Miss Kingsley as the murderer. But turning down preposterous theories is one way, if a negative one, of helping to arrive at the truth. Anyway, we'll say she didn't do it, and we'll look at the possibility of Miss Beaton's having killed Jane."

"Are you suggesting she called first on Miss Beaton, and they left the house together without the dogs? No one saw them go."

"Wait a minute. A rendezvous with someone in the village doesn't necessarily mean a house call. Say instead she arranged to meet Miss Beaton in the woods at the spot where she was killed. The dogs? Yes, they're important too. On an outing of that nature Miss Beaton wouldn't have had them with her."

"When Jane Kingsley left the bus early that afternoon she was seen to walk in a direction *opposite* to the one taken to enter the woods."

"Agreed. But it's quite reasonable to assume that she arrived in Greeting too early, because we know that the Stoneacre bus doesn't run there frequently enough to time it more exactly. We know when she was killed. In the lengthy interval between alighting from the bus and her death she wouldn't spend the whole time at the bench in the woods, surely."

"Then, sir," said Brook, who had been doing some hard thinking, "do you mean she started writing to Mrs. Wild on the postcard that was found, in the actual presence of her murderer? Because if she'd begun it while still waiting to meet the other party she wouldn't have broken off at the address, would she?"

"The postcard isn't much of a snag," Raikes pointed out. "Remember the pen was in her hand when she was struck. Maybe they'd already parted, and Jane, unsuspecting, lingered there to get her message posted in time in the letter box in the wall of the Place, and the murderer *came back* and killed her."

"Could be," Lecky muttered.

"Alternatively," Raikes went on, "she did call at somebody's house and, the interview over—or so she thought, poor girl—was desperate to get in touch with Mrs. Wild as soon as might be, and went to the bench to wait for her bus home and to write the p.c. meantime. And the murderer she'd left at home crept up on her in the wood."

"And that house," said Brook, with gloomy relish for a thrashed-out subject, "could only have been—"

"Miss Beaton's-the Place-Mile House-the Loggerheads-the locked-up Keepsake-the Rectory-Uncle Tom Cobleigh's an' all," Raikes sang out. "I know. But it needn't have been a house at all, nor yet the glade. Why not the garden of the Keepsake, where Blanchard was stripping the gooseberry bushes?"

"Of course," Lecky agreed. "That counts as the cottage itself, though. If Jane called there it was because she didn't know the house had been bottled up on Arthur Tidy's request."

"Unless, sir," Brook ventured again, "she *did* know, and the garden was the arranged meeting place for her and Blanchard, and gathering the fruit a pretext till Miss Kingsley arrived."

Nobody answered him directly. Each knew what, more or less, was in the mind of the other two. Then Raikes said quietly, "Things will be clearer tomorrow when I get the second report from the north. Let's leave the Greeting end open till then. Take a look at Ravenchurch—"

"Not *again*," Lecky groaned. "We know you've hankered to pin it on one of the staff—"

"Look here," Raikes, with a glint of temper, caught him up, "I'm not yearning to bring Bertha Tidy's murder home to one of the girls who worked for her. And you know it. I don't want to see a girl in the dock. But none of us dare lose sight of one or two factors in this ugly business. One, that while Tidy sat there o' nights she could let into the teashop whom she damn well liked, so that the question of entry, of how the murderer got in, never arose. Ergo, anybody could have got in that night. Again, because Tidy was a blackmailer doesn't *necessarily* mean she was killed on that count. Ten to one she was, but we simply can't afford to rule out motives not impinging on blackmail. A corrupt man or woman is corrupt in more than one sense. If she could blackmail, there were other things she could do. You've emphasized that her staff's individual incomes could be no temptation to Tidy. I agree. But say £.s.d. never entered into it? Then I say, and shall go on saying till it's disproved by facts, that Samela Wild, Crystal Bates, Jane Kingsley, and, yes, Marion Oates too are legitimately on the list of suspects."

"You're right," Lecky said, taken aback at this warmth, "and I wasn't suggesting you wanted Mrs. Wild or one of the others charged with murder. But I still can't see it other than the red herring—"

"Of course not," Raikes said more genially. "After all, you've lived with Mrs. Bates and Co.—oh, quite platonically, I mean—in a manner of speaking, you know, and to you they're still the Three Little Girls from School, not yet emerged from the cocoon of innocence and all that—"

"Pipe down," Lecky shut him up. "Let's admit you're justified in suspecting all of 'em, and get off your chest whatever's on it."

"It was really removed before," Raikes said, "when I indicated that Mrs. Wild had made the case against her blacker than need be by her behavior at the time of the discovery of the murder—crashing in without first ringing up the Keepsake, tampering with the teashop key which was found in her handbag, and invariably putting on a bad show in an interview. *Not* a satisfactory lady. On all such points as those the case against Mrs. Bates is a weak one. It's true she turned up last that morning, which may have been engineered to make her a passive spectator of Mrs. Wild's or Miss Kingsley's discovery of the body. In any case I doubt very strongly if she has the brains to murder anyone and not betray herself in the first quarter of an hour."

"Well, sir," said Brook on a heavy note, feeling that Marion was under his peculiar patronage, "I think you may feel safer where Miss Oates is concerned—I don't mean exactly from the standpoint of brains—"

"Oh no," Raikes returned, "decidedly *not* on the standpoint of brains."

Lecky looked surprised. "I wouldn't say the child had more than average."

"With the possible exception of Mrs. Wild," the inspector said, "I'd say she has more than the other two put together. And not so much of the child business. There's a bitter core of maturity, or perhaps prematurity, about Marion Oates. She leads her aunts blindfolded. She's the Dark Horse of the Minerva. And though murder by adolescent girls is a rarity, thanks be, the likelihood can't be discarded if you consider how far she may've been pushed."

They were all silent, two of them at least reflecting on the enormities of human nature that did the pushing.

A spark in the inspector's eye warned Lecky that the insatiable man was probably hot on a new trail. He was right.

"What say," said Raikes pleasantly, "to Mrs. Weaver as the murderer?"

Lecky astonished him by putting up no opposition. "Opportunity, ability, she qualifies for those all right. Motive? Oh well, you'll say same old hidden hand there."

"No, I won't," said the inspector. "Because blackmail's a possibly better answer in her case. Mrs. Weaver, remember, is turning a pretty penny with her rare books, and probably has been doing for years. And she *was*, on the evidence, invited to call that night—the only one we know that was."

"She's a very strong woman, though old," Brook said gravely. "But if it was blackmail, sir, what would she be paying Miss Tidy to keep quiet about?"

"Every life can turn up something worth a blackmailer's while," was the unhopeful reply.

Lecky and Brook began a hasty and wordless examination of their own. Raikes yawned.

"Merely tired's not in this," he said. "I've got myself giddy. I'm nearly in the state to believe the Rev. Mr. Buskin may've done both murders."

"Make it Mr. Trumpington," Lecky complained, "and I'm with you."

"I could make out a lovely case against him," Raikes confessed with a final gleam of humor.

CHAPTER 14

Pray, when will that be?
Say the bells of Stepney.

The Rev. Daniel Buskin was curiously unaware for the most part of what was going on in his immediate surroundings, though he was not blind in Mrs. Weaver's rather wilful sense of the word. Too much alive to issues outside the common ken, he ignored overlong the things close at hand, forgetting that it was those, cumulatively considered, that were apt to become too weighty for easy handling.

Broken windows, anonymous messages scrawled in public, potshots in the dark, had not been part and parcel of his daily experience. They were unfamiliar stains on the Long Greeting landscape, hitherto so quiet a corner of the background to the Ravenchurch picture that it had failed to attract that rougher element which looks to the twilight hours for such practices.

He walked in the churchyard frequently these days, liking the company of the great untended trees, elm, chestnut, lime, forced by proximity to struggle skywards, too lofty even to murmur to the dark yew and cypress crouching far below. They had their music, though, like that of heaven, whose doors they seemed to brush; they were bird- and squirrel-lively, quick with dumb motion, for song was rare here except the robin's. Once he had seen a hedgehog, soundless too, snouting withered leaves between the thrusty roots of oak. Here the grasses were long and undisciplined, embracing the tilted headstones of two centuries, wiping the crumpled faces of cherubs that simpered their grief above them.

There he could think, and feel, which was better than thought. But over here, where he came more often in the past weeks, was the newer, tidier ground. The grass was trim and cropped, the graves for the most part raw, or where stones had been erected not gray-green, flaky, and enriched by time, but chaste marble and granite polished till it gave the lie to its name.

A few of the mounds were still strange, uneasy comers to this patch of earth. The spiky grass grew meanly about them, almost with timidity, as if, he told himself, conscious of their yet unsettled state. He bent now over the one closest to the path, shadowed by no boughs, open to the liberal spending of the sun. It was here he had read for Iris the burial service for the dead.

There were the roses again, twelve of them, perfect, their narrow heads still glittering with dew. Roses had appeared, with other flowers, ever since the funeral, but none like these till the last few days. Yesterday he had come on Mrs. Kane arranging aquilegia in the vase at the foot. He spoke to her of the beauty of the roses.

"They're not mine," she said in a cold, remote voice without lifting her head. She always spoke like that, without either rancor or warmth. He left her.

Perhaps they were Christopher Froggatt's. But he never saw him place them here. The roses that were a day old in the evening, in the morning were fresh ones again. In all Long Greeting and Stoneacre he knew of one garden only that grew roses like these.

Mr. Buskin was assailed by a torment of doubt and a certainty that was worse than doubt. Years ago he had learned how to resolve worry into purpose and intention. He knew now that he wanted to see his friend, Father Connolly, to whom he had not talked for nearly a month, more than anyone else on earth.

He took the next bus into Ravenchurch, looking with his white, hatless head and glowing eyes like a prophet astray from his world. When he reached the presbytery they told him that Father Connolly had gone down less than twelve hours earlier with a sickness the doctors, awaiting analysis, had suggested might be food poisoning; he was delirious and could not see anyone.

2

Scotland Yard outlined its plan to catch a murderer, and Ravenchurch, in the person of Superintendent Lecky, listened.

"I don't expect you to see eye to eye with me over this," Raikes admitted, precluding objection. "I suggest only that we try it. You see, where a killer has already accounted for two victims, the law of diminishing returns begins to function with regard to caution and lying low, and things of that sort which in the ordinary way are obstacles to running him down."

"You mean he's more reckless than the one-man murderer?"

"As a rule. Let him kill two, and temporarily get away with it, and he's only half as prudent—or twice as imprudent, if you like—as the man who does his single murder and lets it stop at that."

"I know that applies in general to poisoners," the superintendent said slowly. "But these are crimes of remarkable violence, crude in execution for all their effectiveness, and I would have thought—"

"That the hand that committed 'em in heat and turmoil was frightened now of its own achievements?"

"More or less," Lecky said after a moment's reflection. He did not always follow the inspector's more agile mind.

"Don't you believe it. Poison seems the more deliberate method, because it's quiet, slow, cumulative—I'm thinking, of course, of arsenic rather than cyanide—but don't from that get the wrong inference that the apparently more brutal murders, which agitate their locality like rocks flung into a pool, are *not* committed by cold and calculating people. Because they are. Practical violence needn't be the outward and visible sign of impetuosity, you know."

"Well, if it's who you say it is," Lecky said, "I'd have agreed there was very little of the impulsive there."

"So I thought. Which brings me back to my muttons. I'll warrant it's easier to commit one's third murder than the first. For, besides the recklessness which grows with power, the lapse of time which leaves the murderer uncharged with his crime also gives rise to a slow passion of resentment against being thwarted. *At all costs* he will continue to defend his personal security, so he paradoxically imperils it as often as not, since the costs may well be successive murders."

Lecky was nervous of these academic considerations, because he hated them. He much preferred brass tacks, even when they were spiky and unpleasant. He recalled Raikes to the here and now.

"That's all very well," he said firmly. "And it would look nice on paper. But, as it happens, we don't want a third murder. We can't *have* a third murder—*at all costs*, as you said just now, we have to avoid a third murder."

"We shall." The superiority Lecky had from the first found offensive in Raikes edged the assured phrase, and the smile intended to mollify his own earnestness did not improve matters.

"It's not *your* life, nor mine," he snapped, "you propose risking."

"I don't," Raikes retorted, "propose risking anybody's life. What I do propose is persuading the murderer to *believe* that another life is being risked. That's a different matter. As I see it, the temptation will be too great. And a third attempt, which we *know* will be unsuccessful, will be made. And it's voluntary cooperation I'm looking for from the one who's to run the apparent danger."

Lecky came as near a snort as his mild-mannered nose could compass. "The voluntary part of the business doesn't make the plan a more defensible one."

"You're too good to be true," Raikes sighed. "To my unregenerate mind it's at least as defensible as trapping would-be blackmailers and kidnappers and what have you by baiting 'em with the potential victim while the police hide near by."

"I'm not concerned in the very least," Lecky said coldly, "with the ethics of nabbing criminals. Get 'em how you will before their mischief spreads. What I'm defending is the cheese in the mousetrap, whether it was put in or walked in—"

"Like Gorgonzola." Raikes grinned. "Well, maybe my cheese will refuse to go in. Then you'll be perfectly happy, and I'll have to think up plan number two. Now, to clear up our other business. Catch a murderer by all means, but first I've got to see Léonie Blanchard about the anonymous letters."

The superintendent brightened. Anything providing even temporary relief from Strictly Murder business was more than welcome.

"Queer," he said with the thoroughly cozy note that banishes exacerbation, "that we didn't spot such a characteristic at once."

"In a way, you know," Raikes replied, "we did. All our fuss and faddle about the stilted phraseology, the odd inversions and punctuation—remember? We grew hot, as the children say, but never quite made it, and it took a reading aloud to make me tumble to the fact it was a foreigner's English."

"We did read 'em aloud in the beginning," Lecky reminded him.

"I know. I should have said, a reading aloud by the right person."

"By Miss Beaton." The emphasis the superintendent gave to her name was as if he were breaking a spell by overcoming the reluctance to speak it.

"Yes—somebody who could read with intelligence and expression. She's a novelist, so, I assumed, had the necessary imagination and skill to read an unprepared script and interpret its finer shades. She did, with complete success. Listening to those letters in the Beaton rendering I knew exactly what it was had bothered me that day at the Keepsake with Léonie's terse conversation in my ears. The accent was precisely that of Poison Pen."

Lecky blew a gusty sigh. "Well-a-day, we know now what was behind those letters."

Raikes looked grim. "Yorkshire leaves us in no doubt, eh?"

"And the Kanes at any rate knew. They admit it now."

"They've no alternative. Of course they knew. Income from the money settled unofficially on Blanchard by the father—no names, no pack drill, and he's not of consequence now—has been paid over by her at regular intervals, first to the Yorkshire Kanes, then to these, up to the time Iris was earning a wage."

"Fleur-de-Lis," Lecky reflected. "It means an iris." He spoke as though pathos attached to that alone. When Raikes said nothing, he went on, "A funny thing that Léonie was content to leave her in ignorance of the relationship. The girl never guessed it, that I'll swear, and the Kanes have pretty well sworn it too."

The inspector nodded. "Mrs. Kane offers a sort of explanation, though—that the woman was waiting with all the patience you'd expect, hoarding and scraping for pride's sake so as to be able to leave Tidy's service and come to the child not penniless. An ambition which the girl's coming marriage precluded. Having sacrificed so much for twenty years, Blanchard wouldn't jeopardize such a match for the daughter she idolized by declaring herself."

"Abnegation," Lecky said with surprising insight. "It breeds abnegation. Easier to go on keeping silence twenty years afterwards than it was when Fleur was a month old."

"No doubt. But as to its being funny she kept the relationship a secret from Iris, *is* it so funny after all? Blanchard's a Breton peasant, a Catholic, an uncultured woman of limited intellect, boundless intelligence, and rigid principle—oh yes, unprincipled, if you like. It makes no difference to what I've said. And because she was these things, she believed Iris, who was her darling and her blessing and the very core of her life, was also her sin—her Sin, in prominent and red capitals. It was an unconfessed sin, for by claiming her as a daughter she feared to extend the stain to her too."

Raikes leaned back, a little out of breath at his own warmth. Meeting Lecky's stare, he stretched in a yawn, then, tilting forward again, thumped the arm of his chair.

"God, how I sometimes hate the muck of police work!"

Lecky was silent. He knew what track his mind was traveling on now. His had run onto the same line. The end was at hand, but it had not yet come, and suddenly, invaded by funk, he wished himself into the day after tomorrow.

Raikes stood up. " '*Aux armes, citoyens!*' " he hummed with the old brittle carelessness, and then, "That's done with, and there's work to do. There's Léonie to tackle with the letters. There's volunteers to invite, or rather one, for the harder job of arresting a murderer."

"If only," Lecky said, "you weren't looking for your volunteer among the innocent and——"

Raikes gave him a quick look. "You sound very sure of the innocence."

3

On the afternoon of the day on which Raikes engaged the necessary help for setting his trap, Samela Wild was walking alone in a street behind the cinema. George, who had first bothered her to stay indoors and then bothered her more fiercely to let him come along too, was in the flat absorbed in an essay on Meredith the *Timekeeper*'s editor had asked for and he himself, as she very well knew, was longing to get to work on.

She walked with spirit, for all that she was miserable. How ridiculous, in any case, to be afraid to walk abroad in Ravenchurch in daylight, Ravenchurch where she had been born and gone to school and had a great deal of fun and met and married George. It was worse than ridiculous, it was treachery. But Ravenchurch had changed these days. She had to admit that. The street was moderately busy at this hour approaching teatime, yet though she encountered a half dozen and more shoppers she knew no greetings were exchanged. What made the omissions particularly horrid was the unpurposive way they each ignored her; nobody made a point of cutting, everyone looked gently past her and was gone. It might all have been accidental, so ordinary it was. Was it? Had nobody seen her among those shops where everyone, like the heedless ant, was intent on individual business? Perhaps so, and perhaps she was just fancying slights like a touchy adolescent. That would never do.

She was worried, of course, because of the weight on her mind. Then she saw, bearing down on her, a woman whom she knew quite well as a client of the Minerva beauty culture. They met, and the rather prominent eyes behind tortoiseshell rims looked squarely into Samela's. The woman turned with a gesture of impatience as if at her own forgetfulness, and abruptly mounted two steps into a jeweler's close by. That, thought Samela, *was* deliberate. The next moment she had recalled how shortsighted Mrs. Falkin was. But this vacillation of hers did nothing to dispel worry or remove the weight from her mind. And when she thought about that she felt sickish and cold.

She stuck her chin out and smiled faintly at her resolute reflection in the windows. Then she looked across the street for no reason whatever, at the fishmonger's almost deserted shop, and caught sight of Léonie Blanchard, standing like the specter of a grenadier beside the naked slab.

Samela's heart thumped, and she went on walking without properly knowing what she was doing, because there was something she had particularly to say to Léonie, and in the ordinary way saying it would have meant either a call at Mile House or else a letter. Both were distasteful. Better this way, perhaps. Now or never.

Even while she considered she stopped at a florist's window and looked searchingly at a display of sweet peas she did not see. Was she always to be like this, shirking contacts, evading responsibility? Heaven forbid. If Léonie were still in the same place when she turned round she would at least fortify her crumbling morale by getting one little piece of business over.

She spun round. Léonie was still there. Sammy crossed the road without hesitation and stood at her side.

She did not, after all, have to open the ball. Léonie, who apparently gave no attention to her entry, went on addressing the fishmonger with a scorn as icy as his unaccommodating slab.

"No, I cannot take *that*. I will 'ave the bream, if it is *all* that you 'ave."

Without moving, scarcely without pause, she lowered her eyes to Samela and added, "Mee-sis Vild, is it not?"

Sammy was disconcerted. Here, it was true, was somebody who made no attempt to avoid her. But the way Léonie had thrown in the remark as tailpiece to her unsatisfactory purchase might, she supposed, be interpreted as an insult even more direct. *This would not do*, she told herself for the second time that afternoon; and the gust of anger she felt for her own hypersensitivity rallied her to smile at the woman.

"Yes indeed," she said. "I saw you over here. I've wanted to run across you. I haven't seen you anywhere since—since—" She blundered to a stop. "I haven't seen you for weeks."

Léonie took her fish from the hapless man and carefully selected the exact sum in payment. She walked out, and Samela went with her.

"Is it so long?" Léonie said with devastating indifference. "I was at the inquest."

Samela knew she did not mean Jane's. "Oh yes. But I couldn't speak to you then."

"No? What is it then that you would say?"

Sammy stopped walking and Léonie, after a moment's hesitation, stopped too.

"I can't tell you here," Sammy said with quiet difficulty. She glanced up and down the street and wished it were all over. "There's something, though, I have to be sure about. You can help me, if you will. But first I shall have to show you something."

Léonie shrugged. "But if you do not tell me here, you come to the 'ouse of Mees-ter *Gray-tor-ay, hein?*"

"I don't want to," Samela confessed frankly. "But if you liked, I could meet you at the Keepsake. The police have done with it from tomorrow morning."

Léonie said nothing for a moment that weighed heavily on Samela. Then she declared firmly, "That may be. But Meester Tidy, no. He 'ave it locked."

"Oh, but he's not going to. The padlock business was only while the inspector was bothering about it too." She added with a rush, "That will be removed tomorrow. If you've got your key—well, I could meet you there, and—it would be private."

There was another uncompromising silence. Then Léonie asked almost dreamily, "Why is it that you 'ave to be sure of something?"

"So as not to go on thinking wrong of a friend," Samela blurted, and was annoyed at her own confusion. Really, she was treating a simple discussion like the bull the china shop.

Léonie frowned. "So? When is it, then?"

"When's what?" said Sammy stupidly.

"When you come to the 'ouse?"

"To the cottage? Oh, I'd rather come in the evening, if that's all right. I'm freer then. And this is private." She felt she had said that too often. "Say—"

"Yes?"

"Nine o'clock?"

"Too light. Eleven," said Léonie.

"That's late," Samela answered doubtfully. She braced herself. "All right."

4

Crystal Bates took out her bicycle, though it wasn't far to the Slip, saying nothing to Ken, who was sniffy these days anyway and would have objected strongly even to this innocuous errand if he had been told about it.

He had had his own ideas about the murders from the beginning; that is, about Miss Tidy's, for Jane's had rather shaken his original theory of a homicidal maniac who had crowned his successive "suicide" killing with the attack on Bertha Tidy. All the same, he had retained his own opinion as to the identity of the killer and had hinted more than once that he could tell the police a thing or two if they cared to consult him. That they had shown no inclination to date to do so did not better his judgment of their intelligence. Well, they might yet live and learn.

Crystal wondered if a cartoonist's work stimulated observation in the direction of selecting a murderer by his physical attributes. Nobody surer than Kenneth for spotting cragginess and muscular potentialities for the purpose of line caricature; perhaps, as he claimed, he had also a flair for more deadly discernment? He was so much brainier than she was anyway.

She shivered a little, feeling the prickle of goose flesh, when she remembered where his suspicions lay and what she had had in her mind this afternoon. Not exactly *on* her mind, of course; responsibility and thought alike had a flittermouse quality for Crystal. Because she was mentally superficial and ultimately insensitive, the significance of any charge laid upon her by herself or others worried her little. That was why she sometimes carried out successfully tasks that the more intelligent failed to achieve.

She was glad she had not told Ken she was going out. After yesterday's outrage on Sammy he had grown fussy about solitary expeditions. Not, she argued, that you were so likely to be attacked cycling. It gave you a kind of advantage. But of course she wouldn't be on the bicycle all the time.

What an age since she'd even glimpsed Mrs. Weaver! She'd never at any time come across her as the others had done, not so frequently, for example, as Jane and Marion, who liked poetry and messing about with old books. Books were not much up her street. Staying beautiful took a big slice from the leisured snippets of one's day, and makeup and hairdo were more absorbing than reading. Awfully heretical, of course, but one ought to be frank, and that's how it was. And *old* books she thought rather smelly.

She jumped off her cycle and ran it into the Slip just as they used to do.

She was glad she was able to pass the silent Minerva without a shudder. She had nerve, she told herself; and that was what Inspector Raikes knew too.

The next minute she was not so sure, for when she pushed the door of the bookshop and went inside a hideous jangle rose from her feet. She was not used to the device, or else had forgotten it, and, stuffing a hand to her mouth, stupidly stood her ground and heard it shrilling. Then she gathered what was the matter and bounded off the mat.

"Hell's bells!" she exclaimed, unconsciously describing them.

She waited, as in other shops, for someone to come. The world of books was unfamiliar to her; she did not grasp that other conditions obtained there. She waited, but nobody came.

This chilly reception, or lack of it, she found eerie, but was not much perturbed on that account. Words to Crystal were flat-bodied symbols, never experienced in the round, the bones of them not felt. While she chattered excitedly of the uncanny and the disturbing, their fingers never knocked at her ribs.

"Funny show," she commented in a soft voice, and decided that the angular shoulders of the bookcases with their indeterminate shadows did not invite exploration. She stood her ground and called in a clear voice, "Mrs. Weav-er!"

"Here."

She was startled then, in her own impermanent fashion, for the voice coming from an invisible presence might have issued from ground or air.

"I'm here," the words were repeated with a hint of autocracy that suggested Mahomet must come to the mountain, "if you want me."

"Funny show," said Crystal, whose vocabulary was a limited one. "Funny way to treat customers." She went in quest of Mrs. Weaver.

The bookseller sat in her corner writing a letter with extreme care. She was using an old-fashioned wooden penholder with a hard, pointed nib, and indited each painstaking word in thin, wavering lines, like—like, Crystal thought in a strenuous burst of imagination, the filaments of a spider's web.

She watched, fascinated, without disturbing her, till in another half minute Mrs. Weaver lifted her head and regarded her quizzically. Crystal saw what she had not noticed before, that she was wearing steel-rimmed spectacles, behind which her eyes looked smaller and indrawn. Mrs. Weaver, however, removed them at once, wiping the lenses with slow movements that missed nothing, and, shutting them down in a worn case, addressed Crystal.

"Ah, another of the handmaidens of Athene," she said, ponderously attempting a joke. "You honor me, my dear. You know, I always thought *my* place would have been better with that title—Minerva, you know, learning and all that—and yours should have been the Aphrodite, perhaps."

Crystal, always befogged by classical allusions, assented with the sort of sickly smile one proffers as camouflage for ignorance. Mrs. Weaver eyed her with some curiosity.

"*You*'ve not been after the books before, have you?"

"Oh no," Crystal said hastily, alarmed at the thought, though she didn't really suppose Mrs. Weaver was imputing pinching to Sammy or Titus or poor old Jane. "I—I came in to see you because I had something to say which I think you ought to know."

"That's a change," said Mrs. Weaver, chuckling in a way Crystal did not altogether enjoy. "Most people come to hear what *I* know. Won't you sit down—and perhaps take a cup of tea with me? Earlyish, I know, but I have to push all my meals on to fit in with my busy hours. Now over a cup of tea—"

"Oh, really no," Crystal cried with a fervor she herself felt was overdone. "I daren't stop for tea. I've a little shopping to do, and then I must go back to feed my husband."

Mrs. Weaver's expression became benign. "That's very nice," she said indulgently. "Not that I'd poison you, you know, if you did drink a cup with me. Oh no. That sort of thing's all right if it's a party of you, but with only you and me it would soon be traced to me, wouldn't it?"

Crystal made an effort to counter this sally with a fitting outbreak of mirth, but was a little alarmed at her own stridency. She caught herself wishing Ken were outside looking in at the window—or, better still, inside. But he'd be mad, anyway, if he knew she were here.

"I'm growing quite reckless, don't you think?" Mrs. Weaver went on primly. "What did you want to say to me?"

Crystal said it.

There was a considerable silence. Mrs. Weaver was seen to be smiling faintly.

"I dare say," she said, "everybody knew that was always what I wanted."

"We guessed," Crystal agreed.

"Of course. I was probably a little obvious. Not *too* obvious, I hope?"

"I don't think so."

"Do you think I was foolish to bide my time?"

"No-o. You—you couldn't exactly have hurried it."

"Not with Bertha Tidy." Her tone was so unamiable that Crystal made no reply.

Mrs. Weaver looked at her. "And what, Mrs. Bates, do you suggest?"

"Why, nothing really. I thought I'd leave it to you. But it *will* be unlocked tomorrow, and—"

"Yes?"

"Well, Mr. Tidy will be there—later."

Mrs. Weaver stared at her, then suddenly bent herself backwards in a peal of laughter Crystal found anything but agreeable.

"Dear child," she gasped, ending as she had begun, "*are* you implying I should get in first and ...?"

"I only meant," Crystal explained, "that he *will* be there—tomorrow."

She wanted now to get away. Mrs. Weaver, defining her anxiety, rose, almost inch by inch, thought Crystal, impressed by her stature. She was accompanied on her way back to the door; in the narrow alley between the stacks it was Crystal who was obliged to walk in front.

She wished her a breathless good afternoon and slipped out, the bell jeering shortly at her dismay.

In such a hurry was she that she spared no backward glance for Emmie Weaver, and so missed in her eye the glitter of anticipated triumph that even the spectacles would have failed to dout.

5

There was time, however, for Marion to look back before she turned the corner of Thistle Square. Yes, there was the movement of the curtain she had come to expect; one or other of the aunts watching her out of sight—watching, watching, always watching. If it were not that they were so self-effacing and she herself so enmeshed by another interest, unremitting solicitude of this sort would have driven her crazy. As it was, she accepted it as part of the stagey horror they were all living in. Behind the scenes, she supposed, life must be going on much as before. But not for them, who strutted and postured before the curtain that, descending, had shut them off from the best of all enjoyments, common, unsuspecting intercourse with one another. Instead were there sidelong exchanges, dumb evasions.

Now there was this task imposed upon her. Oh, no compulsion—she had voluntarily assumed its burden. That was why it was impossible to get rid of it except by performance. Self-loyalty was a far grimmer taskmaster than the loyalty you gave to other people. This was something she owed to herself, to Crystal, to Samela—how much to Samela—above all to Jane. They used to think at the teashop—she knew, though they kept it dark—that Jane harried her a bit at work, was sharp because she was sometimes clumsy. What did they know? Jane ... she had loved Jane.

The bus for Long Greeting would have left if she didn't hurry. She pressed on, as if in response to a summons so imperative that there could be no question of procrastination. She must know. She must *know*. Running the last few yards, she mounted the step as the bus began to move, and sat down close to the door, a little breathless.

She felt again all hands and feet and ugly perspiration; a pang of the self-consciousness that assailed her at odd moments brought the familiar discomfort. Never would she have the poise and self-confidence of the others, though Dr. Hare had told Aunt Win it was only growing pains. How could she expect to make the right impression this afternoon? It was important not to blunder through gaucherie; if she did, how easy it would be to put her off and withhold the knowledge she had to have.

She gazed at the country, sleeping and stretched along the road they traveled. Summer, hot and enfolding, was at its loveliest in the afternoon when clouds lay anchored in the tideless blue, and the flat shadows of field and stream were like hands soothing to slumber. Summer had been Jane's season. All the tawny glow of her was drawn from it, and all extinguished now. She bent her chin low, so that nothing higher than the hedgetops met her eyes, and watched, stern lips set, the ranks of lacy cow parsley slipping by, with here and there flashes of beauty from the crane's bill that looked like patches of the sky.

She got out at the Loggerheads and walked back a short way along the road they had come.

The house, she thought, looked as shut-eye and moldy as ever. Summer might endow meadow and water with every sort of grace; it left this four-square block untouched by warmth or renewal.

"It may as well be winter," Marion muttered, and walked up the path to the front door.

The knocker made rather more noise than she had reckoned for, yet it did not equal the clamor which broke out at once inside. She breathed relief, though her heart bumped quickly. The dogs were at home, and that meant that Miss Beaton would not yet have started on her afternoon walk.

Marion clenched her hands, waiting. The door was opened by Miss Beaton herself, who paid no attention to the babel about her. When the dogs saw Marion their uproar diminished to servile curvettings and whines.

"They like you," Kate Beaton said. She was clad unexpectedly in a much worn dressing gown of brickish hue that gave her a barrellike appearance. Her short tousled hair stuck out in all directions. Marion thought she looked rather like a harassed Father Christmas at the end of a day in a London store.

She blinked, frowned, and examined the girl's face uncertainly.

"I *do* know you," she said bluntly, "but I can't put a name to you."

"I'm Marion Oates," Marion said without cordiality. "I worked in the Minerva teashop."

"Right," said Miss Beaton. "Come in."

Marion hesitated, then plunged into the hall with an unintentional fervor which dashed even the Airedales. It was dim in here, with unguessed regions behind. She turned a little wildly to Miss Beaton.

"Don't shut the door!"

"Oh, but the dogs will get out." She scrutinized the pale, earnest face. "What is it—claustrophobia?"

Marion, a little uncertain of the term, nodded.

"Deary-dear," Kate Beaton clucked. Well, everything might be turned into copy. But she had discerned the panic. "Look, I'll shut the beasts in the kitchen. Then we'll talk here."

She drove the dogs hastily into that dark recess Marion sensed rather than saw, vanished, banged a door, and was back at her side in a moment.

"You want me?" she asked, and contrived without marked friendliness to hearten her visitor. "What is it?"

Marion told her.

CHAPTER 15

I do not know,
Says the great bell of Bow.

In the housekeeper's room at Mile House, temporarily relinquished by the dazed Mrs. Phail, who might be said to have reached the light-headed stage, the inspector sat in silence waiting for Léonie to comment on the letters which lay on the table between them. Superintendent Lecky, hands in pockets, stood with his back to them, gazing out of the window onto the kitchen garden that did not grow gooseberries.

In his study Owen Greatorex gnawed his nails decorously and wondered why it was taking three policemen to conduct this morning's enquiry.

Léonie, thought Raikes, was changed, though the change might be an indefinable one. The eagle-eyed look was waning. She seemed to be indulging a fatigue she had not had time for till now. It lent at least a veneer of submission to her bowed head and the big hands knotted in her lap. He wondered what she would say when she found her voice.

When at last she spoke it was in words they had not expected. Without lifting her eyes she announced, "There are many others that I write also."

Lecky, who had been chinking coins in his pocket, fell silent. After a moment Raikes asked quietly, "To Miss Tidy?"

"But of course. There is not any other."

Raikes pointed to the sheets on the table. "There was Miss Beaton."

"Yes. But one has not to warn *her*. I ask that she should warn Mees Bert'a."

"I know. But why were you so anxious for Miss Bertha to be warned?"

She looked at him heavily. "That she may not die with the sin upon her."

"What sin?"

"You *know* the sin. You think *I* do not?"

"I'm asking you."

"The sin that make others pay for theirs."

"That makes people pay for errors committed?"

"*Mais oui*. That is what Mees Bert'a do—oh, but all the time."

"We call it blackmail," Raikes said. "So you knew Miss Tidy was a blackmailer?"

Léonie shrugged with a wealth of expression. She seemed to be rousing herself. "I? I do not know these names. I am a simple woman."

Lecky, flashing a glance at the inspector over her head, saw that Raikes had momentarily shut his eyes as if in prayer for the audacity.

"You know exactly what blackmail is, if you don't know its name," he said. "How did you find out?"

"But that, it is not difficult. I live with her."

"Blackmail is more secret than—murder."

"So? But I, I work for her twenty years—more. There are no secrets."

"I believe you," said Raikes under his breath.

"Mees Bert'a, she talk. She must talk, sometimes. I am always there, you understand, like the chair, like the table in the kitchen." She spoke the last words loudly. "One is accustomed to me. It is not thought that I have the mind, the mouth, the eyes, but only the ears—to hear when the tongue, it would take a holiday from prison."

She checked herself on a breathless note, afraid, it seemed, that she had said too much.

"And what," Raikes asked softly, "did Miss Tidy's tongue let slip when it had escaped from prison?"

She gave him a cold look. "I do not know—now. It is long to remember. I am a simple woman—and the memory, it is not good."

"Oh come now, it's only a little while ago," the inspector reminded her cheerfully. "When you were writing these letters."

"I warn her," she said dully, as if repeating a lesson.

"Yes, of course. You warned her. But how could you know that she was going to die?"

She gave him a look full of chill pity. "I do not know. I do not know that she will die. But I know that they who live by the evil money, it is often that they die."

Raikes sighed. "And just as often they don't."

"People do not pay for their sin to people," she went on in a steady voice. "They pay to God only. She forget that. And she forget that God, His eye it is on her." She flicked a thumb at the letters. "I tell her. That is all."

"Not quite all." Raikes was firm. "Why did you take the trouble to paste together unsigned letters? You lived with her and could have spoken."

Léonie spread eloquent hands. "But I—*I* who am the servant? I who serve and not speak? I who do not know? You understand, it is I, Léonie Blanchard, who am but the mat for the wiping of the feet. Who look to the mat for counsel? If a nail hurt the foot also," she added with sudden craft, "one does not think to blame the mat at the door."

"So you don't think she ever suspected these letters came from you?"

"*Mais non.* Nev-aire. I try to stop her before she get killed. Oh yes, in *speech* I warn her that she go too often at night to the café, that one will kill her there. She laugh. I write the letters to stop her being evil to others. I write many. Some I send to the café."

"But if, as you say, she talked sometimes, there perhaps was the best reason for her to suspect you. You were the one who had listened to things that had, perhaps, better not have been said."

"She does not," said Léonie scornfully, "talk as you suppose. She does not say to me, 'I blackmail 'im, I blackmail 'er.' Mees Bert'a, she is the clever one. Sometimes she say, 'Léonie, 'ow I 'ate some people. If only I knew to make the little image and stick in it the pins.' "

Both Lecky and Raikes looked at her sharply.

"I think," Léonie added, "she make the little image. But I think she do not stick in it the pin."

"No?"

"*Mais non.* I think that she drown it."

"Mercy on us!" muttered the superintendent, and turned back to the wholesome if uninspiring potato crop.

"Whom," asked Raikes casually, "did she make the image of?"

"Of a beautiful one who live near."

"Mrs. Livingston-Bole?"

She veiled her eyes slowly. Her face was blank. "I do not know."

"But there is a great deal that you do know. I wonder if you recognize this?"

From an envelope on the table beside him he drew the photograph Miss Livingston-Bole had sent him and, with splayed fingers pressing it firmly, pushed it towards Blanchard.

He saw her whiten and suck in her breath. Her fingers made a predatory swoop on the picture, then she withdrew her hand and shrank tightly, almost timorously, in the chair.

"Where you get it?" she whispered huskily. "I take it, I burn it—it is nothing any more." She collected her wits. "This, it is not the photo I put in the fire. You 'ave another."

"Why," Raikes asked, "did you burn the one from the locker?"

"She give it to the Evil One."

"How?"

She pointed at the girl Phoebe without touching her. "She—the beautiful one—she destroy her with acid. When there is no face on her, she keep it by her bed, always."

Raikes took it back, and with it the letters. "I see," he said, pushing them into the envelope. "These were dangerous letters to write. They are not only a warning against *being murdered*. Some would read them as a threat *to murder*. You know that, don't you?"

Léonie shook her head. Her eyes, under their drooping lids, looked at him glassily. "I do not know. I am a simple woman. Yes, it is I who write the letters. I write the letters to warn her."

Lecky, moving up to the table, looked down at her. "Léonie," he said quietly, "is there anything further you would care to say before we go?"

While she answered him she looked still at Raikes. "But no. There is nothing."

Lecky chinked a coin or two uncertainly. "When you thought Miss Tidy would die, who did you think was going to kill her?"

A door closed gently in the house.

Léonie's stare left the inspector's face and wandered blindly to the wall. "I do not know," she said.

2

It was somewhere about lunchtime when Inspector Raikes and Superintendent Lecky left Mile House as unobtrusively as they had entered it, exchanging no remarks until they were out of the village. Perhaps to avoid the more conspicuous exit of a trio, perhaps because he had still some business of his own to attend to, Sergeant Brook did not leave with them.

Long Greeting in the afternoon was still, golden, somnolent as a cat, chin up in the sun. It was very hot, and Miss Beaton was not seen to go out with the dogs. The Place lay shuttered in wall and trees, Mile House showed no wink of life, the blinds Arthur Tidy had insisted should be drawn in the Keepsake remained down, so that to Clara Livingston-Bole spying drowsily from her window the timber beams above them looked like pennies on dead eyes.

Presently animation was imparted to the landscape by the appearance of the postman attending to the four o'clock delivery. He was a blithe and uninhibited soul who cared little about murders and himself ranked them inferior in importance to the punctuality of the postal service in Greeting, of which he was justly proud. Not that he wouldn't like such a business cleared up as much as any; for one thing he didn't like the imputation that, unbeknownst, he'd been carrying nasty poison-pen letters tainting the more artless productions in his bag.

Well, it looked as if these police had their work cut out for them, an' all it did. The super, he was a nice chap, always ready with a word of greeting, and Sergeant Brook, he'd sometimes debate the merits of vegetable marrows and the difficulties of feeding laying hens. The dark bloke from London who was putting up at the Loggerheads he didn't know, but he didn't want his job off him, bet your life, thank you. His ambitions didn't climb that road. Give him a good row or two of celery, and some bean sticks and a chicken run, and you could have your nasty murders.

No letters for the Place today; there was few these times since the colonel and his lady had gone and died. That left only the rectory, and then he'd have finished.

He trudged up the weedy path, its outline merged into an overgrown herbaceous border, and, pushing three letters into the rector's box, returned the way he had come to the tenderly subdued notes of "Annie Laurie."

There was nothing to tell him that he had just taken part in the final act that was to play out the Ravenchurch murders.

3

The old man Mr. Buskin had visited that afternoon was an unconscionable time a-dying, and the rector did not leave him till close on six o'clock. Although he was one of his remoter parishioners he walked home, as was his custom, choosing the less frequented paths by field and stream and covering the ground in astonishingly short time with his spindly strides.

Tea was waiting for him in the study, and beside his tray the afternoon mail. Because he had no interest in superficialities he did not examine the envelopes of his letters to ascertain before splitting them open who his correspondents might be. Handwriting to him was neither familiar nor unfamiliar; it existed only by its content. He drank a long-standing cup of tea, then inserted a thumb in the first envelope that came to hand and drew out the folded sheet. It was a rather wildly expressed begging letter of a not unusual type. Reluctant to reject anything at first sight, he put it on one side for further consideration and picked up the second. This was a brief note from Father Connolly's housekeeper. He read it twice, taking a long while over so concise a message. Then he laid it down quietly and sat without moving for a long time till his old maid, reckoning he must have finished, came in to take away the tray.

When he was alone again, he was brought back to consciousness of his surroundings by the white square of the unopened third letter beside his hand. Now that the table had been cleared it looked conspicuous lying there. He opened it, to find several large thin sheets of close writing penned with extreme deliberation. After he had read the opening lines he turned a little gropingly to the close of the letter in quest of a signature. Then he resumed reading the first page. Mr. Buskin's third letter was from the murderer of Bertha Tidy and Jane Kingsley.

Daniel Buskin was an early riser who spent a great deal of physical energy in the daylight hours and passed the evenings with equal concentration on his books and papers and writing. By ten o'clock every night for five or six years now age and lack of reserve force had induced the sheer fatigue that cannot be gainsaid, driving him to bed and sleep. Tonight was no exception, though the hour after nine o'clock was not spent in the study. The maid who heard him leave remarked that he took the private path leading to the church.

There, with the blue summer twilight pressing on the plain glass of north and south aisles, and only altar and chancel dim, the Rev. Daniel Buskin wrestled with demons. Perhaps they were angels. It was a question he could not resolve.

Nor, when his uncertain steps had found the rectory stairs and, a tired old man, he had mounted to his room, did he know whether he had lost or won.

But sleep that other nights drew him down into its inflowing waves lapped now only the edge of thought. He turned his face to the window, catching the last opal and green of the western sky, letting his eyes travel to the deeper but still luminous zenith. Wakeful as he was, he must at last have dozed because when next he caught himself gazing at the pane of glass all color had drained from the horizon, and in his ears was a curious sound he could not recapture on rousing. All color? No. For a disturbing gleam, not aquamarine or translucent, had pressed open his eyelids; it made now a baleful patch on the ceiling, then was gone, only to return next moment in a kind of quivering rage. Ebb, flow; ebb, flow; he closed his eyes, then opened them at once as the night grew suddenly rough with clamor. He propped himself up in bed while the red glow winked and went out, and relit itself against the walls of his room. There were shouts from somewhere outside, cries that could not be dismissed as the catcalls of horseplay, words and commands filled with a menace the import of which his old ears could not catch. The night was suddenly a tranquil sea lashed to foam and fury.

He got out of bed, trembling from the sharp emergence from sleep, and fumbled quickly among his clothes. While he was pulling them on he heard his maid's door shut and her voice calling to him from the landing above. He did not answer, because at the moment all his attention was for the downstairs window of the Keepsake, where a great rosy light swam and sank and rose again.

"Mr. Buskin! Mr. Buskin, sir! Poor Miss Tidy's place—it's on fire!"

He was on his own landing now. He soothed her with a word, and together they ran downstairs. As they reached the hallway the knocker of the front door fell loudly three times. The rector got there first. While he was drawing the bolt the grandfather clock close by broke into unhurried chimes and struck eleven serenely.

Clara Livingston-Bole stood in the doorway, still in a day suit, her feet thrust into ankle boots. She opened her mouth to speak, when above her voice rose the sudden groaning of a siren. The wailing arc of it swooped above the yells still breaking on their ears and took more than one listener back to those lightless nights not so long ago when even Long Greeting had been bomb-conscious.

"Thank God for that," said Miss Livingston-Bole as it moaned into silence. "And I see you haven't needed rousing. It's not the fire I'm particularly worried about, because the cottage is unoccupied, we know. It's all that horrid uproar—*who* can it be, and what in the world is possessing them?"

"But I think it may not be unoccupied," Mr. Buskin replied. "The locks were removed this morning."

All three were hastening in single file down the rutty path, so that the clangor of voices, louder now, swamped her reply.

In the lane and the road beyond, it seemed to their bewildered eyes as if a mass of people moved, flitted, pounced, and jostled one another. Confusing crossbeams from the headlights of a number of stationary cars gave an inaccurate impression, so that a couple of persons darting restlessly from light into shadow and out again were multiplied to five or six. And the beastly hubbub from the direction of the cottage in some obscure way added, Miss Livingston-Bole was convinced, to one's estimate of the crowd.

"What a Roman holiday a fire is!" she muttered to Mr. Buskin's maid, who, frightened now and having somehow lost sight of the rector, kept close to her side. "People you don't suspect exist flock, thumbs down, to the show."

But a few minutes later she was not so sure that the fire was the attraction.

4

The N.F.S. from Ravenchurch were invading the scene and, with the group of police officers arriving just before them, had poured themselves and their implements over Miss Tidy's once model garden. Brook and a constable kept the gate against a milling but on the whole unvociferous company. The worst of the business seemed to be behind the cottage, where Brook soon withdrew to the help of constables tussling with the yelling boobies whose screams rang out above the crackle of the flames.

"Burn the witch! Burn 'er out then! Why don't she come out? We'll burn 'er out! Burn the furrin' woman! Burn the witch!"

Flames licked from the windows and shone between the rafters. Reconditioning had not arrested the seasoning of three centuries, and the Keepsake was ripe for fire. It was the drawing room and the bedroom above that burned now with furnace ferocity, rolling dense masses of smoke into the tiny entrance hall, obscuring the stairs, and setting to a ghastly shimmer the heat-laden air.

They had not to batter in the front door. It opened easily enough onto the drifting coils inside. While the hoses played and the flames roared their song it was George Wild who, with Inspector Raikes, their mouths and nostrils swathed, dived in on the heels of a fireman. The man made for the stairs, but Raikes, hesitating only a second or two, blundered on to the kitchen in the wake of George, whose newly acquired leg had still put him ahead of the rest.

The kitchen was dim and vaporous with grayscarves of smutty smoke, heavy with explosive heat, but not yet smothered in the black billows that surged about the hall. Raikes sent an incoherent shout to the man upstairs to come down, but paid no further attention to anything but the figure seated at the table to which she clung with clawing hands.

"Léonie, Léonie!" cried George in an agony he might not have been able to explain. "Woman——" He gripped her arms and stopped.

Raikes helped him to pull her from the chair.

"She's dying," he said shortly. He said it to no one in particular. They were both heedless of the moisture streaming down their faces. Above the stench of smoke and old crackling timber rose, as they bent to lift her, the arrogant, deathly scent of bitter almonds.

On coats spread upon a cleared space at the bottom of the garden, fragrant with trampled nepeta, they laid her down. An ambulance man put a blanket about her. But, at the close of a life of few wants, Léonie Blanchard wanted nothing now.

"She's past help," said Lecky, who knelt beside her.

Light from the burning house that gave ghastly illumination to the rigid, convulsed face and violet-hued lips flickered too on those who stood behind the group gathered about the dead woman. They it was who had entered the garden before the police kept intruders out, and who now stood, isolated from one another, helpless spectators of activities they were not permitted to share.

George, standing with Raikes and the ambulance men, watching Hare's neat examination, was overwhelmed with sudden longing for Samela. He lifted his eyes to where, against the laurels where their bicycles leaned, her face shone white in the glare that flooded them. She must have been looking for him too, because she smiled instantly; but she neither moved nor called to him. He was glad. She must not come here. Response so immediate had brought him her presence without physical contact. A few yards off he could see Owen Greatorex, his face upturned to the glow of the sparking roof like that of an avenging angel. Near him a curiously bundled shape, hands in pockets, was to be discerned as Kate Beaton.

Hare straightened up, while at a word from the superintendent the ambulance men prepared to take away the body. The fire, its more spectacular rage quenched, was under control, though still burning fiercely. Dark figures passed in and out, crisscrossing one another in unending pattern, as rugs and furniture piled up on the unrecognizable flower beds. When there was time to notice it was remarked by more than one how quiet the place had grown.

The doctor, stroking his scrubby hair in an abrupt gesture, met the inspector's eye and said, "Bottom fallen out of your case, I shouldn't be surprised?"

"You might be yet," Raikes said.

Hare turned away. His business lay in another field.

A policeman ran out of the weirdly lit darkness like a demon in a pantomime and exchanged swift words with Lecky. When he had melted again into the strangely still region behind the cottage Lecky returned to the group lingering about the plot where Léonie had died.

"They've nabbed five," he said with a jerk of the chin towards the house. "This will be something worse than stones at the cops and slashing a lady's frock. It's arson now."

" 'Burn the witch,' " George quoted with curling lip. "And not one of them with the guts to walk through that unfastened door to fetch an old woman they were prepared to roast alive. Medieval scum like that want medieval punishment."

"Don't worry," Raikes said. "Life won't be very comfortable for our young friends for a long time to come." He looked up at the sound of a recognizably rich voice in his ear.

" 'The tumult and the shouting dies,' " Owen Greatorex announced sonorously.

"But," Raikes retorted, fetching up a grin from nowhere in particular, "the captains and the kings"—he parodied a bow in the direction of Greatorex—"are still here."

That banality loosed tension a little. Only George who was young did not smile.

"Well," Lecky observed, "seeing Brook's off with his Big Five, what do you say to us clearing out too? The N.F.S. will see their job through pretty soon now, and we can leave a couple of constables on duty, with a relief later to carry on till daylight. All that stuff strewn about, and what not, may be too much temptation for some other toughs." He sighed. "I never knew Ravenchurch had an underworld till now."

"Blackmail's a nasty poison in the system," Raikes said. "Sets going no end of organic trouble."

"Big fleas have little fleas," a voice remarked on a note of forced cheerfulness, as Miss Beaton scuffed towards them.

She got no acknowledgment because everyone's attention was drawn to a disturbance at the gate.

"Too late for the show, my lad, whoever you are," Raikes said as the altercation reached their ears.

"Moxon will deal with him all right," Lecky added with a glance at the constable's unyielding back.

But the man was looking in their direction now, and the hesitation in his movement made the superintendent join the scene of the pother.

"Ah," exclaimed Mr. Arthur Tidy, an irritable bantam challenging the senior rooster, "perhaps now you're here, Superintendent, you'll see fit to admit me to my own property—or what's left of it."

Lecky motioned to the constable. "All right, Moxon. You were quite in order. Come in, Mr. Tidy."

The solicitor flounced up the path, sarcasm and ill temper struggling in his face, and gave vent to his spleen at being ejected at midnight from a comfortable Ravenchurch bed.

"Fine result of a cock-and-bull plot," he sneered. "Removing the lock to help the police do their fancy work! What have *I* got out of it? Lost as nice a bit of property as I'll find in a day's march, and that—that old she-*devil*, fire raiser, eh, as well as——"

Raikes put a hand on him that was a push too.

"Léonie Blanchard's dead," he said. "And she didn't burn the house."

"A Man of Property," Owen Greatorex murmured.

"Or, Brotherly Love," said Kate Beaton, "in Tidy terms, Bertha to him was a nice house and garden. Dead woman's shoes."

5

Though it was after one o'clock when Lecky and Raikes walked towards their car, Ravenchurch was not after all to be their destination for another hour or so. In the dimmed headlights a tenuous figure advanced.

"Mr. Buskin," Lecky muttered, and went to meet him. When they had heard him, all three got in the car and Raikes drove to the rectory. Lights welcomed them downstairs, where Clara Livingston-Bole lingered to share the old maid's solitude till the rector returned. Now she withdrew, only wishing them good night and reminding the shaken old man that there was a hot drink and a fire in the study. He accepted her solicitude and her presence in his home with the simplicity that never looks for the unusual, and drew the others in after him.

In the study, where warmth and the familiarity of a quiet room and fatigue itself began to dull the horror of the night, the Rev. Daniel Buskin's trembling fingers presently passed Léonie's letter to Inspector Raikes.

"But this came by post," Raikes said stupidly, glancing at the envelope.

"Oh yes."

The inspector frowned. "Your last delivery is round four o'clock, sir?"

Mr. Buskin looked bewildered. The superintendent gave Raikes a look of mingled impatience and warning. But the rector spoke.

"You see," he said gently, "she must have believed she had missed the morning collection. She writes that I shall have her letter on the morning following her death."

"Yes, yes," Raikes said in annoyance. "But you didn't. You got it in the afternoon. You got it seven hours before she died. It was your duty—"

"It was my duty," Mr. Buskin said in passionate tones, "to respect her wishes." He added, with contrasting gentleness, "Father Connolly, you see, is dead."

He closed his eyes with a finality that left the rest to them.

"Get on with it," Lecky urged. "It's something outside you and me." He nodded towards the letter. "That isn't."

6

When they had each read it Lecky said, "She wrote it last night. Before she was taxed with the anonymous letters."

"But not," Raikes replied, "before Mrs. Wild had approached her. She knew the game was up."

"The game was up for her when they took Iris from the river."

Raikes made no reply. Lecky took up the letter again.

REVEREND SIR,

When this letter come to you I am dead. I write to you because the good Father Connolly die tonight. The law I do not know, I am a simple woman, but if the law permit I desire that I may be buried in the holy ground beside my little daughter Fleur. The money which is in the bank, and that also which is in my room at the Mile House, is now for Mme. Kane, who also care. I write to you who understand the things of the heart as the good Père Connolly understand.

This night Mrs. Wild meet me in the Keepsake at eleven. It is a trap the police make, and the little one she is troubled and not so clever that she hide it. So I understand. But you say perhaps that it is not necessary that I go in the trap, because I can meet her and not kill her. But it is not so, then they set another trap and another. They know it is I. And I, I am tired. I like now to die, without first the slow questions, and the judge.

So, when she come I will be at the rendezvous, oh yes, but having taken the poison there is left for the wasp in the little tin upon the shelf of the kitchen. There she meet me and ask me the question she say she wish to ask. But I, being dead, I do not know.

It is I kill Miss Bertha. It is a very simple kill, I am a simple woman. She say entrez to many, oh so many, at the Minerva by night, me she will never shut out. I have only to whisper through the door, it is I, Léonie, let me in, and she let me in. Miss Bertha, she is vain, so vain, she do not ever believe Léonie may harm. Léonie do not suffer, Léonie do not even think. So all is well. And I, I walk from Greeting to Ravenchurch in the night with the scarf she wear winters.

That is mistake, the scarf. Mademoiselle Kingsley come first to café, always. Some days she come at the moment Miss Bertha come. Such a day is that before the night I kill. She talk to Miss Bertha while Miss Bertha she take off the things she wear and prepare herself for business. And there is no scarf. But when Miss Kingsley, she see the scarf that choke her, she remember it is the scarf of Miss Bertha in the cold days. But not this day. So, she believe it is only I bring it when the others they have gone away. That which she think, it is reasonable. So I must kill her also. She do not know Mr. Tidy lock up the house. She do not know I dwell in the house of Mr. Gratorix. She come to knock on the Keepsake while I pick the gooseberries. But I hear. She come to me in the garden. She tell me of the scarf. She tell me that she do not tell the others what it is she know. She ask that I explain. But I, I do not talk. I say that I do not know. I continue to pick the gooseberry. But she know that I know. I know that she know. She say, I wish Sam to be here. It is, perhaps, her husband? I say nothing. She go away. I follow. I take from the coalhouse the stake. I go to the wood also. She is there, in the wood. She write. I kill her. She has wrote only a name. Let it stand. It is a simple kill. I am a simple woman. But les gendarmes, they do not look for the simple thing.

I kill Miss Bertha, because she is the evil woman. She kill me first, you understand, who might be happy, years before she kill Fleur. Because she work evil to many, so many, the police they confuse themselves. It is not thought that I, Léonie, shall murder. There are the great ones who may desire that she die, n'est-ce pas? But I am tired. It is I, Léonie, who destroy her. I am a simple woman. But I do not kill Mrs. Wild. Now tonight I die also. After that I do not know.

I thank you, reverend father.

Yours respectful,
LÉONIE BLANCHARD

The superintendent folded the pages carefully and slid them towards Raikes.

"A simple woman, yes." He broke silence at last. "But a remarkably lucid one."

"They'd have pleaded insanity," Raikes reminded him, "and not, I think, unsuccessfully."

Lecky glanced at the clock. "Ten past two," he said, "and a day and a half's work tomorrow. Come on."

Their eyes fell on Mr. Buskin.

"The rector's asleep," Raikes said.

EPILOGUE

Here comes a candle to light you to be. ...

Two evenings later a small and chastened company met in the Wilds' flat in Moat Street.

Marion Oates was at first reluctant to come; in her own eyes the enormity of her offense against good-fellowship should in decency have kept her away.

"But, Titus, light of my eyes," Samela remonstrated, "you couldn't possibly have suspected me more than I did you! If it's horrid, darling, it's mutually horrid. When I saw your grim face that night, I—well, I just thought you looked like somebody out of a Webster tragedy. And then when——"

"But my face," Marion protested, "was like that partly because it's made so, and partly because I'd seen *you*, and was so sure you'd seen *me*, poking about the wretched place so late."

"Even if she had," Crystal complained, "there was no harm in it. Neither of you knew then that Tidy was murdered—or going to be."

"Mrs. Bates, how bright you're getting," her husband murmured. "But you see, both of 'em knew about the nocturnal visitors and were keeping what they knew to themselves. And Marion, what's more, had already had a peep behind the dirty scene, so to speak."

"Yes, of course," Sammy said. "Iris and—and everything. If only you'd have let us share the worry of it all, Titus."

"I couldn't. You all thought I was too young. You were all so—incredulous. All, except Jane."

"*I* don't think you're too young, any more," Crystal pronounced solemnly.

"But when all's said," Marion cried in a sacrificial outburst, "it's just unthinkable I should have doubted Sammy, and gone on doubting too. I'm beyond the pale, and nobody ought to forgive me."

Her eyes brimmed, and none of them knew that the tears she kept back were for Jane rather than Samela.

"Look." George was gruff. "Don't be masochistic, Titus. And I'm not going to explain that to you, because you're an adult same as we. And, let me say this, between equals there is no forgiveness."

"Forgiveness," said Kenneth scornfully, "is patronage."

"It's divine," George said. "It's not for us."

They were all quiet, remembering how for each of them the range of comprehension had been extended in the past two weeks.

Then Crystal said, "Besides, think how we'd all have to go round begging somebody's pardon. Ken here was *sure* it was Mrs. Weaver—and after all she is somewhat *spooky*, don't you think?"

It was a relief to laugh, while Kenneth defended his choice stoutly. "Physical type all right—and quite *in*human, somehow, which is what Crystal means by 'spooky.' "

Marion nodded. "She just put the last straw on me, anyway. I was in the shop, you see, when she practically told Miss Beaton that somebody on the Minerva staff, somebody young, was mixed up in Miss Drake's death. That's why I had to go to Greeting to find out. But I told you this. Sorry."

"Yes," Samela admitted. "How all occasions did inform against me! But *you* couldn't help it, Titus."

"Nobody," said George with a deliberate descent to flippancy, "could help anything. Or very nearly not. I dare say even Tidy wasn't snubbed enough as a kid."

"Or too much," Sammy said, trying to be flippant too. "You're frightfully old-fashioned, darling."

"If he is," Kenneth retorted, "he's absolutely in the swim. To be old-fashioned these days is to be the newest fashion there is."

"In that case," Samela cried, hugging Marion and Crystal with happy impartiality, "let's go all Victorian and forgive one another!"

2

Kate Beaton broke through the bramble bushes, negotiated the ditch with more speed than grace, whistled invisible dogs, and came face to face with Owen Greatorex in the little clearing.

"Diana of the Uplands," he greeted her, standing his ground.

"What did she do? Hunt the moon? No, she *was* the moon, wasn't she? Anyway, I'll bet she cried for it, like me." She appraised him with a shrewd eye. "You do haunt this ghastly bit of earth, don't you? It was that first gave me the idea."

"What idea?"

"Why, that you—*you* were the secret'st man of blood! Returning to the scene of his crime, don't you know. At one time I thought you'd killed Bertha and the girl."

"Really, what does one say to this—this ...?"

"Flattery? Charge? You pays your money and you takes your choice. We pen-pushers always yearn to be men of action, eh?"

"Men of action, perhaps. I wouldn't say that murderers qualify for inclusion among them."

(Pen-pushers, pen-pushers, indeed! *We.*)

"Of course," she went on with irritating disregard, "when the Oates child called the other day because she'd eavesdropped a couple of words in the bookshop, and adding two and two made ten of it, I began to see how almighty wise she took me to be and how little I really knew about any of it. A lesson in humility. She almost took me by the shoulders to shake the truth out of me, poor lass—and, do you know, there was nothing there to shake?"

"I believe you," Owen Greatorex said with such enthusiasm that she stared at him doubtfully.

"Mutual ambiguities." She shook her head. "I wonder if you and I will ever properly appreciate one another."

"God forbid!" he cried still more fervently.

She gave a shout of laughter, smacking her knee for the Airedales to come to heel. But it was he who made the first move, retreating with mustered dignity along the path that led to Mile House where Mrs. Phail, at least, took part in no pursuit, unless in some Freudian dream which never upset masculine equanimity.

He saw quite plainly that there was nothing for it but to keep on running. ...

3

It was Mrs. Weaver who had the last word, or very nearly.

"I'm so pleased," she told Raikes. "Mr. Tidy agreed to let me have—at a price, of course—the old sampler that hung in the teashop."

He looked, she thought, a little blank.

"My one ambition's been to possess it. But Miss Tidy, you see, got to know that, so she took a quite abnormal delight in refusing it to me. Then young Mrs. Bates—so kind to an old woman—dropped in the other afternoon to say there would shortly be a sale of effects at the Minerva and that Mr. Tidy would be there later in the day if I wanted a word with him beforehand."

"So it worked," Raikes said curiously. He had always been interested in Emmie Weaver.

"Oh yes." She nodded. "After the house was burnt down he returned to Yorkshire grinding his teeth. But I was lucky—I saw him before he'd had to start grinding. And he was quite amenable. He sees *nothing at all* in dear little Adelaide Bascombe's work in 1842, and he couldn't anyway resist a fancy price for it. So I've got it. I've actually *got* it. *So* unusual, such a nice change from all the other pious samplers that must have been worked tongue in cheek."

"Mrs. Weaver," the inspector said in mock reproof, "how you do go on! Pious, indeed. No, I remember it, of course. Most impious. 'When will you pay me?' A historic document, reeking of blackmail."

Mrs. Weaver had no notion what he meant. She didn't mind. Adelaide Bascombe's bells were hers; as for policemen, they were, she supposed, paid to be cryptic.

THE END

About the Rue Morgue Press

"Rue Morgue Press is the old-mystery lover's best friend, reprinting high quality books from the 1930s and '40s."
—*Ellery Queen's Mystery Magazine*

Since 1997, the Rue Morgue Press has reprinted scores of traditional mysteries, the kind of books that were the hallmark of the Golden Age of detective fiction. Authors reprinted or to be reprinted by the Rue Morgue include Dorothy Bowers, Pamela Branch, Joanna Cannan, Glyn Carr, Torrey Chanslor, Clyde B. Clason, Joan Coggin, Manning Coles, Lucy Cores, Frances Crane, Norbert Davis, Elizabeth Dean, Constance & Gwenyth Little, Marlys Millhiser, James Norman, Stuart Palmer, Craig Rice, Kelley Roos, Charlotte Murray Russell, Maureen Sarsfield, and Juanita Sheridan.

If you enjoyed *The Bells of Old Bailey*, ask your bookseller about its four predecessors, *Postscript to Poison* (0-915230-77-1, $14.95), *Shadows Before* (0-915230-81-X, $14.95), *Deed Without a Name* (0-915230-82-8, $14.95) and *Fear and Miss Betony* (0-915230-86-0, $14.95). The Rue Morgue Press intends to publish all five of Bowers' books. For information on The Rue Morgue Press, turn the page.

To suggest titles or to receive a catalog of Rue Morgue Press books write P.O. Box 4119, Boulder, CO 80306, telephone 800-699-6214, or check out our website, www.ruemorguepress.com, which lists complete descriptions of all of our titles, along with lengthy biographies of our writers.